~

[Solomon & Solomon, Attorneys at Law: The following manuscript was discovered in a concealed safe-deposit box in the home of Fr. Caleb Faraday by the Oxford Police Department, following Fr. Faraday's tragic death. Per the instructions of his Order and his will, all personal items are to be auctioned off and the proceeds donated to the Children's Home, Westchester, England. Although the authorities are still conducting an open investigation into his death, the auction will proceed as planned on 12 August 1999. The manuscript in question has not been previously published, and the new owner will retain full rights and privileges regarding any future publication, sale, and any royalties that may therein accrue, etc. Please be advised that Solomon & Solomon cannot be held responsible for the truth or falsity of any element of the manuscript. The bidding structure is noted on our website, and will be strictly adhered to. Please reference item #TM126]

~

To The Most Reverend Caleb Faraday, SJ:

In response to your letter (now several months old) questioning me about the original catalyst, the original spark of curiosity, for my present course of study, I have considered the best possible way to answer while doing justice both to the spirit of your query, and to our long friendship. Your seemingly innocent and innocuous question has cost me much sleep. You will find this surprising, perhaps, but I have spent in my lifetime considerable effort hiding my past (I hope you will not be scandalized by this revelation). That is to say, not hiding, as though I had, in fact, something to hide. Rather, I have been cautious, overly so, in revealing too much of my fantastic young adulthood, for reasons of prudence. The wicked hide when no one is searching. The righteous man is as bold as a lion, but is also, hopefully, as wise as a serpent. I will leave to your judgment the category into which I happen to fall.

Yes, I have used the word 'fantastic' in describing my youth. Ah, I imagine your face now as you read, and your eyebrows arch incredulously! I will leave also to your judgment whether my word choice is in any way accurate or adequate. You have asked me about my past: the answer to your question is contained in the following manuscript. Longer than you anticipated, I am sure, but I think that, after you have read it, you will agree with me that a shorter answer would be dissatisfying. Even so I have shortened my tale considerably. I have revealed only what I was most directly involved in. Whatever remains to be told at the end of this manuscript is not my tale to tell.

Through the many years that we have been acquainted, you have shown a great interest in my work, and this because, I think, of your own work, your own interests and gifts. We both have truth for a mistress, and wisdom we both seek as a treasure. I seek as an academic with interest in the esoteric and obscure, and you as minister of sacramental grace. Both of our vocations have what may be termed a supernatural bent, but your work may be even more appropriately deemed supernatural, and for this you are accustomed to earn either the approbation or vilification of your fellow man. There is no middle ground. But it is precisely because of your vocation that I think you will have little trouble believing,

Contents

Part I-The Garden... 10
Chapter I...12
Chapter II.. 19
Chapter III...33
Chapter IV...40
Chapter V..57
Chapter VI...69
Chapter VII..80
Chapter VIII...95
Part II-The Valley...113
Chapter IX...115
Chapter X..138
Chapter XI...163
Chapter XII..197
Chapter XIII...233
Part III-The City..255
Chapter XIV..257
Chapter XV..281
Chapter XVI..309
Chapter XVII...330
Chapter XVIII.. 357
Epilogue...382

~For My Children~

at least conceptually, what I have conveyed, or attempted to convey, in my manuscript. Indeed, men with your vocation have long tread the most narrow and dangerous paths of being and reality, and so are not often dismayed when confronted by things that creep from dark recesses and wastelands in the forgotten corners of the universe, or surprised to find that the universe is more wild and mysterious than many of our present philosophies allow. You will not even be surprised, I think, to find that there are many beings both wicked and dangerous in the vast reaches of creation. You know that man is not the only fallen creature. So your view of the cosmos is higher and clearer than mine, and it is in this light that I have decided to answer your question, but in a manner that you will, I think, find unexpected.

You imagine me long ago, perhaps, as a young student poring over dusty books, following one interesting and ancient story to the next, diligently unlocking the secrets of archaic languages, and lo, a spark of flame, as it were, alights above my head, and I see suddenly the question whose answer I will make my life's work! For many men of my vocation, that would not be a guess too far off the mark. But, for good or ill, I am unlike my fellow intellectuals in many respects, not the least of which is the genesis of my career, the awakening of my present vocation. Following truth with steady tread has brought me here, but it was truth under the mode of action and not of intellectual rigor. Only later, after traveling the strange road upon which my soul was tried as in a furnace, did my vocation change, and only then did I take up the mantle of learning, and sit down upon my philosopher's chair.

I will add, though I hesitate, that while the following tale has ended, I have not. That is, I still live and breathe, and for this state of affairs I cannot fault the timidity or sloth of my enemies. You think, perhaps, that I am exaggerating? I assure you I am not. Revenge is a potent motivator. I ask, therefore, that you keep the following in confidence. Let this tale remain between us two.

And, after you have read what follows, I will look forward to your commentary and critique. I know that you will have much to say, and will, perhaps, barely believe what is written. You may

think that your friend has become mentally unstable, or, what would be worse, dishonest. Or you may split the difference, and label me a mentally deficient liar. I am willing to accept the risk. I trust our friendship will survive even this. And so, after you have read and judged, I look forward to many more conversations in your study or in my library, surrounded by clouds of smoke, and with a glass or two at our elbow. There is always light and hope in the world, and this never more apparent than when two friends meet, in mind and spirit, and enjoy the more excellent things, pursuing together both truth and wisdom. In this way, I think, we can sometimes catch a glimpse of a new heaven and a new earth far off in the distance, no larger than a man's hand, and we know that the storm will soon break, cleansing the cosmos in a flood.
Affectionately Yours,
Dr. Thaddeus Michael,
Oxford, England
The Feast of Christ the King
The Year of Our Lord, 1997

P.S. I have included, for your benefit, excerpts from certain stories, books, and letters, some quite old, that I hope will help you with the context, and perhaps illumine elements of my manuscript that may be obscure. Some of these excerpts are directly applicable, some tangentially so. You may recognize all or some of these from my academic work, or perhaps you have seen them in my library. There are countless others that I could have included. But I trust that what I did include will prove helpful.

"We must believe, since the poets tell us that they have discovered a kingdom greater than the world, that an angel is pleased sometimes to tip their bark, so that they take a little "of that water" of which the Gospel speaks and do not get away without some inquietude, and some great and mysterious desire."
~Raissa Maritain

Part I
The Garden

The Beginning

Come walk with me these starless nights,
Come tread the sodden turf,
And drink with me the sacred sights
Not seen upon the earth.

Wild does the wind now roar,
But be you not afraid!
Come beat with me upon the door
Until the storm is staid.

Strength of will, and iron pride,
Unbroken and unbent,
Belong to those who never die,
Their power never spent.

Merry, let us dance and knock
Upon the many doors,
When the Book from 'neath its rock
We tear like open sores.

For then the clang of many doors
We'll hear the echo nigh,
Though rain may pour
And lightning crease the canvas of the sky.

Our feet will beat a wider way
And many lords now risen high,
Will soon begin to swoon and sway,
And then begin to die.

Click and clang, clang and click,
The doors have now been locked and blocked,

And all inside are weak and sick,
And dread the violent path we walk

We laugh aloud at wrong and sin!
Though ash and torment be our bed,
And though the death of many men
Be heaped upon our head.

The sacred sights, the hidden way
Cannot be bought with gems or gold.
But still we seek it, night and day,
Though terrible what must be sold,

Though all in shadow we must stay,
And terror and the darkness weigh,
And with our breath and life we pay,
The power gained is worth the cold.

It's worth our souls, the Book of old.

~Excerpted from *The Nightmare of Percephilous,* circa 1300AD, translated from the original Latin by Dr. Byron Fairmont, 1818

Chapter I

"My good blade carves the casques of men
My tough lance thrusteth sure,
My strength is as the strength of ten,
Because my heart is pure."
~Tennyson

When I was a boy of maybe ten or eleven, my father took me to see my grandfather, my mother's father, for the first time. My grandfather lived a long way away, and my own mother and father had not seen him in many years. When I asked my father why they were estranged (even as a young boy I knew that all was not right between them, and I had heard the whispered arguments of my parents when the subject of a visitation was broached), he looked at me and said, "I will tell you when you are older, but only know that your mother is a very special woman, and a child of your grandfather." At the time, of course, I wasn't sure what he meant, but even a young lad like myself could see that my mother was different, very quiet and serene; thoughtful, almost as though she were pondering something too difficult to contain, but too dangerous to let out. But she was kind, and I loved her dearly. As a child I remember watching her praying on her knees in the Cathedral, and seeing the light of the autumn morning pour through the huge stained glass image of Saint Catherine and fall on my mother, shrouding her in sunlight, and giving her an aura of otherworldliness, as though St. Catherine herself was giving my mother homage. My mother's name was Charity, and it seemed to me as a young boy that God required charity of mankind just to honor her.

My father, Hubert Michael, was a tall man, kind and strong. He taught at the University, and he would often be writing in his notebooks, or reading his volumes of *Plato*, or *St. Thomas*, while smoking his pipe. He loved both my mother and me very much, and I remember him fondly, and think of him every day. I remember how he looked and the smell of tobacco as he walked me to the train station on that fateful morning. We had kissed mother good-by, and she seemed happy but perhaps a little pensive, as she fixed the collar on my tweed jacket. She looked at me with her large brown eyes and smiled, "Go with God, and give my love to your grandfather. And whatever happens, know that he loves you." It was a strange way to send off a child to meet his grandfather for the first time, but I was excited and ready for the adventure of traveling with my father, so I promised her, and set off down the lane, my small hand held tightly by my father's. I glanced back over my shoulder toward our house, and saw my mother standing on the porch, her hands hanging down by her sides, smiling at us; but I imagined that I saw tears shining in her eyes.

It was the first time that I had ridden a train, and so the three-day journey was very enjoyable. I had my father all to myself, and he gave me his full attention, so that the memory of the train ride has stayed in my mind to this day, and in the dark days that were to come I would often return in my mind to the train, and to my father's voice, as he described the landscape as it passed our window, or told me stories of great warriors, and forgotten kingdoms, and of fairy tales and monsters.

"The world is old," he told me, "and she feels the weight of her years. There are things, ancient, cruel things that creep about the earth that she would shake off as a fever, if she could. And there are few any more with the courage see these things, to face them. There are few who labor in her vineyard."

"I will face them," I said, eagerly and sincerely, "I am brave, like the knights of old, and I would labor, if I were allowed." My father looked at me, across the small table that separated our window seats from each other, and smiled.

"You are brave, and you will labor. Only do not be too eager, you are young yet. But the day will come, sooner rather than later, I am sure, when you will understand all that I say to you, and then your mind will be an equal to you heart. That day is fast approaching, and then you will not only be allowed to labor, but will be compelled."

"Compelled? Does that mean I will be forced," I asked, "against my will?"

"Truth is compelling, Thaddeus, and obligates those with pure hearts, not against their will, but as a completion, a consummation, of their will. A pure heart wills what is good, beautiful, and true. Evil binds, turning the will into a mockery, a self destructing mechanism, but truth frees." My father looked into my face, and he knew that I did not understand.

The train rumbled on, and I heard the lonely shriek of the whistle drift down from the engine, several cars ahead of ours, and through our cabin window I watched the countryside roll by.

We arrived at the train station in South Hampstead, the small country town closest to my grandfather's estate, and were met by a strange, skinny, wrinkled little man in a baggy black suit. He shook my father's hand, and it seemed to my young eyes that he was proportioned so strangely that he had an almost frightening appearance, and when he smiled at me from beneath his drivers' hat I remember thinking that his eyes were tinted yellow. He said that his name was Sylvester, and that he worked for my grandfather.

Sylvester drove us through the wooded countryside to the great, old house that was my grandfather's. It took the better part of an hour to wind our way through the deep woods till we finally reached an arched entrance that stood

14

along side of the small, winding road. This was the entrance to the estate.

The house was almost a castle, old and built with great blocks of stone, with two great towers rising above the mass of turrets, arches, and buttresses, one on the east wing, and one on the west. We were escorted through the great hall of the house, and into my grandfather's enormous library. It was a long room, with a sort of second level, a balcony that followed the perimeter of the room. The library had very high ceilings, and a huge stone fireplace at the far end. The walls were lined from floor to ceiling with bookshelves, and there were stacks of books, papers, strange stones and mechanical contraptions on the desks and end tables, and even lying haphazardly on the marble floor. As my father and I walked towards the great fireplace, I saw a wooden display case, with curiously carved legs and a glass lid. The case held the skeleton of a very long creature, which almost, it seemed to me, to be that of a snake, only much too large, even for one of those ferocious jungle snakes that made a habit of swallowing whole crocodiles and explorers, if the stories that I had read were true. But as we continued to walk, I saw that the there were strange fragments jutting out from the spine, fragments that looked vaguely familiar to me, as though I had seen such a creature before. I supposed that they might have been some kind of appendage, perhaps wings. The skull had a frightful appearance to it, almost too large for the rest of the skeleton, and with jagged teeth that seemed too large for the skull. The empty eye sockets stared darkly at me as I passed. I thought that I would not want to meet this creature in the flesh.

There was little space on the walls that was not covered up by the ubiquitous bookcase and cupboard, but there did hang in one open spot a long, double-edged broad sword, and, in another, a round mirror, dusty with age and neglect (as, indeed, was the rest of the library). So dusty, in fact, that as I walked by, it did not show my reflection, though I think that I may have seen some movement on its dark surface beneath the filth. As we walked I was able to catch some of the titles on the aged jackets of the shelved books; names like *The Nightmare of Percephilous*, *The Castle and the Gargoyle*, *A History of the Prehistoric Peoples of Almata*, *The Darkness and Her Enemies: What Lies Beyond the Door*, and *The Book and Its Contents: A Likely Scenario*. There were books with strange pictures on the covers, and books with strange covers that seemed to be not leather or cloth, but rather a hardened material that looked as though it could have been some sort of metal. I thought that it would be very uncomfortable to read while sitting in an overstuffed chair by the fireplace (as was my habit at home). Other books were printed (or, in many instances, handwritten) in foreign tongues; Latin, Greek, what looked like Arabic, and many in languages with which I was completely unfamiliar, and was unable to even guess at.

My mother's father's name was Cornelius Ramsey. He rose from behind his high-backed chair, his wild white hair framing his thin, long face, as the firelight glowed red behind it, and his gray handlebar mustache paralleling his warm smile, while his kind, brown eyes shone brightly from beneath his bushy eyebrows. He greeted my father, and I could sense my father's affection for the older man. "Hello, Cornelius."

"Welcome, Hubert. I am glad to see you have safely arrived, and judging by my daughter's letters on the subject, and from your appearance, I believe that the years have been good to you. It has been a long time, perhaps too long, but I am glad to see you again, and to finally greet your son." The old man embraced my father, and then turned to me. He kneeled down, took my hand in his, and looked at me for a moment with a smile. His eyes were my mother's, and like my mother's, they hid something, something far away, a longing or a hurt that was either waiting to be satisfied or to be healed, I could not tell. I loved the old man immediately, for the sake of my mother, and because I could see the kindness in his face was like my father's, and I trusted and loved my father.

"Welcome Thaddeus, welcome to my home. It was once your mother's home, and when she was a child like you she walked these very halls with me and with your grandmother, God rest her soul. I have waited too long to finally see you face to face."

~

The New England Post Gazette,
August 4th, 1888

*Clifford, CT. ~ A Connecticut baker disappeared on Tuesday under very strange circumstances, and in full view of over one hundred people. M. Adams was attending the Tailor County Fair, and was in the process of examining an Indian artifact on display there, when he touched the stone and simply vanished, according to witnesses. This particular artifact had been pulled out of lake Kallihoosah, in Maine, by local fisherman M. G. Greenley, and was on loan to the County Fair so that, "All could have themselves enjoyment and cultural enrichment, " according to the artifact's owner. The wife of the disappeared man, Mrs. Adams, was in a state of hysterics, and threatened to get her gun if the artifact's owner did not restore her husband, or if they did not tell her where he had gone. M. Adams had been in front of a line of fairgoers who were also eager to examine the stone artifact when he touched the display in question and vanished. "Like a door opened and he just walked through," said one witness. The local Police are investigating the matter. ~ **M. A. Ferneley, reporter.***

Chapter II

And there was war in heaven, Michael and his angels fought
against the dragon; and the dragon and his angels fought back.
~The Apocalypse of Saint John

I was to spend the summer with my grandfather. My father remained with me for a week longer, and then he returned to my mother. "Learn from your grandfather, Thaddeus, and I will return for you when the leaves begin to fall." He removed from around his neck a piece of rope, loosely knotted, with an old key hung upon it. He put it over my head, saying, "Keep this close, always. It is your inheritance, but I want you to have it now, for who can tell what the future holds." He kissed my head, and then Sylvester drove him away, towards the train that would take him home. And I was left with my grandfather. I would never see my father again.

My grandfather smiled at me, after we turned from the porch. "Well Thaddeus, so begins your adventure. I hope that you enjoy your time here. It is, for me, a great privilege to have my only grandchild beneath my roof, after all these years. This castle is yours for the summer. Roam and explore it and the grounds to your heart's content. The bell will ring at mealtimes. In a few days time, after you are more settled, we will begin... you will be able to learn much, about yourself and about your family."

I ran off, excited to explore the extensive grounds,

and the sprawling old house. Indeed, I spent not only the next few days, but whenever I had free time that summer, wandering my grandfather's property. The house itself was so large that to this day I am not sure that I explored it all. While it did not take long to adequately become acquainted with its bulk, it soon became clear that this house was like a well written and intricately contrived book: no matter how many times it was read, a returning reader always found something new, something that he had not before seen.

I would sometimes stumble upon strange winding passageways that would lead to a room filled with antiques, a balcony overlooking the grounds and decorated with potted plants, or a room decorated with sublime and beautiful artwork. In some of these rooms there would be paintings of recognizable classical scenes, perhaps from Homer, or Aeschylus, or from the Bible; but many of the paintings were of stories or histories that were strange to me. Strange, and even ominous...

One room in particular was very isolated, and even after I had discovered it, it would always take some doing to find it again. It was a square room with very high ceilings, a room with only one entrance, and three windows at the top of three walls provided the light. The walls were decorated with a series of paintings, very large, and the story illustrated seemed to begin on the left of the room, and work around to the right. It began as happy, peaceful scenes, with noble looking people, elegantly gowned, at leisure in faraway kingdoms. They were tall and fair, with straw-colored hair and striking eyes, almond shaped and green. But as the scenes progressed they became more and more morbid, more and more sad. The people were no longer happy, and there was something in the background, something not quite visible, that made the paintings dimmer, less colorful and bright. The last few paintings had lost most of the earlier beauty and vibrancy, and there was a woman who walked among the noble people, and seemed at first glance to be very much at home among them, but when I looked closer, I realized that it might be this woman

20

herself who threw the shadow over the paintings, for there was something not quite right about her, though it took me a moment to tell what it was. It was in her otherwise beautiful face, and could only be seen when standing at a certain angle to the painting; it seemed that her eyes glimmered red, as if they concealed a burning fire.

The grounds of my grandfather's house were comprised of large gardens that completely surrounded the house (which seemed to me to be older than the trees), and that was surrounded completely by a dense forest, isolating my grandfather's house from the rest of the countryside, which was in turn isolated from the quickly moving modern world. There was a small cottage at the edge of the wood, on the east side of the house, in which lived the gardener and his wife (who acted as the housekeeper). Sylvester kept a room on the first floor, in an isolated wing of the house, and the woman who did the cooking lived in a flat above the kitchen. Such was the household in which I found myself that summer, and (with the possible exception of the unpleasant Sylvester) it was not a disagreeable group of people. In a place like that there is always something for an inquisitive and adventurous boy to find and to do.

The gardens were fabulous, with twisting paths and old, crumbling stone steps that led to secluded pools, with statues of strange creatures standing in the center, their waterspouts rusted and broken. These gardens were a strange combination of immaculate shrubbery and decrepit masonry, as though the trees and bushes were alive, and full of youthful vigor, while the statues, steps, and walls had died long ago, and the gardener was unable or unwilling to revive them. Perhaps the climbing vines (which seemed intent on forever hiding all signs of masonry) proved too formidable an opponent for even Mr. Sedgwick, the gardener. Or perhaps he loved the sprawling, wild chaos of life more than he loved pruned and clipped order.

Mr. Sedgwick was a curious man, methodical and slow moving, but his eyes sparkled, and were full of wit and

21

wisdom. His wife, Mrs. Sedgwick, was very pretty (despite her age; both she and her husband seemed to be quite as old as my grandfather) and happy; she would sing while she worked, and she was very fond of me. I was very taken by the both of them. They seemed not at all like the other couples of similar age and circumstance that I knew at the time. There was something about them, an air or a disposition, that I could only describe as otherworldly. I don't quite know how to describe what I mean. But Mr. Sedgwick seemed sometimes to not merely tend the various plants in the garden, allowing them the most favorable conditions in which to flourish, but seemed rather to be himself the favorable condition. He did not so much prune as speak, and thereby draw from the soil plants of radiant beauty, whose leaves and flowers opened to greet the aged gardener as if to embrace him. At his merest touch, it seemed to me, he could transform a withered and decrepit plant into a thing of vitality and joy.

As for Mrs. Sedgwick, she would not, I was sure, so much walk as glide, and even float, over the grass or stone, her feet never quite touching the ground...

And yet in both I sensed a restlessness, a yearning, perhaps, for something, I knew not what. Often in the evenings they would stand, hand in hand, looking out over the garden at the setting sun, and reflected in their eyes was a longing, or a sorrow. And it seemed that they were looking for something in the setting sun, something only they could see, far away, at the edge of the last bit of light, just before the world plunged once again into night.

Mrs. Phelps, the cook, spent all of her time, as far as I could tell, bustling about the kitchen, preparing whichever meal was next, and talking or yelling to herself the entire time. She was, unlike the Sedgwicks, very "this worldly." I am not at all sure that she didn't sleep in the kitchen, for no matter the hour of day, if I walked into kitchen (I would sometimes go in search of a snack), she would be hurrying about with bowls and saucepans in her arms, or elbow deep in flour and dough. She was a wonderful cook (though not, I think, as good a cook as my mother), and it was great fun to have such a variety of delicious meals, prepared with flair, and punctual to the minute.

So it was in this strange setting that my adventures began. A few mornings after my father boarded the train back home, I was wakened in the early hours by a disheveled and distempered Sylvester, and told to report to the veranda within ten minutes. Sleepy and shivering with cold, I did as I was told, and from the veranda I followed Sylvester through the dew-soaked morning to a wide alley of grass, bordered on both sides with tall trees. Throughout the alley were dispersed at random intervals paper cutouts of strange and varied shapes, like creatures recently crawled out of a book of mythology, all tacked to stakes of different heights, rising from the mist. My grandfather was waiting for me.

"Good morning, Thaddeus," he greeted me, "I hope that the hour is not too early? I know how you young people value your sleep."

"No grandfather, I am perfectly awake. What is this place?"

"This is the gun range, where you will begin your instruction. Here I will teach you some very practical skills, and the kind of skill that you will find enjoyable to practice. The heir of Cornelius Ramsey must know how to shoot!"

So saying he directed me to a small table close by. Laid upon it were handguns of several makes and caliber, and also several rifles. I was very surprised, and looked at my grandfather again. He was looking down the range, as the early sunlight splintered through the trees and mist, with a smile on his wrinkled face, as if taking a gauge of the yardage of each target, and how the wind might play on each shot. Turning back to me he said:

"Put these ear-covers on, Thaddeus, step back, and we will begin."

I did as I was told, and watched in wonder as he took up a pistol, inserted a magazine, worked the action with deft and fluid speed, and let out a burst of fire downrange that echoed and rebounded through the wood, and sent all the birds in the vicinity racing startled into the sky. Each bullet found its mark, bursting through the paper targets one after another, so quick that my eyes could barely take it all in.

We spent all that morning, and every morning over the next few weeks, learning how to shoot.

My grandfather was full of strange surprises. He was very unlike what I would have imagined to be a normal grandfather. His age did not seem to be a factor for him, for he was as limber and strong as a much younger man. In the evenings he and Sylvester would usually spend an hour or so in the gymnasium, which was situated in the eastern wing of the mansion, boxing. Only it wasn't boxing, really, so much as a whirling dervish of blows and counter blows, kicks and strikes requiring amazing dexterity, and leaps and acrobatics requiring both dexterity and strength. So fast they would engage each other that I could not follow the moves closely, but it seemed to be very much like a game of chess. How a man of his age could fight like that I did not know. Sylvester could also fight well, but not so well as my grandfather.

In addition to his wild athletic habits, I would often find my grandfather in his study, poring over his dusty books or manuscripts, or staring into the fire, or out one of the two huge windows that framed the fireplace and chimney, and looked over the gardens, all the while smoking his pipe, or puffing a large cigar. In hindsight he seemed to be, at least in our earliest conversations, tentatively establishing a confidence with me, to be attempting to build a relationship with his grandson after a ten-year absence. His conversation was earnest and pleasant, but I had the impression that he was not at all used to talking with children, and was unsure of himself. But he was an intelligent man, and even then I could easily see from where my mother derived her superb wit, along with her inquisitive mind and her quiet warmth.

And yet, behind the warmth and wit, there lurked always, it seemed, a hidden sorrow. I could see it in his eyes sometimes, as he looked at me while we talked. He might be asking me about my school or my playmates, and listening to my answers intently with a warm smile on his face, but behind the smile I could see both pain and sadness. Once I walked quietly into the library unannounced, and saw from a distance my grandfather, who, unaware of my presence, was sitting with his head in his hands, weeping. I left quickly, before he noticed that I had seen him.

Thus I spent the first month or so at my grandfather's house, and I enjoyed it thoroughly. But the excitement and joy of that initial month did not last, and was soon transformed into... into something most unpleasant. I will now relate to you the incident that I consider to be the first of the bizarre happenings, though it might appear to be of little consequence: One morning, as I was exploring the garden, I came across a narrow path between two great trees, standing like the pillars that used to guard the entrance of the ancient Greek temples. As I looked through the trees, I heard a cry of a raven, somewhere in the branches above, and I was shaken with a chill. The path beyond the trees was shrouded in gloom, for the trees were so large and tall, that they cast a long shadow, obscuring the path. The shrouded path seemed to me to be the entrance of a sacred place, a place of power and beauty, and darkness and despair.

As I looked through the trees, my heart began to race, and my imagination began to run faster than I thought possible, as it conceived of dark towers at the edge of the world, and great kingdoms and mighty rulers; rulers who were hard and cold, ruthless and cruel, like the quarried stone of this strange pathway. It seemed in that moment as though a vision passed before my eyes, and I saw red banners against the sky, and heard trumpets blow, and with great fanfare and amidst the rapturous applause of great, swelling crowds of people, both young and old, women and men, a mighty queen climbed the steps of a great, white castle; its stones were alabaster, but the castle was a whitewashed grave. In my mind I saw the queen turn to face the cheering masses, and it seemed that she looked at me, and my blue eyes met her green eyes. It startled me, and it seemed to startle her, for it appeared that she could see me as well; she stared for a moment, and then, like a veil lifted, her green eyes flared ember red, and her lips pulled back from her bare white teeth, and she smiled at me.

The vision vanished suddenly, but my chill turned to a choking, sickening fear that welled up into my throat, and I had the irrational, almost irresistible urge to turn and run. I stood shaking for a moment, but I held my ground, and it seemed at that moment of indecision as though the sun came out from behind a cloud, and I was once again in my grandfather's garden. "It is silly to be afraid," I said, "for I am in a well-kept garden, and I can hear Mr. Sedgwick trimming the lawn over by the large fountain," but my voice trembled as I spoke. I mustered my courage, and, as little boys often do, I armed myself with a broken stick that I found beside the path. I pictured myself as a great warrior, and with a determined (but nervous) step, I entered the mysterious way.

I found the gloom was not as intense as I had anticipated, and was a little cheered. The broken flagstones were covered in moss, and the way was hedged by great trees like the ones at the entrance (but somewhat smaller) as though they had been planted centuries ago to line the path, and not that the path had been wound between them as an afterthought.

"It is strange," I thought, "that I did not notice this grove before. These trees are so large, and planted with such precision, that they should certainly stand out, even in such a strange place as this garden."

The path ended at short stone steps, built into a little knoll, which was surrounded by the great trees, and so was hidden from view of the rest of the garden. The steps ended at a stone wall, perhaps eight feet high, set in the center of the knoll, and was so covered by climbing vines that the gray of the stones were barely visible. In the center of the wall facing me (for the wall seemed to be a great square, like a secluded garden within a garden), stood a door, also covered in ivy, but it appeared that the ivy had been cut away at the edge (which was how I knew there was a door underneath the ivy at all) so as to allow the door to be opened. I thought that Mr. Sedgwick must come in here from time to time, to tend whatever was inside, and so kept back the vines from completely entangling the entrance.

I approached the door with great curiosity, and with no little effort, succeeded in pushing it wide. As it creaked open, I noticed that there were strange carvings in the stone arch that framed it. They seemed to be words, but I did not recognize the language, and was unable to guess at the meaning, except that they gave me the impression that the language must be a harsh one, and the message inscribed could not merely be a fanciful limerick, as is often found carved on garden walls. I stepped into the secluded garden.

The enclosed garden was almost completely comprised of a well-kept lawn. The bright, manicured green carpet covered most of the floor. The enclosure was perhaps about thirty feet long and maybe twenty feet wide, with the lawn covering the ground from wall to wall, with only a small stone walkway directly down the middle. At the far end of the enclosure stood a curious pedestal of stone, square, and perhaps four feet high, almost completely covered in ivy. There was something set on top of the pedestal, but I could not at first see what it was, because of the tangled vines. I slowly approached the pedestal, not at all sure what I would find. It seemed to me to be an odd sort of thing, to build this wall simply to enclose, or protect, another garden decoration. There were certainly plenty of statues, sculptures, and other such things spread throughout my grandfather's garden.

I walked completely around the pedestal, for it sat

several feet away from the back wall, and the lawn wrapped completely around the strange bit of masonry, but the stone path ended at its base. Finally, I began to untangle the mess of vines that kept this stone shrouded in mystery. Using my trusty stick, I was able to uncover the front of the pedestal, and saw that there were more of the strange carvings that I had seen on the doorframe. Most of them were faded until they were almost invisible, but a few had withstood the ravages of years and harsh weather. However, directly in the center was a new carving (or, at least, newer than the strange language; it still may have been a hundred years old or more, it was impossible to tell), lines that had been chiseled over the old words. It took me a few moments to clean the vines and grime away, so that I could see them clearly. The words were Latin, I could tell, and I knew enough Latin to make out some of the meaning, but its complete translation remained a mystery. It seemed to me to be a Biblical quotation, for I recognized some of the words from the readings in my missal. This is what it said:

Et factum est proelium in caelo
Michahel et angeli eius proeliabantur cum dracone
Et draco pugnabat et angeli eius

But I was unable to completely ascertain the meaning, and I began to untangle the vines that kept the sculpture atop the pedestal a mysterious mass of green. This took some doing, since it was almost out of my reach. As I tore away a vine, I caught a glimpse of what was underneath, and it brought me up short.

Instead of the gray stone, that I had expected, it was black, like ebony. I quickly tore away the rest of the vines and stepped back to look. It was a statue of a dragon, grotesque in appearance, but beautiful and intricately carved, jet black, but with strange flashes of color that could be seen on its scales, like fish scales, when viewed at the proper angle. It was in pristine condition, and it almost seemed not to be a statue at all, but rather some terrible, prehistoric creature that had been frozen in time, perhaps by some wizard, or by a powerful knight, as a punishment for

28

razing a village and plundering its treasure. But on second thought, this did not at all seem like a dragon from the stories, for it seemed to me that even those dragons, for all their malice, would not be able to match this serpent's cruelty. I thought that if this thing awoke from its sleep, there would be no safe place in the world to hide.

I could not understand how it had maintained its immaculate condition, for it must certainly be as old as its pedestal. But even where the ivy had clung to it there was no mark, neither of grime nor dust. It was such a fascinating sight, with such dark, alluring beauty that I wandered around it for several minutes, just examining the intricate detail, and marvelous craftsmanship. I could not tell what it was made of; it appeared to be some kind of stone, but of a kind that I had never before seen. It was not as though the stone had been dyed black, the color was too *real*, too *alive*, for that. I wondered if perhaps it was a metal of some sort, because it seemed so smooth, but I was almost certain that it was stone. Finally, I reached out my hand to feel the surface. My hand touched the smooth, cold stone, and instantly I jerked my hand away, and staggered back!

I do not know exactly what it was that caused the horrible sensation; it was not that something had hurt my hand, or even that my hand had felt anything unexpected, but it was as though the world had shifted, and a sickness, a nausea, had gripped me, and my head spun. Everything stood as if upside down, and I had the sensation that my very existence, all that was real, was suddenly turned back-to-front. A door seemed to open in my mind, a window thrown back, and something clawed at the entrance, scratching to get in. It seemed that I had only to allow it, only to give the word, and this stranger who stood at the door would come in. I knew only that I must not allow it. All this I experienced in an instant, and it was a sensation that is, I now realize, quite impossible to explain.

The world righted itself, and I stood for a moment somewhat shaken and confused, looking at the statue. The statue stared back, with cold, black eyes, as though it could see me, as though it knew that I was there, and that I had touched it. It was at that moment that I saw past the beautiful craftsmanship, and I was no longer concerned with the curious quality of stone, but rather I knew then that this thing was indeed evil; it represented something evil, and was crafted with evil intent. As I stood looking at the thing, and as it seemed to stare back at me, I had the terrible fear that it would come alive and devour me. Panic gripped me, and I turned and fled. I raced out of the secret garden, down the hidden path, and out into the safety of my grandfather's garden, tumbling onto the fresh, green lawn, my broken stick still clutched in my fist. Mr. Sedgwick had just rounded the hedge as I collapsed, and he paused for a moment, looking at me; then said, "Playing knights and dragons again, are ye'?"

~

The Serpent

A strange [man] came from the high mountains in the west, on foot, wrapped in a tattered cloak, his dirty gray hair long and ragged. He spoke naught, save to ask for food, and then he left, traveling east, into the sunrise...[the fragment breaks off here, but Prof. Wuin believed that the narrative is resumed in fragment 796.003. He cannot with certainty enlighten us as to the nature of missing manuscripts, but it is clear that what remains is very important in our understanding of the development of certain mythologies that have arisen in southeast Asia, specifically those of the "Krishnag," or the "mountain serpents," during the time-period in question, roughly 1500-1000B.C.] -narrative resumed, fragment 796.003: *...Had warned us not to follow, not to question him concerning whence he had come, and from what he was fleeing. It was to no avail that he warned us; it was near twilight on the third day when she* [note the curious use of the feminine case] *came, rushing down from the mountain forests like the wind, and we were stricken cold with terror. I saw her, the demon with eyes of flame, the serpent* [Prof. Wuin has translated this word (or, more precisely, symbol) as "Serpent", but has commented on its notorious difficulty of translation in his notes: "We are unable to use any word with complete accuracy, and the word "serpent" is almost certainly not the creature, or idea (as with Prof. Chung Lee's interesting interpretation that this whole story is completely symbolic, and represents the 'shock' of a culture's exposure to new realities, or new religions) that is implicit in the word; the word (and creature) "dragon", (though the dragon as a mythical creature is, in one form or another, everywhere present in Chinese culture and religions) would also be a poor translation, but because of our limited knowledge of this sophisticated language, we must content ourselves with an inaccurate, though roughly equivalent, translation." from *Notes on the Gongha Shan Fragments*, p.p. 278-279, Harper,

London, 1928] -narrative resumed: *from the netherworld, awakened from her sleep at the roots of the mountains. She devoured us, young and old, and like a thunderbolt was gone, into the east, leaving destruction in her wake.*

Fragments 742.012 & 796.003 from the *Gongha Shan*, circa 1200B.C., Translated from original (Chinese) dialect by Prof. Wuin, 1928, and currently held in trust at the London Museum of Archeological Discovery

Chapter III

"All men by nature desire to know."
~Aristotle, The Metaphysics

After my frightening experience in the garden, I spent more time indoors, exploring the house, and talking with my grandfather. I eventually (maybe three days later) told my grandfather about my strange experience in the garden, though I was worried that he would think it merely the product of an overwrought imagination.

He sat quietly until I had finished my story, the smoke from his cigar disappearing into the dimness of the huge library ceiling above us. He paused for a moment or two, after I had finished my story. "That statue is quite old, as you have guessed. It was here before I came, and even before this house was built, which was over two hundred years ago. I think I should tell you..." he paused. "I think that you will find it interesting to learn that I moved here to this home precisely for the sake of that statue. I am not at all surprised to learn that you had the reaction that you just described. It is indeed an ugly thing. And I would suggest that in the future you avoid that particular corner of the garden; it is not a safe place to be exploring alone." He gave me a peculiar glance from underneath his bushy eyebrows, one that was full of sadness. Then he looked up at the ceiling, perhaps thirty feet above our heads, and sent several smoke rings soaring up into its beams.

"I hesitate to tell you *why* precisely it is here." Again he paused, and then abruptly changed the subject. "Do you know why I have only just met you? Why you are almost a young man, and you had never seen your grandfather before now?" He looked at me, his face bearing a curiously mysterious expression, and again I had the impression that there was something hidden about him, a longing, or a pain, some burden that he carried, and I was instantly attentive. I shook my head, "no."

"First," he said, "I am sorry that I have missed so much of your life, and I want you to know that it was not my choice. That is, if I could have chosen something else, without unfortunate consequence, I would have." Another cluster of smoke rings sailed towards the rafters. "I have been doing some traveling, some investigation, relating to some issues that concern you directly. It was in the course of this investigation, that I encountered some... well, problems and circumstances that kept me away from home, all these ten years." At this point I noticed a pained expression in his eyes, as though the burden that he hid had momentarily come to the surface. For a moment only, and then it was gone. "This, shall we say, 'investigation,' concerns you in this way; it involves your ancestry, and your vocation. What do you know of your distant ancestors, Thaddeus?"

As I thought for a moment, I realized that I knew very little; indeed, I knew my paternal grandparents, who lived in Kent, and my uncle and aunt, and their three small children, who were in London, but I really knew nothing beyond this, and certainly nothing of my family on my mother's side. I guess that this had struck me before as being a bit strange, for, during the Christmas season, we would often visit Grandpa Jimmy and Grandma Joan, and perhaps see my uncle and aunt, but we would never see, and indeed we would never mention, my mother's family. As a small child this anomaly was something to which I gave little thought, but in the recent years I had asked my mother about it. "Well," she had said, "my mother has gone to heaven, and so you will have to wait many years before you will be able to meet her." At my age, I understood well this rhetorical phrase, "gone to heaven," and I asked how she had died. My mother had begun, quite unexpectedly, to cry softly, and she answered, "She grew very ill quite suddenly, and when the pain was too much to bear, she left us. It was very hard on both of us, your grandfather and I, and also your father. You had only just been born..."

"And what of my grandfather?" I had asked, "Has he died also?"

"No, he is alive. But you will not be able to meet him, just yet. But come, no more questions. Let's talk about something else." I obeyed, because I hated to see my mother cry.

"Very little," I answered my grandfather's question. "Well," said he, "you will soon learn more. I have asked you to stay this summer so that I could teach you something of your heritage, with all the privilege and responsibility that is implied." I did not understand what he meant.

"Responsibilities?" I asked.

"Of course." He said, "there is no such thing as a heritage without responsibility. Surely you can see that? Being born into a family means that you share in the life and duty of that family. The pauper or the king, each has his own duty, his own responsibility. It is certainly no less true of this family."

"Well, I am not born a king, so what are the responsibilities of *this* family?"

"I will tell you in time. Not royalty, perhaps, but yours is a special family all the same," He said, his eyes twinkling. "Come, I will show you something."

He rose from his chair, and I followed him to a section of bookcase against the eastern wall. I was again struck by the enormity of the library, and the strange vastness of the house. He reached between two volumes, and I heard a soft 'click'. My heart leapt with surprise as the bookcase quietly pivoted, as if on a central axel, and revealed a secret tunnel in the wall. We stepped into the low passageway, and trembling with excitement, I followed my Grandfather down a series of steps, and past several diverging branches of the tunnel. I had read of such secret places in stories, but had never expected to see one myself. The tunnel was made of stone (as was much of the rest of

35

the house) and lit with the soft glow of electric bulbs, which were hung every several yards or so. I wondered where we were in relation to the rest of the house, and what rooms were above us, or even below us.

We had wandered through the passageway for several minutes when we came out abruptly into a small, cozy sitting room (if a room with stone walls and lit almost exclusively by electric lights can be considered cozy). There were rugs on the floor, and a few sitting chairs. A large crucifix hung from the wall at our left, and there were also a couple of bookshelves, and a sturdy end table with an intricately carved wooden box set on top of it. There was a slight breeze flowing from a vent at the top of the wall directly across from the door, and the fresh air was a relief from the musty air of the narrow stone hallway. Along with the breeze there was a ray of sunlight, broken into squares by the lattice of the vent, and thrown against the wall above the door.

"This room is devoted exclusively to what I am about to show you," Grandfather said, "though I sometimes come here to do some quiet studying. It used to be an escape route, in addition to a hiding place, for the original owners of this house had many enemies." He laughed (I am not sure what it was that he found so humorous), then he walked to the wooden box, opened the lid, and took out a piece of stone. It was perhaps as large as a dinner plate, and the upper edge was rounded off. It looked for all the world like illustrations I had seen of the stone tablets, inscribed with the Ten Commandments and carried down the mountain by Moses.

"Look here," he said, "can you make out any words?" I looked closely, and saw that there were some kinds of symbols chiseled into the face of the tablet.

"I can see writing, but I can't read it."

"In time you may be able to. This is something of a genealogy, a family tree, if you will. These are the names of some of your ancestors, all great men. It does not tell the names of any of your women ancestors, with three

36

exceptions. But you will learn all that soon enough." (Unfortunately, due to the events that were soon to transpire, I would learn very little).

I held the cold stone in my hands, staring at the worn etchings, and thought of all the lives that this represented, all the mysterious past, stretching back God only knew how many years. I wondered what place I had on this stone, if any. And if these were the names of my ancestors, then who was I?

"We will begin your education in earnest, Thaddeus, this next week. We have been learning thus far the practical things, but soon we will begin the more difficult task of the study of history, languages, and... mythology. Every summer you will stay with me, until I have taught you all that I can, all that will be necessary for your future."

"Grandfather, what of my schooling when I am home? Is it replaced?" I asked.

"No Thaddeus, it is supplemented. Learn all you can when you are at home, and then learn what you can with me. What I teach you will be specialized; it will be important for the task that lies ahead. You will be joining the names engraved on this tablet, and their duty will be passed to you."

"What is the duty, Grandfather? Can you just tell me?"

He hesitated for a moment, but then laughed and shook his head. "I could, Thaddeus, but then you might not believe me!" He smiled warmly at me, and laughed again.

We left the hidden room, and made our way back into the library.

I had a difficult time sleeping that night. I tossed and turned in my bed, as my mind mulled over all that my grandfather had said. It was all so mysterious, but also exciting, and I didn't know what to think of it. What was the duty that was to be mine, and what was so different about my family? My young mind could only conceive of adventure as fun and exciting (like learning to shoot on a beautiful summer morning), and it knew nothing of the

37

danger, heartache, and struggle, the joy of success, and the despair of failure that is the stuff of real adventure. And though I did not think it then, I now realize that our entire sojourn in this life is an adventure. We wake one day to the strange realization that we exist, and that beings who are other than us also exist and interact with us, and then we stumble about, as though in a dream, spending our lives on a pilgrimage trying find our true selves, our true home, and our true purpose. I know that there are those who scoff at such notions of transcendence, but I am incapable of understanding their skepticism. I find the fact of my existence to be so strange that it does not seem so strange to think that I might exist for a reason. Our life may be a tragedy or a comedy, but it is always an adventure; in fact, it often seems to me to be something of a faerie tale.

I was thinking about the mystery of my summer at my grandfather's house while tossing and turning in bed that night, and finally, after what seemed like several hours, I slept; and as I slept, I dreamed a dream. It seemed that in my dream I was awake and sitting up in my bed at home. I looked through the gloom of the night at the clock hanging on my wall, and as I looked the clock struck three a.m. In my dream I felt that I was not alone in the room, but that in the corner something waited, watching me from the shadow. I reached for the light beside my bed, but it would not turn on. So I sat and stared, trying to see what was in my room, but my sight could not penetrate the gloom. I was choking with fear, and I tried again and again to call out for my parents, who I knew were just in the next room, but I could not get my mouth to make the sounds. My eyes strained to see into the gloom, and all the time the menace in the shadow stared back.

I awoke from the dream with a start, and I was in a guestroom at my grandfather's house, and the gray light of dawn was visible above the trees outside my window.

~

The Door to Faerie land

~So, my lads, do not go
With the faeries down below.
Their hair is soft, their eyes like coal
With clawing hands to steal men's soul.
If thee hear the sound of drum,
Marching through the midnight glum'
Or of little hands upon the door
Do not open, nevermore!
For like a grave-stone on the moor,
So are doors to that ope' to her~

Lyric from the old English folk tune, <u>The Door to Faerie-land</u>, circa 1300. Translated from Old English by Dr. Seamus MacAllistor, 1905.

Chapter IV

"Once man ate the bread of Angels, for which he now hungers;
now he eats the bread of sorrows, which then he knew nothing of."
~Saint Anslem

It was late June, and I had been living at my grandfather's house for one month. This was the longest I had ever been away from my parents, and it was difficult. My loneliness was assuaged somewhat with the frequent letters that they would send, telling me about the goings on at home. My father would share anecdotes from his summer classes that he taught at the University, and my mother would send bits of the poetry or short stories that she was writing, or tell me what my friends were doing at home with their summers. I came to rely on these letters, for the summer was very long, as summers used to be when we were young.

I would spend the next two months in study. I will explain what I learned from my grandfather in those two months of formal training that I received from him (only two months, for, as you will shortly learn, my adventures soon began in earnest, and my chances for further learning were ended).

He began with a genealogy, obscure and ponderous, comprised of the names from the stone tablet. The names were difficult to pronounce, and more difficult to commit to memory. My ancestors, it seems, were all dedicated to a particular task, and each in turn would hand the task on to another member of the family when they were finished.

"Not just a task, but a vocation." said my grandfather. Many of the older names had to be phonetically transcribed, since they were of an original language now completely lost. "And under tragic circumstances," I was told. And yet it could not have been completely lost, because my grandfather could speak it, if only a little.

"It is a majestic, beautiful language, and almost impossibly difficult for us now to speak and understand, or to read and write." He spoke some words, and it was as though the sound of a quiet breeze was heard, or of the ripples of cool water on a hot day, flowing over smooth stones; more still it was as though he spoke the sound of silence, and the room seemed to grow a little brighter.

"Very difficult," he repeated, "and with good reason. Language seldom goes from simple to complex, but rather from more complex to less. And this is indeed an ancient language."

After I had studied the names, he handed me a small, leather bound book, entitled *Thelmer Ludwig: a Strange Life and Too Early Death*. I read it with great interest over several days, sitting in the library with my Grandfather, or on the lawn of the garden, while Mrs. Sedgwick was working in the flowerbeds. It told the strange tale of a farmer in rural England during the early 1800's, and how the farmer had met somebody who claimed that he was from another world, and how that person (named 'Phleama' in the story; it certainly seemed an invented name to me, the kind of name someone might think up when writing science-fiction, or something similar) had enlisted the aid of Thelmer to get them back to his (Phleama's) home. The farmer had, in good faith, agreed to help the stranded alien, but the alien (or Faerie, as it was called in the story) had tricked him, and once inside Faerie-land had used poor

Thelmer as a slave, and taken him all over the other-world, showing him off like a circus animal. Thelmer had many adventures in Faerie-land, and had finally, and with the help of some "good faeries", managed to escape and return home, much to the surprise of his family and friends, who had by now (the period of several years) expected the worst.

The story was so poorly written, and in such sensational fashion, that I could not understand why my grandfather would waste my time by having me read it. Surely not to learn to write well, or to demonstrate the work of a creative genius, and it obviously had nothing to do with my family. The story was enjoyable as a story, I suppose, but colored by the poor writing and the pretense (so I thought) at being an actual history. But at the end of the story the tone changed. The narrative up until now had been told in first person, seen through the eyes of the protagonist himself; now, the last few pages, the narrative voice changed to that of Thelmer's nephew, Winston Ludwig. The style of writing was remarkably improved, and the tone changed from one of sincere expectancy to that of somber warning. Winston relayed the sad news of his uncle's passing; but more than sad, it was actually frightening.

It seemed that a few weeks after his return, Thelmer began to have strange visions and violent episodes, in which he would sometimes cry out in terror that something had followed him from Faerie-land, and was trying to take him back. This lasted for a period of a few months, getting gradually worse and worse, with no hope for a cure. His family could never quite believe his extravagant tale, but believed (as I did) that his story was nothing more than a product of an excited imagination, or perhaps even a spiteful exaggeration, the kind that a malicious person might tell to draw attention to himself. They thought that Thelmer had left his family and gone off traveling around Europe or Asia, and when he had had enough he decided to return home with his bizarre story (and maybe some obscure Asian illness). The family consulted doctors and priests to try and fix him, but to no avail. Finally Thelmer was advised to write down his experience (the product of that advice is the manuscript which I now read, apparently) to try and exorcise his demons, and this worked to settle him down for some time, and his visions and episodes became more and more infrequent, until his family had hoped that he was cured.

But then came the fateful evening. He was out walking with his dog and his nephew, just outside the quiet country village in which they lived, when he seemed to hear someone call his name. He said that it sounded like someone he had known long ago, and had loved dearly, but he could not remember the person's name. Thelmer had begun to call out in response, and to move toward where he imagined the sound to be, and when Winston tried to slow him down (for he could sense that there was something strange going on), he broke free and started to run. The nephew, Winston, had heard nothing, but it seemed that the dog also heard the voice, for it was going mad with barking and yipping, gnashing its teeth to foam, and leaping about as though it were being driven into a frenzy of either terror or joy. As Thelmer began to run, tears flowed from his eyes, and he laughed out loud and cried in a loud voice, "I am coming to you, I will see you, and I am yours!" He disappeared with the dog over a knoll and into a small wood, where they were lost to the sight of Winston, who was by now quite frightened, but determined to follow his uncle. It was to no avail.

When Winston reached the edge of the wood he saw a figure, hooded in black, leaning over the body of Thelmer. The dog lay sprawled on the ground, some few yards away, as though the poor thing had been flung by some inhuman hand. Perhaps it had. The hooded figure looked up from Thelmer's body, and stared into the eyes of Winston, who was by now numb with shock and fear. Winston could make out no face underneath the hood, but he had the terrible impression that the fiend had smiled at him.

The hooded figure snatched up Thelmer's body and disappeared into the wood. Winston, first calling the attention of a couple of shopkeepers to his plight, had raced off to rescue his uncle. The wood was searched to no avail, and the three had set about awakening the countryside to the trouble. Much of the town emptied to find Thelmer, and several hours later they, along with their hunting dogs, succeeded. Well, they succeeded in finding some of Thelmer. The dogs led the group of townspeople to a wide meadow in the wood, and in the center of the meadow stood a lone tree, ancient, gnarled, and enormous. The dogs began to whine and cower, and would not cross the meadow or approach the tree. Cautiously the townspeople did approach it, and there found poor Thelmer. Or at least they found Thelmer's legs... His two legs stuck pathetically out from the base of the tree, rigid, as though the tree had suddenly grown two unnatural appendages. It was as though Thelmer had attempted to dive into the very center of the tree, and had not quite made it all the way in. It would have been an impossible feat, but there they were, flush in the wood, and the townspeople could not tell how they got there. The legs actually entered the bark of the tree, not as though they had been stuck there, but as though a door had opened in the tree, and then had closed in haste, before Thelmer was all the way inside... The great tree was cut down, and split open, but the rest of Thelmer's body was never found. The legs were removed, but only by cutting a piece of the tree out with them. Thelmer's legs were buried, wood and all. The stump of the great tree was burned.

I set the book down in some frustration. I did not at all see why my grandfather found it necessary to waste my time in this way. Surely there was more to learn than the peculiar fable of some English farmer. The story was barely enjoyable as a story, poorly written, and with a most dissatisfying ending. It was also frightening.

I got up from the couch where I had been reading in the library, and made my way to the kitchen, as the bell was rung for dinner. As I walked through the long hall that was the library, I passed again (as I had many times) the peculiar skeleton in the display case, and determined to ask my Grandfather about it at the next opportunity.

I took my seat at the large dining room table with the rest of the household. Mrs. Phelps was bustling in and out, from the kitchen to the dining room, carrying dishes and trays, mugs and plates, and all manner of food items. Mr. Sedgwick, Sylvester, and my Grandfather were already seated, chatting back and forth about the weather, politics, and whatever else grownups usually discussed around the dinner table. Mrs. Sedgwick was helping Mrs. Phelps to set the table for the household, and she smiled at me as I sat down. "Hello, Thaddeus. Did you enjoy the story that Mr. Ramsey gave you to read?"

"Well, I am not sure. It was enjoyable, I suppose, but I am not at all sure why I was instructed to read it. It wasn't even well written."

"Ah, Thaddeus," interrupted my Grandfather, "you finished it then? What are your thoughts?"

"Well Grandfather," I began, "It was…Well, I am not sure why you wanted it read, I guess."

"Well, to further your education, of course," he responded, somewhat surprised. "Everything that you read here will be for that purpose."

"But a novel of Faerie land?" I asked.

"Surely not!" exclaimed my Grandfather. "Are we speaking of the same book?"

"Now then, what on earth did you have the boy read?" interjected Mrs. Phelps, who had apparently caught enough of the conversation to be indignant, and was attempting to come to my aid.

"Now, Mrs. Phelps," began Mr. Sedgwick, "Mr. Ramsey wouldn't give the boy anything to read but what's good for his education. There is probably a misunderstanding," he added, trying to be helpful.

"A misunderstanding?" asked Grandfather. "Did you not read *Thelmer Ludwig: a Strange Life and Too Early Death?* The little leather bound history I gave you yesterday?"

45

"Well, yes, I did; but a history? I thought... I mean, wasn't it a fiction?"

"A history is not, by its very definition, fiction. Wasn't it clear from the text?"

"But all the talk of other worlds," I stammered, "wouldn't that disqualify it as a history?"

"Only if there are, indeed, no other worlds. But if the story related by Mr. Ludwig actually happened, and he really did travel to another world, then it seems safe to categorize the tale as a history."

"Oh, Mr. Ramsey, don't fill the boy's head with such nonsense!" Exclaimed Mrs. Phelps. "All this talk of other worlds, magical happenings, and the like. This house is strange enough as it is, without dragging your bizarre worlds and stories into the mix!"

"Now Gladys," (this is Mrs. Phelps' first name, though Mrs. Sedgwick was the only one who addressed her as such) said Mrs. Sedgwick, "Not all such talk may be edifying, but neither is it all nonsense."

"Well, perhaps not nonsense, but neither is it history. Let's call fanciful stories by their real names, even if we don't label their authors as charlatans."

"Surely you are not saying..." began Grandfather.

"All I'm saying is that the boy should be reading something healthy, like a science book or something," she interrupted defiantly. "Something that will do him some good."

"A science book!" Grandfather gave me a piercing look. "What do you say to that, Thaddeus?"

"Well, Grandfather," I began, slowly, "Its just that... I don't know that the story didn't happen, I suppose, but the existence of Faerie land seems to me to be so... unlikely."

"Unlikely?" My Grandfather repeated, giving me a strange look from underneath his bushy white eyebrows, "Unlikely? I am not at all sure how one would even begin to calculate those odds. It does seem, however, that to assume that one's own limited experience of the universe, and of the possible universes, has exhausted completely what is

46

possible to be experienced…well, that stretches credulity to the breaking point. But if there is anything that one can safely assume, Thaddeus, it is that one does not know everything. Since none of us… well, unless, perhaps, there are exceptions… has ever been to a different world, we assume that different worlds cannot possibly exist. This seems to me to be eminently unreasonable. You speak of 'science books,' Mrs. Phelps", he turned back to the cook, "Do your books of science chart the paths into the spiritual, into the non-material? Can they say for certain, nay, can they give empirical evidence as to whether there could possibly exist things outside the bounds of their own domain and competence? If I lay eyes upon an elf or a gnome, or even a spiritual being made manifest, do the books of science call my sight in error, or can they admit the possibility that modes of being may be found in the cosmos in the presence of which the empirical sciences must necessarily remain mute?" As he spoke, his face betrayed his amusement. Mrs. Phelps merely muttered something like "I know what I know," and clattered out of the dining room, her arms full of empty trays.

"Wisdom will die with that woman," laughed my grandfather. "It is a poor education and a poor imagination that equates all knowledge with the empirically falsifiable. There are many questions which our physical sciences are not qualified to answer, and we must turn to philosophy or other disciplines to find answers, if any are to be had."

"Well, then how would one know whether Faerie land is real?" I asked. "So it cannot be disproved, and so 'science' cannot be brought to bear on it. That doesn't mean that it is true, does it? I mean, it is not fair to say that, well, we can't come up with a mathematical formula or something, therefore Faerie land exists?"

"Of course not, of course not! I do not advocate a naïve acceptance of every fantastic story that one hears, just because it cannot be proved true or false. That would also be unreasonable. Most stories that one hears of other worlds may be false, but we must be careful not to fall off the other edge of the knife; we must not preemptively narrow our conception of the real. This is what I am trying to say. We should not suppose that all the known universe is all knowable reality. The world is wide and strange, and, as you say, pretense at knowledge, scientific or otherwise, is a fool's game. But maybe, just maybe, your grandfather is not a fool. 'There are more things in heaven and earth then are dreamt of in your philosophy,' Thaddeus." he smiled at me. "Shakespeare."

"But Grandfather, are there other worlds, or gnomes or something? I...I don't think I understand." I was becoming more and more confused by this time. Sylvester, who had been eating his dinner, listening to all the talk with a cynical, condescending expression on his face, broke in:

"These kind of folk can't know what we know, and they won't change their small minds, Cornelius. They are the rabble for which the genius exists. The genius that they lock up in their white, sterile hospital rooms, who they mock and belittle, it is he who defines the world, who sees beyond the provincial, the shallow, and the ordinary. It is he for whom the worlds were made. The rabble cannot see, for they have no eyes."

I have, I think, already mentioned that I found Sylvester disagreeable. This bitter, bizarre tirade served to galvanize my perception of him. It seemed that I was not the only one who was offended. Mr. and Mrs. Sedgwick, who had been eating in embarrassed silence until now, both looked up with indignant expressions clouding their kind faces. Mr. Sedgwick seemed especially offended, and remarked that it was a small mind indeed that considered itself the enlightened, brilliant one, and maintaining all the others who lived more simple lives as somehow inferior "rabble." Sylvester merely grunted and returned to his meal, and Grandfather had to interject, saying that he considered the conversation closed, and he thereby disallowed Sylvester the opportunity to respond, had he been so inclined (he was not, I think).

I myself did not know what to think, or how to

respond, even if I were allowed the opportunity. I finished my dinner in silence, and afterwards helped Mrs. Phelps with the dishes.

"Don't you listen to everything that your Grandfather says, Thaddeus, no matter how much he tries to persuade you," said Mrs. Phelps, as she clattered around the kitchen. "You know how the aged can be, always imagining farfetched happenings, and thinking that when they were young, things were better somehow. He may think he has been to other worlds in his wanderings, but I doubt he has been further than Paris."

"He does think he has been to other worlds, then?" I asked, surprised.

"Well, maybe I've said too much... But then, lord, one can't go around watching everything they say, or nothing will ever get said! Now, I've never heard your Grandfather say so himself, mind you, but that is the talk. All the townsfolk are saying it, and even my old ma. They call him the 'mad scientist in the castle.' Me, I don't know. He was missing for quite some time, you know, before you were born. No one knows where he went, and Sylvester was in charge of the house. We were all here; we make good money, keep good hours, and we are quite fond of him, you know, for all his foolishness and eccentricities. Of course, Sylvester assured us that he was all right, and that he would return, but we were all very worried. You see, that was right after your grandmother... Well, I guess you need to know sometime. That was when your grandmother died, Thaddeus. I think it broke your grandfather's heart, and maybe... well, maybe it tipped him over the edge, so to speak. I shouldn't say that... But something terrible happened that night, during the great storm. He found her himself, you know, lying on the grass in that little dragon garden. I hated that wretched garden before, and I hated it all the more after. Why she went there at all, at night and in the storm, I will never know. She had been sick with fever, and maybe delusional. She had been struggling some time with an illness that was very unusual. He carried her back

49

here to the house himself, his face white as a sheet, and never left her side for three days and three nights. The doctors could not understand how she died, just as they could not understand her illness. They chalked it up to fever, I think, as doctors will when they don't know what's really going on, which is often. Your grandfather buried her, and then he disappeared. I remember it clearly. But he had a terrible look in his eyes, he did. Like his eyes had been set on fire, like they were burning with melted silver... I don't know. It frightened me a little, though, I will admit. I've never seen him like that. That was a terrible time for all of us, Thaddeus. Did no one tell you all this yet? A boy your age is old enough to know his family history, I think. I was very sad, Thaddeus, not to have known you earlier. I helped raise your mother you know, but I only met you once, just after you were born, and before your grandmother died.

"Anyway, some thought that Sylvester was trying to get the house and Mr. Ramsey's considerable means after he left, but there was nothing came of that. Sylvester is unfriendly and pretentious, but he is devoted to Mr. Ramsey. Things continued on like that for a long time, a decade actually. We did our jobs, and lived our lives. And then one day Mr. Ramsey showed up at the house, looking like he had aged thirty years instead of ten. Things were always strange in this house, mind you, but things got even stranger after his return. Weird comings and goings in the middle of the night, visitors from Asian countries, and goodness knows what else. Even our good Sedgwicks, bless their souls, are not your normal folk, as you probably have noticed. They showed up here just after Mr. Ramsey took me on, oh, thirty or so years ago now (when I was a young lass). 'Very queer, very peculiar they are,' I says to Mr. Ramsey. 'Don't you worry Mrs. Phelps,' he says, 'they have had a bad run of it, and need our help. Take care of them, will you, and see that they settle in well? They may be with us a long while.'

"But anyway, that's a long way of answering your questions; I think he thinks he has been someplace strange, but I have never heard him say it outright. I think his mind was a little gone after your grandmother died, and his decade of wandering didn't help matters. I've heard that a broken heart can do that to a person, you know, can bend and break even a strong man's health."

I did not know what to think. I was at the age where children become more skeptical of the strange and mysterious, while still retaining their lively imaginations. It was not as though I was incapable of believing my grandfather; it was just that I was coming to realize (as most children do) that many of the stories that we hear and believe (like Father Christmas) were not literally true. I believed, of course, that other worlds could be "out there," and further I actually wished that they were, but I did not want to be made a fool of, or to be thought merely a foolish child (though I was, in truth, merely a child). I still was not sure my grandfather was not joking with me, and I did know what, exactly, I was supposed to be learning. Surely my grandfather did not think that we were a family of Faeries, or some such thing? But then what did *Thelmer Ludwig's* story have to do with me or my family? Why were the names of my ancestors chiseled on that stone tablet, and why was it all so secret? And where had my grandfather been those ten years? I was beginning to really miss my home, and my mother and father.

~

Sergeant James Churchman
42 brigade, Her Majesty's Imperial Army
June 2nd, 1903,
Katmandu, Nepal

My dearest Charlotte,

I am writing to you in the most dreary of circumstances, but all is bearable for your sake, and for the sake of our beloved England, for whom I fight and for whom you must suffer my absence. I have little time, and fewer writing materials to accurately convey my affection for you, and the extent to which I miss you, and my heart aches for you. The night sky in these mountains is unlike anything that I have ever witnessed, or hoped to witness, since I last gazed into your eyes. There are more stars out here than the grains of sand that compose the beach where we walked two summers ago. As for my work, I can say that we have done little for over four months, and much of what we have done I am not at liberty to disclose to you, for national security reasons, as you know. I will tell you that there has been progress, if only a little. But I fear that there may be more violence in the near future, if the Tibetan tribesmen do not acknowledge our rights and demands. I think that they might be a more stubborn lot than we first suspected. But they are no match for our superior military tradition and firepower, and we have the strength of an Empire behind us.

I have little space to continue (these pages comprise my whole supply of non-official paper for the whole month), but I would like to quickly relate to you a remarkable incident that occurred last weak. It was quite strange, and I think that you will find it diverting, and quite disturbing. We were on a patrol, which lasted three weeks, and were deep in these God-forsaken mountains (I have already described to you their massive size, which make veritable dwarfs of the Swiss Alps) when we lost our bearings. After wandering for two days trying to find our way back, we

52

stumbled upon an ancient path of huge stone steps, leading up into a remote pass between two rugged mountains. Intrigued, we followed it for many weary hours, until it finally led us to a small, beautiful alpine valley, shaped like a bowl, hidden deep in the Himalayan Mountains. We followed the steps (which became a narrow road, paved with ancient quarried stone) across the small valley, until we reached the entrance to a cave, in front of which sat a strange, haggard old man, clothed in tattered rags. The cave seemed to be carved by human hands into the side of the mountain. Now, we have seen many small caves before (the nomads use them as shelter during the winter months), but there was something different about this cave. It was as though a stone door had once hung in the entrance, and now lay in ruined shards in the stoop. The entrance to the cave was framed by an intricately carved stone pattern, interlaced with words from some strange language that we were unable to identify. The carving seemed to be of a dragon, or huge lizard, terrible to behold. It was such a strange situation that we did not know how to proceed. We tried to question the old man, who wore a bizarre, wild expression, and laughed for no apparent reason, revealing his almost toothless, diseased gums. It was clear that his sanity had been compromised, probably the result of sitting alone in this vast wilderness for too long.

He spoke to us in English, which he spoke quite fluently; he was not, I think, English, but we could not establish his heritage with any certainty. His eyes were a strange hue of gray, and his European features made the whole affair that much more odd. He might have been an American. He warned us not to enter the cave, because if we did we would not come out. "All who enter are lost, and those who are lost will certainly enter. All who go down drown in her depths, and all who go up drown in her heights. One you may have, but you cannot have both; choose the cave of this world or the world of the cave." He raved on like this for some time in an unbearably high pitched, raspy voice, and we were unable to get anything sensible out of him. We asked him who he was, and why he was sitting in front of the cave, and he answered thus: "I am the gatekeeper, the watcher; I am he who has beheld Her face to face, and lived; I am he who shut the door, and waits till the worlds end, in ice or fire. I am he who lives, but I am dead to this world; I am old, but there is one who is older than I; I have looked into the dark recesses of time, and seen the light of the past, and the decay of the future. The shadow draws closer, night is coming; who knows the terror of the darkness like I do? I, who have been to the ragged edge of night, who have looked into the very eyes of the void, I am he who sits before you." Needless to say, we were quite perplexed and more than a little disturbed by his speech.

This brings me to the most upsetting part of my tale. Two of our more adventurous lads (I do not wish to disrespect their families by revealing their names) volunteered to enter the cave. We took all necessary precautions, and attached them to a rope, and we held the other end. They took torches and guns, and entered the cave. The old man was by now in hysterics, writhing on the ground and foaming at the mouth, one moment laughing in his high pitched, horrible way, the next moment crying and rending what was left of his tattered garment. I now wish that we had heeded his warnings. The two soldiers disappeared into the darkness, and have not been seen since. You will not be surprised to hear that, after waiting for some time, feeding out more and more of the rope, until observing some panicked pulls on the line, and then feeling it go slack, we plunged into the cave ourselves to find out what was wrong. We proceeded carefully, in case there was a crevasse, or chasm in the floor, so that we would not meet the same fate as out two comrades. But we found that the way was quite smooth. The tunnel was perhaps ten feet high, and ten feet wide. The floor was shaped stone, smoothed by human tool, and worn by constant use (though it was now covered with dust, except where our comrades had passed through, it seems that at one time it had been quite a thoroughfare), so there seemed to be no immediate danger. The walls and ceiling of the tunnel were completely covered with fantastic carvings and etchings, and they were almost exclusively of writhing dragons and serpents, terrible to behold. The path held straight, leading down, deeper into the roots of the mountain, and we followed until we reached a place where the tunnel suddenly opened up into a huge cavern. Our lights only just reached the limits of its interior, and it was here that the cave seemed to end. This stone chamber was a mass of the horrible carvings, and our lights cast strange shadows, and our imaginations began to fool us into believing that the very walls and ceilings of this massive chamber were alive, and that it was one great serpent that writhed and circled the dome, choking the blackness with its scaly embrace, as coil after coil of its terrible body wrapped around us like a nightmare. It was here in this subterranean room in hell that the line of rope ended, and the trail was lost. There was nowhere for our comrades to have gone. They had simply disappeared.

We left the cave in a kind of controlled panic, with the intention of harshly interrogating the old man, but when we made our way back into the light, we found the old man already dead. We had left two of our men to guard him, and they were more than a little embarrassed. It seems that the old man had continued his ravings, going gradually more wild, until the soldiers were unable to restrain him, and in his violent gyrations he struck his head against a rock and died. His features were awfully contorted, his mad smile permanently fixed to his grotesque face.

So that is my story. After several days of wandering in the mountains, we managed to find our way back to civilization, and then to our base. I have been unable, because of other duties, to return to the cave and continue the search, and I doubt it would be worthwhile to try. I do not think that I could find the place again, even if I wanted to. But it still haunts me, and I do hope to return someday, or I fear I shall never be at peace. I have, as you know, seen death many times in the course of my career, and have personally lost men in battle, but none have affected me like this. I cannot rest until I establish for certain that my men are indeed dead, and if so, how they met their fate.

But enough of that. I look forward to your response, and your opinion on this matter. I must end here, on this dismal note, for I am come to the end of my writing paper. I love you more than I can say, and I think of you often. Remember me to our families, and write when you are able.
All my love,
Your Affectionate Husband,
James

~ The author of this remarkable letter was, unfortunately, never to return home to his beloved wife or country. He deserted his regiment six weeks after the letter was written (those closest to him believed it was to find this very same "cave") and was never heard from again. This odd story again illustrates the emotional and mental trauma that soldiers often suffered during combat in the harsh climate and conditions of the Tibetan Plateau. ~

From the Appendices of Great Britain and Tibet: a History, By Dr. Desmond Bedford, (Shuster & Shuster Publishing, London, England, 1925) P. 372-374

Chapter V

"Now, too, the night is well along, with dewfall
Out of heaven, and setting stars weigh down
Our heads toward sleep. But if so great desire
Moves you to hear the tale of our disasters,
Briefly recalled, the final throes of Troy,
However I may shudder at the memory
And shrink again in grief, let me begin."
~Virgil, The Aeneid

The next morning after breakfast, my grandfather sat me down in the library to talk.

"I must apologize to you, Thaddeus," he said. "In my exuberance I have not acted wisely. I have been unjust to you, attempting to teach you what you need to learn in a roundabout way. I was afraid to come to the point quickly, for fear that at your young age it would be too much for you. I see now that that was wrong." He lit a cigar, leaned back in his chair, and puffed a series of smoke rings into the air, and a ray of morning sunshine caught them as they drifted slowly toward the high ceiling. A bit of ash fell from the cigar and settled on the collar of his woolen sweater.

"I suppose the best thing to do will be to start at the beginning, and simply tell you all there I to tell about our family. And then you can accept it as it is, or not. But I think you will accept it, and even embrace it. You are, after all, your mother's son!

"All right then... Let me see, how to begin. Well, I suppose I should summarize for you the main contours, and then we can work on filling in the details as we go." he paused, took a breath, and began:

"There is, Thaddeus, a little bit of truth in even the strangest of tales. It cannot but be so, because the human mind is finite. It can only deal with what it experiences, can only speak of mystery by way of analogy, and even the most wild of imaginings must begin with basic premises, like existence, or the ability of language to communicate. These tales involve people, human beings, or if not humans, than beings which think and act like humans. The world is strange and varied, and so the tales that people tell are strange and varied, but they all operate within the same human condition. So even the most bizarre story must have elements in it that are reflections of the real. Now, of course many stories are simply fiction; that is, they did not actually happen. I think this is self evident, but I say it because, after our conversation last night, I do not want you to uncritically accept everything that you hear, or to suppose that I would advocate such a thing. But I want you to understand that just because something seems to be fantastic, it is not therefore necessarily untrue. In fact, it seems to me that the only thing which might disqualify a story *a priori* from being true would be one in which the moral fabric, or the ethical framework of the world, was distorted. If you encountered a universe in which murder was lauded, for instance, or where hate was commended, you would know you are dealing with a fabrication. There are eternal truths, and these cannot be in one universe proscribed and in another commanded. Of course, there may be universes or worlds that have become so twisted and broken that the Good is no longer recognized, but it can never be so that the Good is in one world Good, and in another Evil. The story would not be meaningful; it would have no purchase on the real."

He paused for a moment, looking at me. I was having trouble following him. What had this discourse on stories to do with me? My grandfather could see that I was confused.

"Hmm… Let me see. I guess, in all this, I want you to understand that your family has always trod the thin line between the fantastic and the ordinary. This truth you must understand first, before all else. I have hinted, time and again, that you are a member of a special family; one called out and set apart. Thaddeus, let me put this as clearly as I can: there are indeed other worlds in the cosmos, and many of these are connected to our world, connected by doors that lead to and from this world and the others. Yes Thaddeus, and to and from these other worlds come creatures both good and evil."

He was looking intently into my eyes as he spoke, and he leaned forward in his chair. The smoke from his cigar swirled around his shock of white hair, and I again saw in his eyes the distant ache, the sorrow or longing, that had first struck me when I met him. At his words my heart seemed to leap, and my youthful imagination raced at the thought of strange worlds, and the doors that connected them. In that moment I no longer doubted, and all the fantastic possibilities came rushing into my mind. My face gave my excited thoughts away.

"Ah, I see that you welcome such a revelation! It is easiest for the young to embrace such truths, I think. And, you are the last heir of Cornelius Ramsey," his eyes twinkled as he spoke, and I could see that he was pleased. "Yes, the doors. They are the gateways to the universe, to the far corners of the cosmos. The doors are usually hidden, sometimes permanent, yet they sometimes fluctuate and change, being one moment a door, and the next simply a stone on a hillside, or an entrance to a garden, or whatever it normally is," my grandfather continued. "There are many stories and legends about doors to other worlds: the land of the Faeries, Leprechauns, strange creatures that stalk lonely mountainsides, visitations, and every other conceivable kind of tale, some true, some partially true, and some, of course, outright fabrications. All these have their source in something that is real. Do not ask me why or how these doors exist, why some are always available, or why some change. I do not know. I have heard some explanations based on the physical nature of creation, but these (assuming that they accurately describe reality) offer only mechanical explanations, at best a "how," not a "why". In happier times these doors might have been great thoroughfares, like the modern day railroad, or the great international highways, that make travel so easy and so enjoyable these days. It may have been that there was commerce, cultural exchanges, and even a common language. This is not purely speculation; in my studies and research, and in the research and studies of others (some of whom you may meet) we have found much evidence to support this."

At this point I interrupted him (I was a little too young to appreciate the importance of such research, and I desperately wanted to know how all of this so closely involved me and my ancestors). "Grandfather, what of those names on the tablet, and the book that you gave me to read? What does all that have to do with me?"

"Yes, of course, Thaddeus, I am coming to all of that. Whatever the history of the doors, all of those more happy times have come to an end. Many thousands of thousands of years ago (I do not know with any certainty how long it has been) a shadow entered the worlds, and went to and fro amongst some of them, destroying many. Our own world teetered on the brink of destruction, while through vicious and sustained battles this enemy sought to gain control of the Earth, and to possess the secrets that we alone knew. But there are other forces in the universe, Thaddeus, and other interests. Though evil seems often to reign supreme, and darkness seems stronger than light, we have not been left alone, defenseless, against the shadow. Our world was saved, and is being saved, and will be saved in the end, though it has since become twisted, corrupted, and dangerous. In the meantime there is still much work to be done, and the world is in need of laborers."

He stopped at this point, for his cigar had gone out. My mind was an excited whirl of images, of battles fought long ago, of strange and evil creatures, and strong and brave men, fighting relentlessly against the darkness, of ramparts crumbling, and civilizations wavering, staggering under the onslaught. My conception of the universe had, in an instant, expanded; if it had been cramped and shallow before, it was suddenly broad and deep. In that instant I knew, almost for the first time, that I was not the center of the universe, and that the human story was not the only story being told. But this realization did not diminish, even slightly, my natural, intuitive understanding of the human person's intrinsic value, of *my* intrinsic, eternal worth. Rather, it was no longer a selfish, self-centered value, the kind that required the universe to bend to my will and desires, but was the realization that I was a part of a larger whole, an irreplaceable player in the drama of existence. And this drama was not a mindless, meaningless drama, played to the silent audience of an empty cosmos; there is Another who watches and who is ever participating.

My grandfather re-lit his cigar (he made a sour face as he began to puff it; I have since come to know that re-lighting a dead cigar playes havoc with the cigar's flavor and aromatic quality) and continued:

"All of this is to merely set the stage. Originally, rulers and the wise of our world had, in their possession, all that could be known about the doors; their whereabouts, the specific world that each door led to, and of the Antechamber, which was something of a central meeting place, where all the doors are said to be congregated, somewhere in the vastness of creation. We, of all the worlds, had this information. We alone knew the fabric of the cosmos, and we alone could see into the mind of the Creator. It had been revealed to us. We were (and are) set apart among the worlds. Not, mind you, that we are somehow better; we have more privilege and more responsibility- the first-born of the cosmos, as it were. Our world was a central hub, a destination, and many others scattered throughout the vastness of creation traveled to our world to learn at our feet, and we in turn traveled to theirs.

"All this the Enemy desired. During the Great War, it threw all its strength into acquiring the knowledge that we had been given. Its desire was then, and is still, to dominate creation, to twist it, break it, and drag us all into the abyss with it."

As grandfather spoke these words it seemed that a cloud moved in front of the morning sun, and a chill went through me. I felt in that instant the menace that I had felt in the dragon garden, and knew the same fear that I'd experienced in my nightmare. The excitement that I had had a moment before was replaced by an overwhelming dread, a helpless, hopeless fear. My mind conceived the irrational idea that there was no hope for us, and that the enemy was far stronger than we could ever hope to be, and that we were alone in the cosmos, alone as the shadow drew closer and closer, shutting out the light bit by bit. It was day now, but when night inevitably came we would all drown, swallowed in the darkness of despair.

It was in that moment of fear that I heard the voice for the first time.

It spoke out of the shadow, out of the void, and though I could not see the speaker, I knew who it was that spoke. The sound of it carried from distant memories, terrible stories, and forgotten legends. Darkness shrouded my eyes, and I was no longer in my grandfather's library, but was alone, drowning in the deep. "Thaddeus, Thaddeus, I can see you," the terror spoke, soft and deep, at once both masculine and strangely feminine, floating through my mind like a fog. "Will you see me Thaddeus? Close your eyes, Thaddeus, close your eyes, close your eyes, close your eyes, close your eyes." Panic seized me, and I fought with every bit of strength I had to keep my eyes open, all the while fighting to come awake, to come out of this dream! My wide open eyes could see nothing but darkness, but I knew that if I closed them, even for an instant, I would see that which spoke to me, and the thought was more than I could bear.

"Thaddeus, Thaddeus!" The voice that reached me now was wonderfully different, at once both strong and real, cutting through the darkness like a knife, scattering the terror like wind scatters smoke. My head snapped up and I could see again. It was a beautiful morning in early July, and I was sitting in the library, looking into the concerned face of my grandfather.

"Thaddeus, are you all right? It looked as though you suddenly dozed off, but then you called out, as if you were frightened and needed help. Were you dreaming?" Grandfather was staring into my face, and though he spoke quite calmly, it was clear that he was urgently worried. His face betrayed a sense of concern and also a fearful understanding, as though he may have suspected the nature of my dream. I could feel my forehead damp with sweat. I shook myself awake, rubbed my eyes, and answered:

"Yes, I suppose I fell asleep. I am alright; I did have a strange dream, but now I am alright. I did not sleep well last night, and I may be a little tired yet," I said, stumbling over my words, and looking about confusedly. "I am fine now though. I am trying to understand and take in everything that you are telling me, that's all."

Grandfather kept looking into my face for a moment longer, and then, as if satisfied that whatever it was that he suspected had not occurred, he straightened up and said, "Yes, we will take a break. This is a lot to accept all at once. Let us have some lunch, and then we will begin where we left off."

After lunch, we sat out on the veranda overlooking the expansive garden. The rolling, forested hills stretched from the edge of the garden as far as the eye could see, and I was struck by the ancient, secluded beauty of my grandfather's house. From where we sat I could just see the giant trees that lined the path to the dragon garden. There was a series of knolls that blocked them from immediate view, and a network of walls and paths, fountains and flowerbeds, that would make all but the most fortunate explorer sure to miss the path that marked the way to the mysterious stone enclosure.

I was still upset and disconcerted about my dream (or vision, or whatever it was), but my curiosity far outweighed my fear. I think that even then, deep down, I suspected that my dream was connected to all that I was learning, but I did not want to really consider the ramifications. So I told myself that it was a strange dream, brought on by the strange stories, and that was all.

"So, Thaddeus, we will begin again. First, are there any questions that you would like to ask me?" Of course I had probably a hundred questions, but I asked the ones that were in my mind the most pressing.

"Yes grandfather, I would very much like to know exactly how these worlds concern me. What is it about our family that makes learning about all of this so important, besides the excitement all this affords, I guess. Also, what of that book you had me read, and where were you for all those years? I guess that you went to another world, but why were you gone so long? And what of that skeleton in the library, and what happened to this "enemy", and what of the knowledge that it wanted?"

This was more than I meant to ask, but every question prompted another. I would have continued like this, hardly waiting for an answer, but grandfather interrupted: "Yes, Thaddeus, those are important questions," he laughed. "I will begin with the story of *Thelmer Ludwig*. I wanted you to read that story because I happen to know that it is a true account. I just wanted to introduce you to the idea of traveling through these doors, and the danger that such travel now poses. Beyond that, it is of little interest to us. It is just one of many accounts that I could have had you read, but I thought that it would be helpful to introduce you to the strange life that you will (probably) lead. Poor Thelmer, kidnapped and taken to that wretched world, the world we call 'Archea,' to be made a slave. It was once a beautiful place, or so I have been told. Now it is violent, indolent, and decadent. But there is good in most worlds yet, and virtuous Archeans aided him in his escape."

I could barely believe what I was hearing. And the way grandfather spoke, such a tale seemed commonplace to him.

"That is something anyway," he continued. "But then to be tracked down by an assassin... And, to top it all off, to have the door close on his legs, is terribly unfortunate. Still, I suppose death was better, in poor Thelmer's circumstances, than returning to captivity. I know his family, you see, and I also am friendly with the very Archeans who rescued him. They live much longer than we do. Anyway, so much for the tragic story of Thelmer Ludwig; as for the skeleton, it is intimately tied to my ten year absence, and I will get to that soon." His eyes clouded over, and I could sense that the subject was painful for him. "As for the information, the secret knowledge that the enemy wanted, you have touched upon the central issue; this is why our family is unique.

"To begin with, all that was known about the doors and the other worlds that make up what we once knew of the labyrinth of created reality, all that we have access to, was transcribed long ago in a book. This book, the Book, is the key to all of this. The history surrounding the Book is long, and you will learn it all soon enough, but I will give you a condensed version. Long ago, during the First War, most of the rulers of these different worlds were able to shut their doors, thus keeping the darkness from invading their realms. They sealed themselves off from our world, and their civilizations were lost to us forever; lost to us, but safe from the darkness. Unfortunately, some could not lock out the enemy, and these fell into shadow, and were destroyed. Entire worlds like ours, some even more vast, more beautiful, more intricate, lost forever. It is a fearful thing." He paused again, his eyes staring into the sky, as though he could still see those worlds, and could feel the agony of their too early deaths. He roused himself, and continued:

"But all that was known of them, and all that was known of the worlds that are still alive, and that are still, perhaps, happy, thriving, and beautiful, was recorded in a book. The location of every door, the way into every world, everything that one would find in any world, all the accumulated wisdom of the great fabric of the cosmos, was in this book. The enemy could not get to the fortunate worlds whose doors were closed, unless it had the book. And if it had the book, all hope would be lost. The darkness that enveloped so much of creation would have spread, and even our own world might now be in shadow." He paused, thinking for a moment. "No," he said, "I go too far. There are other forces in the universe, and we cannot know what might have been. We can only be sure of what has been. But suffice it to say, the information in this book is very important, very important indeed."

"But grandfather," I interjected, "if all the doors to the worlds that survived have been shut, and all the worlds whose doors were not closed were destroyed, what of Thelmer Ludwig, or of any of these stories of travel to and from different worlds? It doesn't make sense."

"You forget, Thaddeus, that our world was the first to be invaded, and we have survived. It is not a zero sum game. There are other worlds that have also survived, and continue to survive, though they have been altered and distorted, much like our own. The enemy does not rest, and though it has been wounded, and its head has been bruised, it is still alive, cunning and crafty, full of malice and deceit. But it is not all-powerful, and there are many who fight against it." He smiled, and sat back in his chair with a satisfied expression.

"Yes, there are those of us who still fight. But," he added, turning to me, "we are becoming fewer and fewer."

Down in the garden Mr. Sedgwick came into view, following the line of a hedge, trimming it back with a pair of shears. The sound of their *clack, clack* carried up through the air to us. My Grandfather lowered his voice:

"The book, Thaddeus, the book was saved from the destruction of the First War." His eyes were fixed intently on mine. "It still exists. All the knowledge of the stars, all the wisdom of our fathers, it still exists. And Thaddeus: we are its custodians."

~

Of the mission of the
Bellator.

When night had fallen, then came the Enemy. With implacable fury and with terror in its wake, it threw down our ramparts and heaped the cold stone with our dead. The Princes with the Antistita and the last remnants of the guard fled into the temple chambers, to make their final stand. All was despair and sorrow, for the end was near. The Antistita, knowing what the end would mean, spoke to the Princes, counseling them concerning their greatest treasure: "Listen, Lords of the Earth, and inheritors of divine light; look to thine inheritance, and guard what has been entrusted to thee, for all is not lost if the Book is safe. If the Enemy finds it, thou hast failed; if it is safe, thou will have forever triumphed, and wherever thy names are again spoken, in the heavens or on the earth, or in the worlds between, it will not be to thy shame, and thou shall not be a byword to the race of Man."

So he counseled, and so the Princes acted. The Book was resurrected from its tomb, and given to the Bellator, and as he took it from the hand of Antistita, he kneeled, and swearing to protect it with his life, he kissed the Book. The Antistita blessed him then, marking him for all ages as the protector of the Book. "To thee Bellator, I give this grace: that thy hand shall never falter, if thy spirit fail not."

The Bellator left the Princes and Antistita to their doom, and as he fled he heard the echoes of the last battle, and grieved in his heart, for he knew that at last the night had fallen. He found the tunnel, which had been carved into the heart of the mountain, many centuries ago, when first the rumor of the shadow began to spread. Fearing this very day, the wise Princes had made secret plans to protect their treasure, and had made what they hoped would be a way of escape, if all else had failed. It was into this darkness that the Bellator plunged, and sealed the stone behind him, so that none would know his path.

So the Bellator escaped into the mountain to protect the divine gift, as the city fell in flames atop the entrance to the tunnel.

Excerpted from _The Fabulae,_ circa 600 A.D., translated from the original Latin by Prof. Byron Fairmont, 1819.

Chapter VI

"By the pricking of my thumbs, something wicked this-way comes."
~Macbeth, William Shakespeare

We were the custodians of the Book. What did that mean, I asked grandfather.

"Simply this: it has been given to our family, to our distant ancestors first, and then passed on, from father to son, or from grandfather to grandson, and even, on several occasions, from father to nephew, until this very day, to care for the Book, to preserve it, to protect it. It is our treasure, it is our vocation, our duty. And someday, many years from now, I hope, when I am too old to carry the burden, the vocation will pass to you. It is both our family's joy and sorrow. Long ago, as war raged, and world after world shut its door, or slipped into shadow, the Book was given to the great Bellator, a warrior of a noble family. With the responsibility was given certain gifts, the promise of certain grace, in order to fulfill his duty. Always we have been true to our duty. Many of our ancestors were hunted down and killed, but always we outwitted the enemy, and always the Book passed safely into the hands of another. Through many worlds they fled and hid, and through many they were pursued. Finally the Book came back here, back to this world, the very world that originally birthed it, and here it has remained. It was my grandfather, your great-great-

69

grandfather, who returned the Book, in stealth, to its original home. Here the Book has remained, until now. "

"For how long must we keep the Book?" I asked.

"How's that, Thaddeus? What do you mean?"

"Well, I am trying to say... What is it all for? That is, why are we protecting it? Do we get to read it?"

"Ah, yes, I see what you are asking. No, we are not able to read it. We are not allowed. The time when such knowledge was widespread, at least among the wise, is past. The Book was sealed, and given to us, that we might keep it until its rightful owner is revealed. Yes, there is a rightful owner! It has been foretold, Thaddeus, that someday there would arise one who could take hold of the Book and use it, use it as it was meant to be used. For in it is contained much more than just the locations of the doors. It contains secrets that only the very wise and very strong could understand or even bear to know. In some sense the Book may be described as analogous to a map of the mind of God. Such light would blind most men, indeed, all men, unless given a special grace. Thus it is said that such strength will be given to one, to one who will wield the knowledge with wisdom, and who has the virtue to lay hold of the text, and to see what has been written. To actually see it, Thaddeus... And, perhaps, that person will use the wisdom contained therein to build a kingdom of virtue, and also to destroy our enemies, especially the Queen. I do not know."

"The Queen?" I asked. "Who is she?"

Grandfather's face grew grave. "Thaddeus, it was she who began the war, the Great War, long ago. It is she who pursues the Book to this day. I hope that you will never meet her."

At this moment grandfather looked away, and his voice cracked. He stared away for some time, and when he looked back, great sorrow clouded his face.

"I have sacrificed much, Thaddeus, to have you sitting here next to me. I have sacrificed much for our vocation. The Queen is not alone our enemy, for she has many friends, many slaves, and, perhaps, she is herself the slave to powers greater than she. But she is wicked, and maybe our most dangerous enemy. I hope that you never meet her."

He sat for some time with his head bowed, and would say no more.

For three days more we talked, and spoke long of the Book and of our vocation. On the third day, my Grandfather received a telegram, the contents of which seemed to disturb him greatly.

"Pack some clothes, Thaddeus." He said, "We will leave in the morning for London."

"What's in London, Grandfather?" I asked, excited at the prospect of a holiday.

"Well, I need to check on something, and it might also be beneficial if you were to meet some interesting and noble people while we are there."

So the next morning I met him in the library with my small overnight bag gripped tightly in my hand. It was very early, the gray light of dawn just visible through the large windows of the library. My grandfather greeted me.

"Good morning, Thaddeus, are you ready for a little adventure?" As he was speaking, he was removing a wooden box from behind a stack of books. He set the box on an end table, and flipped open the lid, revealing two silver pistols, decorated with marvelous detailed etchings. Inscribed on each barrel, etched in calligraphy, was the word *Veritas*. He glanced at me while he tucked the pistols into his belt out of sight beneath his tweed coat. His clear eyes met mine, and they twinkled when he spoke:

"Even little adventures require some preparation and foresight." He smiled, and then selected a walking stick from the coat rack beside the large library doors. He had probably twenty or more walking sticks of all shapes and sizes, all strewn haphazardly in the coat rack. The one he chose was a simple, cherry cane, with a plain, silver horseshoe shaped grip, the kind of cane that any gentleman might carry when on business. He gave the cane a twirl, smiled, and said: "Now, let us go find that Sylvester."

And so it was that Sylvester, Grandfather, and I, left the great house and went to London.

While aboard the train that took us to the city, grandfather continued to relate to me many things about the book, about its history, and about the doors and the other worlds. He also explained to me who we were going to meet.

"I have mentioned before," he said, "that there are others who fight with us, who know our cause and aid us when they can. You will meet two such figures in London. It was one of these who sent me a telegram, informing me that there may be some complications that we had not foreseen."

"You know how I feel about Jacoben," interrupted Sylvester, his voice grating and bitter, "and I don't think that the boy should meet him."

"Yes, Sylvester, I know. But Jacoben has been invaluable in the past, a true ally. And Thaddeus must meet him sooner or later. You must have faith in people, Sylvester, and don't underestimate my Grandson."

"I hope that I don't underestimate him, and I know they must meet. But I think it too soon." Sylvester turned to the window, and glowered at the passing landscape.

"Don't mind him, Thaddeus," chuckled grandfather, "Sylvester is an honorable man, though he has little tact, and fewer social skills. But in a tight corner there is no one else I would rather have by my side. He has seen many dangers, and walked through many a dark night. Someday I shall relate to you the circumstances under which we first became acquainted; it is a chilling tale. But for now, trust him. He is a good man."

He glanced at Sylvester with a smile, and continued:

"Now, as for the complications that I mentioned; we have taken the task of watching the doors that we know about, strewn all over the world. It is through one of these doors that our doom will come, if it comes. So we keep a careful guard, and are ever vigilant. It is a difficult task. We do not always know where an individual door leads, and some doors lead one moment to a world allied to our cause, and the next to an unknown world, or perhaps to the antechamber, the meeting place of all the doors. Historically, there have been several times when we managed to see the attack coming, and so ward it off, due to the diligent watch that we keep. It seems that there may have been a disturbance at one of the doors, and that is why we go to London."

The train rumbled on, and I realized again that I missed my parents.

I had been to London once before with my father, and I had thoroughly enjoyed the experience. The city was alive and exciting, at once mysterious and dangerous, and welcoming and magnificent. I loved the bustle of the crowds, and always wondered where everyone was going in such a hurry. I imagined that it must be someplace marvelous and important, though in truth most were simply on their way to and from work. Holding grandfather's hand, we made our way through the masses, and deep into the city.

We went first to a hotel, checked into our rooms, had breakfast in the lobby (it was only about 8am), and then set out to meet Jacoben.

Jacoben kept a curio shop in an eccentric corner of the city, frequented by artists and anarchists, and all manner of odd people. The streets of this particular burg were narrow, and cobbled, and wound through very old, tall buildings, of a peculiar architectural style. The crowds were thick here, and the sidewalks full of strange looking people, sipping coffee and tea outside cafes, or going in and out of antique shops or rare book stores. It was a very fun place to walk about, being so much out of the ordinary.

After wandering around for about an hour (I was on the verge of asking if we were lost) we turned abruptly down a side street, narrower even than the particularly narrow streets of this burg, and stopped in front of a low wooden door, over which hung the sign, *Amos Jacoben, et al: Curios, Knickknacks, and Impossible to Find Memorabilia.*

"Here we are," said Grandfather, "the charming store of Amos Jacoben."

"Grandfather, if something is impossible to find, how did Mr. Jacoben find it?" I asked, more than a little intrigued.

Sylvester snorted, "It is for exactly that reason that I tend to distrust our friend Jacoben," he said, and then pushed open the door to the shop.

The shop was so small that it was only with great difficulty that all three of us managed to squeeze in at all. To the left was a desk, stacked high with dusty receipts, ledgers, and ink jars. This desk was next to a dirty window, through which the sun entered only with much effort, splashing light on the dust that we had disturbed, which floated and bounced through the air as if it had been etherized, and could only move if violently compelled.

In front of us were dusty glass cases, filled (as I imagined- it was very difficult to see in the gloom, and the glass was very dusty) with all sorts of odd contraptions, statuettes, knives, and even a shrunken human head. I hoped that the latter of these curios was merely an artist's rendition. There were old books and manuscripts piled high against the wall to our right, and also against the glass display case, and against the desk. And everything was dusty, neglected, and disheveled. The whole place smelled of mildew and ink.

Grandfather stepped to the desk, and I saw for the first time that there was someone sitting behind it, poring over a ledger, a large magnifying glass studiously pressed to one eye, while the other eye remained tightly closed. The face was a mess of wrinkles and age spots, and a shock of white hair framed his wrinkled head, while tufts of thin white hair clung to his cheeks, presumably a desperate attempt at a beard.

"Cuthbert, my good fellow!" Grandfather said, banging his fist into a little bell that sat precariously on the edge of the desk. The bell let out a dull "bing," and the man behind the desk startled and dropped his glass.

"Why, good day gentlemen, good day, I hope that it has found you well, and thank you for your kind patronage…" he spoke rapidly, nervously scrambling for his glass, while trying to catch the papers that went sprawling from their appointed places.

"Cuthbert, old fellow, look up!" exclaimed grandfather, "It is I, Cornelius. Sylvester and I have brought someone for you to meet."

The addled shopkeeper finally looked up, blinking through the gloom, and then, apparently recognizing Grandfather, startled again.

"Ah yes, Cornelius, so good of you to come, you have been away too long! Please, Please, sit down, and allow me to bring you some refreshments. Tea! Yes, that will do, tea is the thing. Would you gentlemen care for some tea? And who is this? Hello young man! It is pleasant, very pleasant indeed to make your acquaintance! And Sylvester, so good to see you again! Thank you for blessing this humble shop with your esteemed presence." He rattled on like this for some time in a high-pitched, whiney voice, until Sylvester interrupted:

"Yes, Yes, Cuthbert! It is very good to see you also. We have traveled a long distance. Is Jacoben here?"

"Quite so, yes, he is here. How very rude of me! He has been eagerly awaiting your arrival. Please sit down, I will fetch him."

Of course, there was no place to sit down, even if we had been so inclined. It was so stuffy and dusty in this small shop that I was beginning to feel as though I were suffocating. Cuthbert hopped down from his stool with a creak of aged joints, and disappeared through a small doorway next to the display case. The store was so dim that I had not noticed this doorway until now.

Cuthbert returned in a moment, followed by the strangest looking man that I had ever seen. He was no taller than I was, and slightly portly in build. His ears were

75

elegantly shaped, an S, like a musical note, and much too large for his head. His head was perfectly round, and he wore a sharp goatee and mustache, jet black, and the only hair on his head. When he smiled he flashed the most brilliantly white teeth that I had ever seen, except for one tooth that glinted gold. He had a studious air about him, and his gait was composed and dignified (I couldn't help but wonder at his height; I had never seen such a short man before).

"Jacoben," said grandfather, extending his hand (downward, for it was for him like shaking hands with a child, for my grandfather was very tall) and smiling warmly, "So good to see you again."

"Ah Cornelius," spoke Jacoben, in a soft, quiet voice, "The pleasure is all mine. You are always welcome, even, or should I say especially, in these dark times." Jacoben smiled warmly at grandfather, and then turned and looked at me, his eyes glassy and reserved, but not unkind. "You must be Thaddeus, the last heir of the Ramsey's! It is an honor to make your acquaintance. Your grandfather has spoken frequently about you, though I fear that he has not had the opportunity to spend much time with you. That is indeed unfortunate, and I know that such a privation can be difficult for a young man. I have not seen any of my family, not mother, father, or brother, for over one hundred years. Tragic. But we must be strong, mustn't we?" he spoke deliberately and slowly, as though each word was well thought out in advance. I had the feeling, although he spoke fluently, without trace of accent, that English was not his first language. He smiled warmly and shook my hand, holding it in his for some time, and looking directly into my eyes, as though trying to read my thoughts.

"Thank you, sir, it is a pleasure to meet you." He continued to hold my hand and to look into my eyes for a moment longer, and then released it with a smile.

"Good." He turned back to grandfather. "Now, Cornelius, as you know, I did not invite you here socially. There is a matter of extreme importance that I wish to disclose and discuss with you. If the young man wishes to go in the back room to wait, I am sure that Cuthbert can keep him company."

Grandfather paused for a moment, as if considering. "Thaddeus is to learn all that I know. It might be better to allow him to hear what you have to say."

"Perhaps," answered Jacoben, "That is a prudential judgment that only you can make. But you may want to hear what I have to say first, and then relate it to the young man as you see fit, and in your own words."

Grandfather considered this, and then turned to me.

"Thaddeus, follow Cuthbert. I will call you in a few minutes." So I obeyed.

The back room was, if possible, more disordered than the front. Cuthbert, talking incessantly, led me to a small couch, almost buried beneath manuscripts and knickknacks, and gave me a book to read. Unfortunately, he misjudged my age, for the book he gave me was a picture book. But it was interesting. It told a story of a knight and a dragon set in a time long, long ago, and although there were no words, the pictures were so glorious, so alive, and the tale was so tragic, that I was almost in tears by the time my grandfather called me.

"Thaddeus," He said, "we must be going. There is some trouble, and you may get a glimpse of the kind of responsibility that you are destined to shoulder sooner than we had anticipated."

Jacoben kneeled down in front of me before we left (this made him even shorter than I was) and clasped my shoulders.

"Thaddeus, you have been learning many things, things that the wise men of old longed to know, but could not. You may, in your life, see the dark side of these many worlds, and you must not falter. Strength of will is your only friend. Your heritage, your responsibility, may bring you to the very edge of the void, so be wary. Do not stare too intently into the void, for the void can stare back into you." His hands gripped my shoulders tightly, and his wide eyes looked earnestly into mine. Then he smiled, and stood up.

"Go with the gods, Thaddeus. I will see you again soon, and hopefully under happier circumstances."

With that we left the shop, stepped out onto the cobbled way, and took a deep breath of the smoggy, city air. It was like a breath of heaven after the dusty shop.

~

I saw a moonlit lady
Upon a moonlit hill
The stars were bright and steady
The air was deathly still

"The sun is gone forever"
The world is lost," she said
"The darkness is eternal
And night my shrouded bed"

I saw a moonlit lady
Her eyes were embers red,
"The sun is gone forever,
And all the world is dead."

~Excerpted from *The Nightmare of Percephilous*, circa 1300AD, translated from the original Latin by Dr. Byron Fairmont, 1818

Chapter VII

"The righteous, like sandalwood, perfume the axe that strikes them."
~Rouault

"There is more danger here than I had first anticipated, Thaddeus." We were back at the hotel, sitting on the patio, watching people walk by in the busy street while we had lunch. "We will act quickly. We may not have many days to prepare."

"Should I attend to the preparations at the castle?" Asked Sylvester.

"No, I don't think it will come to that so soon. And in any case, I will need you here with me. But do send a wire telling them to vacate immediately. They will know what to do. Thaddeus," he said, turning back to me, "you are probably wondering what is going on. You will recall I mentioned that we are watching certain doors, guarding against any contingency? Of course you do. Well, it seems that two of these doors have been breached."

"We don't know that, Cornelius," interrupted Sylvester, "we only know that we have lost contact with the guardians."

"We must assume the worst, Sylvester. Had we only lost contact with one, then I would be inclined to agree with you. That is not the case. So we must assume the worst," repeated grandfather, "and we must assume that they will come for the rest of us."

He paused here, and looked at me. "What did you

80

think of our friend Jacoben, Thaddeus? An interesting gentleman, is he not?"

"Yes he is, interesting and strange. He said he had not seen his family for one hundred years, but he looks younger than you, perhaps as old as father. And he is very short."

"Yes," laughed Grandfather, "very astute. I wondered if you caught that. He is indeed much older than I am. I believe he is something like one hundred sixty years of age. You can probably guess why. Our friend Jacoben is not from our world, originally. Jacoben is, in fact, a being from another world, an alien, a faerie. He is a refugee from a dying land, and he only just escaped with his life, many years ago. My grandfather, your great, great grandfather, found him, and aided his escape. And since then, Jacoben has been an ally, always loyal and brave. He is one of our most trusted associates, even if some of his methods we tend to distrust. He is rumored to be, or at least to have been, a necromancer. But he denies it, and I for my part believe him. Our dear friend Sylvester does not."

He paused here, and sat as though in deep thought, perhaps remembering the adventures of his youth, when he was first initiated into his heritage, as I was being initiated now.

"Who will come for us Grandfather? You said a moment ago that they might come for us as well. Who are 'they'?" I asked.

Grandfather sipped his coffee, while staring absently across the street.

"Our enemies, Thaddeus, or rather, the Messengers of our enemy. The Messengers are cruel and ruthless, and if they find us it will not bode well. But they cannot find us. Even the guardians of the doors do not know where we are, or where the book is."

"Grandfather, you just said that we should assume that they will find us."

Grandfather looked up, and I thought for a moment that I saw fear pass through his eyes, and I knew in an instant that he did not fear for himself.

"We must get you to safety, Thaddeus. Our treasure is safe, for now. There are but three people in the world who know where it is hidden. We must activate our protocol, as planned, and then get you to safety."

He finished his coffee, and sat back in his chair.

"Thaddeus, ten years ago we had a breach of security. Ten years ago I had to journey deep into the Himalayan mountains, and into the very heart of the earth, to protect our treasure. I saw with my own eyes the door to the abyss, and I went into the shadow of a lost world." His voice shook, and his face seemed to age in an instant. "I saw her, Thaddeus, the Queen of darkness, I saw her and I wept. I did not leave that place unscathed. I fought with the Captain of the Messengers, and I survived. I cut down an assassin on the streets of the City of Dark Dreams. I wrestled with a *Krishnag*, Thaddeus, a demon snake, a guardian of the Antechamber, and I slew it, and carried its carcass across the border of her world and ours." As he spoke, it seemed that the sun went behind a cloud, and I shivered. "Thaddeus, we cannot allow our world to be dragged into the void."

He shook his head, as if to shake away the memories, and then smiled. The sun seemed to come back out, and I heard a bird singing in a tree next to the patio.

"I am growing old, Thaddeus, and you are my heir. Sylvester is also old, and we hoped that you would be ready and trained before this day ever came. But it is here. Or rather, it may be here. Let us hope for the best, but prepare for the worst. Sylvester," he turned to the glowering man, "we must contact the others if we can. Jacoben is contacting many already. We must send a telegraph to America."

At that moment, the hotel concierge stepped onto the patio, and, after locating our table among the other diners, hurried up to grandfather.

"Ah, Mr. Ramsey, I am so glad I found you. We received an urgent message for you, perhaps a quarter of an hour ago. We tried to find you, but were not successful until just now." He handed grandfather a sealed envelope and bustled away.

Grandfather opened it, and turned pale as he read its contents. "We must go at once, there is no time to lose," he said.

Ten minutes later found us racing through the city in a cab, as grandfather relayed the information of the note.

"Our worst fears have been realized. Jacoben has heard from the others, or rather, learned that the others are dead. All of the guardians in Asia are gone, and Manlowe, here in London could not be contacted. If the Messengers are here, then poor Manlowe is certainly dead. Jacoben thinks they are not yet in London, and that they cannot know the location of the book, but they may find out (how *could* they know about London?). He thinks that we must take our treasure to a new hiding place. You know where I mean, eh' Sylvester?"

"It was I who found the alternate hiding place, Cornelius," responded Sylvester, "I know what to do. What of the boy?"

"He will remain with us, for the time being. This may serve as a great lesson for him, and help prepare him for the day when we are not here. Do you understand what is going on, Thaddeus?"

"I think so, grandfather. Are we in danger?" I was filled with both excitement and dread, and wanted, on one hand, to be at home with my parents; on the other hand I wanted to be nowhere else than right here.

"I don't know, Thaddeus, I don't know." Grandfather sighed.

"Where are we going?" I knew we were going to move the book, and had guessed that it was hidden somewhere in London.

"Why Thaddeus, we are going to the great Library of the British Empire, built three hundred years ago for the sole purpose of housing one book!" He smiled, and allowed himself a short laugh. "It has kept our treasure hidden and safe for all this time, but it seems, if Jacoben is correct, that it

83

is safe no longer. All the great beauty of classical architecture, and more wealth than Solomon's, and we still cannot keep our treasure safe."

"Perhaps we should hide it in the Vatican next time," chuckled Sylvester. "Then maybe God would protect it." This was the first time I had ever heard Sylvester laugh.

"Don't blaspheme, Sylvester. It is unbecoming," Grandfather responded shortly.

The cab rattled on, and Sylvester, after looking out the window, commented, "A storm is brewing."

"It is no natural storm." Grandfather's voice sounded strangely hollow in the confined space of the cab. "Let us hope that we will be in time."

The evening was growing late before we finally arrived at the magnificent Library of the British Empire, a huge building that looked as if it could be one of the ancient Greek temples. There were great marble steps leading up to a domed edifice, surrounded on all sides by massive marble pillars, and fountains and statues. It was one of the most impressive buildings in London.

"Jacoben should be meeting us inside. Let us hurry." As we climbed up the stairs, I heard in the distance the rumble of thunder, and felt a drop of rain, carried in by a cold north wind. In the west the sky was still clear, and the sun was just beginning to set. It would most likely be a beautiful sunset. We met no one on our way up the stairs.

As we pushed through the massive doors that guarded the entrance to the library, grandfather turned around, a puzzled look on his face.

"What is it?" I asked.

"I don't know," he answered distractedly, "but the storm is moving in fast."

We crossed the foyer of the library, and we met no one. The whole library seemed deserted. We entered the massive main room that housed the general collection, and the sight was stunning. The great dome of the roof towered overhead, its stained glass windows coloring the last rays of the sun, as they illuminated the otherworldly library. The library was fourteen stories tall, with level after level of bookshelves, all heavy with volumes that ranged from the most popular to the most esoteric. There was a huge desk for the librarians near the center of the vast room, and the floor was pristine marble. Ornate spiral staircases gave access to the other levels, and the effect of it all was overwhelming.

Such a magnificent sight would have been an occasion of joy under almost any other circumstance. But neither Grandfather nor Sylvester seemed to take notice. There was an eerie feeling that pervaded this massive building, and the silence and emptiness were strangely disconcerting.

"There is nobody here, and yet the doors were open." Sylvester's voice echoed under the great dome, startling me from my absorbed trance. "Something is wrong."

"Quickly Sylvester," responded Grandfather, his voice no more than the faintest whisper, in stark contrast to the harsh sound of Sylvester's loud exclamation, and the look in his eyes was reproachful; surely such an outburst by Sylvester was not appropriate. Who knew what might be listening, hidden among the towering shelves and pillars? "Go to the vault. See if anything has been disturbed. Thaddeus, stay with me." Sylvester obeyed, disappearing into the depths of the library. "They could not know, how could they possibly know?" Grandfather murmured to himself.

"Thaddeus, we will wait here. Perhaps Jacoben has had the library closed early, so that we could remove the book unseen." But his face betrayed his doubt. Something was wrong. Jacoben was not here. Perhaps the Messengers were indeed in London, and he also had been killed.

Grandfather and I wandered aimlessly around the confines of the main library for a few minutes after, and his eyes betrayed his concern. His gait was composed, as though merely exploring the rows and rows of bound

85

editions, but I could tell that he was not at all concerned with the books, but only the Book. I did not know what he was looking for (if he was looking for anything at all), but he was watchful and preoccupied.

As we walked the circumference of the room his head began to sink to his chest, and for a moment his breathing seemed to come with difficulty. He paused for a moment, and his eyes closed as if in prayer.

"Thaddeus," he said, his head rising, and his voice shaking only slightly, "In my haste to teach you, I hope I have not made a mistake...Thaddeus, I hope that I have not too quickly initiated you into your vocation."

I did not know what he meant.

My grandfather was lost in thought, his head leaning forward, his eyes looking at something far away, something that I could not see, and he seemed to hear something that I could not hear. He spoke as if to me, but he seemed to be far away, fighting some battle that I could not join.

"Our enemy, Thaddeus, is very cunning. I am beginning to see... Well, it may now be too late. But I think now that I can see. The snake will swallow its prey, but it will find that it has swallowed a scorpion. Thaddeus, the stars are falling from heaven, and the very sky is twisting and buckling under their weight. They are calling me, calling me to meet my destiny, and I, like a fool, have chosen this moment to have you along with me. Of course they want you too. The last heir must not remain to fight the continuing battle. Thaddeus, can you hear them calling?"

His voice sounded strange, like an echo from far away, and I felt a chill along my spine as he spoke, and was momentarily dizzy, the shelves and marble spinning about me.

"But they do not know you, Thaddeus, they do not know who you *are*, nor what you have inside...they only know me. That is their weakness, Thaddeus, and that will be their undoing. Do you hear them, Thaddeus, do you hear them calling?"

I heard and did not hear, at that moment, a soft

voice, chanting in a strange tongue, words like snakes running across the marble floor, entering the books, the pillars, the walls. The chanting was becoming loud in my ears, rhythmic, like the roar of the tide, and the words began to twist and wrap themselves around my feet, my legs, and run up my body and into my very mind, encircling my head like a crown of thorns. And suddenly, as though in a dream, I was outside the building, flying above the library like a passing bird. There below me, on the great steps in front of the doors a small figure stood, hooded in brown, twisted like a terrible lie in the light of the failing sun. His face was shrouded, and his body cast no shadow. The sky was black in the east, and he stood at the dividing line between the sun and the storm, as if between heaven and hell. All the city of London seemed to be split in half, each side sucked into the vortex of the line, sliding and falling into the hooded figure. His white hand was raised palm forward to the building, his grey lips softly chanting the poisonous ruin, calling something, inviting something, something that should not even be named or thought. This image flickered through my mind, and suddenly I was back in the building, standing next to my grandfather, trembling like the frightened child that I was. The noise of the chanting had ceased.

"Thaddeus, did you see?" Grandfather's eyes were stern and inquisitive, but, as always, kind. He was no longer distant, but immediately present. "Did you see what I could not?"

I had no time to answer. It was at that moment that his face turned pale, as if he had been struck deathly ill in an instant, and he reached down and gripped my arm. "Thaddeus," he whispered, as his fingers dug into my shoulder, "Thaddeus, you have seen him; you know now that we are betrayed! You must find Sylvester. He is at the vault. Get the Book. They are here. Run!" He pushed me away violently, and I turned, confused, to the vastness of the library.

"Grandfather, what will I do if I find it? What will I do?"

"Your inheritance Thaddeus, your inheritance! Remember who you are! Now run!"

And indeed, I ran. As I ran I could see somehow, in my mind, the figure in brown, and at the moment I saw him his white hand closed tightly into an inflexible fist, blood dripping from between his fingers and falling onto the stone steps, and it was heavier than the stone. The drop burned through slab and kept falling, falling like a cinder from hell through the floor of London, through the dirt and stone of England, into the crust of the world, till it was consumed finally in the fire at the center of the earth; all this I saw clearly, and at the moment that I saw the cursed blood strike the fire I heard a splitting crack (which shocked me out of the vision) that I at first took to be lightning striking the building. But it was not lightning. The massive doors of the Library blew off their hinges like they were made of paper, and the crash of glass and crack of marble echoed through the library. The windows near the entrance shattered, and a blast of yellow flame exploded through the splintered doors and windows. I raced up a flight of steps to the third story, and slid behind a case of books, and so it was from this vantage point that I beheld the last battle of Cornelius Ramsey.

My grandfather stood in the middle of the floor, the vastness of the domed library looming above him. He leaned heavily against his cane, his jacket hanging loose around him. His hair looked a dirty gray in the half-light, and he seemed, as never before, to be merely an old man, in the twilight of his years, shouldering a load too heavy for his aged shoulders.

Through the wreck of the doorway walked a nightmare. A figure of a man, taller than normal men, clothed in black, with a large black fedora on its head, its face was as white as chalk. Though the hat hung low, obscuring its eyes, I could see that they glowed like red fire. Its long slit of a mouth pulled away from its teeth, stretching almost to its ears, revealing a double row of white, fang-like teeth. A red, snake-like tongue curled like a whip between them. The Messenger stepped across the shards of the door, and walked into the library, its long black coat billowing behind it. Like black phantoms, a hoard of similar creatures followed, thirty or more in number, slowly spreading out along the edge of the vast interior, moving in a swaying, undulating gate until they had completely surrounded my grandfather.

Grandfather did not move, only stood, leaning on his cane, his face downcast, and his shoulders heavy.

"Ramsey!" The voice was like the grave, gray and heavy, throaty and terrible. "We meet again. Too long have you avoided us, ever escaping our subtle net. Too long have you and your despicable kin kept what is rightfully hers. For that you shall suffer. But tell us now, and perhaps we will show leniency. Where in this miserable building is the Book?" The fiend's voice rose to almost a shriek, and terror like I had never before known gripped my heart.

Cornelius Ramsey did not move.

He stood as if in prayer or meditation, like a sapling before a hurricane. He looked so frail, so weak, and I knew he would be killed in an instant. I knew also that I should run, that I should find the book and keep it safe, but I could not tear myself away from what I was watching. And though I knew that it was real, I felt as though I were watching it in a dream, and that maybe this nightmare would end, and I would wake up in the real world, where monsters did not roam.

"Ramsey!" Shrieked the Captain of the Messengers, "will you not answer? Where is the book?" Its voice echoed under the vast dome.

Cornelius Ramsey looked up, for a moment only, across the massive desk and into the face of the fiend.

"You will never find the book. It is hidden. It is safe. You will never find it."

The creature opened its awful mouth in a snarl of rage, and in one massive stride it leapt to the desk, its great, black boot cracking the surface, scattering papers and pens, and then the Captain of the Messengers vaulted high into the air.

What happened next I will never forget, indeed, I cannot forget. Its memory is seared into my mind, and I see it now as plainly as if I were there. I only regret that I cannot communicate it more clearly.

The monster vaulted into the air, higher than humanly possible, its black coat spread behind it like the wings of some prehistoric bat, and it seemed at that moment that time slowed down.

As the fiend hung high in the air, suspended between earth and sky, his great gloved fist cocked back, and I saw jagged spikes attached to the glove, glinting like fire. At that moment the last light of the setting sun shone through the stained windows overhead, and its rays poured down on my grandfather, waiting helplessly for his doom. As the light caught his white hair, it seemed that a halo was formed, as though Cornelius Ramsey was a Saint of old, crying in the desert. It was at that moment that he looked up, and I saw that there was no fear in his face. It was peaceful, serene, as though he had seen this moment coming all his long life, and had prepared himself for it. His face was serene, but his eyes seemed lit with silver flame. Then he lifted his cane, grasping the handle with his right hand and the shaft with his left, his head turned for just a moment, and he looked up at me, and across the distance his shining, silver eyes met mine, and though his lips did not move, and he made no sound, he said, "Run, Thaddeus, run!"

The cane twisted in his hand, the shaft slid away from the bladed handle and clattered on the marble floor. The last glimmer of light caught the edge of the sword cane's blade, and the ghastly smile on the fiend's face froze in horror. It could not stop its descent, and Grandfather sidestepped with elegant ease. In one fluid motion he swept the fiend's head from its shoulders, and the Captain of the Messengers struck the ground, its body a shattered heap, broken on the cold stone floor. Its head rolled to the edge of the circle, stopping at the feet of its followers, its teeth clenched in an eternal rage, but the fire in its eyes had gone out. The Captain of the Messengers was dead.

There was a pause, a moment of complete silence, as Grandfather stood, sword in hand, over the body of his fallen enemy, and in that moment I dared to hope. And then, with a roar of bitter anger, the Messengers rushed en masse at Grandfather, like a great tide of darkness rushing against a candle. But the fire burned bright. Cornelius Ramsey smote the onrushing hoard with the fury of vengeance, cutting like a scythe through blackened wheat, his sword moving so fast among them that it seemed to be a thing alive, a blaze of light cutting through the darkness. He ran the first fiend through, and with a backhanded blow he smote the next in the face, so that the horror of chalky white disappeared in a splash of crimson. Moving like a dancer, he hewed the outstretched gloved hands from the reaching arms, and cut the legs from under his attackers. Grandfather's movement was so fast and so graceful, that he seemed to be a young man, a youth in his prime, battle-ready and all his skill honed to a point.

The fight was so violent and ghastly, and the cries of the demons, the dying and the living, which reverberated through the library, were so grisly and awful that it was a shock to see and hear, and all the while I prayed that grandfather would escape. For a moment it seemed that he might. The bodies of his foes were heaped around him, and the hoard of black was thinning. He struck this way and that, and with every blow he dropped another fiend, bleeding and dying, to the stone floor. And then there was a moment's lull in the fight as the Messengers stepped back, parting, for a champion of the Messengers, a huge fiend, larger than the others and shrieking in rage, came rushing forward wielding a long jagged knife. The monster swung the massive blade at Grandfather, but Grandfather deftly parried the blow, and stepping forward underneath the reach of the creature as it came on, ran the full length of his sword through its middle. The creature threw his hands in the air, choking as it died, but its inertia kept it moving forward, and though Grandfather stepped out of its path, the sword twisted in his hands, and the blade snapped off at the hilt with a loud crack. The champion lay dead at grandfather's feet, with the length of the blade sticking straight up out of its back, like a nail through tarpaper.

Cornelius Ramsey stood for a moment, the broken sword still clasped in his hand. Then he dropped the handle, both hands flew beneath the tails of his jacket, and then they swept up, the pistols gripped tightly, and I heard again, as if in my head, "Run, Thaddeus, run!" The last glimmer of sunlight saw him standing, his enemies strewn about him, his arms outstretched, his silver, burning eyes looking up to heaven; and then the storm broke against the library, and the sunlight vanished. With a scream, a shriek of unearthly rage, the Messengers rushed at grandfather, and I jerked my head away, tears blinding my eyes as I scrambled to escape. The roar of the pistols was deafening, a sustained blast echoing off the walls of the dome. My ears seemed to explode, and I could hear nothing for a moment but a pitched ringing as I blundered through the bookshelves, trying to escape.

I could barely see through the gloom and through my tears. The gunshots ended abruptly, and I knew my Grandfather was dead; I could do nothing now but run.

~ We all thought that Dr. Valiune was insane. Of this I can assure you. There was no expense spared, no possibility that we did not explore, and no fewer than twelve specialists examined him thoroughly, all arriving at the same conclusion: he had lost his mind. So either the science that could cure him has not yet been discovered, or his story, his fantastic story, was true. I have already related the specifics; a map carved upon a stone, a map that revealed the location of a lost city, hidden deep in the Indian jungles. Against our better judgment he had insisted upon making the journey alone. I still regret letting him go, but what could I have done? We tried to follow after he had disappeared, no less than two expeditions, and we could find no trace of him or the city. I sometimes wish that I had accompanied him initially, but if I had then perhaps I too would be dead. He disappeared for four years, and was finally discovered in a ghetto outside of Calcutta, half dead. After we had transferred him to a hospital in London, he began to frighten his nurses and orderlies with his fantastic ravings. He could not explain to us what it was that he had seen, except that he warned us over and over not to go to "the dark city." If it was not insanity, and if he had actually seen something, or found some strange city, it would mean that we had all failed him, that all of modern science had failed him. This scenario is not feasible. But what if reality consists in more than our sciences have discovered, or even can discover? I know this is reasonable to you, leaning, as you are able, on your crutch of faith. But if our physical science fails, perhaps it is because our metaphysics is too weak? Your metaphysics can handle what I have seen, mine cannot. The possibility that Dr. Valiune's illness was induced by something supernatural, or something from another world as he claimed has haunted me for some time, and this is why I have written to you these several letters. I lie awake at night, seeing in my mind his emaciated body thrashing against the restraints, screaming and crying, his eyes wide and shot with blood. I still hear him, before he finally died, foaming at the mouth and convulsing uncontrollably, as he repeated again and again the strange mantra, "She lives there, she lives there, in the dark city, the city of dark dreams."

~Excerpted from a letter written by the world famous neurologist Dr. Ebenezer Crilley, to the Reverend James Aston, S.J., of St. Nicholas Parish, South Hampton. This and the other letters referred to are recorded in the critically acclaimed study, *Insanity, Hysteria, and Mania: When Doctors Lose Their Minds* (Bartley & James, New York, N.Y., 1909)

Chapter VIII

"The trick, my friends, is not in avoiding death, but in avoiding evil, for evil runs faster than death."
~Socrates

He had said that I had to somehow find the vault, and get the book to safety, but surely that was hopeless now? What could I do that my grandfather could not do? What chance had I where he had failed? My head throbbed and my ears still rang, and the tears would not stop. Perhaps I could just hide, just wait until those monsters had found the book and were gone?

A hand like a steel vice gripped my face, smothering my cry, and a harsh voice whispered violently in my ear, "Quiet, don't make a sound!"

For an instant I was sure that I was dead, that the Messengers had found me, and when I realized through my fright that it was Sylvester, I sobbed with relief. But the relief was short lived. He never released his hold, but dragged me through the maze of bookcases, to a door and then a narrow stairway, and then down, down, down, into the depths of the library. I had been hiding on the third floor of the fourteen story building, but this stairway seemed to lead twice as far down as I had been up. It must lead to a basement, deep below the streets of London. Sylvester was holding me under one arm and with the other he held my mouth closed, never softening his grip. At first I thought that we must be going to the hidden vault, that we must be going to rescue the book. But then why was I a prisoner, and where had Sylvester been during grandfather's battle? If he had been there then perhaps grandfather would still be alive. My faculties were in a pitiful state of confusion: the horror of my grandfather's fight fresh in my mind, and the fear for my own life now obscured all coherent thought. It was through this cloud of emotion that I recalled my grandfather's words: "we are betrayed." In an instant my mind was clear, and I realized with a shock that it must have been Sylvester!

Who else knew of the hiding place, of London, or that Grandfather would be here this night. Probably then Jacoben was already dead, and now Sylvester would be the only one who knew of the book's existence. Was he working with the Messengers, planning to deliver it into their hands? This did not seem feasible, for why would he need the secrecy, why was he sneaking down to the vault without them, leaving them to find it on there own? I could occasionally hear loud noises, crashes and what sounded like thunder from overhead, somewhere up in the main edifice of the library. The Messengers were searching for the book. So he wanted it for himself, the knowledge, the power, he had waited all these years to betray grandfather, and steal the book. I felt sick to my stomach, and my eyes clouded over for a moment. Then I would surely also be killed. But why was I not dead already?

We entered a vast underground storage space, piled with books to be catalogued, shelves to be repaired, and couches to be delivered to the main library. It was lit by pale electric light, and Sylvester never paused, but ran, weaving through the warehouse till he reached a metal door. He burst through it, and down a narrow corridor till we reached a narrow stair leading back up. Here he stopped, and turned to the wall just left of the stair. He released my mouth, and began tapping the stone wall, as though he were counting bricks. He found what he was looking for; he pressed the palm of his hand against a particular brick, and it snapped up, revealing it to be a false front, concealing a lever. This lever he threw, and the stairwell in front of us lurched, and the first ten steps shifted a few feet towards us, and then with the creak of gears the ten steps moved up over the stairs above them, revealing another passage underneath the stairs, leading down. We plunged down this passageway, pausing only to throw another lever, which shut the door behind us.

We reached our destination shortly. It was a gate of iron, a door like a prison cell. Beyond it lay a wide room of steel; floor, walls and ceiling. On the far side of this room was a massive steel door, seemingly impregnable. This could only be the vault.

Sylvester released my mouth, and dropped me roughly on the stone floor.

"The key," he hissed, "quickly!"

For a moment I did not know what he meant. Then it struck me; my inheritance, the key that my father had given me when he left grandfather's house. This key must open the gate. And then I realized, and my stomach turned; this is why I was still alive. Sylvester only needed the key.

It still hung about my neck, for I was never without it. I pulled it out of my shirt, and drew the rope over my head. The key was old and large, and its mechanism was a very curious shape, like a pair of wings. What a strange lock it must be that could be opened by such a key.

I handed it to Sylvester, but he refused it.

"No," he said, "open the door."

So I did. The lock turned easily, and the iron door swung wide. We entered the steel room, crossing to the door of the vault. It was massive, thick and imposing, with a large handle like the wheel of a ship in its center. In the center of the handle was a wide keyhole, much different than the keyhole of the previous door.

"Quickly, open the vault," Sylvester still whispered, his face set and cold, and I supposed that I saw fear in his eyes.

"I don't think my key will fit this lock," I protested, "it is not the same."

"You fool, do you not know what you have? Has no

one told you? There is in existence no lock that your key cannot open, though no key can open this lock except yours. There are only three keys in all the worlds like it, and one may have been lost or destroyed long ago, for no one knows where it is now. Your grandfather has the other. But that means our enemies may have it now, unless Cornelius was wise enough to leave it somewhere safe. We cannot take the chance. Open the lock."

So it was that I realized more fully what my inheritance, my responsibility was. This key must have been my mother's, and before her perhaps my great-grandfather's, and on and on, deep into the past. It may have been in my family for centuries. Was it even of this world? Perhaps it had come from a lost world, saved from the ashes by some miracle, or from an allied world, as a gift to my family for their work.

With trembling hand I used my treasure, and the great door of the vault swung open.

The vault was the size of a large room, perhaps thirty feet square, made completely from steel. On the opposite wall was another door, just like the one we had entered by. All around the perimeter there were drawers of different sizes, like safe-deposit boxes at banks. Sylvester went directly to an obscure drawer along the right side of the room. It was low to the ground, in the second row from the floor and maybe one-third of the length of the wall.

"This is the one. Be quick."

Once again I used my key, and the drawer slid open. Inside the felt-lined drawer lay a small metal box about the size of a bible, a small silver revolver, and some coins which looked like the gold doubloons I had seen pictures of in pirate story books. Sylvester grabbed the metal box and the pistol and stowed them in his jacket. He tossed me the gold (it was held in a small leather bag) saying, "you can keep these," and then he slammed the drawer shut.

He strode to the door we had just entered by, and pulled it closed.

"This should hold them for some time, when they

find the stairs. And the drawers will hold them even longer. They all hold exactly the same thing as our drawer, except the book and the gold are not real, and the pistol does not shoot. But we must hurry. We need your key again."

I opened the far door, revealing another set of stone steps leading up a narrow, dim passageway. We closed the door behind us and began our ascent.

"So that…is that the book?" I asked, breathless as we climbed. The stairs seemed to never end.

Sylvester laughed, a harsh, grating noise. "Yes, this is it. Or rather, it is in this small box. The bane of the worlds, and I carry it in my pocket. Much blood has been spilt over this throughout the ages, and more will be shed tonight. Let us hope it will not be our own."

On and on the stairs ran, and on and on we climbed.

"Are you going to kill me?" It was, perhaps, a foolish thing to ask, but I genuinely wanted to know. I felt now that I really did not care whether I lived or died. My whole body ached with weariness, and the pain and shock of seeing my grandfather die was almost too much to bear. If he had betrayed grandfather, then he was acting very strangely. I wasn't sure why he had not killed me in the vault, or why he had bothered to give me that gold, but I was too tired to think, and so I decided to find out once and for all. It did me little good. He merely glanced at me with an odd expression, and continued to climb, taking two steps at a time.

After climbing for what seemed like hours (though was really probably about a quarter of an hour or so) we finally reached the end of the stairway. It ended abruptly at a metal door set at an angle to us. Sylvester pushed this open and stepped through, pulling me behind him. We had emerged through the floor of a stuffy, dark room, lit only by a street lamp shining through a grubby window. There were tools and assorted lawn equipment strewn about the small space. Sylvester stepped cautiously to the window, stared out for some time, and then, satisfied that it was safe, opened the creaky door to the shed. A blast of cold wind blew rain into the narrow space.

"Quietly, follow me." He grabbed my shirt sleeve, and pulled me behind him onto a gravel path in what appeared to be a park. We immediately left the path and plunged into the wooded park, weaving in and out of the trees and shrubs. Sylvester seemed to know exactly where he was going. The rain came down in sheets, and the sky was lit by occasional bolts of lighting, while the roar of thunder hid any other noise of the park or surrounding city. Branches lashed my face as we rushed through the shrubbery, and I was chilled to the bone.

It did not take long to reach the edge of the park. Here we stopped, and crouched beneath an overhanging branch. Before us lay a level grass lawn, stretching to the street, which was lit by lamps. Beyond this loomed the city of London, dark and forbidding in the grip of the storm. And then, moving slowly down the street came a car, its lights off, creeping as though it did not wish to be noticed. Sylvester gripped my arm tightly.

"Jacoben! I knew he would come through. The contingency plan has been successful." He spoke quickly, excitedly, and his voice shaking with relief.

I looked at him, the strange wrinkled little man in his oversized suit, looking even more absurd in the pouring rain, his hat misshapen, its brim dripping water like a fountain, and his dark hair plastered to his disproportioned head. "Successful?" I thought. How could this be considered a success? Grandfather was dead. The book was far from safe. Perhaps Sylvester was indeed stealing the book, and then it might be considered a success.

The car stopped underneath a lamppost, sitting silently in the rain. Sylvester, after looking carefully around again, gripped my arm and pulled me to my feet. He looked at me through the darkness and rain, and for the first time I saw what looked like kindness in his black eyes.

"Thaddeus, we are almost safe. We must make one last effort, and then we can grieve for Cornelius. He was the greatest man I have ever known, and I live today only

100

because of his kindness. We must steel our hearts for one last rush, and then we can pick up the pieces. Thaddeus, your grandfather would want you and the book safe, before our grief dampens our resolve, or dulls our nerve. Do you understand?" His hand tightened, and his face was earnest. For the first time I felt that I understood what grandfather had said about him, and in that instant I doubted my previously held opinion of him. Perhaps he was a true friend and a true ally. Perhaps he had not betrayed grandfather.

I had barely time to shake my head in acknowledgment of Sylvester's words, when he said, "Come on! To the car. We must leave this town before they find us. Go!"

We left the relative safety of the tree and raced across the open lawn, our feet bogging down in the rain-soaked turf. At every moment I expected to hear the sound of pursuit, the hideous shrieks of the messengers signaling our doom. But we reached the street without incident.

The doors of the idling car sprang open, and Jacoben emerged from the passenger side, while old Cuthbert clambered unsteadily from the driver's side. Cuthbert looked even more ghastly than usual in the driving rain and wind, his wisps of hair clinging to his aged, wrinkled face. His crooked smile revealed nearly toothless gums, and he muttered incessantly under his breath. Jacoben seemed even shorter than he had before, and he raised his arms to us in greeting.

"You are safe! We almost gave up hope. We have been driving past this spot again and again for almost an hour. Hurry, it is not safe here in the open. But there are only two of you; where is Cornelius?"

"Jacoben, I have never been so glad to see you, my friend! We have lost our leader; Cornelius has been killed. It is the Messengers of the Queen. They are here, in London. But of course you have realized that. Cornelius killed many, and I managed to kill a few, but there are many more. We are well beyond outnumbered. We must flee now and live to fight later."

Jacoben's face showed a strange expression, a twisted look that could have been mistaken for fear and sadness, but was something else. I could not tell what, exactly.

"Oh may the gods preserve us!" he exclaimed, "this is disastrous! But the Book, Sylvester, is the Book safe?"

Sylvester looked at him for an instant before tapping his breast pocket and answering, "Yes, I have it here."

"Well, then all is not lost. We must hurry. Get in the car."

And then several things happened at once. As we turned to the car a great bolt of lightning cut across the blackened storm clouds, illuminated the sky and everything around us, making it as light as day for an instant. In that flash I saw Jacoben, his face contorted into a sickening look of rage, pull a slender dagger, curved like a moving snake, from the sleeve of his jacket and raise it in the air behind the back of Sylvester. I opened my mouth to shout an alarm, but my cry was lost in a roar of thunder that shook the very ground and rattled the windows of the waiting car. The knife fell violently, and Sylvester's arms flew up, his face a mask of surprise and pain. Then a brutal shock went through me as I myself was stabbed in the heart. The blow sent me to the ground, my head struck the stone walk with a terrible violence, and I lay stunned, looking up through the falling rain into the awful face of Cuthbert leering over me, a jagged bloody knife gripped in his bony fist. He seemed almost giddy, his cloudy eyes alive with perverse pleasure, and I realized what now seems so obvious. Jacoben had betrayed us, and now it was all too late. The knife of the aged wraith who stood over me dripped with my own blood, and he raised it now to finish the job. The shock of pain and despair washed over me, and for the instant that the knife hung in the air all I wanted to do was to see my mother and father again.

And then Cuthbert, his face frozen in the leering smile, seemed to be snatched from before me by some great

102

invisible hand. There was a simultaneous blast as Cuthbert's broken body was literally thrown cart-wheeling across the street and stopped with a sickening crunch against a streetlamp, almost cut in half by the violence. In the corner of my eye I could see Sylvester lying face down on the sidewalk, his arms outstretched before him, his hands gripping the smoking revolver. His eyes met mine for an instant, and I could see the despair in them. They seemed, in that rain and blood soaked moment to say, "I'm sorry."

And then Jacoben's knife fell again, and Sylvester's eyes blazed with pain for an instant only, and his teeth clenched. And then he was dead.

I did not move, but lay with my eyes half closed, my tears mixing with pouring rain. Jacoben stood stiffly, looking briefly at me, and then across the street to the mangled body of Cuthbert. The bloody knife was gripped in one hand, and then the other turned the body of Sylvester on its side, and he reached into Sylvester's coat and removed the metal box holding the Book. He put this in his own pocket, and then wiped the blade of his dagger on Sylvester's jacket. He must have thought that I was as dead as Cuthbert or Sylvester, for without looking again at me he quickly got back into the idling car and roared away, the tires spraying dirty water over the body of Sylvester. And then he was gone, and I was alone.

I lay for some time staring up into the pouring rain, tears streaming from my eyes, while I waited to die. It was the darkest moment of my life. In the matter of a few hours my grandfather had been killed by creatures from out of a bizarre story, Sylvester had been stabbed to death before my very eyes by someone whom we had considered to be a friend and trusted ally, and I had been stabbed by the kindly old man who had, only hours before, given me a picture book to read. How I longed to wake up from the nightmare! How I wished that I could open my eyes and be in my own home, my own bed, with the voice of my mother calling me to wake up, to come into the light, to not waste the day. I would have given anything at that moment to hear my

Father's voice, strong and reassuring, telling me that all was right in the world, and that monsters only roamed in Faerie tales.

How long I lay in that condition I do not know. It may have been an hour or longer. And then it occurred to me that I had not died, and that although there was a sharp pain in my chest, it did not really feel as though I would. I sat up and began to examine my wound. The knife had struck my breast pocket, right over my heart, but had somehow been deflected and cut along my ribcage, drawing some blood and making a nasty cut, but nothing that was life-threatening (in fact, most active boys my age have been wounded much worse in the course of normal games and childhood adventures; I myself had my leg stitched up two summers before after a fall gave me a much worse scrape than the one that I now examined). After the initial relief of discovering that I was not dying, I realized that what had turned the blow was none other than the gold coins that Sylvester had given me. The disagreeable Sylvester had saved my life twice. At that moment I remembered his words, that he had killed several of the Messengers in the library, but must have gone hunting for me, to get me and the Book out of harms way. I realized then that I had misjudged Sylvester, and I wept.

It was not long before I began to come to my senses. I could cry no longer, and I had to figure out what to do next. I moved over to the body of Sylvester and retrieved the pistol. The training my grandfather had given me came back easily. The cylinder swung open, and I saw that there were still four live rounds. I removed one of the rounds, for I was curious about the power of the weapon. Cuthbert was very thin, but it still seemed that the force with which he was thrown across the street was not proportionate to the caliber of this handgun. Upon examining the bullet I realized that this was no ordinary gun. The casing of the shell was silver, with tiny, beautiful etchings. The bullet itself was also silver, with one small rune pressed into the very top. I had never seen anything like it, and I came to the conclusion that it must be an extraordinary weapon. So I dried it off and put it in my pocket.

I had been subconsciously noticing a red glow emanating from somewhere behind me while I had been examining the gun. I now turned, looking over the park from which we had emerged, and saw the great dome of the library several blocks away, looming high over the rest of the city. Great tongues of red flame were leaping from its roof and shooting out its many windows. So the Messengers had finished their work.

My first thought was to try to find my way back home to my parents, and explain as best I could what had happened. And then I considered going to the police, but I doubted that they would take my story seriously. Even being as young as I was, I realized that they would not find any corpses of the Messengers at the library. There would be nothing to verify what I had to say except the bodies of Sylvester and Cuthbert. I wanted to go back to my home, but how could I tell my mother that her father had been killed, and that the family's treasure and responsibility had been lost? But what other choice did I have? How could I know where the book was now, and even if I did know, what could I do about it. It is hard to describe the emotions that I experienced during those dark moments, the loneliness and sense of despair. I knew that I was not to blame for grandfather's or Sylvester's death, but I *felt* that in some way I was. Perhaps if grandfather had not had me close by to burden him, he could have escaped.

As I sat in the puddle, the rain and wind howling around me, watching the great dome of the library which was by now a mountainous inferno, I heard, as if a voice had spoken in my mind, "You can waste no more time."

Then I suddenly realized what I had in some way known all this time; I knew where Jacoben would go. I was startled by the clarity of the realization. But I knew, I knew without any hesitation or doubt. He would take the book to the dragon garden at grandfather's house, then over the threshold of the world.

I stood up, unsure how to proceed but without any doubt about my goal. Jacoben would be driving, so perhaps if I took the train I could beat him there. Of course, what I would do if I found him I could not say; I just knew that I needed to rescue the book. It was, perhaps, very naive of me to think that I could succeed, but I turned nevertheless and began slogging through the rain in the direction of the train station. (There may be those reading this now who might be somewhat incredulous at the idea that a child would attempt such a task on his own, and after such a traumatic experience. It is true that, in retrospect, the obvious thing would be to contract the aid of my parents, who would understand what was at stake, and would be willing and able to help. As I review these events in my mind, I can only think that there was something else to be accounted for here. I was not just a child in terrible circumstances, but was now a participant in drama that was far beyond normal human affairs. There were other forces at work that night, for good and for evil. Also, I think that I had a subconscious fear, after seeing my grandfather killed, that if I involved my beloved parents, they might meet the same fate. I doubt that I could have articulated this to myself at the time, but I think that it is true nonetheless).

Allow me to say only a few brief words about the rest of that terrible night which sits like a shadow in my mind even to this day. I somehow managed to make it to the train station without being "rescued" by the police (most of their excitement that night no doubt involved the fire at the library, and perhaps the eventual discovery of the bodies of Sylvester and Cuthbert) or any good-Samaritan citizen. I had just enough money for a ticket, and I boarded the almost empty train that went through South Hampstead at 1a.m.

For two hours the train raced through the night, and I sat sleepless and alone in the car. I remembered the trip that I had taken with my father, and remembered how eager I had been for adventure and noble battle. Oh how I longed to have my father with me that night! There were many

106

moments on that dark journey when I wanted to turn back, to go home and sleep, and when I woke up maybe everything would be normal, and maybe all of this would turn out to be only a terrible nightmare. But when the train pulled into the station, I disembarked and began walking out of the sleeping town, through the night, towards my grandfather's home.

It was a very long walk, and the storm could be felt even here. The rain fell as steadily, if not as severely, as in London. There were no street lights on this lonely country road, and it was illuminated only by the occasional flashes of lightning. It was a frightening trip for a boy, especially under those terrible circumstances. I think that if I had not been so exhausted, and the hour had not been so late (both these realities served to dull my senses), it would have been difficult to finish at all.

When I arrived at the gate of the estate, I realized with a shock that I had been too careless. A car, definitely the car that Jacoben had been driving, was in the ditch across the road, haphazardly hidden behind a tree, and the massive gate itself lay in a shattered heap next to the broken stone pillars from which it used to hang. I cowed quickly behind a tree, thinking that Jacoben must be near. My first thought was that the car had broken through the gate, but I quickly realized that the car was perfectly intact, and, as it was on the far side of the road, probably played no part in the destruction of the gate. "Of course," I thought, "Jacoben did not make a wreck of the gate! It must be the Messengers!" Unable to find the book at the library, they must have come here. Jacoben must have the same problem that I do; he wants to avoid the Messengers.

I began to make my way down the long wooded drive, slinking cautiously from tree to tree. When I finally rounded a curve near the castle, I saw that the sky ahead was lit by an unearthly red glow; my grandfather's castle was burning. It was a ghostly site, the great black mass of turrets and buttresses, with its windows glowing with fire like great red eyes, and the surrounding gardens and out-buildings lit with fantastic glow. It seemed that I could see movement on the great stone porch, a blackness that was darker even than the surrounding night. The Messengers were still here, searching for their prize. I hoped that the household had received Sylvester's warning and had fled.

As I lay in the grass at the edge of the wood, watching the spectacular site, my eyes caught a faint movement illuminated briefly by a burst of flame, at the edge of a low stone hedge on the west side of the garden. I recognized the short, round silhouette instantly. Jacoben!

He was crouching low, dodging from hedge to fountain, avoiding the glare of the fire as he tried to make his way around the main garden and to the Dragon's Garden. I had a chance; if I was clever I could beat him to the statue and preempt his escape. I watched him for a moment longer, and then I moved. I raced around the circumference of the woods and through the underbrush as far as I could go until it was too dense to go through unheard. I was now almost around to the west side of the castle, its length stretching like a great glowing wall perhaps one hundred yards from my hiding place. Here the huge front lawn and drive ended, and the expanse of the garden, with all its twists and turns began. A tool shed stood twenty feet to my left, and with this as my destination, I began crawling, completely prone, through the rain-soaked grass and away from the sheltering forest.

I was halfway across the grass, muddy and soaked to the bone, when I froze with fright. A tall shadow, as black as the depths of night against the burning castle, was striding across the lawn towards me with a burning brand in one hand. The fire lit its chalky white face and long slit of a mouth, making it appear even more grotesque than I had remembered. I lay completely motionless, my face buried in the wet grass, and prayed that it would not see me. It passed maybe fifteen feet in front of me, and threw its flaming torch into the dark confines of the shed. The wooden building instantly ignited, the flames engulfing it entirely within moments. As the fire leaped up, the entire stretch of lawn was illuminated all the way to the forest. If the creature had been facing me I would have been done for. But it remained with its back to me, staring into the flame until the shed was reduced to embers. This took the better part of ten minutes, and when it was over the creature strode back toward the castle, its black coat flowing like a cape behind it.

I waited until I was sure that it was gone, and then I began shimmying as fast as I could through the grass towards the nearest hedge. I made it safely, and sat with my back against it, trying to regain control of my breathing. I was shaking terribly. After a few moments, I began to run toward the great trees that marked the path to the hidden garden. It took some doing in the eerie half-light and falling rain. The garden was varied and confusing in the best of circumstances, and the hidden Dragon's Garden was difficult to find even in broad daylight. The constant fear that I was experiencing certainly did nothing to help matters. The statues and strange fountains all seemed alive tonight, and the twisting ivy seemed to move and grow like snakes around the masonry. I feared to meet a Messenger around any corner, and I feared that Jacoben knew that I was following him and was waiting in ambush, his crooked dagger poised to finish what old Cuthbert had begun.

The great wall of trees stood like silent sentinels, moving and murmuring in the wind and rain, and towering over the shrubs and fruit trees of the garden. They were dark against the darkness of the night, and I had the strangest thought that they might try to stop me from reaching the walled garden. Perhaps they would wait until I was on the stone path, and then slowly move together, wading through the ground like water, their branches grasping and choking, and I would disappear forever into their clutches. I crouched in the wet grass behind the knoll that protected the path from view, my teeth chattering with cold, my sopping clothes clinging to my weary body, and I could not make myself move. Jacoben must be in there, I knew, but perhaps the trees were friends of his. He used to be a necromancer, didn't he? Of course the trees would be on his side.

To my left the great castle of my grandfather was burning to the ground, along with all the out-buildings and the cottage of the caretakers. I urgently needed to move, to act, but I was frozen, my limbs would not function, and it was as though all the terror and pain of this night had at last taken its toll. It may seem strange to some that after all I had gone through during this terrible night I would be struck numb with fear at this juncture. All I can say in my defense is that it was no ordinary fear.

It was at that moment, as I crouched before the dreaded path, that I felt a little warmer, as though the rain was not so cold, and the wind did not cut so deeply. I raised my eyes to the east, and I saw that there the sky was lighter, that the unnatural black storm clouds of the night were giving way, as I knew that they eventually must, to the natural movement of the heavens and the earth; the dawn was breaking. A single ray of light escaped over the horizon, cut through the storm and fell on the towering trees before me, and in that instant I knew that they were only trees. And trees are never on the side of the necromancers. I staggered to my feet, and plunged into the darkness between them.

The trees offered protection from the wind and rain, and I hurriedly slipped and scrambled over the smooth paving stones till I emerged at last in front of the little knoll upon which sat the dragon. Even through the darkness and falling rain I could see the doors of the garden were hanging open; Jacoben was here. I took the pistol out of my pocket, holding it down at my side. It was surprisingly light, and fit my small hand very well. I cautiously climbed the knoll, disdaining the stairs for fear that I would be seen through the doorway. Then I crouched against the wall next to the doorframe, and carefully contorted my neck so that I could peer around the door and into the garden.

The interior was even darker than the surrounding woods. I stared intently for a moment, but could see no sign

110

of movement. But as I continued to look, I began to focus on something at the far end of the enclosure, something that I at first took to be a product of my imagination, or a trick that my eyes were playing. I realized quickly that it was neither of these things. Something red was glowing, like two small embers, at the end of the garden. As my eyes adjusted I realized what it was, and I turned away quickly and vomited against the stone wall. The eyes of the dragon statue were awake and wide open, burning red, and had been staring right back at me.

The effect that this produced on me is difficult to describe, except to refer to my previous adventure with the statue. It was a sickening fear, quite unlike merely fearing for one's life; it is more like fearing for one's soul. With terrible force I knew that whatever had wanted access to my mind before had not left, and was again scratching, clawing to get in.

"Thaddeus, Thaddeus, will you see me?" the voice spoke inside my mind, and I almost screamed, but instead choked on my own vomit, as I again was sick against the wall. "Thaddeus, Thaddeus, Thaddeus, Thaddeus, it is I, won't you see me Thaddeus." It was mocking, taunting, and wavering back and forth between gratingly masculine to a serpentine feminine, as though it was possessed of two natures. The oppression that I felt was overpowering, a physical weight crushing me, and the surrounding darkness was no longer only the night. The voice was not as distant as it had been before; it seemed as though it was right here, all around me, and clawing at my mind, threatening to drag me into its void like a sheep to the slaughter. "Thaddeus, Thaddeus," the voice was insistent, commanding, and I began to crawl as though through a fog, on my hands and knees, still clutching the pistol. It was as though I was crawling through a wall, or as if I was trying to crawl in a dream, moving inch by inch through the arched doorway and into the garden. I could see the eyes glowing red across the lawn, and as I moved forward the voice became garbled and distorted, angry to the point of incoherence, an enraged

111

opponent incapable of controlling his passions. It was screaming now, meaningless and violent, as though a spigot of death and chaos had been opened wide, churning filth into the air. The eyes of the demon statue stared at me, devouring me with their cruelty, and I had the terrible sensation that it was the statue itself that spoke, or that it was possessed of whatever it was that tried to possess me. With the last of my energy I staggered to my feet, and with a shout I stumbled forward, the pistol raised, and I pulled the trigger.

The noise of the blast seemed to break the fog and chaos like a hammer, and the dragon statue exploded into a thousand black fragments, its eyes winking out like candles in a bitter wind. It was as though I was released from a physical hold, and I fell forward, grabbing at the pedestal with my free hand, and then plunging into a gaping hole at the pedestal's base, unseen until it was too late. I frantically grabbed at the sides of the hole, but found myself tumbling down an almost vertical narrow stairwell, and deep down under the earth. When I finally came to a bumpy and bruised halt, I looked back up, and saw perhaps fifty feet above me the entrance. I could see the clouds whirling in the air, illuminated by the gray dawn, and then the door to the entrance, which was the pedestal itself, rolled back in place, sealing out the light, and sealing me in the darkness.

So it was, though I did not know it then, that I, Thaddeus Michael, left the only world that I had ever known and stumbled across the threshold of another.

~

Part II
The Valley

~What does another world consist in, and where is it located? Yes, I suppose that is the most important question, and perhaps the most difficult to answer. Plato tells us in his **Timaeus** that God has created only one universe based on the model of the Supreme Good, and not a plurality of worlds. There are not two or more Supreme Goods, and so only one universe. This is not repeated to give simplistic, unqualified support for a Platonic cosmology, of course, but merely to buttress our thesis with a metaphysical (and poetic) authority. You see, I think that there might be some who accept this concept, but who tend to misunderstand what we are, in fact, proposing: not that these multiple worlds are extrinsic to the known universe, or would have required multiple acts of creation (so to speak) on the part of the divine. Rather, wherever these worlds are located physically, they are still integral to the fabric of the universe per se, writ large, if you will. This is, I think, (and this is what Dr. Maynerd was alluding to in his excellent lecture earlier this evening) why we can know of the existence of these other worlds at all. They are part of our universe, the only universe that exists, as Plato suggests, and, indeed, as a Christian cosmology might also suggest (Father Thabian will, as you know, present a lecture tomorrow evening on just that topic). It is just that the universe is more vast, more complex, more mysterious, than we have often assumed. I say often; of course there are many exceptions, historically. If this were not so, that is, if there were multiple universes, I am not sure that we could travel to and fro between the worlds, or, as I have said, could even know of their existence at all. How could we? They would be radically "other" than us, than our world, and this (unless by a special act of God) would make

113

any sort of worldly adumbration impossible. Now, whether these worlds are simply other planets, as Dr. Barnes has proposed, or if they exist in another dimension of some sort, another "strata" of creation (as I am personally inclined to believe), is a question less important philosophically, at least for our present purposes, than whether they do, or can, in fact, exist at all. But I think we have successfully answered that question affirmatively in the course of this discussion. As to where they are, and how we could harness the means by which travel between them and us could become not merely normal, but also self-instigated (that is, if we were to understood the mechanisms by which this travel is actually possible; if we could understand the nature of the Doors, then perhaps we could travel at will), those are the questions that must be answered, and hopefully will be successfully answered in the near future. ~

-These bizarre words are from the minutes of the International Counsel on Inter-World Travel, 7th Annual General Assembly, April 22-25, 1938. This group composed of scientists, philosophers, and several wealthy patrons, was dedicated to the idea of multiple worlds whose existence they believed accounted for and legitimized many of the stories of strange creatures, disappearances, and "fairy tales" that are ubiquitous in every culture and age. The lecture was given by Dr. Edmund Shullmen, Chairmen of the Counsel, and the excerpt recorded here is taken from the question and answer session of the final meeting. Unfortunately, the advent of WWII caused the Counsel to disband, and many of the scientists and academics tragically lost their lives during the course of the war, including Dr. Shullmen, who was killed by Hitler's SS in Poland. Much of whatever research and discoveries that the Counsel may have made were lost during those chaotic years.

~Excerpted from <u>*Cults, Magic, and Eccentric Clubs: Man's Fascination with the Esoteric, 1800-1960*</u> *(Cramner & Sons, London, 1972)*

Chapter IX

"Was never man lived longer for the hoarding of his breath;
Here be dragons to be slain, here be rich rewards to gain…
If we perish in the seeking,… why, how small a thing is death!"
~Desdichado, Dorothy Sayers

I crouched in the musty darkness for several minutes, with bated breath, listening for any sound from the depths beneath me. Not knowing how far down the stairs descended, it felt as though I was standing on the edge of a cliff in the dead of night, with a thousand feet of empty space a hair's breadth away. Nothing stirred in the stairwell, so I scrambled back up the stone steps, and tried to move the stone base, to slide it back somehow and escape this hole, but the slab would not give. I sat for a moment, my heart racing, trying to gather my thoughts and to keep from panicking. The sickening terror from the attack above was gone, but had been replaced by the cold fear of being trapped alive beneath the earth, of starving to death in the blackness, my bones sealed forever in this stone crypt.

But of course I soon realized that Jacoben must have opened this door, and must be following these very steps himself. If he had entered this stairwell, then it must lead to somewhere safe (for Jacoben perhaps, but not necessarily for me). So I gripped the pistol tightly, and began to cautiously descend the worn steps into the blackness.

Keeping my free hand on the wall of the cramped

passage (the stairwell was no more than four feet wide, and the roof no more than three feet above my head) I sat on a step, and with my feet I explored the next step, testing their strength, and only when I was convinced of its integrity did I slide down to it. In this manner I began my descent. The face of the cold stone wall under my hand began as a smooth surface, but gradually began to change. My hand began to detect variations and undulations in the stone, which startled me at first. I was desperately afraid that there would be an opening in the wall, an opening to the den of some dark creature of the night, waiting for an unsuspecting traveler to pass by. But as I proceeded I began to discern the nature of the carvings; they were detailed renditions of writhing serpents.

As I continued to descend (it seemed as though hours and even days passed) the carvings became so dense and ornate that they seemed to move beneath my hand. Finally I could bear it no longer, and I took my hand from the surface. The carvings now completely covered every square inch of surface on both walls and the ceiling, and the tunnel was becoming more and more narrow, until I felt as though the whole tunnel was a giant snake, choking me in its scaly embrace, blocking the sun with its massive coils. I was perspiring heavily, and felt as though I was suffocating. It seemed as though I had spent a lifetime in the darkness, and it was only with the greatest effort that I kept from screaming in panic, and I was sure that I would soon lose my mind. The desperation was reaching a tipping point, and I began to slide and jump down the steps, heedless of the danger, only hoping that I could reach the end of the darkness. All around me the tunnel writhed and curled, and I scrambled, tripped and raced down the stairs faster and faster, until I lost control and tumbled head over heals through the gloom.

Bruised and shaken, I landed in a heap on a small landing about fifty yards further down. Here the tunnel seemed to end. Twenty feet ahead, to my surprise and inestimable joy, was a splinter of light, jetting out from what seemed to be a partially closed door. I could have cried with relief, but I kept my head, remembering that this could only mean that Jacoben had been through here and had left the door cracked. I arose shakily, holding my pistol, and crept cautiously to the door. The light coming through was not, as I had hoped, the bright, warm light of the sun, but rather was a dull reddish color, almost the color of a brown rust. It is difficult to accurately describe. The door itself was composed of solid stone, thick and heavy. It was short and narrow, as though it had been made for children (or for very small people like Jacoben).

Slowly, holding the pistol ready, I inched the door open and peered through the opening. The dull light bathed the scene in a somber, rusty hue. Directly in front of me was a massive pillar of stone, cracked and aged, and to my right was what looked like the corner of another wall, as though this door was set back in an alcove and guarded by the pillar. It took some moments for my eyes to adjust to the strange light. Moving carefully into the room, I noticed something lying at the base of the giant pillar. It looked like a pile of dirty sticks next to a large dinner plate. As I looked closer my heart nearly stopped, and I leapt back to the shelter of the doorway, wildly waving my pistol. The pile of sticks was a human skeleton, and the plate was an ancient shield, the kind the Greeks or Romans might have used. Shaking, I waited to regain control of my breathing, and then moved out into the alcove again. The person had obviously been dead for years, perhaps for centuries. The skeleton was covered with dust, but otherwise was perfectly preserved, and if it were not for the old armor and shield, I would have thought that the skeleton was only perhaps fifty or one hundred years old. But it must have been much older. I could not guess where I was. Perhaps this was a hidden city, buried beneath England for a thousand years, only waiting for someone to find it. But that did not make sense. This had to be one of the worlds of which my grandfather had spoken, for why else would Jacoben have come down here? But what kind of world could it be- an underground world perhaps? I moved stealthily past the skeleton, and around the pillar, my pistol held tight. The sight that met my eyes was astonishing.

I had stepped into a cavern of enormous size, seemingly carved out of the very heart of the Earth, with pillars of solid stone, one after the other, extending away for miles on end, receding beyond view into the red depths of the cavern. They towered hundreds of feet into the air, supporting a stone ceiling, from which were hung great chandeliers, suspended on thick chains, perhaps one hundred feet above the floor. The ornate iron chandeliers held the source of the strange light: great candles, burned almost completely down, with only a dying red glow defiantly resisting the impending darkness. The lights were covered with thick layers of cobwebs, which could be seen hanging from them like dead lace, choked in dust. The candles were slowly blinking, randomly, one after the other, blink, blink, blink, and with each blink one section of the cavern was momentarily lit with the dull glow, and another receded into gloom. Patches of pillar and stone would blink in and out of shadow, all at different and irregular moments, so that one moment the nearest pillars might be more visible, and at another moment the decaying orange-red light would momentarily reveal some other pillars, deep in the bowels of the endless chamber. It was as though the candles had been fighting against the darkness for a thousand years, and would not admit to defeat, even now. But at any moment, I thought, the candles could burn down. I would not allow myself to think about it further.

The whole room (if I could call such an unimaginably massive space a room; I could not even see to the other side, but only row after row of pillars running forever through the slowly blinking orange light) seemed to be a circle, for I could just make out the sweep of the curve on my right and on my left. The breathtaking size was made even more somber and foreboding by the complete silence; not a thing moved or made a sound, and the dust lay undisturbed as it must have lain for centuries. The only thing that seemed to be at all alive was the flickering light of the candles, burning down forever in that dead hall. But more disturbing and unnerving than all of this was the wreckage strewn across the stone floor, in groups here, singly there, stacked in perverse, mangled piles around the base of the pillars, or on the huge steps that led down from the doors onto the main floor of the cavern. The bones of people, warriors and soldiers, their armor and weapons mixed with their broken bodies, were spread like a ghastly carpet throughout the cave.

Shattered skulls and splintered armor, skeletons with the arrows or spears struck through their ribcages, some corpses still locked in a deadly embrace, their knives forever fixed in their enemies back. The empty eye sockets of the dead stared darkly at me when the candle overhead was brightest, as if they were angry that I had disturbed their tragic rest; and then they would disappear into the gloom again, becoming merely lonely shadows. A battle of epic proportions had been fought here, thousands of years ago perhaps, and the winner, whoever it was, had not seen fit to clean the battlefield. I could only guess at the number of bodies in that room, but it must have been hundreds of thousands. I had stumbled into a subterranean crypt, and like a shock of cold water I realized that if I could not find a way out of here, I would most certainly join these bones, lost eternally in the anonymity of the dead, known only to God.

On either side of me, set about fifty yards from each other in the face of the sheer wall, were massive doors of iron, framed with stone, ornate and beautiful, stunning in their ancient glory, and large enough for a modern train to pass through. There were many of these doors set around the circumference of the chamber as far as I could see, hundreds of them maybe, all shut tight, with the skeletons of the ancient warriors piled up against them, as if they had hurled themselves against the doors in desperation but could not break them down. The small door from which I had emerged was set between two of these massive doors, tucked in a narrow alcove, hidden from view by one of the massive pillars, and made to look exactly like the face of the stone wall. The whole place was so stunning, so awe inspiring, so tragic in its eternal death that my knees failed me and I sat down on the top of the stone steps.

I sat for some time, listening for any sound, any sign of life, and trying to adjust myself to this strange place. Jacoben must be here somewhere, but where? Which direction did he go? What if he had already entered one of these doors and closed it behind him? The stillness and the strange flickering light, the vast loneliness, the silence of the dead warriors, the mysterious ancient doors, was so surreal that I almost convinced myself that it was a dream. But soon I noticed a rusty spear lying across a step a few yards down, and I could tell by the disturbed dust that it had been moved, perhaps kicked from its position by someone in a hurry. Jacoben had passed here not long ago, and because the spear was closer to the right side of the hidden alcove than to the left, I made the decision to begin walking to the right. So I began to move carefully down the stairs, until I reached the floor, and then began to wind my way through the ghastly remains, keeping the steps and doors always on my right. I did not dare venture into the depths of the room, between the endless rows of pillars, for fear of losing my way. And of course, before I began, I marked the entrance to the hidden passageway with two broken spears, leaning them against the pillar at the top of the steps in the shape of an "X."

What a strange journey, as I watch it now in my mind's eye, walking through that somber cave, that antechamber of despair. My footsteps on the cold stone floor were muffled, and if I stumbled over some aged armor or the bones of a long dead warrior, the sound seemed to leave the floor only with great effort, and then simply died in the heavy air. I walked past door after massive door and saw that great engines of battle were also strewn throughout, catapults and battering rams, some splintered against closed doors in a futile effort to breach them. Also amongst the carnage were skeletons of strange animals and bizarre creatures, perhaps bred for war by these prehistoric peoples. Before these I paused, and felt a shiver run down my spine at a terrible thought: what if there were other things in this cave that were alive, besides Jacoben and me? What if something had survived this battle, and was even now crawling through the bones and rubble, more horrible than either Jacoben or the Messengers? The huge teeth and empty eye sockets of corpses seemed to smile hungrily back at me, coming in and out of focus through the shadows cast by the blinking light. I looked hurriedly around, deep into the cavern, but saw nothing except endless carnage. I continued to walk.

After having walked for some time through the blinking light, I suddenly noticed that one of the great doors stood open. I stopped for a moment, thinking that this might be Jacoben's escape route. The mouth of the open door was as dark as night, and the bodies of the slain were piled in the entrance, as though the darkness had vomited them out into the cave. I slowly began to make my way up the steps towards the open door, but then stopped. A chill swept over me, and I could not make myself go closer. The darkness of the entrance was complete; nothing could be seen beyond the threshold. Even as the candle swinging high above was at its brightest it did not penetrate the impossibly dark opening. When the light dimmed the darkness of the door was like that of a mouth opening in the night. The tangle of bodies was high, and it would be very difficult to climb over the bones to reach the entrance. But it was not the difficulty that held me back. Coldness could be felt pouring out of the opening, not a breeze, but the chill of the darkness itself. And it was not the cold of the night, or even of ice and snow; it was the cold of the grave. I kept staring into the darkness. But was there something that was looking out, that was even now watching me from the shadow? Was there something beyond that door that *wanted* me to enter? Something that even now was hoping that I would climb over that pile of bones and enter, and was even calling me, encouraging me to disappear into the darkness? Whatever was beyond that door I knew I could not face it. Whether Jacoben had gone through or not, I could not follow. I stood for a long while staring at that open door, and began to shiver violently, but I could not take my eyes off the door. I could not climb further, and I could not go back. It may have been hours that I stood there, I do not know. But finally it seemed that I awoke, shook off the chill, and hurried down the steps and away from the door. The moment my back was turned I began to run, tripping and stumbling over the bones and armor in the half-light, trying to get as far away from that door as I could. Not until I was far away from that door did I stop running.

I somehow knew that Jacoben had not gone through that open door. Surely there were things that would frighten even a murdering necromancer like him, and if so, that door was one of them. I even somehow knew, or at least hoped, that whatever was in that darkness could not pursue me now, not in the light, not while the candles still burned. But what if the candles went out? What if the slow, pained flickering stopped, and the wicks finally burned down, flashing their last bit of orange light against the impending gloom? Then the antechamber would be plunged into darkness, and I would be alone, alone in the dark. Alone with whatever was beyond that door. I kept on, looking for signs of Jacoben's passing as I walked, but I was no longer awe-struck by the strange place in which I found myself; now I was afraid. Suddenly anything was possible; suddenly this place was full of spirits, ghosts of the dead soldiers, and monsters behind locked doors. Even in the flickering lights I imagined I could see shapes moving in the distance, burning eyes behind pillars, even the faces of the dead suddenly come to life for a moment, following me with their empty eye sockets. It made no difference that deep down I knew (or hoped?) that I was imagining it; the fear was too great. On and on I walked, further into the chamber, and further into fear.

Where had Jacoben gone? I had now walked so far that to even turn back would be impossible. I did not think my strength could last. It may have been a full day that I had been walking, perhaps longer. I had to rest, but fear was pushing me on, pushing me to find a way out before the lights failed, before the night fell. But in the end it was too much; I had to rest. I found a nook beside the stairs that offered some hiding spot. I crawled in between a pillar and the stairs, pulled a heavy shield in front of me, and tried to sleep. It was almost impossible. I drifted in and out of sleep like in a fog, dreaming only of dark doorways and flickering candles. I was running, but the shadow beyond the door was following, always a step behind. The bones at my feet were coming alive with a rattle, grabbing my ankles as I ran, calling to me, calling me to wait, to wait for the door. "The door," they cried, "let us go through the door! You must come with us, come with us through the door!" Then I woke up.

I was shaking and sweating, and had no idea how much time may have passed since I had fallen asleep. The lights still flickered, but they were much more dim, and the shadows much longer. Indeed, it was difficult to see at all. I pushed the shield away, and stood up, somewhat panicked. I had slept too long! Any moment now the darkness would be complete, and I would be lost forever. I scrambled over the bones and armor blocking my nook and started to run again. I ran and I ran, always seeming to stumble and to trip, never seeming to get anywhere. The candles were so low now that I was sure at any minute they would go out. Finally I tripped over some bones and fell flat on my face. At that moment I looked up, my head spinning, and saw the last of the candles wink out. The darkness was instantly complete. Fear indescribable! Darkness, all was darkness. Too long I had tarried! Too long I had slept! But wait… the darkness was complete, except there (could it be true?), there ahead somewhere was one oasis of light, one halo in the center of hell, one candle that had not burned out! I scrambled up and headed for this light, feeling my way through the suffocating darkness, hoping to reach the light before *it* found me, before the thing beyond the door caught me. But the light seemed to recede even as I pursued it, being one moment just a few yards ahead, and another moment there, beyond the pillars. In a panic I realized that I had followed it far into the depths of the chamber, far away from the stairs! Deep despair mixed with panic now, and I was all but sprinting, falling and stumbling over the bones, running into pillars, but sprinting. Finally the light was just here, behind the next pillar. In relief I rounded the pillar... but I saw that I had been mistaken. It was not a candle at all, hanging high above in the iron chandelier. It was the light of a small lantern. A hooded figure stood, holding the lantern, his back towards me, in a clearing of bones and armor, between two pillars. The hand that held the lantern was white, like snow, and the hood and cloak were brown. The flickering lantern light cast strange shadows on the ground and on the pillars. I stopped and stared, fear welling up within me. I had been led deep into the antechamber, led away from all hope, into the darkness. The hooded figure did not speak, but only reached his other hand into the lantern, and with a pinch the light of the lantern went out.

And then I woke up.

I knew that I would get no true rest here. Indeed, I was even wearier than when I had first attempted to rest (how long ago, now?), and I was more frightened of dreaming than of whatever I would find in this chamber. The lights were (to my relief) no lower than when I had found my nook. I scrambled out, and began to walk.

On and on I walked.

I was on my guard at all times, my pistol always in my hand. I had seen no sign of Jacoben since finding the dislodged spear, and in the back of my mind I knew that I might have made a mistake. He could just as easily have gone the other direction. Or, perhaps, he had gone into the depths of the room, where I feared to go. This cave might not be a great circle, as I had at first supposed, but might be infinitely large. Of course, it wouldn't have to be infinitely large to be too large for me to navigate. Suppose it was the size of England? Or like walking along the bottom of the ocean? I couldn't help but think of these things, even though I tried not to. But the stark fear that I had been feeling was subsiding. Not because there was anything less to fear, but rather because of the time that I had spent so far in this world. I think that my psyche was incapable of that kind of sustained fear, so in its place was merely a dull, constant somberness, an aching dread.

But sometimes I was sure that I heard something, far in the depths of the chamber, some movement, some shifting of bones, but it was never clear, never obvious. I would stand for some time, listening, but it would not repeat. Then I would move on, stealthily, running from pillar to pillar, hoping that I was unknown and unseen to whatever I imagined was out there in the far reaches of the gloom. Then sometimes I would reproach myself for my cowardice, for what if the sound was that of Jacoben, maybe as lost as I was, trying to find a way out, trying to stay hidden from me? But still I would not leave the curve of the steps. If there was any way out of this place, it must be here, through one of the doors, or through a hidden door like the one I had entered. But the sounds that I imagined sometimes echoed through the musty depths were unnerving.

Once I was sure that I saw movement, some shadow that was deeper than the surrounding shadows, deep in the interior, lit briefly by the blinking lights. This brought sheer terror to my soul, and I hid myself, listening intently, watching to see if there was anything else. But how could I be sure? The lights, those terrible blinking lights that I prayed would not go out, they cast all kinds of shadows in the depths, all kinds of strange shapes and whirls. I would go mad staring into the distance as those lights blinked, and blinked, and blinked… I continued walking.

On and on I walked.

I think that I may have even dozed off, my eyes downcast, watching my feet weave around the obstacles, always keeping the stairs on my right. I was startled out of my delirium by a distant scratching sound and a dark shadow that seemed to pass over the floor just on the corner of my sight. My eyes went up, and I paused, looking at the line of chandeliers high above me. One chandelier, perhaps halfway down the pillared corridor (or at least halfway down the length that my eyes could penetrate) was moving, swaying just slightly, as though a breeze had struck it. A breeze? Here, in the depths of a cave?

I stood a moment frozen in place, watching the hypnotic pendulum movement, unable to register the potential danger. Did my eyes deceive me again, or had they ever, on this whole devilish walk, deceived me? Was the chandelier really moving, or did the shadows around it only create the illusion of movement? Maybe it was my head that was moving like a pendulum. A very rational panic gripped me, and I scrambled to hide from I knew not what. I knew only that it was not Jacoben who had induced the motion. I hid behind a pile of bones, my pistol gripped tightly, and from this vantage point I watched as the chandelier finally stopped swaying. And then I heard a sound.

It was a scratching sound, and the rustle of movement, far off in the distance, but away from the moving chandelier. It was ahead of me now, closer to the stairs. And then silence. I waited and waited, crouched and hidden, for what could have been an hour or more, sweat dripping from my face, and my hands so damp that they could barely hold the pistol. I was shaking all over. But there was no further sound. Finally, I cautiously began to move again, to creep out from my hiding place. Still nothing. The chandelier had long stopped swinging, and there was no movement, no sound. The lights continued to blink slowly.

I continued walking, my heart hammering in my chest. I was sure that if there really were something out there it would hear my heart, like a drum, echoing in the chamber. But there was nothing.

Further and further I walked, and I began to believe that what I had heard and seen had only been my imagination. Here there were bones and armor piled higher than in the other areas in the cave. They were massed in high mounds, and I sometimes would walk for some minutes before the mound receded. At these places I could not see far beyond, far into the chamber. It was like walking between small foothills, with the mountains of the pillars rising up behind them. I imagined that I was walking beside a silver creek, running between the hills, and that the sun was setting in the distance, or perhaps it was lightning, for blinking lights threw strange patterns on the pine-covered hills. I thought that there must be beautiful birds here in these hills, in these trees... I shook my head violently! What was happening to me? I was losing my mind in this terrible place. I had to get out! Panic rose in me again, and I started to run. I raced between the piles of bones and armor, leaping over broken machines of war, and rounding pillars like I was being chased. I had to get out, I had to get out! Blink, blink, blink went the lights, the chamber spun, and the piles of bones swayed like they could come crashing down at any moment and crush me.

As I ran blindly around the next pile of bones I heard something else besides the rush of wind in my ears and I pulled up to a stop. Ahead of me was an enormous pile of bones and armor, not only high but long, stretching away to my left, away from the stairs. This pile came to an end almost at the edge of the stairs, with only a narrow passage between it and the stairs, which were also strewn with wreckage. Other piles were littered around, so that it was like walking into a circle, a cul-de-sac, with the only exit being the small opening by the stairs. The pile around which I had run was the entrance; the exit was before me. But it was not this unique sprawl of bones that made me pull up to a stop. There, on the far side of the circle, was movement. An ancient helmet had been somehow dislodged, and was even now in the process of rolling and falling off the long pile, down to the ground. I watched in fascination, not really sure what I was seeing, as it bumped off a protruding bone, struck a breastplate with a clang, and finally clattered to the floor, coming to rest some feet in front of me. The noise was like cannon fire in this silent crypt.

The lights kept blinking slowly.

I was not so far gone that I did not recognize danger. I began to slowly back away, wondering if Jacoben had just climbed that pile, and was awaiting me on the other side, beyond that narrow opening, with drawn knife. But the thought of Jacoben was short lived. As I stared at the mass before me, backing slowly up, I realized that there was something wrong with the pile. There, right near the narrow gap, was something dark, something large protruding out, like a black tarpaulin full of sand... only, not completely black, but with a flash of color. But... the tarp was moving, there was a flash of fire on its surface, like spark leaping in the night; the black bag was looking at me with two bright red eyes! The whole pile began suddenly to move, to suddenly shift, like the foundation had been removed from a house. Bones and armor came rattling down, bouncing off the stone floor, and something dark was beneath the pile, something that stretched the entire length of the pile, something that was rising up out of the carnage. I was turning and running in the same instant that I saw all this. Behind me I heard the crash of bones and armor; and then I was out, away from the entrapping piles and running.

It had been waiting for me, it had been waiting for me! It knew I would be just there! "Don't look back," a voice in my head was screaming, "don't look back!" Passing pillars and piles of bone I ran, hearing behind me the crash of armor and remains as the black creature smashed through the piles moments after I had passed them. "Just the right shot," I told myself, "just the right shot!" I was somehow distancing myself from the creature at a rapid pace, darting in and out of the piles and pillars, for it must have had to take the time to search for me. "Quick," I thought through my terror and tears, "just behind here, I will wait and ambush the creature as it passes! Just the right shot, that's all it will take!" I dodged quickly behind a large pile between two pillars and crouched down, trembling and listening.

I could hear crashes and movement in the distance, but then it suddenly died out. For some minutes I could hear nothing but the beating of my own heart. I held the pistol ready with shaking hand, ready for that one perfect shot that I had to make. But I could hear nothing. What could this mean? Had the thing lost me, and had now gone back to where it thought I would pass by, if I continued walking again?

I then heard a sudden noise.

It was this sound that saved me. It was like a rush of wind, followed by what sounded like a release of steam from some great locomotive, bearing down on my hiding place like a runaway train. I leaped headlong away from the sound as the mound of bones exploded with a scream that nearly struck me deaf, and I only just caught a glimpse of blackness, as though the night itself was tearing through my hiding place. The shock of the attack knocked me sprawling among the bones, thirty feet at least, and I struck the hard stone with a jolt, the pistol spinning from my hands into the shadows. Rolling over in a blind panic, I saw the creature. It was a Krishnag (I would later realize), a prehistoric horror from out of a faerie tale.

It was moving like a bullet through the pillars, gliding along the stone, a horribly huge snake, black as midnight, its red eyes glowing as it swept the chaos, looking for its prey, looking for me. And oh! The ghastly sight, as it turned, its muscles rippling like waves under the black scales as they scraped the stone floor like sandpaper, and wrapped itself around a pillar, moving up it with furious speed, one hundred feet above the floor at least. How can I describe the sight? The terror was so great that I am almost at a loss of words, all these long years later. Its head was far too large for its body, and was horned, pitted and diamond-shaped like a viper. Its black scales, when they caught the orange light just right, reflected a rainbow pattern, which (as strange as it may seem) made the creature appear all the more evil, as though it was mocking beauty itself. I had the bizarre thought at that moment of the stories that I had heard, of the flood with which God had judged the world, and how God had given a rainbow as a sign of his favor. No flood perhaps, but surely there could be for man no greater punishment in all the universe than the existence of this dragon.

With a horrible serpentine roar the fiend gripped the stone of the pillar with jagged claws, and its long body whipped around behind it, unwrapping like a rope from the pillar, and then it leaped like a striking snake! It flew through the air, undulating in an "S" pattern, and then its arms and legs stretched out, and four bat-like wings unfolded from its sides and beat the air like a hurricane, the force of the wind knocking me flat on my back. For a moment the light of the candles was made dark as they sputtered and flickered from the blast, and the giant shadow of the dragon passed over me like a storm. The Krishnag struck the pillar directly behind me, and it cracked like it was made of wood, and for a moment I thought that it would come crashing down, perhaps bringing the roof of the cavern down with it. The creature did not pause, but with a scream that echoed throughout the antechamber, bouncing off ceiling and stone, and bursting upon my ears like a air-raid siren (it is difficult to describe the sound; a scream like a roar, but a serpentine roar), it turned and flew straight down the middle of the row in which I was now lying prone, only a few yards in the air above me, undulating in the S shape, and I could see the incredible length of the creature as it passed over me. It seemed to run on forever and its arms and bat-like wings were far larger than I would have thought possible. The cavern was now choked with ancient dust as the wings churned the long dead air, and scattered bones in the blast. The snake flew so far down the aisle that I almost lost sight of it, and could only make out where it had been by the flicker of the candles that it passed. Then it flew straight up among the chandeliers, snaking through the chains in a mad but agile dance. The sight was sickening as the black body writhed amongst the chains, almost extinguishing the lights with every beat of wing. It then swooped down, dropping to the floor, alighting like a bird of prey; then its red eyes saw me, and it began to run, straight towards me, on all four legs like a jungle crocodile. Still at a dead run, it suddenly dropped to the floor, its legs with their bat wings folded up against its side, and it was a snake, gliding forward towards me at an even faster and smoother pace, its mouth open in the awful scream.

I scrambled and lunged for the base of the pillar in a desperate effort to find the pistol, my eyes streaming tears, blurring my sight. My ears rang with the screaming cries of the dragon, and I had mere moments to avoid its attack. Indeed, it was only by chance that I did. In my panic my foot slipped on a piece of rusted armor, and I fell rolling behind a pillar as the dragon swept by, close enough that I felt the heat of its breath, and saw the white fangs like swords as they crushed the pile of bones mere inches away. I leapt behind the pillar, only just avoiding the whipping tail that struck the pillar with such force that a shower of small stones rained down like hail. And then I saw my pistol, lying against the base of a pillar across the aisle. I did not pause, but ran as I had never run before, sprinting across the open ground, praying with every step that I would be in time. The creature had turned its long body with incredible speed, its arms and wings tucked against its sides, and its burning eyes found me.

I reached the pistol, gripped it and turned; the sight still haunts my nightmares to this day. Through the dust and chaos the Krishnag came at me from out of my darkest fears, its mouth wide open like a grave, its forked tongue moving among the white fangs like a thing possessed. I raised the pistol, closed my eyes, and squeezed the trigger as fast as I could.

All was heat and blood, pain and shock, as the Krishnag hit me with the full force of its body, throwing me like a rag doll into a scattered pile of bones. My head seemed to explode in pain, the breath left my lungs in a ragged burst, and all I could see was darkness and blazing points of white light. All around was thrashing violence, noise and dust, and I knew that I was dead.

My mind was a foggy haze when I opened my eyes some time later, and saw only the stone floor, soaked in blood. I lay for a while, trying to remember what had happened, where I was. My head felt as though it was on fire, and it was all I could do to roll over, for my body was wracked with pain. But I was alive! Trembling, I managed to raise myself to a sitting position, to divine what had happened. All around me was a disaster of carnage, gore and blood. Piles of bones and stone obscured my view, so I stood to my feet, and looked at the battlefield.

Ancient bones mixed with fresh blood, and pieces of aged armor with pieces of the mighty demon serpent, the Krishnag, whose still writhing carcass lay splayed out in the aisle, the orange light casting a terrible sheen on the blackened scales. It was shorter now than it had been, for its head was completely gone, leaving only a horrible mess of destruction on its stump of neck, a testament to the strange power of Sylvester's pistol. I realized that I still held the empty gun tightly in my shaking hand. Indeed, my grip was so tight that I could not now let it go, though I tried. I was shaking all over, and was covered in blood and gore, and I soon realized that the blood running down my face was my own. There was a huge gash in my head, and only with much pain and difficulty did I staunch the flow, wrapping my head with my handkerchief. It seemed that my head had struck the edge of a helmet when the Krishnag threw me, and this wound, unlike the earlier knife wound, was very painful.

I sat for some time on a stone, viewing the battlefield in a kind of pain-wracked daze. It is a strange scene, if you can see it now in your mind's eye. A little boy, his wounded head wrapped in cloth, sitting alone in a vast cavern, his only companion a slain dragon, a creature from the pages of a storybook. I felt ill at the sight of the carnage, but yet strangely invigorated by the victory, like the hero in the story of Jack the Giant Killer, or David and Goliath. I too had killed a giant; even more, I had killed a dragon, a Krishnag, a demon serpent. I had stepped into my role, my vocation, filling the place of my grandfather. Only this creature was at least three times the size of the one in my grandfather's library. Or, perhaps I am merely projecting what I feel now, all these many years later, onto that moment and that little boy. Perhaps the pain and the loneliness of the hour are best left hidden in the recesses of my memory, while only the glory of the hour is related.

What glory I may have felt at the time was short lived. I was dizzy and disoriented (which is hardly surprising given the circumstances); the head wound was still bleeding, though not as severely. I finally roused myself, and began to make my way around the scene to the stairs, which I could still see down the aisle. As I stepped around the mess, I noticed something white, almost glowing among the bones and debris. I bent down, and saw the perfectly preserved tooth of the Krishnag, almost as large as a sword, and certainly as sharp as one. I (painfully) removed my coat, and wrapping the tooth in it I carefully hung it from my belt.

What hole in the universe had those worms crawled from? How many thousands of years had it been since, like maggots, they had been spawned from the darkness of a dead world, from a land that had burned like a dying star? Nesting among the bones, feeding on pain and chaos, crawling through the holes and passageways and into other worlds, the demon snakes, the Krishnag, had long been the guardians of the fabled Antechamber, the gateway to all the worlds; and my grandfather had once killed one. In that terrible place it was only by the narrowest of margins that their vengeance had not been paid to me.

Walking past the creature was like walking in my grandfather's library, past the skeleton in the glass case. It seemed to go on for so much longer than it should. I couldn't imagine how grandfather had managed to drag his carcass anywhere, let alone all the way to England (although his carcass was, as I have said, much smaller). I was more than content with my souvenir. Perhaps ten minutes later I had reached the steps, and then began to continue my journey.

I need not, I am sure, recount the events of the last day (or days; I do not know for sure how long I was in that ageless room). I had neither food nor water in all that time, had not slept, and had endured enough tragedy and trauma to last anyone a lifetime. My wounds were severe, and as far as I knew I had lost my prey; who knew where Jacoben was now? What's more, my weapon was now empty. Even if I met up with him, what could I do now? Nothing. I was no match for Jacoben and his serpentine knife.

Having no other options, I began to walk on. I could certainly not go back the way I had come. But Jacoben must have a destination other than this horrible place, so I decided to keep going, hoping for some sign of him, or at least some way out of here.

I will not describe the rest of that journey in detail. Indeed, I hardly remember it all very clearly. It seemed that I wandered for days and days, step after step through the decaying light and dead air. My pain was great, and I had trouble thinking clearly, or even walking in a straight path. But soon it was my hunger and thirst that overwhelmed the pain of my wounds, and it became a constant torment, until I was sure that every step would be my last, and I would finally give in, lie down, and die. Door after door I passed, and the sight of bones was no longer strange. I was in too much agony to even fear that another of those dragons would be lurking in the shadows somewhere, to finish what the other had begun. But I think that mine was the last battle that anyone would have to fight with a Krishnag. Miles down the cavern I found the nest of the creature, a great mass of bones and twisted strands of something so grotesque that I chose not to even wonder from whence it came, or from what it was made. I climbed the mass of smoothed-out carnage, worn from centuries of use, and found there three large eggs, as large as I was, terrible sacks of the demon's offspring. Three ancient swords I put to final use, running them to the hilt in the leathery hide of those accursed eggs. Blackness and foul stench oozed from the gash, and I could not help but wretch. I left that horrid place as fast as I could.

Hour after hour I walked, mile after mile, and I was sure I would go mad in that chamber. Surely the light would go out, the candles finally snuffed by time, and I would be alone in the dark. I walked until I could walk no more, and then I crawled on my hands and knees, desperate to find an end to this hell. I remember finally lying on the stone floor, having passed out, or fallen, staring up and up to the great ceiling, almost invisible except for the glint of the orange candle light as it moved in its macabre dance over the carven stone. There were spirits in the candle light, I was sure, and I thought in my delusion that I could see them moving, leaping from flame to ceiling, and dancing about with each other on the tortured stone. They were dancing their last dance, a condemned man eating his last meal, for soon they would be no more, and the cave would finally sink into night. I am sure that I would have died right there in that hour, but I heard in that moment a voice. Coming to me like in a dream, it was the voice of my father. He was speaking to me, but far away, and I heard behind his voice the sound of a whistle, like a train in the distance.

"Thaddeus, you are strong and brave, like the knights of old. The hour is fast approaching, Thaddeus, when you must labor in the vineyard. While it is still day you must labor, for the night is coming when no man can work. Do not sleep the day away!"

My eyes opened with a start, and I realized in a panic that I would die if I stayed here. I rolled over, and began to crawl along the edge of the steps, pulling myself along, determined to somehow escape. I did not make it far before I fell again, unable to compel my limbs any further. I lay there sobbing, and in complete despair. I was lost, and I had failed- failed grandfather, failed my parents, and indeed, had failed all of my ancestors, all those who had come before me, who had worked and fought and bled to keep the Book safe. It had all come down to me, and I would die in this hellish cave, sealed forever with these bones, and no one would ever even find my body. But as I lay, I heard again my Father's voice. "Rise, Thaddeus, rise and face the day. You have not yet begun to labor."

And then I felt something. I could recognize it, and I knew that it was something good, but in that place I could not, for a brief maddening moment, remember what it was. I shivered, and my eyes opened wide. It was a breeze, a cool breeze! And it was a fresh breeze, the clean crisp air of the world outside this cave. I scrambled unsteadily to my feet, my head spinning, and I saw ahead that the next door was ajar, only slightly, just enough for someone small to slip through. And this was unlike that other open door that I had previously seen; there were no long-dead combatants spilling out of it, and the chill that I felt was not the chill of the grave, but the chill of an autumn night. I staggered to the opening, and just managed to squeeze between the massive iron doors; fortunately, there was just enough room, for I would not have been able to push them open to get through in my condition. On the other side was a short tunnel. I could see just ahead the glint of stars, and could feel the breeze on my face. I ran the last few yards, before stumbling out of the entrance, into the blast of cool air, and a stunningly brilliant network of stars, more stars than I had ever before seen or imagined. The night was so lit by these magnificent lights that I could see almost as clearly as if it were midday. I was on a high wind-swept mountain, with jagged, snow-capped peaks to my right and to my left, while just in front of me a massive stone stairwell led down into the gloom below, down the side of the mountain. I dropped to my knees, tears streaming down my face, looking up into the stars; and then the world spun wildly, and I fell face down onto the cold slab, and remembered no more.

~

The wind through mountain crag is carried
Down ragged edge and crooked pass,
To where the Bright Ones, last to stand
Against the Dark Queen, finally buried.
Entombed in broken stone and ash,
They, last of all, eternal, godlike strand
Into the night were finally carried.

Blackened edge of blackened blade
Cracked and broken, helmet, shield,
Eternal, godlike, Bright and winged,
They were our hope when battle waged.
Though pursued and harried, did never yield,
They, like angels, trumpet singed,
And fell, like angels, to darkened grave.

Helena, the evening star, and also Gabriel
The brave, from brilliant sky they traveled once,
And in the autumn night they died.
Water pure was drawn and drunk, from the silver well,
The Bright Ones of the summer month,
While all the heavens wailed and cried,
Have descended into hell.

~Excerpted from *The Nightmare of Percephilous,* circa
1300AD, translated from the original Latin by Dr. Byron
Fairmont, 1818

Chapter X

The night has a thousand eyes,
And the day but one;
Yet the light of the bright world dies
With the dying sun.
~Francis William Bourdillon

There lay a great plain before me, barren and cruel, strewn with boulder and thistle, stretching out from mountain in the east to dark sea in the west. On the edge of that sea an ancient castle sat, white, and towering high into the gathering storm clouds. Fear was in that loathsome tower, and though it was white, it was not pure. No one dared approach that castle to knock its great doors to the ground, to bathe the white marble with pure water, to cleanse it or raze it to the ground. I only knew that if no one either cleaned or destroyed it, then all would be lost. I heard the cry of a great trumpet, and saw an army of strange men rising from the sea, hideous and deformed, like things untimely born. They held aloft a banner of the white rose, a flower beautiful to look upon but deadly to touch. They ringed the castle, spear and shield, while out of the east came a single warrior, noble and silver helmed, and riding on a great horse. From the horse's brow rose a single horn that looked as though it were carven from a thousand pearls. The rider and horse bore down on the army of the dead across the barren plain, his silver tipped lance lowered and his shield ready. I thought that this warrior could surely throw down the castle and route the army. Upon the wide shield was a mark that I recognized from somewhere, a symbol of a key and a scroll, and as the warrior turned and looked at me with eyes set like flint, I saw that it was my father.

I saw then in the clouds, high beyond the reach of the white castle, a woman clothed in blue like the day, riding in the wind and on the rays of sun, scattering the black clouds like the wind scatters smoke. Her hair was long and spun of silver and gold, her blue eyes bright and piercing, and in her hand was a naked sword.

The vision changed abruptly, and behold, a hall of great splendor, alabaster and decked in purple and gold, filled with royal and noble people, all of whom bowed at the entrance of a beautiful woman, sweeping the white floor with their robes. The object of their adulation made her way through the hall, as music played and subjects wept with joy. Slowly she walked, and the train of her elegant dress seemed to float behind her. Her hair was as dark as midnight, and though I strained for a view I could never quite see her face. Even as she took her place on the great throne, surrounded by knights in black armor, their helmets painted in chalky white, her face remained shrouded. And then approached the throne a man of noble bearing, aged, his long beard white and his robe trimmed in gold, bearing in his wrinkled hands the royal scepter of power. He bowed low before the queen, and presented the scepter in uplifted hands. The queen, her face still strangely obscured, took the scepter, and suddenly but calmly, the knight at her right reached out and grabbed the old man by his fingers, and viciously he cut the aged hand from the wrist with a single blow of his knife! The black knight flung the hand into the horrified assembly, and the vision faded from sight.

Red and yellow light was shining from somewhere,

seemingly dancing as through a fog. I heard the soft sound of movement, and a familiar crackling, like that of a fire. I think my eyes were opened, and I saw flames leaping in a cozy stone hearth. There was a black iron pot hanging over the fire, and a small stack of firewood to the side. I could smell something cooking, and could hear the voice of my mother, softly humming to herself while she moved quietly about the room. I could tell that I was lying on a soft bed, covered by a warm quilt, and I thought that I was at my home, and that I must have been having a terrible dream before waking, a dream that I could not quite remember, except for a vague feeling that it had been vivid and painful, and there was a dull ache in my head. For a moment I was perfectly comfortable, perfectly happy. Home! I was so very drowsy that I could hardly keep my eyes open, and began to drift happily back to sleep. As my eyes fluttered closed, I saw my mother come into view, her arms full of blankets and towels. How strange, I thought, as my eyes closed and I fell back into sleep, for I do not remember my mother's hair being so long and silver...

And so I had begun a new stage in my journey. I compose this section with great trepidation, for how does one describe a different world? The categories that I employ can only be taken from what I share with those who might be reading this tale, and in many ways this is sufficient, though in many it is not. Much of the story until this juncture has been of a fantastic nature, and probably difficult for an even an open-minded reader to believe; it certainly becomes no less so at this stage of the journey. I say this perhaps as a way of warning you, the reader, that I cannot flawlessly relate what I saw and experienced, but that what (and how) I do relate is, in fact, adequate. That is, it should disclose the essentials of this tale at least so far as any tale is able to be disclosed, within the confines of a particular language, culture, and indeed, that particular race of beings with which we are most intimately acquainted, the human race.

I awoke to find myself in a strange house, built of roughly hewn grey stone, quite small, a single living space and a separate bedroom. It was furnished with hand-made wooden tables, chairs, and couches, and the walls were warmly enhanced with thickly woven tapestries. A stone fireplace provided the warmth, and some of the light. A single window let in the day. Through the window a cool breeze blew, carried as I would soon find out, from the high windswept mountain passes. The small hut was perched on what seemed like the very edge of an inaccessible cliff. An alpine meadow was behind it, perhaps an acre or two in size, set against the face of another cracked granite cliff that joined the network of mountain range. The meadow was fed by a small stream of melting snow that fell from the towering cliff into a clear pool. A vegetable garden had been planted in the sunny meadow, and a gnarly, aged tree, bearing a strange but delicious golden fruit grew at the base of the cliff, near the falling water. It was a beautiful, restful place, the kind of place that seemed to be at perfect peace.

The sole inhabitant of the tiny homestead was a woman, tall, willowy and silver haired. Tall, but her back had an odd shape to it, as though she were somewhat hunched. She had a strange beauty that defied my attempts to guess her age, but I think that she was very old. It was easy to understand why I had, in my delirium, mistaken her for my mother. They both had an air about them, almost regal, composed and dignified. The woman's name was Charismata- named, she told me, after the evening star.

"In honor of the celestial light first seen in the evening east."

Her voice was like quiet water, or the sound of silence.

Here I must pause, and comment for a moment on something that is very strange, and I am sure the reader has already noted it, although I admit that I did not, at first, realize how marvelous it really was. I am referring, of

141

course, to the fact that the woman spoke, and I could understand. She was not speaking English, obviously, and though I could hear the strange language as it was, my mind translated it without effort. Indeed, when I spoke, I could hear the strange language in my ears, as it were, though my mind only heard my native tongue. What was the nature of this anomaly? I can still only guess. Perhaps it is not so far-fetched to suppose that there was once only one universal language, as my grandfather had suggested, and that it was still spoken here? Maybe when I crossed the threshold of the Antechamber I somehow recalled what I had never quite forgotten? I do not know with certainty. Whatever the case may have been, this continued throughout my journey, and I became so used to it that it gradually became normal.

I would remain in this house for the next month. It took almost that long to recover from my wounds and the exhaustion that I suffered. Charismata had found me lying on the threshold of the Antechamber the very night that I had stumbled from the door in the mountain, and had thought that I was already dead. The night before she found me she had heard strange cries echoing from the doorway, which she could see far below and to the south of her home.

"There has been much movement on those ancient steps of late, and much coming and going. But I have not heard the serpent that prowls the caves awake for many years, and you were not the first person to leave the cavern that night."

Over the course of the month, as I remembered all that had previously transpired, I began to relate it to my host, and to try to piece together what I still could not understand. Charismata earned my trust immediately. Indeed, as I have said, the resemblance to my mother was uncanny (except for her age; it seemed that at one moment she was as old as the mountain, and at the next she seemed as young as the flowers in early spring). In the day, as she worked in the garden, or prepared the food, or busied herself about the small house, she seemed to be a stooped

142

old woman, her back strangely hunched. In the evenings, when we sat on the stones overlooking the far flung valley and mountains and watched the stars, she seemed somehow different, as though the light of the celestial orbs was burning in her own eyes. During the day I could almost believe that I was merely at a mountain cabin, perhaps in the Swiss Alps, recovering from a skiing accident or something; in the evenings, as the strange patterns began their cosmic dance, and the air that I drew into my lungs was cold and foreign, as though it had drifted down from the fiery heavens, breathed out by the gods of those distant lights, I knew that I was an alien and a stranger in this land.

It was not long until I believed I could trust her with my tale. I explained the entire story to Charismata, all I knew of the Book, its importance, my role and the role of my grandfather. I told her of Jacobin and Cuthbert, their treachery, and of the Messengers of the Queen. I told her of my narrow escapes, and of my battle with the dragon. Had I had more life experience perhaps, or more wisdom, I might have withheld some of the more secretive information, and relayed only what I was sure would be safe to tell. I would never have mentioned the Book or its importance. It was a foolish move, maybe, but I often think that it is hard to distinguish between foolishness and innocence and the faith of a child; I think that God can distinguish them. Whatever the case, if ever I would meet someone in whom it was safe to confide, that person was my hostess.

She listened carefully, her eyes sparkling with the strange light of the stars, seldom taking her eyes off the heavens to look at me, but occasionally asking questions, or had me repeat something, or describe something in more detail. She never doubted any part of my story (or at least she never seemed to), and when I had finished she sat quietly for some time.

"That is indeed an adventure worth telling. I have heard something of this Book that you speak of, rumors that have been whispered secretly since the end of the golden age, all those eons ago. I did not know if they were true."

"Then do you know what I should do?" I asked hopefully. "And what does Jacobin want with it?"

"No." Her brief answer was most unwelcome. "I cannot see all things. But I can tell you that the land from which you have journeyed is known here, at least to some, though we take little interest in the business of other lands and peoples. I have heard that it is a tortured land, but one that has been most uniquely blessed. That, at least, is what the legends say. I am not surprised to find that the Book has been in the care of those from your world. It would be a minor honor for such a favored race, but an honor nonetheless." She gave me a strange look, like a parent might give a child when they learned of a good grade in school, or of receiving an award.

"I know what the Messengers are," she continued, looking again to the starry night sky. "And I know the queen whom they serve. Indeed, I know her all too well. All this dark land that you have stumbled into is held tightly by her poisoned fist." She waved her hand across the vast gloom before us, stretching out (as I would learn) hundreds of miles to the sea in the west.

"The Messengers that you speak of are none other than her knights, and the very sight of them is enough to strike fear into the hearts of even the very brave. Your grandfather was truly a great warrior. The queen is powerful, and has ruled here for thousands of years, since the end of the golden age."

"Thousands?" I stammered confusedly, "does no one die of old age in this land?"

"Not all races are as bound to time as yours, Thaddeus." She looked at me with a smile and laughed, and it seemed that in her laugh I could see the earth stop turning, and the stars stop moving, and the constraints of age and linear movement fall away. In that laugh (I do not say 'in that instant') time seemed to be a petty thing that could be cast away like an old coat on a warm spring day. The blue sky of freedom beckoned, and I rose to follow.

I think that in that laugh I lived longer than I have

lived even to this day. Even now, in my old age, I will remember something, a vague feeling or half-way reminiscence, from that life lived in freedom, and I cannot help but weep, and long for my home.

Whether I left that laugh voluntarily, or if even it had to bend finally under the weight of the now, I do not know. But I found myself answering:

"Why would Jacoben take such pains to avoid the Messengers if he was going to bring the Book to this world anyway? Why would he betray us and then betray the Messengers, if he was coming here all along? It seems that there would be other worlds that would be safer places to hide."

"Safer, perhaps, but who would want such a treasure as the Book? This Jacoben has surely not stolen it just to hide it again. It is only of value to those who can open it, read it, and act. It seems that the enemy wishes to possess all the worlds, to drag them into the abyss. Jacoben might have killed and stolen for this end, to assist the enemy, and maybe to earn some coveted reward. Power is ever at the fore of those minds malformed by black magic. Perhaps he thought that his reward would not be assured unless he handed the prize over himself."

"The enemy?" I asked, "Do you mean the queen?"
"Perhaps," She answered, her voice strangely deep, and the stars seemed at that moment to grow dim, "but she is not the only, or the most dangerous enemy. There are others…"

I grew cold, as though the winter frost had settled in my chest, and the stars spun in their orbit. Scratch, scratch, scratch, went the sound at the door, and I knew who was approaching.

"But those enemies have no power here." Warmth flooded back into me, the stars became stable, and whatever I imagined was approaching vanished.

"Do not fear." Charismata was looking at me, her eyes almost glowing with an otherworldly light, and I realized I was breathing in raspy, quick gasps.

"I…I have heard…I mean, I once had a terrible

dream, and I felt like I might..." I was fumbling for words, trying not to seem afraid, but I could not hide the deep panic.

"I thought that maybe I had gotten rid of it, when I shot the statue...It has been following me, you know, and I don't know what to do..."

"Do not fear, Thaddeus. Only go now and sleep. There is no evil that can reach you here. In this home you are safe. If nowhere else in all your journeys, at least you are safe in this home."

I went unsteadily into the house to lie down on the makeshift bed by the fireplace, but was sure that I would never be able to sleep. I was just a small boy in a strange and dangerous world, a world that only seemed to get ever more dangerous, and I felt nothing but small, frail, and frightened. I could see my hostess through the window, silhouetted against the night sky, still sitting on the edge of the precipice, looking up into the stars. "I don't know that she ever sleeps," I thought to myself; it was my last thought before falling into a deep and restful sleep, full of good and pleasant dreams. And in the morning the sun shone bright.

It is surprising how quickly a person can adapt to a new environment, and even to a new life. The startling strangeness of this new world quickly lost its surreal edge, and was replaced by a curiosity and an excitement not unlike that kind of excitement which seems to constantly possess the very young; a passion and wonder for life.

The wound on my head scarred over, and I would have a streak of white hair over the sight for the rest of my life, though today it blends quite well with the rest of my aging head. Charismata showed great interest in the souvenir that I had brought back from my fight with the dragon, for it seemed that the tooth was more than the mere bone of a prehistoric beast; it apparently was endowed with some special significance, but what significance I could not tell. She asked to borrow it one day, and said that it would be gone for some time. I was loath to give it up, but I trusted

146

her.

"It must be turned to some useful end, Thaddeus; it must be redeemed. If it was used to shed innocent blood, it must now be used to protect the innocent. With your permission, I will have it cut into a weapon that you can wield, a Krishnag blade. I think that even the queen and her messengers will find you a worthy opponent with such a weapon."

I do not know where or to whom she took the fang to be altered. But she returned it some two weeks later, and I was more than pleased with the result. The knife kept the same sweeping form as the tooth, but had been honed to a razor sharp blade, thin and light, and covered in marvelous etchings that were in-filled with silver. The silver seemed to glow against the stark white blade. The detailed handle fit my hand perfectly, and was itself a work of art. It was sheathed in a simple leather pouch, reinforced on the inside with flakes from the tooth itself. The blade was so sharp that it needed such protection. The silver etchings on the blade flowed subtly into the word *veritas*.

"To honor your grandfather," She said with a smile, when I had noticed the writing. "I thought that it might help you to remember him, and the vocation that he has handed on to you."

It was a wonderful gift, and at the time I did not even begin to know how wonderful.

I had been able to piece together more of the puzzle by the end of my stay. Wondering about the dragon and the cave, I asked my hostess if the huge antechamber was actually in the mountain (which, as I have said, could be seen along with the beginnings of the cut steps, further down the mountain range and to the south) as it appeared to be. It seemed, however, that what my grandfather had told me was quite accurate; the antechamber was not inside this mountain or any other mountain. Where it was physically located was a mystery even in the days of open travel between the worlds, and remained a mystery still.

Charismata told me that she could remember when she was very young, and the thoroughfare was open, and this mountain pass and doorway was a well-known and busy highway.

"So long ago, in happier times… but it was a product of pride, built by men who would be gods. It is no wonder that doors were found and opened that should have remained hidden and shut. All good things in this world can be corrupted, Thaddeus, even, and perhaps especially, the wondrous ability to harness the powers of the universe, and to stitch and unstitch the fabric of creation."

Now the huge stone door only opened to a stone chamber some hundred yards into the mountain, and there it ended. Unless, of course, the way was open; but as for when that was or how it could be known in advance, was a mystery even to Charismata.

"The stairs have long sunk into neglect, and there is no one has come this way for many years. It is only lately that there has been some activity, some coming and going during the night. I even saw your Jacoben leave the entrance in some hurry before you staggered out. Indeed, I was watching the entrance closely after I saw him leave. As for that terrible dragon, I am glad it will snare no more travelers."

So somehow Jacoben knew when the door would be open, was able to slip past the guardian (or, as I was inclined to think, had some power over the creature) and knew which of the thousands the right door was. He knew about the secret door through the dragon garden, and had somehow timed everything perfectly. This was no last-minute act of passion. Jacoben's betrayal had been premeditated and planned in advance, perhaps years in advance. But why was he here, in this particular world? It must be to give the Book to this Queen, as Charismata had suggested. The Queen must have offered him some great prize, some powerful seat in her government, or at least something that he, whatever strange race of being that he was, would find valuable. Black magic, Charismata had said? He was a necromancer. What would a necromancer value?

It had been some four weeks since I had arrived, and I was now fully recovered. The medicine that Charismata had administered was remarkably effective, and the mountain air was invigorating. It was like and unlike the mountain air of our world; like, in that it was bracing and clean, and unlike in that it did not have the tiring effect that our thin alpine air has. Rather than causing a lack of breath after some time working in the little garden, it seemed that the longer I exerted myself, the more energy I had. But I was beginning to realize that I needed to move on. I had to plan my next course of action. Jacoben and the Book were now long gone, and rescuing the Book seemed less and less feasible. But I could not simply give up on my vocation, and condemn the past thousands of years of my ancestor's work to ultimate failure. I must go on, and trust to luck and to providence. Even (I thought while relaxing in the warm sunshine and safety of the little meadow) if it meant I would never find it, and would meet some terrible end in this strange land, or wander for years until I died an old man, lonely and decrepit. I could not return home even if I wanted to (and I did not want to; I could not come home to my parents empty-handed, and, truth be told, I was more than a little excited about the adventure that I was on), so I decided that I must journey on. I spent long conversations with Charismata about where Jacoben might have gone, and what kinds of peoples and dangers I might expect to find.

She did not seem surprised or disturbed by my decision to continue on, which actually struck me as rather strange. As a child I was used to adults disallowing me the opportunity to do many things that I would have liked, and usually with very good reason. But she seemed rather to expect me to continue. Indeed, the gift of the knife was made with just such a journey in mind. She did, however, offer to let me stay, if I liked, or to try and help me to get back into the antechamber, and from there back to my own world. But I was determined to go on. Now, in the twilight

149

of my life, it is a great comfort to remember the pure courage and faith that I had as a child. To remember that my youth was not spent in vain, and that once I was free of the failures, fears and cowardice that accumulate like cancer to a soul in the course of a long life.

I would leave Charismata's home on the thirtieth day since my violent entrance into this world.

Charismata packed me a satchel with blankets and food for several weeks journey. She also gave me a curios straw-like contraption that acted as a filter against impure water; I could drink from any stream with confidence, no matter how foul the source. I still wore the same clothes that I had on when Grandfather, Sylvester, and I had left for London, only they had been cleaned and the holes repaired. She also gave me a coat, which was more like a cloak, long, warm and hooded to protect me against the elements. I wore my knife hidden beneath my tweed jacket, along with the bag of gold and now empty pistol. The key was in its place around my neck; indeed, it had never left that place since my father had given it to me. Excited and ready for adventure I left the mountain homestead at first light.

Charismata had described as best she could the landscape and the peoples that I might encounter on my search. She had not left the mountain for what must have been many, many years (she was waiting for something, or for someone, I was not sure exactly what or who, a sign or something, a reason to leave the mountain. I gathered this only by things that she had said in passing in the course of our conversations over the last month) and she could only give me vague directions. I was to travel west, down the mountainside, through a terrain of scattered stone until I reached a great river. I was to travel north along the river, following the old North-South route till I reached a bridge. This I would cross, and continue journeying west until I reached the White City, or its ruins. Charismata warned me of the dangers of the road, as there were many powers at work in this land that were foreign to my world. The Queen's power was one, and her influence had been

150

growing, from her castle in the west to the mountains in the east. I was to be careful to keep my business and my face hidden. She could not tell me exactly what I would find when I left the eastern bank of the river. Jacoben's most likely destination was the great alabaster castle by the sea, the ancient home of the kings, and now the home of the Queen. This castle was surrounded by the huge city, once the thriving capital of this land, but it had been leveled in the wars. Charismata did not know what I would find there now.

"I do not know if you will meet any allies on your journey, Thaddeus. You have been open and honest with me; you must be closed and guarded with anyone else you might meet. There are those who yet fight against the darkness, but they are few and they fight in secret. That you will see many terrible things on your journey is the only promise I can give you. You might fail in your quest. But know this; you have been refreshed on the mountain, you have breathed the clean air, and have drunk pure water. And you have me for a friend. These may yet bring you comfort. In the valley the air is thick and unclean, and there are few friends. Remember the mountain, Thaddeus, and remember me."

"And Thaddeus," her voice was suddenly strange, cold and earnest. "In the city you must be careful. If it still stands it will not be a safe place. It is as confused and varied as a labyrinth. It will be easy to become lost. Do not lose yourself, Thaddeus. Take care that you do not lose yourself."

And then a strange thing happened. Charismata reached out her hand and touched my forehead, tracing two lines, and her touch was molten gold. The gold seemed to burn through my forehead, and I saw suddenly, as though from above, a man standing alone in a dark valley, a warrior with broken shield and notched sword, his dead enemies strewn about him on the floor of the valley. His face was lowered, his body wounded and bleeding, he stood alone in the desolation, holding out against an enemy of impossible

151

numbers. I knew in that instant that the dead were only the beginning, only the vanguard, and there in the darkness around the warrior I could hear more of his enemies, hear them circling the edge of the valley, and hear their mocking, distorted cries, and the cruel rumble of their tramping feet, marching forward in the gloom. I wept as I watched, for I knew that he was alone, and that he could not hold against such an onslaught. Alone in the darkness he would die, alone and hopeless. And then I heard a voice call out, like a trumpet from the heavens, "Who stands with this warrior? Who stands with him, in the breach, against the darkness?" And at this call the earth around the warrior moved, the heavens opened, and the stars and stones called in return, "We will. We will." And silver fire fell from the heavens, and the rocks and stones rose up and flung themselves upon the burning enemy. Now the valley was a ring of stone and flame, and I thought that the warrior himself would be consumed. But behold, the ring of fire parted, and the stones made a road, and the warrior walked forth from the valley triumphant against his enemies.

And then I was back, standing blinking before Charismata. My forehead still burned, and it was hard to see for a moment, because of the brightness of the flames...

Charismata was looking at me intently. "What did you see, Thaddeus?" she asked gently. "You were away, away in your mind, and for some time. I called to you and you did not hear me."

"I... I don't know," I responded. The pain on my forehead faded, and my sight became clear again. "A vision, I think, with a knight, and fire... I don't really understand it."

"Do you not, Thaddeus? Do you not know who you are, and what you have in you? But do not fear. I have uncovered it. Indeed, I had already seen it, but it was dim, like a waning moon through a dark glass. It shines more clearly now. So now you must find it, like the full moon breaking through storm clouds, and with this light find the Book. And Thaddeus, remember me; and remember who you are."

I left her standing at the edge of the small path, leading down to the great staircase that would be my path down the mountain.

I enjoyed that first day of travel very much. The path was easy and clear, and I made it to the entrance of the cave and the beginning of the staircase in less than an hour. I could still see where I had spent the last month, but from here it looked only like a crack of rock against the side of a great cliff. The waterfall above it looked like a silver thread stretching up into the sky against the gray stone.

The staircase was huge, each step hewn from the stone, but it was in complete disrepair, and showed no signs of use, except perhaps by the large mountain goats that were common here. I would occasionally see one leaping across the jagged stone, or standing quietly watching me from a distance, their gnarled horns as large as small trees. There was other wildlife as well, birds of all kinds, small and colorful, hopping about the grasses and plants that dotted the stone, or among the small trees that were sometimes precariously perched on precipices, or forcing themselves through too small cracks in the stone steps. Small mammals that looked like rabbits could sometimes be seen as well, scurrying between boulders and tufts of grass. It was a pleasant walk.

Towards the afternoon I took a long rest, and had a little lunch. The bread was freshly baked, and the dried fruit was delicious. I began to think that I rather liked adventures, and the violent episodes that I had experienced seemed today like a distant bad dream.

The landscape began to change as I walked, and the lower I traveled the more the air seemed less clear and fresh, and the more I began to enter the haze that I had looked down on so many times before from the meadow perch. It was like a dreary day, not quite cloudy or foggy, but just kind of hazy. The steps began to become tiring as well, the constant downward, jarring pace. They were too large to be taken comfortably in stride, and had to be taken at an

153

awkward kind of double-step. Smaller mountains rose up around me, and the trees and grasses became more numerous and taller. The trail began to turn more, where it had been completely straight before. Occasionally I would pass a broken pillar, or a landing area. The path became rougher as well, more broken and disheveled.

I spent the first night on a smooth landing, from which I could just see the face of Charismata's cliff, far above me and to the north-west. I had the daylight to travel further, but the truth is I was desperately frightened of the night, and I wanted to spend my first one at least in sight of safety. As the last rays of the sun disappeared behind the great hulk of the jagged peaks, I huddled down into my blanket, holding the knife tightly in my hand for comfort. But I fell asleep almost immediately, and had a restful and uneventful night.

The next day's journey was much of the same. The steps kept descending, and the smaller jagged peaks kept rising around me. I realized that this range of mountains was far more extensive than had appeared from my vantage place on the cliff. But by the end of the tiring day the landscape was more obviously changing. There were more of the small trees, more relatively flat areas, which made the walking much easier. The animal population was changing as well. I saw few of the mountain goats, and more birds and small furry animals. They were small, but still larger than the conies of England, and without the floppy ears, though they had large flat hind feet that propelled them along in an awkward sort of hopping motion. I also saw a large grey snake curled up at the corner of the stair, and I was careful to keep my distance.

That night was also spent in the same manner, curled up under my blanket with my knife clutched tightly. I wished, and not for the first or last time, that my pistol was loaded. But again I fell quickly to sleep, and woke refreshed at the first light of morning.

The mornings were strangely beautiful, again like and unlike the mornings in England. They were refreshing and new, full of birds singing and with a touch of chill to them, but the haze, which I have referred to, made the rising sun seem somehow ominous and distant.

I journeyed in this way for four days, with the landscape changing only ever so subtly. I was beginning to be fatigued, wearied of the same sights. The mountains were beginning to seem endless, and I had long since lost sight of Charismata's cliff. This left me with some discomfort, for while I was in sight of the cliff I had the feeling of relative safety. Now, far from its watchful gaze, I felt truly alone in this vast, alien land.

It was on the fifth day that I finally left the main bulk of the mountain range. I had turned another of the endless corners, following the steps around a small, craggy mountain, when the steps abruptly ended, and a smooth path of quarried stone began. It led across a narrow canyon whose sides rose to perhaps thirty feet of solid, sheer stone. I have called the stone of this mountain range granite, but in truth it was composed of something else. The composition was almost clear, like fogged glass, with veins of white and grey rock running through; quite beautiful, and not unlike granite. These cliffs were of the same sort, only more clear and glass-like, with only the thinnest of white veins encased within. I walked along the bottom of the valley, admiring the stone, when a sight brought me up short. There encased, it seemed, within the very stone, was a figure of a man, formed of the white stone, like a marble statue enclosed in rough glass. I was quite startled by this sight, and paused for a moment, my heart beating slightly faster, to examine this anomaly.

The canyon was, perhaps, one hundred feet wide, with the smooth path itself stretching from wall to wall, the entire length down (maybe three hundred feet). I walked slowly to the wall, my knife unsheathed in my hand, to get a closer look. The figure was completely white, made, it seemed, of the stone itself. It had a crown upon its head, and a great sword was in one hand, the other raised in a salute, as though acknowledging the traveler. It was an intricate and delicate figure, every fold of its robes and every detail of its hard but noble face could be clearly seen, as though it had been frozen in place, in the very act of raising its strong hand. The eyes, which were white like the rest of the figure, still held a power, exuding strength and nobility, and, perhaps, sadness (I do not know how the expressionless eyes could hold such expression). I stared at the sight for some time, captivated by the strangeness.

I continued, after a while, to walk down the canyon, and now could see that there were many more of these entombed figures, some men and some women. They all had the same look, like kings and queens, princes and knights, held captive in the stone. I had the curious sensation that I had seen these people before, that strange feeling that one sometimes gets. I wondered if they had been carved somehow, by some art that was lost to our world, or if they were actual people entombed here, mummified by reverent followers, like the Kings of Egypt. The opposite side of the wall was the same, a museum of kings and queens. But it was at the very center of the walls, one on both sides, that the most interesting figures were housed. They were standing taller than the others, both hands outstretched, as though blessing the royalty on their right and left, or signaling to some enemies that these kings and queens had their protection. They were stunning in their beauty, and they exuded strength and a power that seemed to leap out of the wall. But the strangest thing about them was what seemed to float from their back, and to lift them off the ground. They had great wings, like those of an angel, or a faerie.

I took some time walking through the canyon. It was fascinating, and just a little disconcerting. And at the end of this could be seen the wreckage of stone pillars and a broken stone statue, its face lying in weeds. I stepped out of the canyon, and there below me, stretching far into the distance, was a forest

It was sprawling for some miles, a rolling sea of leafy

green, disappearing into the hazy horizon. At the end of this wood, a corner just visible in the distance was the river, shimmering like a sliver of glass in the warm light of the afternoon sun. Beyond this the sky was obscured by the deepening haze. Past the river it seemed that the air was so foul that it was almost black, like the smoke from a great fire had settled low to the ground, covering the vast sweep of the valley.

Steps led down the final descent into the wood, and then the steps became a broken road, cutting through the forest. I was excited for a new stage of my adventure, and since it had been so far without too much action (at least for the last month or so, since I arrived on this foreign soil) I had been losing much of the fear that I had first experienced, especially at night, after leaving sight of Charismata's home. So I entered the great wood with a springy tread and a light heart, knowing that the river was only a day or so away (of course I had no idea what to do when I crossed the river, or how I would ever possibly track down Jacoben and the Book; my young mind was, unfortunately or fortunately, uncluttered by such details).

The road was mostly overgrown, the heavy paving stones displaced by shrubs and small trees, but it was still visible. The further the distance into the wood that I traveled, the fewer small shrubs and bushes I observed. These gave way to an open expanse of soft grass underneath an incredible ceiling of multicolored leaves high above. These leaves tinted the sunlight with an otherworldly color, like walking in a prism. The trees themselves were larger and larger the further in I traveled, until they were of such enormous size that I am sure they rivaled the great Sequoia in North America that I had read about. The trunks were of a mottled brown and grey, and they were twisted like vines, but of incredible thickness. Some were as thick as a house, and wound up like a pretzel. They were beautiful and enchanting, and that first afternoon walk beneath their bows was quite peaceful and even today I am compelled to compare all my evening walks unfavorably with that one.

At around seven o'clock (as I supposed; I could only make rough estimates of the time) that evening I came to an opening in the forest, a small, circular meadow, and decided to camp for the night. I was hoping for one more chance to see the stars before I was completely in the valley, where I feared the haze would conceal the magical view. I had enjoyed the sight of those strange cosmic patterns when on the mountain, and I knew I would miss them.

I made my little camp in the center of the meadow (I had by now developed quite an efficient system), and lay down to watch the night lights. I was somewhat disappointed. The sky was so very hazy that it filtered much of the brilliance. I gave it up after an hour or so, and fell asleep.

I awoke some time later, while it was still the dead of night.

Though I could only have been asleep for a short time, I felt very relaxed and refreshed, as if it were late morning. So I lay back on my makeshift pillow, and looked into the night sky. A cool, easterly breeze was moving the leaves in the trees, and the whole meadow was much lit by the light of the stars. In fact the stars were quite visible now, as though the breeze had swept away much of the filthy haze of the valley. I lay for some time perfectly at peace, watching the majestic swirl of lights and thinking vaguely what a beautiful land this was that I had stumbled into. And then, as I watched the sky I began to notice that a few of the stars to the west (I was laying with my feet pointing west) had begun to dim. A distant cloud was obscuring them, blotting them from the deep blue sky. At the moment that I noticed this, the light breeze that I had spoken of turned suddenly cold, and a gust shook the trees, rattling the leaves like discordant chimes. And then more of the stars began to disappear, faster, one by one at first, and then in groups, and I could see a darkness from the east, a great black cloud growing, darker than the night sky, and moving west at a great speed. It was as though a jar of black ink had been spilled across the table of the sky. The wind was strong, and it was unclean; as it blew a great dread came over me, as though the filth of an open grave was carried with it, and the sickness that I remembered all too clearly gripped me like a vice. The wood began to spin, or I began to spin, and I felt as though I had been wrenched out of the world of the living and thrown into the abyss. Nausea overwhelmed me, and a sudden and violent pain wracked my head, as though it had been struck a deathblow. The wind was blowing faster now, cold and bringing with it the great storm that now obscured half the night sky. The stars were being snuffed out one by one, and the approaching darkness was impenetrable, like the mouth of a grave closing over an unfortunate soul, buried alive. The trees were moving strangely, as though in agony, writhing to escape from something, something that was slowly approaching. Bit by bit, closer and closer it came, and I could hear footsteps carried in the wind. I was choking with fear and panic, my eyes already running tears, blurring the already obscured line of trees in front of me. If only it would come no closer! I wanted to grab my knife, to have some comfort, something to at least temper the terror, but I found that I was unable to move, that I had lost completely the strength of my body. Though I tried desperately, the knife mere inches from my hand, I could not reach it. The fear was overwhelming.

The sky was almost completely black, and the trees in front of me were creaking and groaning, writhing away from each other, and through the opening I saw *it* that was approaching, seemingly stepping out of a hole that opened like a mouth in the darkness. A figure, darker than the surrounding darkness, was walking slowly towards me, like a man on a stroll. It walked, but seemed to disdain the ground, or perhaps the ground could not bear the weight of its tread. The trees were now bent almost completely to the ground on either side, straining to escape this presence. The shadow halted on the edge of the meadow, and the wind suddenly stopped blowing, like a switch had been thrown,

159

and I had the strange memory of the stories that I had learned, when even the wind and rain obeyed the Christ. Perhaps they also obeyed the antichrist. For a moment all was still and quiet; and then it spoke.

"Welcome, Thaddeus."

It was the same voice, the voice from my nightmares, harshly masculine, yet liltingly feminine, a tangle of distorted natures. But I could see it now, or at least a shadow of it. It was no longer trying to get into my mind, to enter the window that had been opened, but was now present to me; some defense had been subverted, some wall had been breached.

A moment passed before it spoke again, as though it was waiting for me to respond, but my throat was closed with choking sobs of fear. Though I could not see its face, I knew that it was smiling.

"I have released him, Thaddeus. I have released the Searcher, and he will find you."

The voice changed slightly, like stone shifting against stone.

"Thaddeus, how fast can you run?"

And then it laughed. And I found my voice enough to scream.

My eyes opened suddenly to the bright light of day, as I was awakened by the sound of my own cry, and I found myself lying in the middle of the meadow, the morning already several hours wasted.

~

"John?" I could detect in Mary's voice a subtle inflection, tense and strained with worry and exhaustion. The evening hour was waning, the day had been overly long and quite emotionally difficult, and, as a result, I was in no mood to speak of the matter. I suppose that I considered it moot, simply childish fancies. Or perhaps I simply accepted what Doctor Chester had said, taking it on face value; he was the expert. Damn him to hell. I say "expert" with the greatest disdain, for I have nothing but disdain for that man, and cannot help even now to lay part of the blame for what happened at his feet, for assuaging my fears with his grotesque conjectures. But I think that it is universal to fatherhood, for they have so much invested in their children, their futures and their happiness, that any good father would instinctively shy away from the suggestion that his beloved daughter might be a chronic liar, telling these dramatic stories for such an extended period of time as though they were God's truth. Whatever the case, I buried my head further in my newspaper, offering something off-putting in response, hoping rather to dissuade her from continuing. She was not dissuaded.

"John, I can't help worrying, you know, about Susan. It just isn't like her. I know what Doctor Chester said, and, of course, he should know, it's just that..." Here she paused, and I glanced over the corner of my paper. The eerie twilight cast a strange hew on her pale face, and revealed the toll that the past few weeks had taken on my beautiful wife. She seemed to have aged, and the tears that she had cried for the last several nights as we had tried to understand what was happening to our beloved Susan seemed to have chiseled lines in her smooth skin. But it was something in her eyes that made me pause and pay closer attention to what she was saying. Her voice shook as she began again:

"John, I know what the Doctor said, but I know my daughter better than he. What he claimed was wrong with Susan, that she would just lie like that, to our faces, with no hint of shame...no, John, John I don't believe him. I won't believe him."

She paused again. I think she must have anticipated an abrupt response from me, for she continued quickly, her eyes fiery, determined to be heard no matter what. But there was something

161

else in her eyes, something that I did not at first place, because it was so out of character; I had never before seen such an emotion displayed by my brave wife. Only later, the next afternoon, would I realize what it was: it was fear. Fear, as though she knew what was coming, that she could see what would happen, and knew that we would not be able to stop it.

"John, Susan is telling the truth."

My stomach turned at her words, and my hands gripped the paper tightly, tearing it down the middle, startling both of us.

"John, listen to me! I know that it seems crazy and outlandish; I know how far-fetched it is. But Susan is telling the truth. She has seen what she says she saw, and has been where she says she has been. She is not a liar. And John, you are her father. You, most of all, need to believe her."

With those words, and a look of such sadness that it cut me to the heart (to this day that look lies like a curse on my soul, an unbearable, burning pain) she arose and went up stairs. I could hear her crying as she climbed.

It is difficult to be candid in such a book as this, as though in some muckraking tabloid, to tell the world my greatest failure in life and the source of the agony and shame that will never be relieved. I did not listen to my wife. If ever there was an hour to listen, ever a time when so much was at stake, this was the hour. But I did not listen. And by the next day it was too late. Susan went with her nurse in the early afternoon into the garden to play, as was her custom, and then into the little grotto with the Ash saplings that had been the setting for all her strange stories, and she disappeared. She was seven years old when she vanished, and has never been seen since.

~Excerpted from the autobiography of the famous orator and nationalist, Lord Robert Whinfree, entitled <u>Lord Robert Whinfree: A Life</u>. (Reprinted from the 1890 manuscript by Parliament Publishing, 1905). The kidnapping of his daughter was labeled the "crime of the century" by contemporaries, and his subsequent explanation, with the bizarre insinuation of some supernatural element, sealed his political and social fate.

162

Chapter XI

"Sed libera nos a malo."
~The Lord's Prayer

This new land had, with sudden violence, lost its magical and exciting aura, and was replaced instead with menace and dread. My body ached, as though every muscle in it had been strained to the breaking point, and I had trouble packing up my little campsite. It was some time before I could even stop shaking. I hoped at first that it had been merely a dream, a nightmare brought on by fatigue, but at the edge of the meadow there were several broken branches, and leaves scattered the floor where the trees had attempted to escape the awful presence.

Never before had I actually seen what was speaking to me. In the visions that I had experienced in my own world the speaker was never present to me, never in sight. I suppose the closest it had come to being seen was when the dragon statue seemed to be doing the talking, but I was not laboring under the impression that it had been the actual carved stone that was my nemesis. It was as though my dreams and visions were seeping into the real world, as though the line between my mind and everything else was porous and fragmented. Whether this meant that upon arriving in this strange land I had entered some new dimension where this thing had more power I could not say. I consoled myself that I had not actually *seen* the creature (or being, or spirit, or whatever), but only a vague outline of

163

what could have been a man. Perhaps it had no actual power over me, for why did it not simply kill me then if it could, or swallow me into its nothingness?

What to do now? I did not know what it had meant, what had been released, but whoever this *searcher* was I did not want to meet him. What now of the Book or Jacoben? It had been more than a month since the Book had been stolen, and it and its captor were long gone. Even if I made it across the river, and into the city unseen, how could I hope to find them?

I sat for some time at the edge of the wood, trying to stop shaking, and in that moment I almost turned back. Perhaps Charismata could help me get back home, to my parents, and I could leave this madness, this terrible adventure that I had been thrust into. Yet my obligation lay heavy on me, and even as I thought these things I knew that to go on was my only true option. The chain might break with me, the task too big for my shoulders, and my family's vocation die with me in this land, but it would not be because I turned back.

So I continued to walk through the forest, with the sun at my back.

I was not so carefree and careless as I had become over the last few days. I stalked from tree to tree, listening for unusual sounds, and watching for any danger. It was stressful, and the going was much more difficult in this way. The wood seemed darker and more foreboding now, as though the trees too were traumatized by what had visited last night. No birds sang, and no small animals frolicked in the boughs. There lay a dead stillness over it all, and the small noises that I could not help making as I skulked about were shockingly loud in my ears.

It was several hours later that I arrived at the edge of the wood. The road ended abruptly, at the edge of a steep, craggy slope that landed perhaps two hundred yards below. I cautiously hid behind a mangled stump near the edge, and looked out to see what I could see.

Before me lay an open plain, strewn with boulder

and thistle, stretching to the river, which could now be seen in the distance. It was still a long way off, but was clearer now, and what I saw was not encouraging. It was very wide, and looked from the distance to be black, as though it were polluted and poisoned. But it was what lay on the western side of the river that grabbed my attention. All along the edge, stretching as far as I could see to the north and the south, following the contour of the river like a snake, rose a wall, windowless and dark, an imposing mass of stone or metal (it was impossible to say from this distance) that cast a great shadow over the river and the western bank. Charismata had not spoken of this, so I thought that it must have been built since she last left the mountain, all those years ago. Still, it could have been a thousand years old for all I knew, the way she had spoken of her age. Whatever the case, I did not know how I would sneak past such a mass of battlements.

Beyond the wall I could see nothing except the dense cloud that seemed to hang over the land, like a dirtied carpet, covering the western shore as far as I could see, north, south and east. The city was somewhere beyond that wall, through the dense smoke or fog, and beyond that the White Tower and the sea. My hopes, already dashed and deflated, now sank almost to despair.

I could see a ribbon of road, on the eastern shore, running north and south, paralleling the river, and then disappearing along with the sweep of the mountain range, out of sight on my right and left. The bridge would be somewhere to the north, and I supposed that I could follow that road and find it. Straining to look through the haze, I thought that I could just make out the crossing, where the glint of black water was obscured.

The road up the mountain ended here, and I suppose that it had been forgotten long ago, for there was no sign of it on the valley floor beneath me. Erosion and time seemed intent on hiding all signs of the ancient causeway. I needed to find a way down the embankment, but I did not want to be seen. There did not seem to be any sign of life, but what if there were watchers in the wall, with telescopes or binoculars (supposing that there were such technologies in this land), or spies or travelers along the road who might see movement? But the line of trees at the edge of the cliff apparently extended indefinitely to the south and north, so I decided to travel as far as I could along its edge, using the foliage as cover. So it was that I made my way north, towards the bridge.

It was slow going, for fingers of the mountains reached down far into the valley, finally breaking off at the steep embankment, and these were difficult to navigate. The underbrush was denser here, and contained thistles and thorns, making the travel painful. The dense haze filtered the light, but seemed to trap the heat like a blanket. I was sweaty, dusty, and had many a deep scratch by the time I reached an area where erosion and landslide had created something of a narrow gulley, traversable with care.

I was closer here to the road and the river at this point, for the natural swath of mountain jutted at this point toward the west. The bridge was now certainly in view, and two towers, standing like silent sentinels in the haze, broke the seamless mass of wall at that point. It was a wide bridge, with a series of beams and cables strung across it like the webs of some monstrous spider. It was not inviting.

It was with great care that I scrambled down the gulley to the relatively flat plane. I was worried about creating dust or otherwise revealing my position to anyone that might be watching from those silent towers, but I arrived at the bottom without incident.

The heat was more intense here, and the plane was strewn with boulders and thistle. It was a very uncomfortable place, and the sun still had several hours to travel before evening ushered in a relief from the heat. But the plane was far bigger than I had realized, and the distance combined with the elements and my need to remain hidden made the journey long and tedious. The silence lay like a shroud over this land. No sound came from anywhere in the valley, and none from the wall. It was eerie,

166

as though this land had been abandoned long ago, and perhaps now bitterly resented my intrusion. By the time I reached the road, the last rays of sun were casting a strange glow through the haze as they disappeared behind the city and the wall.

The road was roughly cobbled and elevated above the plane perhaps thirty feet. Beyond this, across the river, the wall towered dark against the sky, as tall as any modern city skyscraper. It was frightening at this proximity, windowless and made of a seamless dark material that could have been iron or steel. I did not dare to scramble the last distance to the road, but instead crept and scrambled among the boulders strewn along its edge.

Evening had definitely set on, the shadows of the mountain darkening the smoggy sky, and though there were no stars visible through the haze, I knew that they would have been visible now back on the mountain. (I need not, I am sure, remind my reader of the previous night's experience. I did not allow myself to think of it, pushing the memory to the back of my mind, focusing instead upon the task at hand. But I dreaded the onset of night.) I was very close to the bridge by now, the towers of the wall standing like the minarets of Muslim mosques that I had once seen in a picture book, dark against the darkening sky. There was a gate in the wall at this point, huge and studded with massive bolts, almost reaching to the very top of the buttressing mass at both sides, only a thin ridge of wall at the very top spanning the divide. The bridge itself was wide and imposing, made, it seemed, of the same dark metal. The network of cables that were slung like a web, from pillar to pillar, were as thick as the trunk of a tree. There seemed to be no way in to whatever lay beyond, except across the bridge and through the gate.

The river was not visible from my low vantage point, but I could smell the water in the air, and it was not a pleasant smell. It was foul and putrid, as though it was a polluted and poisoned stream. But it was very wide, and I could not dare to attempt a swim. Besides the unknown currents and the pollution, who could know what kind of creatures might live deep in the dark waters of this strange land. The mere thought of such a swim left me feeling cold.

I sat for some time hidden (as I supposed) between two dusty boulders, watching the last rays of the sinking sun on the top of the towers, trying to figure a way in. I supposed that if the gate were to open I might be able to sneak in, but I will not pretend that I wasn't very concerned. This was a dangerous place, and it did not seem at all likely that I could get inside undetected. I felt very foolish and small, like a child whose imaginative game is interrupted and made fun of by some insensitive adult. I had been imagining that I, a child, could endure this adventure and even win out in the end. Of course such an idea was foolish. I imagined myself playing knights and dragons with my friends near my parent's garden, complete with wooden sword. It was so real, so perilous, and I was so brave and invincible; and then my father called me in for dinner, breaking the spell. This spell had now been broken, but it would not be a warm dinner that I found on the other side.

It was then that my adventure took a decidedly unforeseen turn.

The silence (which had been constant since I left the edge of the forest; no singing of birds, no sound from the direction of the wall) was broken suddenly by a jarring, echoing noise, a deep trumpet, mournful and menacing, from the towers. At that moment the huge gate began to move, the metal joints screeching with effort, opening slowly outward. My heart seemed to skip a beat, and I went facedown behind the largest boulder, cowering down away from the road. I lay like this for a moment, until I realized that this might be my chance. The horn continued to blow, but as I looked up I could see that the door had stopped moving, perhaps a third of the way open. Still crouched as low as I could, I began to snake my way up the stony embankment to get a better view. There was a large stone almost at the edge of the road, and I crawled behind it, lying prone, and looked out through the hazy twilight.

168

Though the shadows concealed much of the base of the great wall, I could see movement, someone or something was coming out of the gate. At first I imagined it was a great snake, and I was gripped with a great fear, remembering the terrible lizard of the Antechamber. But for only a moment; I quickly saw that it was a group of fast moving people, running in unison, and I could hear their feet as they struck the surface of the bridge, a hollow echoing clang. Behind them I could see that the gate began to close, as suddenly as it had opened. Then the horn stopped blowing, and the only sound was the noise of many feet running across the bridge. The bridge was so long that it took some time before I saw the troop appear on the eastern side of the river, and then turn south, towards me.

It was too late for me to escape back down the hill, so I had to hope that the rocks and dim light would hide me. I could now see the nearest of the marchers, and when I did I desperately wished that I had not left my more secure hiding place below. The leader was riding on something, like a large horse, only with shaggier black hair, and two great fangs, like those of a saber-tooth tiger. The face of this animal was long like a horse, and its nostrils were wide, foaming and frothing. It was an ugly, savage looking creature. Upon its back sat a tall figure, clothed in black, caped and armored, his face hard and cruel, with long black hair hanging raggedly from beneath his jagged helmet. His eyes were wide, completely black and unblinking.

There were about thirty following behind, on foot and running fast in procession. They too were strange looking, like men with long dark hair, and wide, black, unblinking eyes. They were also armored, and armed alternately with long pikes and what looked like rifles, or crossbows. They were drawing close at great speed.

I was numb with fear, hoping against hope that they would pass my hiding place without seeing me. I crouched lower into the dust as they came on, sidling against the stone on my right. They had almost reached my hiding place.

It was too late, of course, to respond when I realized that they already knew where I was, and that they had probably left the confines of the wall with no other aim than to capture or kill me. What had the vision said last night? The Searcher, that it would release the Searcher? Was that who was rushing toward me now? I could see them straining for speed, dust rising from the road like a cloud, their weapons ready. Their black eyes were looking right at my hiding place, and seemed to pierce right through the stones that I imagined hid me, and I knew suddenly that I was no more hidden than if I had a flashing light and a bell hung about my shoulders. In a moment all would be over.

At the very instant that I realized this, the leader riding the great beast suddenly moved, his body jerking oddly, turning abruptly to his left, shifting in his saddle and his ugly face was an expression of shock. There was a simultaneous noise like a dull slap, and a puff of dust lifted suddenly from his cloak. This was followed almost instantly by a burst of the same, noise and dust, and his body seemed to be pummeled by invisible hands. As his body turned I could see his back, and it looked like a pincushion, punched through by bolts or arrows with such force that they were driven almost completely through him! The beast upon which he rode staggered forward to its knees, still at full speed, like a freight train derailing, and I saw that a bolt had pierced through the leg of the rider and into the side of the creature, pinning the leg of the rider to the flank of the beast. The horse (I do not know what to call it) let out a terrible cry, a deep and pain-filled snort, and then horse and rider were a tangle of blood and limbs, tumbling and cart-wheeling in a hideous mess thirty yards or more, before finally disappearing over the opposite embankment.

The double line of runners was decimated in an instant while still at a dead run, more than half knocked violently sideways, towards the river, pierced with bolts from the unseen enemy. All was chaos, a shuffling of dust, and the grunts and cries of the falling and fallen, but only for a moment. There was no time for the attacked to even

170

respond. One of the dark haired men managed to loose a shot from his weapon, a bolt like from a crossbow, into the thickening darkness, but was then almost instantly knocked back down, thrown several yards, struck through with five or six arrows.

All was over in an instant, and I just lay as though paralyzed, hoping that the attackers had not noticed me. I heard some whispered movement, and peaked around my rock in time to see what looked like a large brown stone at the base of the embankment unroll and become a man, so camouflaged that it was like seeing the very floor of the valley come alive! Several more men, disguised just as well, appeared out of nowhere, and I realized with a shock that I had walked almost on top of them mere minutes before.

I was then grabbed roughly and flung headlong down the embankment. Instantly another of the strangers tied my hands sharply behind my back, and wrapped a piece of cloth around my face, nearly suffocating me. I could not speak, but the cloth slipped down far enough that I was able to see something of what was going on. My feet were tied as well, and two of the attackers grabbed my arms while another grabbed my feet, and then we were moving, running across the valley floor, weaving between stone and thistle, all the while crouched low. So low, in fact that my body struck the ground violently several times. My arms, meanwhile, felt as though they were being yanked out of their socket, and I could barely breathe.

The light was by now almost completely gone, only a glimmer that allowed me to catch a brief glimpse of my captor's faces, but these were concealed by scarves the color of the dead earth. I could see at least three ahead of us, and thought that there were at least as many behind; ten altogether, perhaps.

I was in a state of shock, but not complete terror as I might have been. Whoever was the enemy of those other creatures had to be my friend (or so I surmised). This was naive to suppose, I know, but such was my state of mind, as I remember it. I knew that it would not have fared me well to fall into the hands of the black-eyed men, and then, if I wasn't killed outright, perhaps into the hands of the Messengers, or the Queen. The terrible white faces of Messengers came into my mind, and I could see the snake-like tongues writhing between their double row of fangs; then I saw the kind face of my grandfather, and my eyes clouded with tears.

And then, away towards the gate, I heard the sound of pursuit.

A howl went up into the night, guttural, deep, and as cruel as a naked blade, biting and tearing through the filthy air, the violent scream of some maddened prehistoric wolf, and my blood went cold. My captors shot forward like from a gun, sprinting like all of hell was in pursuit, and indeed, perhaps it was.

This mad pace was kept up for some time, and though I listened intently, I heard no other sounds of the beast, and hoped that we had put it far behind. Little did I know...

The darkness found us still running. My captors did not slow their pace. They seemed to know exactly where they were going, and were running full out with great urgency. I closed my eyes, glad at least that I was not the one running, though my arms still ached, and every bump and jolt sent a shock of pain along them. My body was no longer struck to the ground, for they no longer were running crouched low, but ran instead like sprinters; sprinters pursued by deadly enemies.

Still at a dead run we turned abruptly left, or north, presumably along the edge of the same cliff that had given me so much trouble earlier in the day; and then straight on, for several hours at least. Just as I was wondering how they could keep up such a pace without rest, they paused for a few moments, and I could hear their raspy gasps in the night air, trying to catch their breath through the ever-present smog. Then new hands lifted me, and away we went.

A short while later we turned right, or east, and immediately we began to climb. The pace was slower now, and more indirect. We kept climbing and weaving, and I imagined I could smell the trees again, and hear their leaves moving in the late-night breeze. On and on we went, and though my body ached and I felt as though I would die of thirst, I think that I must have fallen asleep, for I awoke abruptly, dropped facedown in some cold grass. It took a moment to try to gather my wits, and I could hear whispered voices, and what sounded like the impatient stamp and snort of horses.

At first I could see nothing but darkness, but I managed to roll slightly to my side, and so could see a waxing moon just over the outline of trees, blurry through the haze. Dark shadows passed to and fro, and the whispering became more fierce. After a moment I could make out some of the voices.

"It was foolish," the first voice said, the sound low and strong, like the voice of one used to being obeyed.

"You will see that it was our only choice. We did not know who he was, nor do we yet, but our enemy was clearly seeking him. We had to act, for better or worse."

This second voice was also strong, and noble sounding, confident yet deferring (it seemed) to the authority of the first.

"For better or worse we are now pursued. Show me the prisoner," the first voice commanded.

Instantly I was rolled roughly face up, and shadows appeared above me, for a moment only, and then they pulled back, and I was shoved forcibly back over into the grass.

"Let us hope it will be for the best," the first voice said, with a note of resignation. "The deed has been done, but we are now exposed, and in great danger. We must move immediately. I have already sent word ahead, and they know of this problem. Feed the prisoner."

I was pulled up to a sitting position, and my bonds

173

were loosed. They gave me water and bread, enough to take the edge off my hunger and thirst, but not enough to satisfy (I had not eaten since early afternoon). Then my hands were tied in front of me, but they did not cover my face. Horses were brought out, and I was put up on one, told to hold the saddle with my bound hands, and then we were off again.

The horses moved at a fast trot, and by the noise I thought that there must be quite a number of horses in procession. It was not long before I began to see the horses in front of me, for the dawn was beginning to break.

The morning was cool and dew covered, and was a welcome relief after the long night. I had not slept, except for the few uncomfortable minutes when I had passed out while being carried, and I was exhausted. But, it must be admitted, I was very glad that the night had passed, and that it had been passed in the company of others, even as a prisoner, for I dreaded the thought of another night spent alone in this strange land. I did not think I could bear another visit by whatever had been stalking my dreams.

I began, in the dim light of the dawn, to make out the horses in front of me, and could see that there were at least five or six (it was difficult to count exactly, for we were riding through a dense and deep forest, like the one I had walked through, only much more grown up, with massive trees and much undergrowth. All was green and alive, and I began to realize that it must be a foggy morning, for even as the sun rose, the mist did not abate. It was not the same as the haze of the valley, but more like a foggy morning near the sea. It was difficult to see very far ahead or to the side, but it was not unpleasant to ride in. Rather, it was refreshing, and as the morning advanced the temperature did not rise dramatically.

It was as the sun began to rise that I had a very pleasant surprise. I had been noticing the shadows of the horses around me, and to see the head of the horse upon which I rode more distinctly. As the horses moved in the gate peculiar to them, I could see something bobbing up and down and side to side with the trotting gate. I thought that it might have been some plumage from a helmet or a fancy bridle. It took me some time to make out exactly what it was, but when I had ascertained the answer to the mystery, my heart leapt for joy! For what I had been confusing for plumage was in fact a single horn, rising from the forehead of the horse. I was riding a unicorn! The horn was white, and flowed upwards in a gentle swirl to a sharp tip, exactly like I would have imagined it. Only it was not so clean or elegant as I had imagined. The horn was somewhat stained, and even slightly chipped, as though it had been used many times, even in battle. The body of the unicorn was also dirty, but it seemed to have been made so for the purpose of concealment. It was unlikely that unicorn had rolled in mud and dust, and the grime looked brushed on, and was the exact color of the saddle and blanket. Indeed, upon further investigation, I discovered that the blanket and saddle covered the other appendages that make the mythical unicorn such an admired creature: wings. They were secured under the riding gear, and blended quite well with its sides. If the "feathers" were actually feathers I could not say, for they looked like something much stronger and more appropriate to the task of bearing such an animal aloft.

This discovery did much to lift my spirits, and it punctuated the strangeness of this adventure. This, combined with my fatigue, made that early morning ride quite otherworldly and surreal.

The ride seemed to last for hours and hours, but the morning fog never burned off. I drifted in and out of sleep, surprisingly comfortable given the situation. The gentle rocking gate of the unicorn acted like a sleeping agent, keeping me in a comfortable doze for most of the trip, and somehow I didn't fall off. Once or twice I caught myself just in time, waking at the last moment. Thinking back on that ride is a happy memory. I have already said that it was surreal; I think that captures the experience. It was almost like I was floating through a happy dream, the sunlit mist obscuring the details of the terrain and only allowing a sensation of refreshing green foliage and coolness.

I came out of the long daydream abruptly. The animals were splashing through a stream of quickly-flowing water, and the spray woke me with a start. The fog was still hanging low, and I could only just make out the unicorn ahead of my own. I turned in the saddle to look around, and discovered that there were at least three more behind us, obscured through the mist. We made our way silently (except for the splashing hoofs) through the shallow water for some time. It seemed that what I had at first taken to be a creek was perhaps a shallow river, and it took some time to traverse it. After a few minutes the stream widened into a quiet pool, a deep, rich green, like flowing liquid emerald. The unicorns dropped into it easily, swimming through in a relaxed and causal pace, the cool water lapping up almost to my waist. They soon came out of the pool and scrambled up a sandy embankment to a flat, grassy edge. It was brighter on this side of the river, as though the water had swept much of the fog downstream. Gathered in a group were those who had been leading our caravan, and two other men, who were not riding unicorns, joined them. (It is still difficult to write 'unicorn' instead of horse, though they have become for me as normal as horses. It is like when a child first learns of elephants, those bizarre, giant creatures, and is amazed that something so strange could actually exist. But even the child soon is no longer surprised by them, but rather takes them for granted, forgetting how incredible they are. They are to him simply elephants. This is how I came to see the unicorns, even by the end of that day; they were animals like other animals.)

I could see my captors more clearly now, in the brightening afternoon light. They were clothed, as I have said, in loosely hanging clothes the color of the dirt or the trees, varying earth-tones of all shades. Their hair (when I could see it; many remained hooded) was light, not quite blond, but a golden brown, like wild grasses in the late fall. Their faces were well-defined, not thin, but long and elegant. But it was their eyes that stood out. They were an earthy green, deep and rich, and shaped like wide almonds.

If they were in every other way identical to humans, it was their eyes that reminded me that I was in a strange land, and these people did not belong to my own race of beings.

The new men were talking to the riders in the advance of my party when my unicorn came out of the water. They looked at me with piercing glances, but not with animus. The faces were stern and unbending, but they were not cruel.

"Bring him forward," said a voice, which I recognized from the previous evening; it was the commanding voice. Another rider pulled alongside of me and grasped the halter of my ride, leading me forward.

"Do not fear," he quietly said, and I recognized the other voice, the kinder voice from last night. "Just do as they say; you will not come to harm."

One of the newcomers stepped up and looked closely at me. His face was wary, and he stared at me for some time.

"All right," he finally said, "you may lead him in. I see no guile in his eyes. Has he any weapons?"

For a moment a jolt of panic swept through me, for I had only just then realized that my knife had been taken. Also my empty pistol and the bag of gold must have been taken, for I could not feel the weight of them in my coat. But my key still hung securely around my neck.

"He had, but we removed them. Here they are." The leader handed him a wrapped bundle, which the newcomer took. He laid it on the grass and opened it; then he stood up, and looked again at me, his eyes stern and surprised.

"Where did you get these? Did you steal them?"

"No," I stammered, "I found them. Well, I found the gun... I found the knife also, only it wasn't a knife, it was a tooth...it was in the cave..." My voice was cracked and shrill, and sounded strange in my own ears. "It was made for me into a knife, but I didn't steal it. I suppose I did take the gun, but it was Sylvester's, and they had killed him. I didn't know what to do...I didn't think he would mind..." I probably would have stammered on like this for some time, but here I was interrupted by my friend (or so I had dubbed the second voice from last night).

"Let him be, he is tired and afraid. Wherever he procured theses weapons we will soon find out, but let them be shown to Ajax. And perhaps Ajax will bring him to the Elder. They will know what to do, and will not make any rash judgments."

The newcomer stared for a moment more, and then rewrapped the weapons.

"All right, proceed. The way will be open for you. I hope that your prisoner has not brought some new danger to us. Already there is movement at the gate, and the watchers on the cliff heard the cry of a dreadful beast; your attack is well known to our enemies. They are even now combing the plane, searching for signs of your passing. Perhaps this boy is important to them. We may soon regret our leniency."

"If he is an enemy of our enemies, than perhaps he is our friend. We may indeed regret our leniency, but I do not think this boy will. We will see whether the Elder regards our actions as a mistake." I was indeed thankful for their leniency and for my friend.

The two newcomers stood aside, and our caravan continued forward.

Some yards from the bank a thick forest began, and we entered it by a narrow track, only wide enough for riding single file. The fog was rapidly growing thinner, until after only perhaps ten minutes of riding we exited both the wood and the fog bank. Before us a cliff reared up, a massive wall of stone rising straight up into the air, so high that though I strained to see, the top was invisible to me. It was a natural cliff, the face of a mountain. The wall of fog behind us was just that: a wall. It stopped a few yards before the cliff, as though it had been cut by a knife. Between the wood and the wall it was as clear as any summer day could be, and it was very much like being at the bottom of a deep canyon.

We rode straight at the wall, and I wondered what

our aim was. Perhaps it was to turn to the north or south, the left or right, and follow along the bottom? But we rode straight ahead, and suddenly the lead rider turned slightly and seemed to vanish! The next rider did the same and the next, and suddenly I was at the wall, and only then did I see that there was a great crack running straight up along the wall, and overlapping the crack was a slight edge of rock, effectively concealing the crack until one was literally face to face with it. Into this crack we all plunged.

It was much cooler and darker here, and so narrow that my feet brushed the side of the walls. The path led inwards for a short distance, and then turned to the left and began to climb. The track was worn of the very rock, and was steep and treacherous. The animals were working hard to make it up the path, and the sound of their hooves on the stone was loud in the narrow confines of the pathway. The path began to move to the right, and continued to climb. It was suffocating in here, cold, and although the light of the sun still found a way down in, it was very dim. Above us the crack of the rock swept up, presumably to the top of the cliff, however high that was. Just as I was beginning to grow very uncomfortable with this leg of the journey, the path opened slightly, and began to level out a bit. It was still steep, but manageable. More sunlight found its way in, and the atmosphere of the path was much more cheerful. We continued climbing this way for more than an hour.

The pathway began to widen some as we continued, and there were periodic spans of flat spaces, like the landings that interrupt staircases, and these were often covered with grass. In these areas a patch of the afternoon sky was visible overhead, and the heat of the sun was a relief from the chill and the dank smells of the narrow crack of stone. Sometimes when looking up I could see men standing on levels of stone high above us, watching us as we passed. I thought that these must be sentries, and perhaps they were sending signals ahead to warn the rest of their group of our approach. The narrow path continued to wind and climb up through the stone.

Soon I began to be aware that I was hearing something, something far in the distance that was echoing down the path towards us. It was a dull roar that grew ever louder, until I could hear nothing else. I could see nothing that might be causing such a sustained noise, nothing but broken walls of stone stretching to the sky. Louder and louder it grew, the further up the path we climbed. Finally, when I thought that it could get no louder, we rounded a corner of wall, and the path opened up into a sort of stone stadium, a broken bowl of rock, and into the center of this bowl a great river fell. It was a cascading torrent of water, a waterfall that fell more than a hundred feet from the lip of a great slab that jutted out from the side of the stadium, and into a pile of huge boulders at the bottom. The roaring water then disappeared into the darkness of an opening in the pile of stones, spinning in a violent vortex down into the mountain, like wine down the black throat of a giant. The noise of the river bounced and echoed off the sides of the stadium, and the mist from the waterfall caught the rays of the afternoon sun, and threw a luscious rainbow across the bowl, a stark contrast to the black stone below.

A narrow ledge followed the circumference of the bowl, and led underneath the great lip of stone, underneath the waterfall. It was a dangerous path, and I clung tightly to the saddle of my unicorn. A fall from here would mean certain death, either by being broken to bits on the boulders below, or sucked into the darkness of the underground river. But the animals did not stumble, and we made it around that bowl and to another ledge of stone that took us to the top.

The top was a wide expanse of flat stone, broken here and there with patches of grass, even a group of gnarled trees. The whole shelf sloped away to a horizon that disappeared abruptly maybe two hundred yards towards the west. Beyond the edge the great bank of fog was still visible, climbing another hundred feet or so into the sky. It was a strange sight.

The sun was near this horizon, and I thought that it

must be four o'clock or so. I also knew that the edge of the great cliff was at the end of the stone plateau, and my stomach turned at the thought of that drop. Behind us another cliff rose, huge and imposing, into the sky. The river flowed out of a v-shaped crack in this cliff, across an expanse of the plateau, and into the hole that we had just climbed out of. Behind the cliff (which was perhaps five hundred feet high) the vast sweep of the mountains could be seen, stretching forever left towards the north, and right towards the south. How far they rolled east I could not say. But my heart sank when I realized what I suppose I had known all along: I was going the wrong way, and now was no closer to my goal than when I was at the home of Charismata.

Our little caravan (there were ten animals and their riders in all) turned towards the cliff in the east and continued to climb. We followed the course of the river into the cliff, and the way was broader than the previous path. It followed the river up and into the mountain, and wound its way at a leisurely pace. As we proceeded, the river was fed by many small streams, springs, and melted snowfall from the high tips of the mountains. The shallower of these we crossed easily, our animals wading and splashing through without slowing. Other streams were spanned by small bridges of stone, of which some were makeshift, and others skillfully engineered. The path was steep and wide, but not as steep as it had been earlier. There was much grass and moss, trees and shrubbery, and there were many more half-hidden sentries that I spied. They were positioned along the high ridge top on either side of the chasm, and also among the trees and boulders near the quickly flowing water. Hoods and wraps sometimes obscured their faces, but when I could see them they were all much like the guards by the river, and those who were my captors. It seemed that I had stumbled on some race of beings other than the creatures that had been killed by the gate, and also unlike Charismata. I wondered if they were only culturally and ethnically different, like the differences between Asians, Africans, and

Europeans in my own world, or if they were, indeed, completely different races of beings.

The path by now had flattened out, and the cliffs on either side had risen to maybe three hundred feet above us. The river flowed deep and still here, and I could see ahead that it was coming out of a dark tunnel, and the wide chasm was coming to an end. A cliff rose now in front of us, and in the face of the stone above the entrance to the subterranean river was carved a great tree with twisted roots that wrapped around the entrance to the cave, its branches heavy with leaf and fruit. The carving looked old and cracked, and there was moss growing on it.

The way inside the tunnel was still wide, and though I was weary of caves and stone, it was not an unpleasant ride. The path was lit with hanging torches or lamps of some kind, and they cast an orange glow across the tunnel and the water. Once into the tunnel the loud noise of falling water was again insistent, and we soon came to another waterfall, only not so fierce and abrupt as the previous one. The path next to it was steep and winding, crisscrossing back and forth, and it took some time to finally reach the top. Once there I could see the end of the tunnel, and the sunlight was welcome. The water flowed quietly again here, and following it we exited the cave and came out into the most beautiful valley that I had ever seen.

Even as a child I had heard the legends of mythical valleys, hidden deep in strange mountains that were paradise on earth, and were inhabited by perfectly happy and content natives, who had no wants or needs that the valley did not meet. It seemed that I had been led to just such a valley. It was like a great amphitheatre, the bottom of which was composed of gently rolling hills with the river running through it. This immediately became steep embankments going up to meet the mountains that encircled the valley on three sides. These embankments were terraced, and crops of many varieties were growing there. Down from the mountain many small streams flowed, meeting finally the river, and then running back down into the tunnel. The main river found its source straight ahead across the great valley, falling in a long waterfall from between two peaks of jagged mountain. There were houses or barns as well, built all over the valley, next to crops and streams, and inhabited by many people. These were made of brightly colored wood, and roofed with thatch. Here and there were even children my age, running through the grass that grew wherever there were no crops, and splashing and swimming in the cold pools of the river. Men were working in the fields and woman were cleaning laundry in the streams and in the river. There were animals about, strange shaggy-coated beasts that might have been cattle. There were birds and butterflies in the air, and flowers growing along the well-worn path. I had arrived at a thriving community of these people, and found it to be very like a community of my own world.

We followed the path that led along the edge of the river, and then was diverted towards the left side of the amphitheater. This rose in a zigzag toward the top of the mountain where I could see something like a plateau of granite coming out from the bulk of the circling mountain. Behind us, where the river flowed into the tunnel, was an impassable hulk of sheer mountain. There were no homes or farms on that side.

We soon arrived at a large terrace upon which was built a great hall, and several outbuildings, probably stables and barns. The hall was painted bright red and built of wood, with beams that were carved into the forms of running animals, birds, and other forest scenes. There were many people here, and children ran up as we climbed into view. Several younger men greeted my captors and helped them from their unicorns. The children ran immediately up to me, and stood around pointing and talking, very curious. Seeing children my own age was both a relief and a comfort, but it also made me feel strangely self-conscious, as I wondered if I would be accepted or if I could make friends with them. I realize how silly and (of course) childish this may sound, but I had not been around anyone my own age for over three months now, and I missed the company.

They were quickly bustled out of the way, and I was helped off my own ride. My legs failed me, and I fell forward on the soft green grass. Embarrassed, I quickly tried to stand again, but I had been off my feet for too long, and I had to be helped forward up the wide plank steps and into the hall.

It was an expansive room, wide and long, and the ceiling was at least twenty feet high. A great table was at the center, and there were stone fireplaces with slab hearths at either end. The walls were lined with shields, brightly colored and very tall, and weapons of all kinds were leaning here and there, swords, pikes, spears, axes, and long bows. Also, the strange rifle-like weapons, half crossbow and half Her Majesty's army-issued carbine that had been so effective at the gate, were ubiquitous amongst the assorted arms. The table was laid, and there were cups, bowls, bread and fruit of all kinds, as well as roasts of meat. The company of men who had rescued (or kidnapped) me was seemingly expected.

I was led to a chair against the far wall, and forgotten for some time. The men milled about the hall for a while, talking to those who had welcomed them home. The women were busy running to and from the table and a door in the far wall that presumably led into a kitchen. Then they all sat around the table, eating and talking, and I wondered if I dared to go up and ask for something to eat. But in a moment one of the younger women brought me a wooden plate filled with food, and I sat alone and ate. I was ravenously hungry. When I had finished I continued to sit, listening to the talk at the table, but I was unable to follow any of the conversation. I was so tired that I began to drift off even as I sat. The room was deliciously warm, and I was more comfortable than I had been in many days. The talking now sounded like the rhythmic noise of a far away ocean, and a breeze blew in from the open door, bringing the smell of freshly cut grass, and my heavy lids closed in sleep.

I awoke some time later, and the shadows in the

room were longer. Through the open door I could see that the sun was going down, and the familiar smells and sounds of evening were at hand. The hall was less crowded, but there were still several people milling around, some talking by the fireplace, and others clearing the table, or otherwise busy with domestic concerns. I was startled to see that someone was sitting right next to me, having dragged a nearby chair (the noise of which woke me up, I think). It was a boy, about my age or a little younger. I blinked my eyes a bit, and then said 'hello.'

"Hello," he responded, in a soft, curious voice. "who are you?"

"My name is Thaddeus," said I, "I do not live here."
I am sure that this came as no surprise to him, but I was still waking up.

"Thaddeus," he repeated, "that's an interesting name. I've never heard it before. My name is Asher. I have lived here for three years. Soon I am going across the desert, but not now. Not here, so where do you live?"

I thought about this, and for a brief moment I could not remember. Then I saw the face of my mother, and heard the voice of my father, and for an instant I could not speak. Where indeed? Somewhere in these mountains, far to the south, as near as I could tell, was a door. Sometimes the door was open, and one could follow it into a terrible cave filled with even more doors, and through one of those was my home. Where it was, really, I could not say. Was it still there? Did I have a home, or did the Messengers burn all of England down looking for the Book?

"I live just near Oxford, in the countryside."
He looked at me for a moment, his green eyes alive with interest.

"I saw you come in with the war party, and I thought that you might need a friend. Are you a prisoner?"

"I think so," I answered, "though I don't know what I have done to deserve it. Actually, I think they may have saved my life by capturing me. Whatever the case, I don't think I am your enemy."

185

Asher pondered this for a moment.

"Well, then whose friend are you? I know you can't be friends with the crooked people. At least you don't look like you could be. But maybe you're a spy. Were you sent by her, to spy on us?"

"No, I don't even know the crooked people. I don't know anyone, except Charismata. And I suppose I know Jacoben, but he is not my friend." I stopped talking, remembering Charismata's warning to be careful about sharing my secrets.

"I don't know those names," he answered slowly, "but Ajax will know. Ajax is a great warrior, maybe the greatest warrior of our age; even you have probably heard of him. And he is coming back soon. He will know who your friends are. But are they with Her? Are they Her servants?"

"Well, I don't know. Who is 'she'?" I suspected that I knew the answer already.

"She," he answered, "the Queen."

"Jacoben might be, but I am not sure. Charismata is not. I don't know who Charismata calls friends, although I am her friend. Who is the Queen? I have heard of her, but I don't know anything about her. And," I added quickly, "do you know who the Messengers are?"

He flinched, as though I had slapped him.

"I am not allowed to speak of them. But they are wicked, that much I know. I saw one when I was little, before I came here, and all I remember is that I was afraid. They are the Queen's, and they come from some other place, not here, not this land."

I was surprised to see his eyes well up with tears, but for a moment only. He coughed, and made a show of rubbing pollen from them.

"They just cut the grass today," he helpfully explained.

We talked for a few minutes more. He told me that he did not think I was much of a prisoner, because I was here in the hall, well fed, and not in chains. And besides

186

that, he had never seen a prisoner brought here before. It seemed that this Ajax was away, but that he would be returning soon, and they were waiting for him to question me.

"He went across the desert, taking many of our people with him. It won't be long before I can go too. We are escaping," he said, with a sly look.

"So Asher, it seems that you are already debriefing our prisoner. Did you learn anything of interest?" Two men had approached us without our being aware, and I recognized my friend, who spoke, and also the leader of the group that had captured me. Asher scrambled up, embarrassed.

"No Beow, my lord, I was only talking."

"Well, leave the prisoner, and allow us to do the talking. Go attend to your duties." Asher gave me a quick glance, and then hurried away. Beow, as my friend was called, pulled a chair beside me and looked intently at me for a moment. The leader stood tall beside him. Beow spoke;

"Well, there is much that we need to speak of. We don't know who you are, or why you were at the gate. If the reason is nefarious, and you are a friend of our enemy, know that you will find no mercy here. We helped you in good faith, and we have brought you here because your life seemed to be forfeit but for out intervention. That action put us in grave danger, then and even now. I hope that it was not in vain."

Here he paused. Although he spoke sternly, there was no unkindness in his eyes; but there was curiosity. Then the leader spoke:

"I am Pallas, guardian of the Valley. I stand beside Ajax, in whose hands your fate lies. I have brought you here, to our safe dwelling, because you are a boy, and because your life was in danger. But if you are a servant of our enemy, and if your danger was but a ruse, know that your life is worthless. She cannot save you, even if she would. What is your name?" His voice was also stern, and his eyes unbending. I answered:

187

"My name is Thaddeus. Thaddeus Michael. I am not your enemy, and I thank you for saving me, for indeed, that is what you did. I did not mean to put you in harm's way, but I am sure I would be dead or worse if you hadn't intervened." It was an effort to keep my voice from shaking, but my answer was controlled and (I hoped) dignified. I thought that I probably had nothing to fear from these people, but they were not sure that they had nothing to fear from me.

"Thaddeus," said Beow, "Who are you, and why were you on that cursed plane? You were armed with a very deadly weapon, the likes of which even the noblest warrior would feel privileged to carry. Why need you such a tool?"

I paused before answering. Charismata's warning was loud in my mind, and I did not want to reveal too much.

"I am nobody," I began, "at least, nobody special. I was just trying to find the White City, which I thought must be beyond that wall. As for my knife, I was accused of stealing it earlier today; I did no such thing. It was made for me by a friend, who wanted me to have a means of protecting myself, that is all. I don't know if I will need it, though I suppose it would have come in handy if I had to fight those people whom you and your men so quickly disposed of." I felt rather silly talking about fighting those black-eyed men. I would have been killed in an instant, I am sure.

"Made for you by a friend? You have powerful friends indeed, if that is true. But such a skill is no longer possessed by anyone in this world, since the fall of the Bright Ones, many ages ago. Do you think that we are so easily led astray? And where was the bone acquired, the one that was so fashioned? Did your friend pluck it from the mouth of a demon snake, just for friendship's sake?"

I was taken aback by the harshness of Pallas' response, and my words stumbled across each other as I tried to answer.

"I...I don't know where she acquired the skill. But

the tooth was mine before I met her…that is, I found the tooth, and she had it fashioned into a knife. I am not trying to deceive you. I speak the truth, and if you do not believe the truth, then I don't think I can convince you otherwise."

At my words both of their faces blanched, and Pallas' eyes burned.

"Thaddeus," said Beow softly, "Who is 'she'? Your friend, what is her name?"

"Her name is Charismata."

There was palpable relief in their faces. I realized quickly that they thought I had been calling the Queen my friend.

"Charismata?" asked Pallas, "the witch of the mountain? The old hag who lives alone above the ancient highway? Is that who you mean?"

"I don't know. She did not seem like a witch. She was very kind to me."

Pallas and Beow looked at each other for a moment. Whether they believed my story I could not tell, but something was wrong. I wondered if my Charismata was this same witch. I felt a little sick in my stomach, thinking about it. She had been very strange, but certainly not evil, or what I would consider to be witch-like.

"We will let that question go, for the moment." Continued Pallas, "Tell us where you found this tooth."

This would be tricky. I did not want to reveal too much, but I felt I needed to give them something, so that they could begin to trust me.

"Well," I began, "I found it in a cave. I did not just find it exactly. I first had to kill its owner."

"You mock us?" interrupted Pallas fiercely. "Do you think that wise?"

"No!" I responded, startled, "I mean, no, I am not mocking you. But if you don't want me to answer then don't ask me questions. It is the truth, whether you like it or not."

"Thaddeus," said Beow softly, "how did you kill a Krishnag snake? How did you even find one? I did not think they existed any more. It is only in ancient myth and stories

189

that we know of the Krishnag at all, or of the weapon that is forged of their fangs. Indeed, as far as I know there is only one such sword that has ever been made, and that thousands of years ago. If your story is true, then there are now two. You see why it is difficult to believe? Tell us how it happened, so that we may understand."

His calm voice was soothing, and his eyes were kind. I did feel I could trust him, but I decided that I would hold back the most important part of my story, namely the Book. I paused for some moments; the story rushed through my memory like a storm, and each sound and color was loud in my mind. I could feel the fear, the smell of the dust and the blood of the dragon's lair, and felt again the wound in my head. The stars on the mountain were spinning again, and I felt the rush of cold, pure air as I left the antechamber. The fire crackled in the hearth, and I heard the voice of Charismata, saying "Remember the mountain, Thaddeus, and remember me. Do not lose yourself, Thaddeus, take care that you do not lose yourself."

Then I answered:

"More than a month ago I stumbled out of my own land and into the Antechamber, deep underground, quite by chance, and then wandered lost for some time, perhaps for days. Too late I learned that the demon snake made its home among the dead in that place. It attacked me without provocation, and in the decaying light of that chamber I fought it, slew it, and took its tooth as my prize. Then I smote its offspring, so that no other traveler would be so molested. I tried to get out of that terrible cavern, but could not, and I almost died in that place. I was afraid, always afraid that the candles would burn down, that the lights would go out. It was only through a miraculous turn of events that I did finally find a door ajar, and I stumbled out into the night, half dead. It was Charismata who found me, and brought me back to life. I owe a great debt to her, and so I am sorry if you think that she is a witch. She is my friend, the only friend I have had since my grandfather and Sylvester were killed. But I did not choose the door, and have entered this world only by accident, as it were. As a stranger and wayfarer I found great hospitality and comfort in the home of Charismata. I hope that I will also find it here." My voice was strong and deep, and sounded strange and old in my ears, as though it was not a child who spoke, but a great warrior, a man in his prime. But I stopped, for I found the memory of my grandfather's death too sorrowful to bear.

There was silence for some time. Pallas was now sitting, leaning forward in a chair watching me intently. Beow still kneeled, and his face had the look of one who has seen a wonder. In the background I could hear the murmur of voices, and the click of dishes, as women were cleaning the great table. Children younger than me were running about the great hall, and I could hear their happy laughter. Finally Beow spoke:

"This is indeed marvelous. I believe you Thaddeus. I do not understand, but I believe you. I can see that there is much more to your story than you are willing to let on. You may, for now, keep your secrets. Only know that Ajax will not settle for a partial account, and the Elder, if his wisdom is sought concerning you, may see even deeper into your mysteries than you do yourself. Only answer me this, and know that if you try to deceive us, you will fail: are you an ally of the Queen? Do you work for her Messengers?"

The image of those wraiths came into my mind like a phantom, and I saw my grandfather as he stood, waiting his doom, and I heard the terrible voices of those fiends as they cruelly cut him down. Tears came to my eyes, and my voice cracked as I answered:

"No. I saw my grandfather, who I loved, die at their hands. The Queen and her Messengers are my enemies, and even now I think that they are hunting me, and wish to kill me."

They spoke no more. After some time, Pallas said something softly to Beow, and then took his leave. Beow looked at me with compassion; "Come Thaddeus, you are weary and afraid. Though you are our prisoner still, you have nothing to fear at our hands, and you will be treated well. But for now you must rest. Ajax will be returning soon, perhaps within a few days, and he will be able to sort all of this out, and even to help you, if you need it. And I think that you do need it. He will take you to the Elder, who is wisest of all, and I think that he will be most interested in your doings. I cannot see through your cryptic story, and I know that you are concealing much, but there is no guile in your eyes. Thaddeus, I am your friend. So now, at least, you have two friends." He smiled. "Even if you cannot yet trust me, I can see that your heart is noble."

His eyes were searching my face as he spoke, but I could not answer him.

"I will have you taken to a private room now. It is comfortable, and you can rest. This valley is a stronghold, safe from the Queen and her allies. But do not try to venture out of your room after the sun goes down. You will be well guarded, for your own sake as well as ours. It is for your sake that I tell you again; do not leave your room after dark. But stay here, I will have one of the women take you there now. Do not be afraid, Thaddeus." He finished with a smile. "Hold here for a moment, and then you can go rest."

With that he arose, and went out the door in the far wall, across the hall. The moment he was out of site, Asher returned, appearing as if by magic from some nearby hiding place. His green eyes were wide, and he looked awestruck and excited.

"I heard everything Thaddeus," he said, his soft voice alive with happiness, "you are a great warrior! I knew it, I just knew it! Well, I mean I thought that there was something special about you. You are a dragon slayer, a wielder of a Krishnag blade!"

"No," I quickly answered, somewhat embarrassed, "I am not really special at all. It is not as exciting or great as you might think, actually. It was really quite terrible."

But Asher paid no attention to my disclaimer, and jumped around excitedly for a moment, letting his imagination fill in all the gaps of my story.

192

"Wait till Ajax hears this! He will be amazed! Even Pallas was impressed, and he has fought with the Messengers hand to hand! I don't think even the dreams would frighten you..."

"Asher!" An older woman was approaching, wiping her hands on a small towel. "Do not speak those words, even in the daylight of the Hall! And leave that boy alone! His welcome has been inhospitable enough without invoking that shadow. He has had a long day, and I daresay those men did not treat him well either, riding all night, tying his arms and talking his poor head off, making him cry and everything... Help me get him to bed."

She helped me from the chair, and then across the hall and out the back door, into the evening. Asher trotted alongside, and I was happy to have his company. The evening was warm and lovely, with dragonflies and crickets flying around, as well as those incredible bugs that I had never before seen: fireflies! There were people still coming and going, walking around on errands, or simply enjoying the evening, and I could hear the stamping and neighing of the unicorns in the barn just down the slope. From our vantage point the entire valley was visible, like a great bowl, though the bottom was obscured in the fading light. The sound of the many waterfalls flowing from the mountains and pooling throughout the valley was the lovely background noise to all this. I was led to an outbuilding, and inside found a small room with a washbasin, and some fresh clothes laid out on a small wooden bed. After first admonishing me to stay inside, the woman and Asher bade me good night, and then I was alone. The room had a small window that looked out over the valley, and I was able to clean up (it had been some time since I had had the opportunity to do so) and the clothes were comfortable and soft. They were loose fitting tunic and trousers, a deep green color, and very much like the styles that I had seen. The light faded completely as I lay on my bed, and a slight cool breeze was moving the sheer curtain over the window. I could see through the window and up to the peaks of the mountains, and far away the stars spun in orbit. The stars! I wondered suddenly, with a jolt of panic, what Asher had meant about 'the dreams?' I didn't think I could bear any more dreams. But I fell asleep a moment later, and the darkness around me was only the darkness of the natural night.

~

"Naturally we were both very worried for our father. My brother still insists, to this day, that his sickness was contracted during his several month absence, when he went on the expedition, the one I mentioned earlier in this letter. Maybe it was. I am no medical doctor, and so can only speculate. "It was those dreams," my brother would say. "I think those dreams killed him, and I think that he 'got' those dreams on his expedition, the one he refused to speak of." My poor mother, she almost lost her own mind during this time. My father never slept, and when he finally passed out after several days awake, he would wake soon after, screaming incoherently. The whole household suffered with him. It was during this time, however, that the obsession took hold of him. I call it the obsession. I can think of no more appropriate word than that. He never left his study, or when he did it was only to travel to the library. Soon the books he collected and piled throughout the house were not enough for him, and he began to travel to the great libraries in Paris, Milan, Rome, and, once, the library in Jerusalem. It was here that he found something he considered important. Sometimes we were able to travel with him, which we enjoyed. But he was always distracted, and tried to tell us stories, stories that he seemed to consider somehow weighted with great importance, but that we thought merely strange tales told by a wandering mind. My mother daily grew wearier during these several years, and I once thought that she might be as sick as my father. Of course I was wrong. Finally, my Father, apparently having discovered what he was looking for, locked himself in his study for three months. Sometimes at night I would hear him scream, and I knew that he must have fallen asleep. He emerged finally, emaciated and glassy eyed, but he seemed better, seemed even happy, as though his nightmares were not so strong. "I have completed my project," he told us. "Now, maybe, we can fight back, now maybe something can be done to stop her." We had no idea who or what he meant, of course, but he was so excited that we naturally joined him in rejoicing. The manuscript that he had discovered in Jerusalem, and had been working on, actually translating, he took to someone he knew at the university. This is,

195

of course, the same manuscript that I sent you. My Father seemed to believe that this person would be able to help him, and would know what to do with my father's discovery. But apparently he had misjudged his friend. My father returned very upset, and in the days that followed his condition worsened. He finally died, as you know, when I was only thirteen years of age. But he left something for us, for my brother and me (and now I get to the point of my overlong story), in his will. Of course everything was left to my mother, but one small package was specifically for us. It was this book, or story, or manuscript. And here is the question that I want to ask you: now that you have read it, what do you think it means? Is it only the product of insanity, or does it have, as my father believed, some greater significance? What does it mean, and, more importantly, is any of it real? And what of its strange title? I can't help but wonder if the title is important, at least for diagnosing my father's illness. Nightmares have become, as you know, something of an obsession for me, and I have devoted my career to understanding them. Please let me know what you think. What does this book mean, and why did my father spend his last days translating it? And what a strange name. 'The Nightmare of Percephilous...' A disturbing name, I think."

~Excerpted from a letter discovered among the personal effects of Father Joseph Bastiolny, SJ, of Milan, Italy, in 1899. Father Martin Camolo, SJ, of the Missouri province, translated it from the original Italian in 1953. The letter was written by Nelson Fairmont, a name probably familiar to students of the occult. Nelson Fairmont was a practitioner of the esoteric (and since disbanded) group, the Dreamers. The goal of this group was to uncover the hidden meanings of dreams. Upon the strange disappearance of Mr. Fairmont, the group fell into disarray, and was disbanded in 1913.

.

~

Chapter XII

"Do not be afraid of sudden fear, nor of the onslaught of the wicked when it comes..."
~The Proverbs of Solomon

I would spend the next week in this strange valley, and in the company of these people. They greeted me with remarkable kindness, and I found myself the special charge of Asher, who never left my side. With him I wandered the entire valley, meeting many of the children our own age, and I was able to participate in all their games and activities. Indeed, it was very much like spending a summer holiday with friends in the countryside. In the mornings and evenings we had certain chores and projects that we worked on, and after lunch we were free until dinner. After dinner we would have more chores, and then would spend the evenings in the great hall around the fireplace, listening to tales told by the older men, or songs sung by the women. But in their eyes I could see a flickering sadness, and, especially in the eyes of those who had most recently arrived in the valley, fear. It was as though they had awoken from a terrible dream, and though the morning light played across their faces, the darkness of the night haunted them still. Indeed, Asher's eyes would sometimes betray some past sorrow, even in the midst of play.

It was here that I first heard about the dreams.

The City of Dark Dreams was exactly that. Every night, Asher told me, the dreams would come to every sleeper, and the dreams were of darkness. And in the darkness something sought them, each dreamer in its own way, hunting them in the night. Madness was not unheard of in the City. And all the inhabitants dreaded the setting of the sun.

Asher's words were cryptic, and I had to piece together scattered statements to begin to understand what he meant, for he would not speak about it in detail, or at length.

The stables were where Asher worked; I helped him with the grooming and the feeding of the animals (which included an odd assortment of domesticated animals, used for their wool and milk), and I was able to spend much time with those amazing, horse-like creatures, the unicorns. These were housed in small, private rooms in the vast stable, each with its own source of water and food, and with windows that looked out over the valley. They had beds of down that were cleaned and changed daily, and the food was only the best of hay and grass collected from specific terraces. They were treated not so much like horses, even the most valuable and loved of horses, but with a degree of reverence and honor that I have never seen given an animal in my own world. Indeed, Asher would speak to them in a low voice, in a language that I did not understand. At first he explained to them (so Asher told me) who I was and why I was accompanying him. The creatures would look at me with eyes that were remarkably aware, but would otherwise act just like a horse might. On the first morning, when I inquired about this, Asher told me that he had to learn the language of the unicorns, passed down from a forgotten time when unicorns roamed free, and had their own culture and customs. The language was at that time known by an ancient race of peoples, the "winged men" (or so they were called), who first dared to ride the creatures. Asher himself knew only a few words of this language; "Just enough for

198

my chores, and I don't know if I am pronouncing the words correctly. But they seem to understand me."

The afternoons were spent with the other children in the valley. We swam in the cold pools of clear water that formed as the streams that fell from the mountain rim made their way to the creeks, and finally to the river and down through the cave that was the entrance to the valley. I was very popular among my cohorts, who saw me as a novelty and a mystery, and I quickly forgot that I was technically a prisoner, or that I was in a hostile land at all. There was, however, a guard whose sight I never left, and who followed us all over the valley, although he was never very close, and never interfered with our games. All in all it was a wonderful and refreshing week.

Because of the strangeness and newness of it all, I did not often think of my own home, or of my parents, or of my mission. Indeed, I think that I intentionally put it all out of my mind so that I could escape for a while. But I would often be brought back to it by questions from the other children, and especially Asher. He was very curious about my family, and where I had come from. It was difficult to give complete answers, because I did not want to reveal too much of my quest. But from him I was able to piece together something of this community that I had been led to. It seems that this was something of a fortress, a hidden halfway house between the great city in the west, and some kind of hoped for land of safety in the east. From what I could gather, Asher's people were the original inhabitants of that city, but long ago had been enslaved. He was evasive on some of these points, and I think that he had had a terrible experience in that city. His parents were not here with him. I thought that they might have been killed, or remained enslaved.

Ajax and others were involved in a counter-revolution, and were systematically smuggling the slaves out of the city and to safety in this valley. Here they would remain for some time, perhaps years, until a way could be made to get them through the mountains and over a vast desert in the east. Across this desert was a fabled land where the arm of the Queen could not reach. It was clear that the children only knew a little of the details, and that there was much that they did not know, including the history that led to this state of affairs. But many of them clearly had terrible memories of the city, and were loath to talk about it.

My peaceful holiday did not last long. By week's end there were rumors circulating through the valley that Ajax was returning. And not Ajax only, but someone was with him. "The most beautiful princess," said Asher, "perhaps in all the world."

There was much activity throughout the valley, as preparations were made for their arrival. With Ajax and the princess were a hundred fighting men, and also the Elder would be here soon, though by some other route. I tried to find out who the Elder was, but Asher had only heard legends. "He is said to be the oldest person in the land, and also to have great power. I do not know much else, except that he is a great ally of ours in our war against the Queen."

On the seventh day since my arrival, in the late evening, we heard the sound of trumpets across the valley, and saw in the fading light a line of unicorns filing down from the eastern edge of the valley, entering this secret place by some hidden trail. All of the valley was at the great hall. The table was laden with food and drink, and the fires were roaring in the hearths. Asher and I had been kept very busy with chores up till then, and now found ourselves waiting with the rest of the inhabitants outside the hall. The warriors, led by Beow and Pallas, were lining the road, and the rest of the people (perhaps eight-hundred in all) were crowded behind them. Asher and I were next to the steps of the hall, and had a clear view of the procession. The sun was slipping away into the clouds and smog in the west beyond the mountains, and the valley looked like the starry, early night sky, so full of fireflies it was. The waiting crowd stood solemn and reverential, but not without joy. The excitement in the air was punctuated by the yells of the little children (who had no respect for occasion), as they ran around the

200

outside of the crowds. The procession drew closer.

Into view they finally came, and I instantly knew which rider Ajax was. He was tall and formidable, and his face carried the weight of his responsibility. Indeed, he looked just like I would have imagined a warrior-king to look. Behind him rode four warriors in a box formation, surrounding someone in the center who I couldn't quite see. Pallas stood forward and greeted Ajax, helping off his steed. They spoke quietly for a moment, and I saw that their eyes strayed momentarily in my direction; I unconsciously moved a step back against the edge of the steps. Ajax raised his arms, and in a loud voice addressed the gathered crowd:

"Greetings, fellow sojourners, my kinsmen and friends! We have been successful in our latest venture; those who traveled with us are safe across the endless desert. This is a time for joy and celebration. Let us feast tonight, and rejoice in our good fortune!"

The crowds cheered, and the newly arrived warriors were helped to dismount and given wreaths of flowers that had been prepared by the women. The entire procession began to ascend the stairs into the great hall, led by Pallas and Ajax.

It was at this moment that the four riders parted to reveal the person who had been their charge; it seemed that an angel had descended from the stars, still glowing with fire and light, and had taken the form of a woman. Beow, who held her hand like it was the most precious and delicate flower, helped her off her steed, and she now turned and made her way toward the hall. All the sound of voices and trumpets faded in my ears, and all the beauty of the valley was dull in my eyes at the sight of this princess. Her hair was gold and knotted with white flowers, and her dress was pale blue. Hers was a loveliness indescribable, and left me with an inconsolable ache and longing, the kind that one might have after seeing for the first time the canopy of the night sky, choked with stars too beautiful to apprehend. It was the strange ache for home, for rest and happiness, those things that cannot truly be found in this life. She walked past us with the gait of royalty, and her face was mystical grace. But it was also careworn and sad. As she passed us and began to ascend the steps, she turned suddenly and looked right at me and smiled, her eyes meeting mine like a spark of flame. I was startled by the look, for in this sea of dark green eyes, hers were as blue as the morning sky.

The feast in the hall was a grand thing, full of music and merriment, with Ajax given the place of honor at the head of the huge table. The princess was at his right hand, and Pallas at his left. Beow stood always near the princess, and waited on her every need. The warriors were feasted at the table with them, along with the older men and women who attended to the daily affairs of the valley. The rest of the inhabitants (those who were not involved in the cooking and serving) ate at tables around the hall, while the children ran around the whole affair, eating while they played. Others were outside on the grass surrounding the hall, chasing fireflies and enjoying the merriment. Asher and I sat at the edge of the hearth, eating quietly and watching everything. Ajax and the rest of the party were festive and celebratory, but there could be seen in their faces something more than weariness from the journey; they were thoughtful and concerned.

After the feast there were songs sung, and stories told, as well as music and dancing. It was a wonderful evening, but through it all I could hardly keep my eyes off the princess, so otherworldly was her beauty. I could not help but think that this was an angel exiled from her place in heaven. Long into the night the celebration went, and all the children began to drift off, falling asleep on their parent's laps. The firelight cast strange shadows in the room, and the songs were enchanting and sublime. I must have finally dozed off, for I was startled awake by Asher nudging me and whispering in my ear:

"Thaddeus, Ajax is about to speak!"

The room had grown quiet, and Ajax stood tall in the center, his presence commanding and kingly.

"My dear friends," he began, "we are grateful for your welcome, and we are grateful for your steadfast courage in these dark times. Indeed, though the times are dark, your courage is a light, a beacon that will not be put out. What happiness is to be found in this land is found here, in this valley, in your strength, and in your freedom. While servility has draped a shadow over your homeland, you will not be made slaves; while our enemies make others cower, you will not be cowed. This is a source of unyielding hope, and more hope is yet to be found. The princess Susana is here with us, and has traveled far and through much danger. After Beow the Brave himself rescued her from the Tower of Grief, fifteen years ago, she has been safe. Now she has come within the shadow of danger to speak with the Elder, and offer her aid to us here in exile. There is much news to speak of, for there has been movement in the sea, the roots of the mountains are groaning with the pangs of labor, and the stars in their orbit are finally speaking. Tomorrow we will convene a counsel, and the Elder will be among us. Tonight we have celebrated and rejoiced; tomorrow we will speak of sorrowful things. Go now in comfort and blessing, for tomorrow we will again be at work."

Thus did Ajax speak. After he had sat down, the assembly moved to leave, the children being taken up by their parents, and the table cleared quietly by the women. It was very late. As Asher and I rose to leave, one of the warriors approached us. "Ajax wishes to speak to the prisoner." My heart sank, for though I knew that this was inevitable, I hoped it would not be tonight. I was tired, and was in no mood to speak of my quest. Indeed, I had put it out of my mind over the last few days, trying to escape from the memories if only for a while. But we followed the warrior to where Ajax, Pallas, Beow and two other warriors and one of the old men from the valley sat. Asher did not leave my side, and his presence was a great comfort.

I stood in front of the group of men feeling small and frightened. The firelight played strange shadows on their stern faces, and made it difficult to judge any subtlety in their expressions. Pallas spoke first:

"This is the boy, my Lord. Thaddeus is his name." He addressed Asher: "Go attend to your duties Asher. Ajax wishes to speak to your friend alone."

"No, stay Asher." Ajax spoke now. "I see in your face that you are concerned for your new friend. It may be that your presence is a grace to Thaddeus, and you might do well to listen to our conversation. Only let Thaddeus speak for himself, and know that we mean him no ill will."

Asher stirred at my elbow, and remained.

"Now Thaddeus," continued Pallas, "we have relayed what we know of you to Ajax, how we found and rescued you on that barren plain outside the gate. We have told him of the weapon that you carried, as well as the strange metallic instrument with markings unknown to us. We have told him how you claim to have killed a dragon, and of your friendship with the Witch of the Mountain. Is there anything more that you would like to disclose?"

I looked at their faces as the firelight danced off them, and answered;

"I do not willingly keep anything from you. You have rescued me, and although I am a prisoner, you have treated me with nothing but kindness. I am not an enemy of yours, and indeed, I know little of my own story beyond what I have told you. But if there is anything that I can answer that will help you and will not endanger my own quest, I will answer."

"That is good to hear, for all of our sakes," answered Pallas. "To begin with, what is this quest that you speak of? Why came you to that gate, and why are you in this land at all? We know that whoever your people are, they are not found in any of the many leagues to the north or the south. Did you cross the mountains from the east? Or did you find a way across the sea?"

"I...I cannot speak of the quest. It is that alone that I cannot reveal. Whether it succeeds or fails, only time will tell; I cannot now speak of it. But I will tell you this: I think that I am from another world. That is, I came through a door into this land quite by chance, and my own home is neither in the East nor across the sea. It…it is in a different world, that is all I know." The late hour made it difficult to decide what to tell and what to leave out. But of course they would know that my journey into this land would be tied to my quest. The men were quiet for some time, and then Ajax spoke:

"From another world, Thaddeus? That is most interesting. I have heard of such things, though I do not know how it could be true. But who can say? You yourself do not seem to know how such a thing could be true. That there might be other worlds somewhere in the vastness of creation, and that there might be doors to these worlds, has long been known to me; indeed, you are not the first person who has told us of such doors." He looked at Beow, but Beow's eyes never left my face.

"We will leave that for a moment," he continued. "It may be that the Elder can enlighten us both. He may know what to make of this other world that you traveled from. But tell me what you know of the Witch of the Mountain. Even as a child I have heard stories of her, and know that even our enemy dares not or cannot disturb her in her alpine nest. But you are her friend, you say, and know her. Perhaps you can tell us something about her?"

"Well," I began cautiously, "I don't know that much. But I can tell you that she is very old, and also that she is good. If witches can be good, I haven't heard, so I do not think that she is a witch. But she is very strange. And…and sort of enchanted, I guess. I don't know how to describe it. At her house there is peace and safety. She took care of me and healed my wounds. I owe her my life for sure, perhaps even more than I owe you my life. She is not wicked. This is all that I really can tell you." Probably this would not be enough, but I really knew nothing more.

"These wounds you speak of, did you sustain them in your fight with the dragon?" Pallas asked.

"Yes, in the cave with the dragon. Also…" I began,

205

but then paused. If I told them of the wound that Cuthbert had given me, I would have to explain a lot more.

"Also what, Thaddeus?" Pallas encouraged.

"Well, I had another wound, but I cannot speak of it."

I looked at the plank floor. The men were again quiet. Then Ajax looked at the others, and spoke:

"Thaddeus, even if you will not tell us about your quest, perhaps you will not mind if I tell you of ours. For yours is not the only dangerous path. In pursuing your mysterious way you might have stumbled into something much greater than you realize. You are here in the safety of this valley. For that safety we pay a dear price. Daily is blood spilled to protect this valley, to keep its location a secret. We have been driven these many ages from our city and are hunted like animals, and even now our kinsmen are slaves in the darkness beyond that very wall that you were attempting to cross. Even in rescuing you we were in grave peril, and in procuring your delivery we were prepared to sell even our own lives. These children who are your companions, even Asher here, have come through fire and sorrow to reach the safety of this valley. We have few allies, and on the western slopes of the mountains are found no friends, only spies and enemies. We have brought each of the inhabitants of this valley, by stealth and danger, out of slavery in the cursed City of Dark Dreams to this secret place. And even then the danger is not passed. Each of them is ferried across the mountains and through an endless desert, by paths unknown to our enemies, to the City of Lights in the East. This is our quest. Your secrets may be of grave importance to you, and I understand why you might wish to hide them from us. But if your quest takes you beyond that wall and into that dark city, then I must know what it is. If you will not tell us willingly, then you must remain here, and your quest will never be completed. I do not wish to pry into your affairs, but by stepping foot on that barren plain you have made your business my own. Indeed, it may be that we can aid you on your quest, for an

206

enemy of the queen is our friend. But we must know. So tonight, sleep in peace, and think of what I have told you. Tomorrow the Elder will be here, and with him you must be candid. He will settle for nothing less. Goodnight, Thaddeus."

With these words he rose, and so did all the rest. They left the hall, and Asher and I made our way back to our rooms in silence.

Even though the hour was late, I could not sleep that night. The moon was full and her beams swept my little room with a glow, cold and soft. Was I right to withhold what I knew? Surely if the Book was of such importance, then it mattered to the inhabitants of this land. And were not my enemies their enemies? And if they knew of a secret way into the City, a smugglers route, then maybe they could show me? But Charismata's warning was still loud in my mind, and I trusted her. How could I not? Even if these people did not know her, or thought that she was a witch, that was no reason to start distrusting her. I wondered what this Elder was like, and whether he would be able to help me. All of this floated through my mind as I watched the breeze move the white curtains of my little window, but most of all I wondered about the princess.

Asher arrived at my door early that morning. He looked tired and worried, but he said that he was very excited to see the Elder. "I have heard many stories and legends about him," he told me, "and they say that it was he who stopped the advance of the Queen during the Great War. He is very old," he added.

After our chores and breakfast, a horn rang out through the valley, loud and clear, bouncing and echoing across the bowl. This was the summons to the gathering. All the inhabitants, young and old, had been all morning making their way to the Hall, but Asher told me that the gathering would not be held there. "Further up," he said, pointing, "along the edge. There is a cave up there. That is where we will meet."

This was the western most wall of the valley, and I had noticed before how the mountains flattened out like a mesa at this point, and how this mesa stretched over the section of the bowl that was a cliff, just above the tunnel entrance to the valley. On the right hand side of the mesa, or the northern side, a finger of stone jutted out of the mountain range, and looked like a ceiling of stone along perhaps half of the mesa. All of the people were now making their way up a narrow path that crisscrossed its way up to the top of the mesa. We joined the line of people and in the morning sun we began to climb. At the first landing, a hundred feet above the hall, a warrior was waiting. He was not one who had been in the valley when I arrived, but had come with Ajax. He signaled to us, and told us that we were to accompany him. So we continued the climb, and I remembered all too clearly that I was a prisoner.

The view from the side of that cliff was expansive and breathtaking, a sweeping panoramic view of the entire valley and of the mountains in the east. The line of people below us looked like ants, and the houses and barns of the valley looked like tiny, colorful boxes strewn across a deep green lawn. Although the path was narrow, it was wide enough to be fairly safe, and it crisscrossed back and forth so frequently that even if one were to fall he would fall only fifteen feet or so to the trail below, and not tumble down the hundreds of feet to the valley.

The trumpet sounded again, echoing from the mesa above us, and bounding off the far walls across the valley. The pace of the climb quickened.

We were too out of breath to talk much on the climb, but our guard was courteous and answered the few questions that we posed him. Yes, he said, the Elder had arrived, but his comings and goings were secret, and how he had arrived unremarked by the inhabitants of the village he could not say. And yes, to my question, the princess would be there.

"Something is going on," Asher whispered. "There are so many warriors with all their weapons around. This is

208

not a normal gathering. I think something has happened that we don't know about."

The top of the mesa was incredible, a wide expanse of flat stone, the surface smooth and clean like the marble floor of a castle. The jutting crag of rock, a high roof that provided shade and relief from the hot sun, covered half of the mesa. On the far side of the mesa, perhaps two hundred feet away, the edge disappeared into the clear blue sky, dropping into space. I trembled at the thought of what a height that must be.

There were warriors stationed along the plateau, and they guided the people into the mouth of a wide stone tunnel that was at the north end of the mesa. This tunnel was rough hewn, but clean and clear of stones and pebbles. Torches hung at intervals, filling the crowded tunnel with dancing orange light. We followed this for some way, and I could not help but compare it to the terrible caves that I had been lost in. I wondered if this was as ancient as those others. Ahead of us I could hear the sound of drums.

The tunnel ended suddenly, and opened up into a wide cavern, lit by a great fire in the center. The ceiling could just be seen by the light of the leaping flames. Drums were echoing in the cavern, and the inhabitants of the valley filtered to the left or the right, sitting along the circumference of the cave's wall. I wished that I could just blend in with the crowds, but the warrior led us both out near the center of the cave, close to the fire. It was very hot, and I was perspiring freely. From this vantage point I could see the expanse of the cavern, and saw that the people were all seated around against the wall, with warriors stationed at intervals, some holding torches. The older men of the valley, those that were in charge of the daily operations, were seated with a group of warriors and others directly across from the entrance. This group had more warriors standing among them, and I could see that Ajax and Pallas were standing next to something that looked like a pile of old blankets propped with a gnarled staff. But what really captured my attention was the person sitting on brightly colored cushions a few paces away from Ajax; the princess seemed to exude some soft light that lit the cavern with enchanting beauty, like a wildflower among stones.

At her shoulder stood Beow, and from across the room he gave me a smile, though his expression remained grave. Behind us the last of the people were coming in, those families with small children and the elderly, who took a little more time climbing the path. The drums continued deep and lonesome, echoing through the cavern. When all the people were settled in, Ajax stepped forward and raised his arm, and the drums ceased.

"Kinsmen, brothers and sisters, the young and the revered old, welcome to the Gathering! It has been a long year since we have convened thus, and there is much pressing business to attend to. All is not well, and the poison in the west is seeping even into this valley."

There was an audible gasp in the room, and a deep panic gripped me; was I the 'poison' that had seeped in?

"Yes, even now the enemy does not rest. All of us here have sacrificed and bled in our struggle against the Queen, and our sacrifice is by no means over. There is movement beyond the walled city, and the secret paths by which each of you was ferried out are being shut, one by one. Our remaining kinsmen are becoming more hopelessly ensnared, and some of our most trusted allies have turned against us and aligned themselves with the Queen, selling their souls along with our secrets. And the dreams are growing worse. This development has made open war even more hopeless, and set our plans back for the foreseeable future. Though we cannot abandon the rest of our kinsmen to slavery, neither can we hope to rescue them by the means we have used in the past. New plans must be formulated, new friends and allies cultivated. Indeed, as you all know we have here today the Princess Susana, recently traveled from the City of Lights, sent by the Lord of that place in gratitude for Beow's courage. As you all know, it was he who treaded that dark path to the Tower of Grief those fifteen years ago, and he who slew the Gatekeeper in order to save the little girl trapped therein. The anger of the Queen was kindled at that victory, so let the presence of Princes Susana be a source of comfort and hope to us, and know that the City that sent her in gratitude has long kept the Queen at bay, and thwarted her desire for domination. Princess Susana will take back to her people all that she sees and hears here, that with wisdom and prudence they might find more ways to aid us. So we have much to give us hope, both the strength of our own, and the strength of our allies, yet there is much now to cast a shadow over this valley."

Here he paused, his face cast down, and the only sound in the cave was of the sparks leaping from the wood in an effort to escape the immolation.

And then the pile of old blankets stirred. I blinked and looked again, for it seemed that from the blanket a voice began to speak, a voice so ancient that there might have been moss growing on it. And then part of the blanket fell away and I saw that there was an old man wrapped in it, so thin that he might have been a pile of dried sticks, and whose green beard (green? But it was not green, it was white) was so long that if he were standing it would certainly have dragged on the ground. As it was, it lay piled in front of him like matted lichen or moss, the kind that might be seen hanging from very old trees. His bony hand clutched a staff, and I could not be sure where the staff began and his arm ended. The voice was old, as I have said, as old as the stone, but commanded a strange power, for when he spoke a warmth flooded the room, a warmth (how shall I describe it?) exactly like an evening in the late spring, and the heaviness that was so pervasive after Ajax's speech was suddenly lifted.

"Fear and fire, Ajax, yes," said the ancient man, "but there is more movement of good than ill. Fate has struck an ugly blow, yes, but who can know the hearts of men? We have been betrayed; those who care so little for their own souls that they would sell them for even their lives deserve our pity, not our hatred. Though they do us grave harm, it is they who are mortally wounded. There is much hope to speak of along with the danger. The Princess is here, yes, and we have on our side the bravest warriors since the fall of the Bright Ones so many ages and ages ago. But there is someone else who brings hope in a different form, someone who has stumbled unknowingly into our arena, someone like the princess, who offers hope not in strength of war, but in strength of character, someone who may play a greater role in this struggle than he knows. Bring the boy forward, Ajax, and let me look at him."

It took a moment to realize that it was I that he spoke of. "Thaddeus, come forward," commanded Ajax. Head down I stumbled forward, and stood alone in the center of the room, with all the hundreds of eyes on me. I realized that I was trembling, and tried hard to control myself. I could see my shadow swirling and leaping in front of me as the heat of the fire burned my back.

"This is the boy, dear Elder, the one who Pallas and Beow rescued. He has been in their care for eight days now, but he refuses to answer our questions with candor. Perhaps he will now realize his duty."

The Elder stared at me with his sharp green eyes, and a strange look spread across his face.

"Thaddeus is it?" he asked, his ancient voice cracking, "Thaddeus the Dragon Slayer?"

"No sir, my name is Thaddeus Michael. I killed a dragon, but that was more luck than anything else."

"Indeed? Luck? The same luck that fitted you with a weapon of kings, and the same luck that saved you from certain death at the gate, perhaps? If luck it was, than you are indeed the most fortunate of boys. Well Thaddeus Michael, fortune's heir, you have been less than candid with Pallas and Beow, and even the mighty Ajax you have refused to answer; will you answer me now?" He smiled as he spoke, and I felt immediately at ease and comfortable, as though he was an old friend. But I still kept an internal guard, determined not to let on too much of my quest.

"Yes, as much as I am able I will answer your questions. Only know that if I keep anything back, it is not

212

because I am ungrateful for your kindness and favor."

"Indeed, Thaddeus, your character will not be impugned here. Will you answer this: why did you find yourself on that barren plain, and why do you seek to enter the City of Dark Dreams, the very place from whence all its inhabitants !ong to escape?"

I paused a moment before answering, and then made a decision: I would tell him everything except what was stolen. I would not mention the Book.

"I did not know anything about that city, except that I think the person I am pursuing is hiding somewhere inside. He stole something that belongs to my family, and it cost me dearly. My grandfather and our brave friend Sylvester both died at his hand, and I only just escaped with my life. But what he has stolen is very important to my family, and with the death of my grandfather the responsibility of its safekeeping lies heavy on my shoulders. I followed this person into the Antechamber, and there I fought the Krishnag snake. I was lost in that timeless place for a long time, and I almost died. But I found a way out, and was helped by Charismata, who you know as the 'Witch of the Mountain'. When I had recovered from my wounds, I continued following this person, and I thought that he would make for the city, and then to what I have heard called the Alabaster Castle. I hoped to find him and get back what he stole from my grandfather. I am well aware that this quest will probably fail, and that it may be completely foolish. But that is my quest, and I can no sooner abandon it than you can abandon the fight against the Queen, and leave your kinsmen in slavery. That is why I was on that plain, and that is why I must enter the city."

There was murmuring among the people, and Ajax and Pallas exchanged looks. The Elder was looking intently at me, and I found that I could not meet his stare.

"So you will not tell us what this person has stolen; very well. I am older than I look, Thaddeus, and I may be able to see more deeply into your story than you do yourself." I did not answer, but wondered how he could possibly be older than he looked.

"Will you give us the name of the person whom you seek, the one who murdered your grandfather, and who killed your friend? Perhaps I may know who he is, and where he is most likely to be found."

I considered this. It would be very useful if the Elder could tell me where to find Jacoben, and I did not see what harm it would be to tell him his name. But the Book would remain a secret.

"His name is Jacoben," I said loudly, a little too loudly. "Jacoben the Necromancer."

Ajax started, and the crowds gasped. Beow looked hard at me, and even the princess blanched.

"Ah yes, Jacoben the Necromancer," repeated the Elder, slowly. "Yes, I am beginning to see clearly now."

"Why did you withhold this from us Thaddeus?" interrupted Pallas. "You have placed us in greater danger than you know! What do you think will happen if you find him? That is a fate worse than death!"

"I...I didn't know what I would find..." I began, but the Elder raised his creaking arm for silence.

"Yes I see clearly now," he continued, "I do not know how such a thing could be, but I understand now that it is so." With creaking joint and aged step he rose, leaning heavily on his staff, his robe wrapped loosely around him, and his beard hanging like a dirty rope to the floor. His voice became louder as he spoke:

"Nine nights ago as I watched the stars, in the deepest hour, they shuddered in their course, and I saw the moon turn her face away in shame at what she saw. Fly, Fly, the wind warned me, for terror has once again been awakened. Then I heard the crack of the lock, and saw the sea churn, and felt the bowels of the earth disgorge the vile filth that had been locked away inside her. Yes, we have now much to fear, my fellow sojourners, for the enemy is on the move; the Searcher has been released!"

The hair on my neck stood on end at his words, and a woman in the room screamed. A sickness overwhelmed me, the room swam, and darkness seemed to overshadow my eyes. I stumbled, and Asher reached out and caught me before I fell. I heard him call for help, but his voice seemed faint and far away.

I awakened out of what felt like a painful dream, and I found that I was propped up against some pillows close by the Elder and Ajax. I felt ill, but I could not understand what had happened. Had I fainted at hearing that the Searcher had been released? But I had known that already. Whatever had happened, my head was now throbbing, and nausea still lingered. It seemed that the gathering was still going on, and that the discussion was still about me. I heard one of the head warriors speaking:

"How is it that this boy can be a source of hope? If the Searcher is loosed, where can any of us hide, and where is the hope to be found? Not with this child, surely? He has brought doom upon us!"

"Nevertheless, we have cause to hope," responded the Elder. "I know now what I only guessed before. The enemy is moving, but is desperate. She has dared to breach another world that is not already lost in shadow, but in stealth she entered it, for she has no strength left for open war after all these ages. And it seems that she has found what she was looking for. Yes, I know what it is that this boy seeks."

"What then, Elder, what is this child's quest?" asked Ajax. "And what does it have to do with us, if it is true that he is an alien from another world? If the Searcher is loosed, how can he hope to accomplish it?"

"Listen, Ajax, and I will tell you," continued the Elder. "I will tell you what the wise of old knew, and what has been passed on to me. Before the Queen had power, the tales say that she came from somewhere else, some other world, that she herself is an alien, though she walked among us as a friend. Ever deceitful, she brought down the kings of old through treachery, and strove with princes of the land through duplicity. She had some power at her command, or she was ruled by some power. Black ships came from out of the sea, and the Dark men came from the mountains. Her Messengers were unveiled, and the Alabaster City was razed to the ground. But her ambition was not for this land alone. Something else drove her to make war against other worlds, back when such worlds were known. But ever the key to her power evaded her, and there were other forces that worked against her. The full extent of the history of the Great War is too terrible to retell here. It was during those dark ages that the Bright ones fell, or were thrown down. Such was our doom. Our hopes rested on them. They alone, we thought, had the power to stand against the Queen and her allies. But the Queen is ever treacherous. And there are other powers, more wicked even then she, at whose pleasure she serves."

Here the Elder paused, and I realized that everyone, including me, was listening with such rapt attention that complete silence reigned in the cave, so that even the crackling of the fire was quieted.

He sighed, and continued: "Yes, there are many strange things in our world, and many sad tales. But ours is not the only tale, and ours is not the only world. What the child tells us is true: he is a traveler from another land, a land that we cannot reach. And there are many more things in creation that are strange and unknown to us. I say that this boy is a source of hope; not because the Searcher has been released, but because although the Queen has thrown everything that she can at him, he has survived and has come this far. Because of him we know of her desperation. And we know now that what has eluded her for so long is finally come to her, that what ever the Necromancer stole from Thaddeus is of great value to her. But, if she possesses it now, why cares she for this boy? Who is Thaddeus Michael that she should fear him? And fear him she must if she has released the Searcher. No, there is cause for hope. The winds have changed and the sea is waking. The Queen, in her pride, believes that finally she has what she has always desired, the Book, the Book of Lost Worlds, and that her ambition can finally be fulfilled. Only this Book, I think, can be of such importance to her. But something went wrong, that much is clear. I think I may know from whom Thaddeus is descended, and I think that the Queen may have bought that Book with a dear price. And Thaddeus lives, and has killed a Krishnag serpent, the guardian of the Antechamber. Now he carries a weapon unlike any I have seen, and he has befriended Charismata, who you so foolishly call the Witch of the Mountain. Do you know nothing of your own history, your own tale? If we know of Charismata, do you think it likely that the Queen does not? And yet upon her mountain she remains. What power or stealth could keep her from the Queen's clutches? For centuries we have kept the Queen at bay, always one step ahead of her, always moving in secret, and striking in stealth; but Charismata does not leave her lofty meadow, and the Queen has not challenged her."

The Elder stopped, his head bowed, and seemed to be lost in thought, his right hand on his gnarled staff, and his left hand knotting his tangled beard.

"This book that I speak of, this Book of Lost Worlds; what secrets are held inside it no one can tell. But there is something locked away, something that the Queen in her malice desires above all. The book has been lost, or hidden, for thousands of years. It must remain lost. The Queen can never be allowed to find it."

Ajax rose again to speak.

"How came a small boy by such a treasure, if this is true, Elder? What kind of family possesses such an heirloom? I know there are strange places in the universe, and I know that Beow himself traveled a dark and narrow ledge between this world and another to rescue the Princess when she was but a child. Indeed, it may be that there are many other worlds, and that there are roads and paths to and fro between them, as some of the old tales claim. But what is this 'Book of Lost Worlds' that The Queen should desire it, and who is Thaddeus that she should release the Searcher to find him?"

217

"Power and domination, if one could read and understand what is contained therein. Knowledge twisted upon itself and devoid of charity, a desire to be the master of the Worlds and all the powers that they contain; indeed, to be the master of all the masters of the cosmos, and to even command the One who summoned the cosmos out of the void. This is what the Queen believes she will find. I thought that the Book had been lost or destroyed long ago, even though rumors surfaced now and then of a family sworn to protect and hide the Book at all cost. But these rumors had long since died out, and even I thought of it infrequently, so consumed I was by our ongoing battle against the Queen." Here he paused. All was quiet in the cave, and the firelight cast strange shadows on the eager faces of those listening. His voice was louder when he continued.

"And then, five years ago, I met a ragged man in the halls of the Underlord, half dead. He was a stranger in the land, and he also had upon his shoulders some quest of which he would not speak. He had seen something that burned his soul, and a terrible sickness had overtaken him. How he had found his way into the hidden halls of stone that are the home of the Underlord he would not say, but I thought that he must have been escaping the City of Dark Dreams, and had fallen down into a well or some other entrance to the Underworld. The Underlord gave him aid, and I have some power of healing. We brought him back from the edge of death, and when he was well enough, we ferried him out of the deep, narrow halls of the Underworld, and into the mountains. But I never could discover his secret, except that I think that he was, like Thaddeus, an alien in this world. Indeed, the likeness between the two is striking. This man possessed some power and strength that I could not discern. Yes, there are powers in the cosmos that even I cannot understand or see." His bright green eyes met mine, and they seemed to pierce me to the soul. "And I have sensed something in Thaddeus, something that he even he may not see with clarity. He bears a mark, a mark that I do not know…" He looked at me for a moment longer, and continued. "Whether this man that I helped had anything to do with the mysterious quest of Thaddeus only Thaddeus can know for sure. But I wonder… in the ancient tales, the protectors of the Book were men called Bellator, warriors schooled in arts long lost to our race. Indeed, these legends describe the protectors as arising from a race of peoples who were graced with some favor unknown to other races. I suppose that this must be so, for they held the fates of us all in their hands. Has Thaddeus this grace? We must hope so. If the Book is now in play after all these long eons, we must hope that Thaddeus has indeed inherited the mantel of the Bellator. Thaddeus, your responsibility lies heavily on your shoulders; this is as it should be, for your success or failure will fall on all of us in this world, and in your own; and any other worlds that survived the Great War, it will fall upon them as well. It seems that our peril has never been greater than at this moment."

Here he stopped, and Ajax rose again to speak.

"If this is true, then it is in our best interest to help Thaddeus continue his mission. Indeed, it is imperative that we ourselves see to the return of the Book, even at great cost to ourselves. For time may be very short. And this is, I think, the right moment to alert all those who abide in this valley, and who seek safety and refuge from the long arm of the Queen, that the day we have long dreaded may have finally arrived."

He stepped forward into the firelight in the center of the chamber and raised his arms.

"My friends," he cried, his strong voice echoing and bounding off the rock walls. "This place of refuge, this valley, is no longer a secret known only to us. The emissary of the Queen is even now ascending the steps outside, escorted by the guard."

There were gasps and startled cries throughout the cave, and several of the inhabitants stood and shouted questions. Ajax called for order and silence, but it took some moments before he again was able to speak.

"Yes, they arrived at the waters edge three days ago, and requested an audience with Pallas, the Elder, and myself. We have agreed. Why she has sent only her agents, and not her army we do not know. But do not fear; we have used the interlude to our advantage. Only know that these are our last days in this valley. When the emissaries arrive, do not speak, and take care that you are not deceived by their words, even if they please or frighten. The Queen is a liar and a deceiver."

At that moment one of the warriors entered and signaled to Ajax. Ajax acknowledged him, and drew his great sword from its scabbard, and placed it point down in the dirt floor, with his hands resting on its hilt. More warriors entered, and stood on each side of the doorway. The air was tense, and all the mothers held their children tightly. Asher, who had been sitting behind me, moved close by my side. The Elder did not move, and his head remained bowed low. Torchlight could be seen in the tunnel.

Into the cavern, walking between an escort of warriors with slow, dignified pace, came three men clothed in white robes. They were tall and very thin, with pale arms that hung to below their knees, and fingers at least three times the length of an ordinary hand, and each finger was tipped with a long, white, polished nail. Their hair was long and white, and their faces pale, with a great red slash of a mouth. Their eyes were clear and colorless, like wide drops of a bottomless pool; and yet there was no emotion or life in them, as though they were useless appendages and these creatures could only see by other means. They were led to the center of the room, next to the fire, and the escort stepped a pace back. Silence reigned.

"The Glorious Queen Lilith, gracious and merciful, greets her loyal subjects with great joy and with great expectation!" The voice was clear and song-like, wavering back and forth as on the crest of a musical note, and it was as though something unseen cracked and broke in the

220

stifled atmosphere of the chamber. My body grew unexpectedly cold, and I remembered the phrase that I had heard used before by my father: it felt as though someone was walking on my grave. The middle emissary was the speaker, and he stepped forward, his red mouth twisted in a smile, and he raised his long arms and fingers to the sky.

"To the mighty Ajax she sends a special greeting! Although there have been many misunderstandings between the Queen Lilith the Fair and Ajax the Loyal, nevertheless, with open arms and joy she invites reconciliation, and a healing of harms. No animosity is held in her magnanimous heart, even after betrayal and rejection." Here he turned towards Pallas.

"Pallas the Brave she greets! Long has she admired your courage from afar, and she notes well how you guard this bit of grass and rock as though it were your own kingdom. She knows how valuable your service would be, and she wishes you to know how great her generosity is. Real kingdoms and castles of gold are the rewards for her faithful servants." The smile never left his mouth as he spoke. He turned next to Beow.

"And Beow the Just, to you she sends a special greeting! You, of all warriors know what service to a lady means! You, alone of the knights and warriors of her realm know what it means to face death rather than dishonor, and you would rather suffer death a thousand times than allow dishonor to befall your beloved. Her majesty's beautiful heart is moved to know that chivalry is alive and well in her realm. Indeed, if the great Queen has a fault it is this: that she covets the love and dedication of her servants above all, and she is perhaps overly generous and lavish with rewards for those who return her marvelous love." He smiled for a moment more at Beow, and Beow returned the gaze with an unwavering stare. The white creature then raised his arms again, and turned in a small circle, allowing his smile to grace the entire cave.

"And to all her beloved subjects, you who live here in poverty and disgrace, camping like animals in the wilderness, to you she expresses her boundless love and admiration! Though her beautiful heart has been broken to hear how you crept away from the comfort and care of her maternal embrace, yet she knows how easily one can be led astray by those whose hearts are not pure, by those who desire not your wellbeing. Indeed, to some you are only foils for their own dishonest gain. How many tears she has shed for you, her children! And how she longs to once again take your hand in hers, and protect you from the cares and tribulations of the brutal life you now lead." The song-like voice broke, and I could almost imagine that those unseeing eyes shed a tear at these words. Last he turned and faced the Elder.

"And to the Elder, for Elder he is indeed; older than the hills, and yet with no hearth of his own to offer comfort, and no reward for a long life lived well, nothing but hard stone and dirty rags. To the Elder she sends greetings, and wishes him to know with what admiration and respect she holds him! He who has wandered like a beggar for centuries across desolate wastelands filled with violent creatures, to him she wishes to offer comfort and a home, and the reward and accolade so richly deserved!" The Elder did not move, and never raised his eyes, but I thought at that moment that he did look like nothing more than a tired old man who had wasted his youth and now was left with nothing.

"We have no words of welcome for you or for your mistress." The voice of Ajax was strong and loud in the room, and commanded authority. "You have come to tell us that the Queen now knows of our secret refuge, and knows how we have smuggled so many of her slaves away, right under the watchful gaze of her Messengers. Very well. What else does your Queen wish to convey to us, beyond the false promises and adulation breathed through silver?"

The thing did not stop smiling. It raised its long, thin, white arms again, and answered:

"Ah, Ajax the noble, Ajax the wise. Do you really think that this lair, this bit of rock and turf that you call your 'secret refuge' has been unknown to our most benevolent

222

Queen? Surely you, in all your wisdom, have not led these poor people who are your charge astray with false hope and security? Long has the Queen known of this hole, and all your diversions of cloudbanks and fog have not blinded her! Perhaps the mists were the work of the Elder, a display of his might and power? How very inspiring. You must be pleased to know that you have such a distinguished magician at your disposal, one who can summon an impenetrable fog to hide and protect you!" Here the white creature laughed, and I thought how flimsy and weak such a defense was. Even Ajax' face was clouded with momentary doubt. The Queen had known all along, and our greatest ally was merely an old man whose claim to power was making fog hide the entrance to the valley?

"You claim that she has known of our presence here all along, and yet she allows us to smuggle her slaves to safety? This is a strange act for a tyrant!" Ajax's voice was still strong, but it seemed to ring falsely. The kindly figure in white laughed again.

"Yes, this would be strange behavior for a tyrant! Indeed, a tyrant would have long ago crushed all resistance, and smashed these very mountains down before she allowed her 'slaves' to escape. But for a mother this is not strange behavior at all! For one who would comfort and love her children this can be easily explained. What mother does not grieve for her wayward son yet hopes and prays for his return? If seven times a child rebukes a mother, then seven times she will forgive. It is her maternal care that has shown such mercy and patience toward you, Ajax. Your great wisdom will no doubt have drawn this conclusion already! Surely you in your wisdom can see the difference between a mother and a tyrant? Thus she asks only for your homecoming, for your joyful embrace, that she may forgive and welcome you. Indeed, it is for this reason that she has sent us, to offer you a chance to redeem yourselves, to leave this wilderness and come down to the City of Rest, the City of Pleasant Dreams. In the city there is no want, no war, no hunger; there is brotherhood, and you will be cared for and nurtured like children. Only one token gesture she asks of you, only one small act of good will."

It was at this point that I noticed that while the first of these magnificent beings was speaking so eloquently, the other two were swaying back and forth in unison, like two pendulums. The room was warm, and I wondered suddenly if I might not be on the wrong side of things after all. Why would all these people have to hide in the mountains, like criminals? It sounded like Ajax and Pallas were kidnapping children and women and selling them into slavery across the desert. And the guards that they had killed at the gate when they "rescued me!" An act of murder and cowardice it seemed now. I looked at Ajax, and saw the face of a brutal, power-hungry man.

"What..." began Ajax, "what is the token gesture that would put us back in her favor? I do not want... I care nothing for her favor, but let us hear what you are offering."

His voice was hollow, and sounded harsh and weak in my ears. The Elder had not moved, and his head remained bowed. Pallas looked lost, as though he was not quite sure what was going on. All around the large chamber the people sat with happy expressions on their faces, and they leaned forward, eager to hear what these wise beings had to say. The Princess' face was covered, her head was bowed, and her hands were clasped over her head, as though she were in pain. Only Beow stood defiant and unwavering, his hard eyes never leaving the face of the beings in white. I was shocked when I saw him, for it seemed so out of character, so unlike him. He was a noble man, so why should he fix these wonderful beings with so ignoble a stare?

"A small token only, Ajax the Wise. In return for this favor the Queen wishes you to know that all will be forgiven." His voice was warm and reassuring, and I was filled with hope. "Forgiven," I thought. "He said that all would be forgiven!"

"Yes, the gracious Queen Lilith will forgive all the injury and sorrow that you have caused her, and will welcome you back with open arms. You will each be given an expansive home, and to each family will be given gold and silver, enough to live on for many generations. Even the most heinous crimes will not be held against you, Ajax and Pallas; including the death of the Queen's soldiers and servants, who died honorably in her service." His voice was like that of a loving father, gently rebuking a wayward son. While he stood speaking, turning slowly so that his words would be heard by all those present, the other two emissaries had now begun to dance, a slow swaying dance around the fire, each in opposite directions. Their white hair glowed in the firelight, and their brilliant raiment seemed to be soaked in moonlight, while their long arms swung majestically, tracing lines in the air with pointed nails. I was captivated. I wanted nothing more than to meet the Queen, whose beauty must be indescribable. Ajax stood with slumped shoulders, and he leaned heavily on his great sword, a sword red with the blood of innocents. His face was ashen and downcast.

"What," he asked, so softly that I could barely hear him. "What is the gesture that would earn us her favor?"

The emissary, who seemed to possess the beauty of an angel, smiled again.

"Only this, Ajax the wise: there is someone among you, a person who is of little consequence to you, but for whom the Queen has great love. All the Queen asks is that you hand this person over to us, that we may escort him back to his true home, in the maternal embrace of Lilith the Fair."

If this was all, I thought, then it is a small price to pay for safety and prosperity. Let us hand him over quickly, and then all our hopes and dreams would be realized, and we could live in peace comfort, with all our needs met by the beautiful mother, Queen Lilith.

"Yes," he continued, "we will leave with him in our care, and you can all follow after, bringing your possessions and your children, and you will be escorted with dignity and honor befitting those whom the Queen loves. Rejoice therefore, and do not let your hearts be downcast! Only hand over him whom we seek, and all will be well."

"Whom do you seek, you leprous deceiver?" The tone of the voice was shocking, hard and strong; I looked up and saw that it was Beow who spoke. For a moment there was a shift in the atmosphere, as though a window had been thrown open on a stuffy room, letting in a cool breeze. But the dancing continued, faster now, the fire blazed higher, and yet not brighter, and the angelic speaker laughed.

"Such animosity from so noble a soul, Beow! Listen, then, and I will tell you whom we seek." The dancers were moving even quicker, in their strange, undulating manner, and the fire seemed to burn faster and faster. The speaker stepped forward, closer now, and his sightless eyes seemed to be an infinite pool of love and affection. I had to catch myself, for it seemed that I might stumble and fall into those eyes, and drown. The dancers now were spinning wildly, their white robes billowing, and I thought in that instant that they looked like falling stars. Closer now the speaker stepped.

"He is the boy you kidnapped on the meadow near the front door of the City of Peace, Beow, when you killed the men sent to find the lost lad and bring him home. Yes, the strange little boy who sits there now, next to the wise old Elder: Thaddeus Michael!"

Like a shock of cold water I was gripped with an inexplicable fear. These noble men meant to bring me back to the wonderful Queen, where I would live in peace and harmony, like I used to before I ran away from her. *Ran away? When did I run away?* My mind moved slowly, as if I were struggling to wake from a deep sleep, and I tried to remember something that seemed important, but no matter how I tried I could not place it. The speaker was even nearer, halfway between me and the fire, his sightless eyes never looking away from me. I was strangely torn, wanting both to leap up and run to him, and also wanting to escape, to escape those clear, hollow eyes, to wake up and get out of this fog. I did not want to drown. A deep panic was welling

226

up inside me, and I could not quite understand why. The cave seemed to be alive with beauty and dancing, the angelic beings leaping and gyrating in fits of ecstatic joy; or else they were demons being driven mad, frothing at the mouth and clawing themselves to death in a ghastly act of self-sacrifice. It was as though I were watching two different scenes simultaneously, one wonderful and the other terrifying. But I could not understand why, or which was a dream, and which real. The cave now seemed to be swimming with chaos, and either the dancers were spinning too fast to be seen as anything other than a blur of light, or my head was spinning and all I could focus on were the two bottomless pools of fatherly love and affection; or were they empty pools of hate, bottomless because they were nothing, only a privation eating and consuming every drop of human affection and charity? Nearer now came the speaker.

"Do not fear, Thaddeus, only trust in the Queen; trust also in us. Rise and take my hand." The white hand was extended, and its long nails looked like razors; I was afraid that I would be cut. I began to rise…

In that instant there fell upon my ears the sound of a quiet laughter, like clear water across smooth stones, softly, but the sound began to grow and to fill the room, and a breeze that brought the scent of roses on a spring day, and the room seemed to stop spinning, and to slow down. And then I looked and saw that the Princess had raised her head, and at her smile my mind cleared, and I could see again. Then the Elder raised his head and spoke.

"Yes, it is enough; reveal yourselves now."

There was an audible crack, like glass shattering, and the dancers stopped their ghastly spinning, stumbling to a halt. The speaking terror stopped his advance suddenly, as if he had hit a wall. Ajax stood taller, raising his slumped shoulders, and all the people seemed to be waking from sleep, rubbing their eyes and looking around. Only Beow stood unchanged and unmoved. I looked without fear at the face of the white creature, and I no longer desired to go with it to certain death at the hands of the Queen. It was hate that

227

was rising up from the endless depths of those sightless eyes.

And then, as I looked into its eyes, the clarity became cloudy and dark, and the smile on the fiends face was fixed and frozen, like a wax statue. Its white hair hung long and straight, falling in front of its face, so that I looked through the strands like through matted cobwebs. Its long fingers were bent into claws that hung down below its knees, and I saw with horror that its nails were growing, extending like living spikes to ferocious claws two feet in length. I looked back up at the face, and saw that it was turning its head to the left, its sightless eyes now dark and cold, and I thought that it was going to speak, but it kept turning slowly, slowly, until it had faced completely around, like the head of an owl. I sat too stunned to move or cry out, looking at the back of the fiend's head, though its body faced toward me, and suddenly I saw through the thin white hair what looked like two burning coals of fire.

It was like watching something in a dream, something that could not possibly be real yet casts a pall of terror so dense that one lays shaking in bed for hours even after waking up.

The other two emissaries were undergoing the same transformation, and I could see their frozen wax faces with their dead eyes staring out even though their backs were to me, and their nails had grown like crooked white spikes. For a moment the whole room was silent, sitting stunned at the horrible change; and then one of the emissaries moved, his white robe billowing like a shroud unraveled, and he stabbed his pitchfork nails through the chest of a standing guard, turning and flinging him into the fire. The fire exploded in a burst of spark and cinder, and I looked again at the creature nearest me. His white hair parted, and I saw that the coals were two flaming eyes, and below these a mouth stretched open on the back of the creature's head-teeth and foam. With a scream of hatred that rent the air of the cavern like a sheet it leapt at me, a white star leaping from hell, framed with fire and ash.

228

In that same instant Ajax moved also, sweeping his great sword up with both hands he cut across the arms of the moving demon, cutting both hands off at the wrist and sending them flying across the room like ghastly pieces of cordwood. Ajax never stopped moving, and he spun through the stroke, turning completely around and falling to one knee, his sword spinning with him, and with force of violence he hewed the creature in mid stride, felling him to the dirt floor. The fiend collapsed like a pile of broken sticks and dirty sheets, rolling forward till he came to a stop at my feet. The burning eyes on the back of its head still glowed for a moment more, looking through the tangle of cobwebbed hair and into my eyes with hatred so vile that it still comes back in my nightmares to this day. And then it died.

Ajax had never stopped moving, but leapt over his dead foe and to Beow's aid. Beow had deflected the attack on the Princess, and was locked in a furious hand-to-hand battle, his face bleeding from a great gash torn by those terrible claws. Again and again Beow stabbed it with his knife, but the screaming white creature struggled still. Pallas had moved as quickly as Ajax, and his sword ran the creature through the chest before Ajax had reached them, freeing Beow from the death-grip of the fiend. At least a dozen bolts from the warriors in the room had felled the third creature, knocking it back into the fire just as he was leaping at the guard by the door. Its body rolled off the fire and lay burning on the floor, a fallen star, and the stench was terrible. The battle had lasted only an instant.

~

"Dr. Bryant is, I think I have already said, quite brilliant. Not, assuredly, in the manner of his colleagues. No, his brilliance is of a different kind, a kind that I am hard pressed to explain following the common course of reasoning. A mystical brilliance, perhaps? But what is 'mystical'? A meaningless word, one that is weighted with all manner of religious and fantastical baggage... No, I will not call him mystical. But what then? And how do I explain what I saw? I will try, nonetheless. If my explanation lacks clarity, it is because of the nature of the phenomena that I am trying to explain, and hopefully not a deficit of imagination or a paltry vocabulary. First of all, Dr. Bryant insisted, as you know, that there exist other worlds, worlds that a person could find, if he knew where to look. Indeed, he insisted also that there were those among us, that is, there were persons (or beings) who walked the face of our very own Earth who were not, actually, citizens of this world. I know that at this point you might possibly ignore whatever else I might have to say, and if you do, I will hardly blame you. And surely there are those, based on his published work, and the constant themes of his lectures, who would love to strip Dr. Bryant of his academic credentials, and throw him from the hallowed University grounds. But I know him, you see, and I know that these wild claims did not stem from a compromised reason. Moreover, as I will relate, I myself saw something that I cannot explain, but could be explained by his theory. Dr. Bryant had insisted that he himself knew someone from another world. Yes, and I myself met this person. He was quite old, and wore a beard of remarkable proportion, but looked in every respect like one of us. He was working with Dr. Bryant, apparently, on the 'other worlds' project. Dr. Bryant claimed that there were some worlds open, and some closed. Open, that is, to us. We could enter, if we found the door. He wanted to open the closed worlds, so that he could visit these as well, if he could likewise find the door. His aged helper thought it unwise to try. Whatever the case, and whatever they may or may not have discovered, the helper was possessed of remarkable gifts. I call them 'gifts,' quite aware of the religious connotation that such a description naturally assumes. Call them 'abilities' if you wish. But, I swear to you, this

230

gentleman was hardly substantially different than the whole network of natural phenomena. He was able somehow to direct the elements of nature, seemingly at will. I know how this sounds; I see it written on the page before me. But I cannot imagine another way of describing what I saw. Once, when the weather was too severe to conduct some experiment that Dr. Bryant had been planning, this gentleman merely suggested we step outside again, and behold! The storm had subsided, and the sun shone. At his merest word! And when we walked through the park, I watched as the grass seemed to rejoice at his step, and to spring forward in anticipation. The very trees bent toward him as he walked, bowing before him in honor, and the flowers bloomed at his touch. I became accustomed to walk behind Dr. Bryant and his helper (I never knew his name; he was always referred to by Dr. Bryant as 'my helper') as they walked and discussed their ideas, just to watch the earth come to life around him. This helper was only with us for a short time, several weeks at most, but it was during this time that I began to believe what Dr. Bryant was trying to teach me. And yet, how my young mind rebelled at what I saw, and what he taught! You understand, I know, for you, like me, will only accept empirical proofs. We are not swayed by elusive moral dogmas, or by appeals to authority, or to 'beauty' or 'love'. No, we are made of sterner stuff. And yet, how do I explain what I saw? Perhaps I was deluded, insane. Or enchanted. I do not know. And, indeed, there is more. This same helper was only with us, as I have said, for some few weeks. Where did he go after this, you may ask? Or where did he come from in the first place? From the sky, he came from the sky. Do not laugh. I can hear your laughter even through this page. I did not see him come, to be sure, but I saw him go. Huge white clouds were in the distance as we walked in the countryside one day, and Dr. Bryant turned to me and asked me to stay here, near the edge of the wood, while they continued on over the hill. I said I would stay, but then proceeded to follow when they were out of sight. At the crest of the hill I watched from behind some foliage as Dr. Bryant shook the helper's hand, and then the aged gentleman began to walk away. And as he walked, the great clouds in the distance rushed down, and the gentleman walked up into them like up stairs, and the white clouds wrapped

231

themselves around him, as though welcoming him home, and he disappeared. The clouds lifted once again into the sky, and then dissipated over the vast space. The man was gone. Like the prophet of old, in the sacred Jewish texts, he was gone. Dr. Bryant seemed completely unconcerned with what he saw. It was after this that I began to take a special interest in Dr. Bryant's theories. My universe of possibilities had, in that instant, become indefinitely expanded. Even religion, or a supernatural element fundamental to realty, the suggestion of which I have until now considered anathema, did not seem so fantastic."

~Excerpted from *The Collected Correspondence of Fabian Smith, 1790-1846*, Barron Hardgrove Publishing, 1890. Jonathan Fair, the Chair of the Divinity Department of Cromwell University, 1830-1840, wrote the letter in question, dated March of 1812 (four years before earning his Doctorate in Natural Philosophy), to Dr. Fabian Pierce, the noted atheist of the Paris University. Fair, who himself was radically opposed to any suggestion of supernatural phenomena, especially any religious explanation of reality, took a dramatic turn soon after this letter was written. He became an adamant proponent of his mentor's, Dr. Bryant's, 'other worlds' theories, and became actively involved in the seeking of these worlds, and in trying to find other persons who might be aliens among us, like the 'gentleman' or 'helper' mentioned in the letter. Dr. Bryant vanished during an expedition to a remote corner of Northern Africa in 1818. Dr. Fair likewise disappeared under mysterious circumstances in 1841.

Chapter XIII

*"Deep calls to deep at the roar of your cataracts; all your breakers
and your waves have swept over me."*
~Psalm 42:6-8

All three of the emissaries lay dead on the floor, and the warriors all stood shaken and dismayed. The warrior who had been stabbed through the chest was dead. Women and children were crying, and voices were shouting. More warriors appeared at the entrance, attracted by the sounds of violence. It took some time for order to be restored. I sat shaking uncontrollably, feeling ill and somehow violated, as though a corridor of my mind had been breached by a thief. Asher moved up next to me, and I saw that he too was shaking, and I think he had been crying. He did not speak. Several of the men took the bodies of the foes out to be burned, while the body of the fallen warrior was carefully wrapped, and removed with dignity for a warrior's burial. Ajax called for quiet and peace.

"What is done is done," he said, his voice once again strong and commanding. "And we have avoided what could have been a much greater calamity. We have been reminded again of the power that the Queen wields. Let us now hear what the Elder has to say and heed his counsel."

The Elder stood slowly at these words, leaning heavily on his staff, and spoke.

"Yes, power the Queen wields. I was wrong to let it

233

go on for so long, wrong to let you all feel the web of deceit that she is able to cast. I knew what they were, even through their disguises, but I did not think that they would attack after they were exposed. These were banshees, emissaries of death, having crept into this world long ago, at the dawn of time, and given over to wickedness. The Queen is more desperate than I imagined. Perhaps if I had disallowed the façade, our brave warrior would still be alive..." His voice trailed away for a moment.

"Elder," the voice of the Princess was a soft mountain lily, swaying in a cool breeze. "What might have been is not our purview. We must act now in light of what is." It was the first time that I had heard her speak.

"Yes, my Princess, you are right. Now we must act. The intention of the Queen is exposed, and now we know how desperate she is to capture young Thaddeus." He looked at me with keen eyes. "What is it about this boy that she finds so valuable, I wonder?"

"Yes," said Ajax, "and why did she send the emissaries at all, and not her armies? I do not understand her action."

"Do you not, Lord Ajax?" answered the Elder. "Do you not see how desperate she is to secure Thaddeus? She merely wanted to get Thaddeus out before her armies razed and burned this valley, killing at last all those who still fight against her. The emissaries lied; she knew nothing of this place until recently. Indeed, it was probably the Searcher, hard on Thaddeus' trail, that alerted her to our whereabouts." His voice began to rise as he spoke. "What we have long feared has come upon us; life in this valley is over. The armies of the Queen are surely at our gates. We must activate the plans that we have laid, and quickly."

"The day we have long feared has come upon us then," Ajax responded. "So be it. It is our generation that must fight this battle, and it is good that we do not leave it for our children, and their children. But I grieve for what must befall our kinsmen in the City of Dark Dreams, now that we have been discovered and this valley falls in ashes and flame."

He turned to all those who were assembled. "All of you know what part you are to play in this conflict; go now and prepare. Darkness will fall soon."

The people began to leave in an orderly manner, but many of the women and children were crying, and the faces of the men were ashen. Ajax addressed the warriors who were assembled. "You all know your duty; this hour will be your greatest, when you are privileged to lay down your life for those you have sworn to protect. The innocent and the weak find in you their salvation; go now and die well."

With hardened faces the warriors left. Beow spoke now:

"Will all our plans be put into effect, even in the city? We are not ready…"

"That cannot be helped," the Elder responded. "For good or ill we must act now. Time has run out. It may be that this is our final stand, and all that is good in this land will finally be blotted out. We must, with full force, move against the Queen, and hope that it will not be in vain. Let us go now and direct the defense."

The Elder moved with creaking joints and slow step out of the cave, and the others followed. Not knowing what else to do, Asher and I followed behind.

"What are you going to do, Thaddeus?" Asher whispered as we walked down the corridor. "The Queen wants to capture you, and the Searcher is also after you. Where will you go now?"

"I don't know," I responded. "I don't really know why she is after me. I mean, I guess because I am trying to get the Book back. But I can't see why she wants to kill me so badly. My chances of even getting close to the Book, or to Jacoben, if he has it still, are very slim. I don't know what danger I really am to her."

"So what the Elder said about that Book is true?" Asked Asher excitedly. "You are the Bellator, the protector of the Book?"

I hesitated a moment.

235

"Yes, I am the protector of the Book. I don't know about being the Bellator, and I don't have any special power or skill, like my grandfather had. But it is my responsibility now that he is dead. So I guess that I have to try to get into the city still, and then see if I can find Jacoben."

We walked out of the tunnel and on to the plateau. The weather had changed, and what had been a beautiful, sunny day in the mountains had turned to a dark, dismal gray, as though a great storm was brewing. Dark clouds were looming high into the air, billowing and rising like dark castles in the sky. The wind was cold, and the chill was the chill of night.

The Elder led the way to the edge of the plateau overlooking the valley, his tattered robes flowing in the wind. Down below we could see the lines of people as they were descending into the valley. There was a frenzy of activity down below, with warriors rushing down to the entrance of the valley, and others leading animals from the stables, or procuring arms from the hall.

"It is time for me to do my duty, and to lead the defense of the valley," Pallas said. "I hope that we will meet again on the other side of this dark hour. Thaddeus," he turned now and spoke to me. "I pray that you are able to succeed in your quest. For your sake and for ours."

He turned and headed down into the valley, followed by three of his warriors.

"Now, Ajax, our plans must be modified," the voice of the Elder cracked as he spoke. "We must decide now what our young Thaddeus is to do. His options and ours are limited; either he can flee with the people, Asher, and the Princess, led by you, or he can go now with Beow, and be smuggled into the city. Thaddeus, what will you do?"

"I...I think that I must continue my quest. Is there any hope in the city?" A great sorrow was in my heart. I felt like I was trapped, and could only choose a lesser evil.

"Hope there may be, but it is small. It is most likely that you will die in the city, or fall into the hands of our

236

enemies, which would be much worse than death. The Necromancer has been in the service of the Queen for some years now, and I think that you will find that his power in the city, so close to the Queen, will be greater than it was in your world. But you will have Beow with you, at least until you are inside the city. After that he will not be able to help you. There is another path that he must travel. And the Searcher will find you; especially in the City of Dark Dreams, the Searcher will find you. But it may be that we are able to throw him off the scent and buy you some time. The other option for you would be to go with Asher and Ajax and the rest of the people. They are even now leaving by the secret, treacherous paths through the mountains and into the endless desert, in search of the City of Lights in the East. That way lies safety, at least for now. The Queen has never been able to find the hidden path across the desert, and so the City of Lights remains a safe haven, even today. You could remain in that city, and perhaps return to your quest when you are older and stronger. In the interim it may be that the strength of the Queen will wane."

He paused for a moment before continuing. "Or the Queen will have used the Book to her advantage, and all the worlds will have slid into the void. Who can tell? It is a difficult decision to make, and I think that there is no obvious answer. Death and destruction may follow whatever path you take."

The wind was blowing stronger now, and I felt the chill through my tweed jacket. Ajax stood some paces away from us, and was in deep discussion with the Princess and one of the warriors. Beow was watching the valley intently, and Asher was sitting on a rock, shivering. The atmosphere was oppressive. It looked as though a violent storm was about to break over the valley, and a feeling of doom hung in the air like a thick tapestry. What was I to do? I felt that I needed to continue my journey and try to rescue the Book. But was I being foolish? How could I succeed when even great warriors might not? The thought of journeying on in the company of Asher and the Princess was like thinking about a warm spring day. To go on an adventure where success was likely, and the reward was the City of Lights, was certainly more desirable than almost certain failure and death in the City of Dark Dreams. But though I longed to escape with Asher and Ajax, I knew that I could not. I had come too far to turn back.

Ajax returned with the Princess at his side.

"It is completed. We now have only to act and hope. Our steeds are waiting for us in the mountains, and the people are even now making their way along the plotted course. We must leave you here to fight and die. But even now I will trade my fate with Pallas or Beow, if only you give the word, Elder. I know we have long foreseen this day, and that I was chosen to lead the people on the journey to the City of Lights, but I cannot help but wish to stay and die with my brethren."

"Be that as it may, Ajax, you are the one who knows the paths across the desert, and you know all the dangers to be avoided. And if your people fall under attack on that journey, then you will have the honor of dying for them. Let Pallas die here, and Beow in the City. We must all face our own fate. And I do not think that Pallas will trade the defense of his valley for anything. He has long guarded it, and guarded it well. The day may come when you can return and fight along side both Pallas and Beow if all goes well. Go now and protect your people and the Princess. Indeed, it is she alone who could turn Beow's heart away from his path to the City of Dark Dreams. Go now and lead your people to safety."

Ajax bowed to the aged man, and then clasped Beow tightly. I just heard him whisper in his ear: "Protect that boy, Beow!"

Then Ajax turned to me. "Much is riding on your small shoulders, Thaddeus, Dragon Slayer. Let us hope that the blood of the Bellator runs in your veins indeed! Fare well."

He turned and rejoined the Princess and his comrade. Asher hugged me tightly, and tears were flowing freely from his dark green eyes. "Fare well, Thaddeus! I hope that you kill more dragons with your Krishnag knife. Maybe someday we will meet again."

"Fare well, Asher! Thank you for your friendship. It was too short a time to know you, and I think that we will meet again someday." He walked away, and it was all I could do to keep from making a spectacle of myself with tears. Loneliness gripped me as I watched him go.

The Princess stood some yards away, and her soft blue dress fluttered in the wind. Her piercing blue eyes met mine, and again I wondered at her beauty.

And then I heard her voice, though her mouth did not move and she made no sound, saying, "Be strong, Thaddeus; remember your home, and remember your heritage. Take care in the city, Thaddeus, take care that you do not lose yourself!"

And then they were gone, down the narrow path to the valley floor.

I stood shivering next to Beow, shaken at the sound of the princess' silent voice. The Elder looked at me with a strange expression. "What did you hear, Thaddeus? The voice of a kinsmen, perhaps? Many have stumbled unknowingly through hidden doors, and not you alone. What do you know of the Princess?"

"I know nothing, sir, except what was told me in the gathering. Who is the Princess, and why was she here?"

"I think that it is Beow the Just who can best answer those questions, Thaddeus. After all, it was he who treaded the narrow way to rescue her, when she was but a child."

I looked up at Beow, who was looking out across the valley, his eyes filled with sorrow and heaviness as though he had lived years in pain and torment. The dark clouds loomed up behind him, and the wind stirred his green cloak like the leaves of a willow tree.

"There are those, Thaddeus, who do evil for the sake of evil. There are those who exist only in shadow. Cerria

Sussana was stolen as a child, stolen away from home and family, and locked away in the Tower of Grief. A night many years ago I had a dream, a vision, and in it I saw a desolate path threading through a valley of shadow. On either side of the path was a great chasm, and clawing hands in the dark reached up to snatch any unfortunate traveler and pull him down into the darkness. On the far side of this valley stood a dark tower, a black pillar against a dead sun. High in this tower I heard a voice cry out, the voice of a little girl locked away. I heard her weeping, and heard her call for help. But at the base of the tower a shadow stood, and I knew that it held the key, and barred the way. I awoke from the vision, and I knew that I had to find that little girl. It took many years, many years of searching and of reading old tales that might illuminate my quest. Finally, with the help of the Elder, I was able to discover the place in my vision. It was a world long lost, that had fallen during the Great War, and now was under the sway of the Queen. She had sought those in other worlds who were a threat to her, or who had gifts that could be twisted to wicked ends, and then taken them in stealth and deceit from their home to hers. How many others she had stolen away and ruined thus, I could not say, but I think that Jacoben may be one such instance. But some also have sought her out, and sold themselves to her. In all of this, I believe she sought the Book that was in your family's care. I did not know that then, but I think now that it must be true. So I found a door into that world, and I walked the narrow path. The Gatekeeper I slew, and I broke down the black doors and carried the little girl out of that fallen world and into this land. But there is no safe place here, and only the City of Lights offers a true refuge. So Ajax ferried her in secret across the desert, and the Lord of that city adopted her as his daughter. Her unique gifts were in time revealed, and she has been a great help in our constant battle against the Queen. But I did not leave that place unscathed, for no one can go into a dead world, or even look into one, and not be pierced to the heart. That is all I will say."

All was silent on that plateau, except for the mournful sound of the cold wind as it swept over the stone. The dark clouds hung low in the sky, and a strange feeling of despair gripped me. This alien land had seen so much sorrow for so long, and I had brought more sorrow upon it. Maybe I should have let the Book go, and then this valley would still be safe, and Beow and the others could continue their efforts against the Queen. But if the Book had the power that it was purported to have, the end would have come soon enough. I realized suddenly that I was crying, and I saw in my mind the face of my grandfather, and of my mother and father. Why had this fallen to me, after so long? Why had the queen discovered my family's secret, kept so well for all these centuries? Now all was lost, and all the bravery and valor of Beow, Asher, Ajax and Pallas, and also my grandfather, and all those who had come before me as keepers of the Book would be forgotten, and the shadow would blot out all that is good.

"Sadness and regret, yes, Thaddeus. But nothing that is truly good will be lost. Even the bravery and honor of the warriors that time has forgotten, those whose graves lie unmarked and unremembered, and even the nobility of Beow, nothing is lost in the end. There are more powers in the worlds for good than for ill. Never forget that. But there are few laborers, few who work in the vineyards. We each must do our part, and we each must choose the good, and forsake the evil."

I looked up at the words of the Elder, jolted out of my thoughts by what could have been the voice of my father! The Elder was looking at me, his ancient eyes still keen. But before I could answer, a messenger ran up to us, one of the several who were posted on the plateau and in the valley.

"My Lords," he said to the Elder and Beow, "the attack has begun. I have word from Pallas that the enemy has crossed the water. We have choked the river with their dead, but they have pressed us to the crack in the wall. We have retreated into the pathway, and from there even one brave man can hold off an army. But Pallas has also reported that it is not only the Dark Men who are in the Queen's service; there are other creatures whose origins we cannot guess. They are vicious and violent, and all the Queen's army seems to have been driven into a frenzy. There is something else on the far side of the river, something that waits unseen, that compels them into certain death at our hands."

"Then we can only trust in the strength of Pallas and his warriors to keep them at bay until Ajax is far enough away. I hope that Ajax does not tarry." We could now see the last of the people, like grains of sand in the valley below, moving up the slope and disappearing into a fold of the mountains. The noise was growing louder.

The clouds that billowed above us were as black as night, and they seemed to blot out not only the light of the sun, but also to smother any hope that I might have held on to. The Elder sat on his rock, looking like a gnarled stump, clinging to the mountain for dear life against the storm. So weak he seemed that I wondered that he did not blow away in the cold wind.

"Is this a natural storm?" I asked, although I knew the answer.

"Not natural, no; in fact, very unnatural. This is the work of the Queen, or at least the work of her servants. She need not stoop to such petty sorcery herself, nor soil her hands with altered weather. Most likely it is the work of your nemesis, Thaddeus, the very one you followed through the doorway and into this land. Jacoben the Necromancer has been in her service for some time now, and is ever active in exposing our plans, and closing our secret routs out of the city. Indeed, it was he who captured and tortured one of our greatest allies and chief conspirators in the city, causing us great pain." The Elder stopped, and seemed deep in thought, his eyes watching the great billowing black clouds as they rolled and convulsed overhead.   We sat for some time in silence, watching the darkening storm.

242

It had been perhaps an hour since the first news of the battle had reached us, when another breathless messenger arrived, having run up the valley and the winding path to the top of the plateau.

"My Lords, the battle has already taken a devastating turn. We have kept the enemy at bay, and they could not breach the cleft in the stone. They suffered great casualties, while we suffered few. But they then retreated to the water, and behold, a hooded figure in brown approached the cleft, and though we loosed many arrows at him he remained unscathed. He raised his hand and spoke a word, and fire leapt forth from the air, and burned the cleft, turning the entire pathway into an inferno, and a tomb for all who were stationed therein. We retreated to the waterfall, and are now engaged in a vicious hand-to-hand battle to hold that bit of rock before the entrance to the valley. We have suffered many casualties, but Pallas fights still, and to him all of the warriors have rallied. But there is little time. The forces of the enemy are greater and more determined than we imagined."

Beow looked at the Elder, his face grave.

"Will Ajax be far enough away?"

"We can only hope so, Beow. But for now we must assume that they will be. You must ready yourself to leave."

Beow nodded, and left with the messenger down the path into the valley. He was followed by several of his warriors.

"Little time indeed," the Elder sighed. "Let it be enough."

The storm was darkening, and the cold wind cut deep.

We could no longer see any people in the valley, except for some warriors hastening to and fro on some errand for the battle, either securing weapons, or consulting with the older commanders who were orchestrating the defense from the Hall. But Ajax and the people had now disappeared into the mountains in the east.

243

Beow and his men returned a short time later, cloaked and hooded, and leading unicorns that had been smeared with dust and mud to disguise their bright white coats. The animals were led under the jutting rock near the entrance to the cave, and packs of provisions and weapons were strapped to some of them. I counted ten warriors including Beow, and ten steeds. Other than these, the Elder and I were alone on the plateau.

We sat silently for some time, watching the movement in the valley. I shivered against the cold wind, and the gloom from the dark clouds was suffocating. The Elder stirred suddenly, and turned to me.

"Perhaps I should give these back to you now, Thaddeus Dragon Slayer. You may need them before long."

He handed me a bundle from beneath his robe, which held my useless gun and my knife. I secured the knife beneath my jacket, and put the gun in my pocket. The small bag of gold was also there, and I put that in my inside breast pocket. I wondered if I would have the opportunity to use my knife before it was all over. All over. It might indeed be all over soon. Why did we not flee, like Ajax? Indeed, I was beginning to feel panicked and nervous up here. If the enemy was so close, why did we tarry?

As we watched the valley a sudden change came over it. There were suddenly warriors running fast towards the tunnel entrance to the valley, much movement along the water's edge. We could also see a messenger running hard up the path towards us. He reached us in only a few minutes, his breath coming in ragged gasps as he fought for air. Beow ran to our sides when he saw him arrive.

"My Lords," said the messenger, "the battle is very near the valley. We have sold every foot of the path dearly, and piled their dead in the stream. But they are like a dark wall, and no matter how many we kill there are more to take their place. Even Pallas the Brave cannot hold them much longer. He has sent word to make ready your escape, for the valley will soon be breached. As I left they were holding the cave entrance, only some yards from the valley. I will now

244

return to the fight, with your leave."

"Yes, return and tell Pallas that all is ready for our escape. He has done well."

The messenger left, running back down the path to the valley.

"We shall now see," said the Elder, "whether some of us shall live, or all of us shall die."

He arose from his seat and stepped to the edge of the cliff, looking down into the valley. I wondered for a moment if the cold wind would pick him up like a dry leaf and drop him to his death.

Then a sound reached our ears from below. It was the hard, cold noise of battle, the clash of steel and the cries of men relentlessly and mercilessly killing one another. We saw suddenly at the entrance to the valley a quick burst of movement as the defending warriors retreated from the cave and into the heart of the valley. My heart sank as I saw them fan out to defensive positions behind rocks and houses, for they were so few. Hardly a tenth of the original force, I thought, remained to fight. And it seemed a hopeless fight. The enemy poured out of the cave like a stream of living darkness, hardly pausing at the volley of bolts and arrows that met them. They seemed an inky flow of death, rolling over the banks of the river, an unstoppable tide of destruction. The warriors retreated further, falling back to yet another defensive position, and raining bolts and arrows into the enemy. Again and again they retreated and then fought, sometimes hand to hand, before again falling back. And each time they retreated they were fewer and fewer. As the enemy advanced they left a trail of destruction, the houses, barns, and fields, which had only hours before been the homes and livelihood of happy people, bursting into flame.

Fear was knotting in my throat as I watched this mad retreat, and saw the approaching doom. There were so few now, so few. Even Beow could not hold them off if they reached this plateau. I wondered again why we did not also flee and try to escape over the mountains like Ajax and the

Princess. But how could we run fast enough? Even with the lead that Ajax had, I knew that it would not be enough. They would all be caught and killed, just like we would be in a moment.

The whole valley seemed to be on fire now, burning with a fury of violence, and the dark flood was rising, encompassing the entire bowl. The desperate retreat had reached the Hall, and I could now make out the individual men who were now fighting for their very lives just to reach the pathway up to the plateau. The enemy was racing to encircle the Hall and cut off their retreat, and for a moment I thought that they had succeeded. The enemy soldiers were like the men who I had seen killed in front of the entrance to the City of Dark Dreams, men with black hair and black, lidless eyes. They had just closed the loop around the Hall, cutting off the path to the plateau, and the Hall burst into flame. My heart sank as he fire soared into the dark sky, thinking that Pallas had at last been killed.

"Fight, Pallas, Fight!" I heard Beow murmur.

I looked again at the battle, and behold, with a flash of steel I saw that three warriors were fighting still and had cut a hole at the narrowest point of the enemy line, breaking free and running towards the path. The enemy was right on their heels, and the three were engaged in a running battle, desperately trying to reach the path.

"Fire, now!" I heard in my ear, and I saw that all nine of Beow's men were lined on the edge of the cliff, bows and crossbows in hand, and at Beow's words they loosed a constant volley of arrows and bolts onto the heads of the enemy, loading and firing so rapidly that they might have been using modern repeating rifles. The line closest to the retreating warriors stumbled and fell, and the three reached the path, sprinting up it like all the diabolical hordes of hell were at their heels.

The volley from the plateau did not cease, and though the enemy scrambled to reach the last of the defenders, the path was too small, and the three pulled ahead. But as they did I saw one of them stumble and fall,

246

pierced from behind by several arrows. The enemy was shooting up at the remaining two, and also at us, but their reach was too short to hit the summit of the plateau. I saw them bounce off the wall some yards below us, or simply fall back down onto the shooters.

The last two warriors were almost to the top now, and I could see that one was Pallas. Hope momentarily flooded my heart as I saw him, but the hordes of dark men were gaining, and though the arrows of Beow's men thinned them out, the mass of darkness did not halt. All across the valley the dark men swarmed, and every building and field now burned with fury. There were other creatures among them, ape-like things with long, shaggy hair and thick fangs, that leaped and ran faster even than the dark men. These were now scaling the sides of the bowl, some trying to reach our plateau, and others seemingly searching for the hidden pathway that Ajax had used to escape. I could see the black eyes of the enemy now, so close were they as they raced up the trail. Pallas and the other finally scrambled up the last few yards, and fell over onto the plateau. But even as they did so, the warrior with Pallas jerked violently, staggered forward, his hands flying up to his throat that had been pierced by a black arrow, and fell onto the rocky surface of the plateau. Struck down so close to safety.

But what safety? The enemy would be on us in a minute more; ten warriors, an old man, and a child would be no match for them. Even as I thought this I saw that the warriors all retreated a few steps back from the edge, with Beow helping Pallas, while the Elder stepped forward to the very brink of the precipice.

He stood, looking out into valley, the place that only hours before had been the happy home of families and children. It was now a bowl of flame and ash, filled with evil men bent on destruction. It seemed as I watched him that even the mountains groaned, and longed to be rid of this filth. I almost imagined that the tips of the mountains in the east, across the valley, were swaying, shuddering, and even that they were crying. The streams that flowed from their tips into the valley, the silver veins of freshness and purity, seemed to be rushing faster now, as though the mountains were mourning the destruction of the valley, and hated the tread of the Dark Men on their roots.

The cold wind snatched at the cloak of the Elder, swirling it about him, and the dark clouds hung low, trying to smother the tiny, fragile old man. The clamor and cries of the enemy echoed up, but the old man stood calm, and raised his arms, his gnarled staff clutched tight. He looked out across the valley, not at the enemy below, but at the great weeping mountains rising in the east. He looked out, and then he spoke a word, a small word, softly, and at the word a calm spread through me, and I thought I saw the word like a dove drift across the valley, through the cold wind, piercing the chaos of sound and violence, under the black clouds rolling, and to the sorrowful mountains in the east.

The mountains heard the word, and understood.

They shuddered; I heard a crack like all the world had split in two, and the plateau swayed under my feet. The silver streams across the valley rushed stronger, and I saw a great slab of stone break free from the far cliffs, slowly, hang in the air for a moment, and then go crashing into the valley, vaulting off the side of the mountains with thunderous noise, and bursting below on the heads of the enemy. It was like a bomb exploding. I could feel the shock when it struck the bottom of the valley, and the Dark Men were crushed like roaches beneath it. I thought at first that the whole mass of those great mountains would tip and fall into the valley. But the baptism of the enemy would not be one of rock and stone alone. The mountains seemed to sway, to tremble, and then suddenly, with a heave of joy like a slave breaking free of his fetters, all the cataracts of the mountains burst forth and a torrent of water like a freight train, chill and foaming, came rushing down into the valley with unimaginable force, freed to clean and purify, to wash and renew all the filth and ash that choked the bowl.

It was as though all the oceans in all the world now rushed down with a fury of vengeance, and the Dark Men had no time to even run. They only saw their doom, and were engulfed. The relentless tide swept down the cliffs, across the valley floor, and into the cave entrance, taking with it every piece of debris and death that had invaded the valley, flushing it out through the cave and over the cliffs in the west. Such a roar and such a sight I have never seen, before or since. I thought that surely the waters would sweep across the plateau and we too would be lost to its power. The entire eastern side of the mountains was a deluge, and even as it destroyed, it purified. It swept around the valley like a bowl, catching even those who were below us on the pathway, and I saw fear in those black eyes as they disappeared into the foam. So much water that the cave was not enough to drain it away, and so it swirled about the mouth of the entrance, and then the bowl of the valley began to fill.

And still the mountains wept.

"Hurry now, or we shall join our enemies!" The Elder turned from the sight with a smile upon his aged face, and began to shuffle towards the overhang where the animals were tied.

We all turned, and as I did I stumbled over a stone and fell to one knee. The Elder stopped, and looking hard at me said, "What is that, Thaddeus Dragon Slayer? Another gift from a friend?"

I did not know what he meant. He reached forward and pointed to my neck where I realized the rope that held my key, my inheritance, had fallen out of my shirt. I quickly grabbed it and stuffed it back in as I arose.

"It's my inheritance, something that my father gave me."

The roar of the water was deafening, and I could feel the spray as it splashed over us. The bowl was now more than halfway full. The Elder grabbed my arm tightly.

"Thaddeus, could this be why the Queen is so desperate for you? The Book, Thaddeus, was the Book sealed?"

"Yes," I stammered, thinking quickly, "It was sealed in a metal box. I never actually saw the Book itself."

"This key, Thaddeus, your inheritance, I know this key. There are no locks made which it cannot open, but only it can open the box that holds the Book!"

I had no time to do more than register his words. Even as he spoke he was fading from my view as though dissipating, and I found that I was no longer standing on the plateau. I was lost in a fog of darkness, standing instead on a crooked path, with great stone statues of goats rising above me on either side. In front of me I could see only fog and the night. But behind me I could hear the tramp of boots, and the rattle of chains. The horned heads of the statues seemed to lean over me, and behind me in the distance I heard the howl of wolves. "I must hide," I told myself, and then I plunged ahead into the fog. I could see nothing but dark grey, and the sound of the chains was getting closer and closer. The howling wolves seemed to be just behind me, and I ran faster and faster through the mist. But it seemed that I was standing still, for the grey never receded, and the boots could be heard growing ever nearer. And then I heard in my head the voice, the voice that I dreaded more than anything. "Thaddeus, Thaddeus, how fast can you run, Thaddeus, how fast can you run? Can you outrun the Searcher?" In terror I plunged further and further through the fog, and it seemed to grow thicker and thicker, until it was like trying to run through a mountain of dirty cotton. I was finally caught in the fog, immobile, like a fly in honey, and somewhere ahead of me through the fog I could see two burning eyes, and behind me I could hear the wolves.

"Fly Thaddeus, fly!" I heard the voice of the Elder as though from far away, in a deep hole. "The enemy has found you!"

My vision came back, and I was staring at the stone floor of the plateau, lying face down. Strong arms grabbed me, pulling me to my feet, and I saw the face of Beow as he dragged me towards the cave. I staggered with him, as nausea gripped me, and I thought that the plateau was moving, rolling beneath my feet. Black arrows whipped by us and skittered across the stone floor. I turned as I ran looking out to the west where the plateau dropped away into thousands of feet of space. And there I saw a wonder.

Rising up out of the dark clouds, seemingly floating on the air, was a flat deck of metal, a wide stage suspended on nothing, and on it danced a horde of Dark Men, shooting arrows and bolts into the small band of warriors. But they were not alone on the deck. Standing unmoving on the edge were three massive creatures, like goblins from a fairy tale. Green and black scales for skin, taller than any man, tusks and fangs for teeth in their massive mouths, and in their clawed hands were gripped double bladed battle-axes.

Beow was rushing me away, half carrying me, for I had no strength of my own. I saw one of the warriors fall, pierced with arrows, and could see the others returning fire, and trying to keep the steeds from bolting with terror. I looked back as we ran, and saw that the Elder was facing the floating deck as it came closer and closer. The Elder raised his arms as arrows flicked around him, and spoke something in a quiet voice, a voice like a soft wind.

At his words the deck stopped moving, as though it had stalled, and the Elder moved his arms, raising them into the air. The deck tilted sideways, struggling, as though the unseen hands that held it aloft were losing strength. The Dark men at its edge lost their balance, and tumbled screaming over the edge and into the mist. They would fall a long time before they reached the bottom. It was as though the Elder was engaged in a duel with an unseen foe, whoever or whatever force was keeping the deck aloft. But the Elder was winning. The deck continued to tilt, rolling and lilting like a sinking ship, and then something gave, and it dropped like a stone into the emptiness below.

Yet, even as the deck fell, the three monsters leapt out into space, off the plummeting deck and onto the

251

plateau, as the cries of the Dark Men disappeared into the mist. The plateau cracked and shuddered as they landed on it, but one of the three's jump was too short. It struck the edge of the rock, grabbed wildly for a handhold, dropping its axe in desperation, and then it was gone, falling into the fog, a piece of broken rock still clutched in its claws.

The water had now risen so high that it lapped over the edge of the plateau, and still the mountains wept.

The goblins stood facing us for an instant, and the flowing water steamed around their scaled feet. The Elder stood between them and us, a candle against the night.

At that moment I thought I saw, swimming above the goblin's heads, swirling and spinning like a snake, a black cloud, twisting and rolling in feverish excitement. And in the cloud I could see two burning eyes. Then I heard the dreaded scratch, scratch at my mind's door, heard in my head the whispering voice, the voice that was possessed of two natures, saying, "Thaddeus, Thaddeus, will you see me now?" I think that I was flailing violently, convulsing as Beow tried to hold me and drag me towards the sheltered unicorns.

The Elder did not move, and all that stood between the monster in the smoke and me was the little wizened man. The goblin creatures held no fear for me, only the thing in the smoke, the thing I dared not see.

With wild roar the goblins raced forward, their huge barbed feet splashing in the flowing water, their axes high overhead. In a bound they would be on the Elder, hacking him apart, and then would be on to us. But as the goblins leapt forward, I saw a sudden flash like a spark on the wind, and Pallas the Brave leapt faster. His sword glowed with fury, and he intercepted the goblins, reaching the Elder first. The leading creature tore into Pallas instead, and all was foam and fangs as Pallas was hurled down, his body torn and gashed by the huge claws and double-edged axe. The beast flung him through the shallow water, and then leapt with axe raised and mouth open to devoir.

But Pallas the Brave had long protected this valley,

long given blood and sweat to its safety, long stayed the reach of evil. He had kept the Queen at bay for all these years, and protected the women and children from her white hand. He did not, then or now, suffer the shadow to creep uncontested, nor suffer his charge to die while he still lived. "The innocent and the weak find in you their salvation." Pallas hewed the great goblin to the ground, spilling its dark blood into the flowing water even as it mauled him, and together, light and darkness, they fell over the side of the cliff, swept away in the purifying stream.

We had reached the unicorns now, and the warriors were struggling to control them. They neighed and pawed the air with their hooves, and the men had to duck and avoid their savage horns. Beow was yelling something to his men, and the water was sweeping fast around our feet. The Elder still stood in the middle of the plateau. Beow had mounted his steed, and was hauling me up behind him, but I could not take my eyes off the swirling smoke above the last goblin, the cloud of darkness and burning eyes. Across the expanse of the plateau it watched me, and then the goblin began to advance. But the Elder barred the way.

The goblin wielded his battle-axe with two hands, and swung it down onto the waiting elder. The Elder met the axe with his upraised staff, but the staff cracked in two in a shower of sparks and splinters, and the blade of the axe struck the elder, knocking him backwards into the water.

The Elder fell backwards into the shallow water, his aged head striking the stone floor of the plateau, and I saw blood flowing through his white hair, a gash open on his forehead. He rose to a sitting position, blood and water flowing down his long ragged beard, and he looked back at us. His eyes met mine and I saw through them great forests of tall trees, mountain meadows and raging sea, cracked stone and fertile soil, birds racing and dawn breaking. Ages and ages I saw, and the night sky burning with a thousand golden stars, and then all the light of those stars burst forth from his fingertips and feet like molten gold, and flashed a halo around his bleeding head, brilliant flame, lighting the dark storm around us with shining radiance. With fiery hand he cupped some water, lifted it to his mouth and spoke a quiet word. The water heard him, knew who it was that spoke, and slid from his burning fingers to the stone floor, and the mountain heard the water and understood. The goblin stepped forward once more, but no further; the plateau gave away under it with a surge of jubilation, and water like chariots of white fire swept over it, consuming it, and the goblin disappeared in the deluge of stone and water pouring down the mountain.

The Elder leapt up as the waters broke loose, struck through with golden flame, and he ran lightly along its surface like on springy grass, and then he rose, through the spray and foam, up, up into clouds, the wind and storm lifting him, and he was gone.

The unicorns surged forward, the water sweeping them along, and I gripped tightly to Beow as they crested the edge of the disintegrating plateau and launched into space. For dear life I clung to Beow's cloak, and the unicorns spread their wings, the valley disappearing behind us. We were flying west through the clouds, towards the City of Dark Dreams.

And still the mountains wept.

Part III

The City

~

"There is a similar story of Nordic origin, the author notes, dating from the thirteenth century, in which a demon possesses a tree like Legion did the swine, and in this version we find that the paradigm has shifted, and although it may certainly be supposed that the concept of the 'living earth' is by no means done away with, it has been severely truncated. Not so much the primitive notion of beings who inhabit, or who, in fact, are the trees or the water or the rocks, have been put to sleep, as it were, or have been enchanted, but rather that there has taken place a certain respectful 'bowing out,' so to speak. If the Gods have entered the world, as in the Christian mythology, then it follows that the gods must be shouldered aside, leaving only demons and angels in the extra-human domain. There is no room for non-human, rational beings that do not readily fall into these categories. While Dr. Munson presents this popular interpretation faithfully, he assures the reader that he finds with it a certain coarseness, a crudeness which, he suggests, that quite possibly misstates the whole thing. A 'living' cosmos, Dr. Munson says, has room within its embrace for a variety of life, and found within these varieties are certain modes that do not readily give themselves to what he calls 'psychological impotence,' by which he apparently means an inadequately robust imagination. That there might have been 'spirits' in the trees and water, he says, hardly necessitates that a Christian cosmology is to blame for their demise. Rather, he suggests, (a quite fatuitous suggestion, as I argue further on) that a Christian cosmology actually embraces, at least implicitly, the notion that there could once have been elements to creation that we today call mythological. Only it was not God who killed the satyr and the nymph, but was rather 'sin,' or the prehistoric 'fall'... Man has killed, and God resurrects. God and religion restore the spirits, the mythological creatures, to their rightful places, neither as objects of worship nor of demonic origin, but rather as beings with their own mode and dignity, and their own work in the universe. Hereafter he launches into the most bizarre element of the work, in which he suggests a correlation between mythology and the vastness of the cosmos, bringing this notion to bear on his 'multiple worlds' hypotheses. Needless to say, the bulk of this latter portion of his work I find both incoherent and childish, and quite at odds with the modern scientific community."

Excerpted from the *London Review of Books*, 4th Issue, *Volume 7, 1909*. Dr. Ebenezer Sledge is reviewing the latest work of the noted Oxford Professor of Literature, Dr. James Munson, entitled *"More Things in Heaven and On Earth: Bridging the Gap between Anthropology, Mythology, and Religion."* Kepler & Sons, 1909.

Chapter XIV

"We have lingered in the chambers of the sea,
By sea-girls wreathed in seaweed red and brown
Till human voices wake us, and we drown."
~T.S. Eliot

Many are the experiences that those who travel in foreign lands may boast of, but who has felt the cold air of that alien world sweep over his face, or heard the beat of the wings of fantastic creatures thought to exist only in the strangest of tales as he winged through the dark night to rendezvous covertly with saboteurs and rebels in the City of Dark Dreams? But I, Thaddeus Michael, found myself in just those circumstances. My stomach churned at the height and the speed at which we flew, and my eyes still held tears of sorrow for the loss of all those warriors, the valley, and for the death of Pallas. But so great was my relief at our escape that I could have laughed with joy. My head still ached with the strange sickness that seemed to sweep over me whenever I heard that terrible voice speaking, or felt the scratching at my mind's door, and every muscle in my body was sore from the violent convulsing that had overtaken me. But we had escaped!

Escaped from certain death, and were now flying to almost certain death.

"Thaddeus, how do you fare?" Beow's voice came back to me on the wind, shaking me out of my thoughts.

"I am fine, I think... What happened back there? Is

the Elder alive?"

"I do not know, but I think that he still lives. He is very resilient, and has faced down worse enemies than those. And yet that was a near thing. Long have we planned for such a contingency, for an attack on the valley. We knew that it would not remain secret forever. And we were given three days to prepare, from the time that the emissaries arrived at the waters edge, till today. So desperate was the Queen to secure you that she was willing to give up her element of surprise. But we were surprised on the plateau. I had not foreseen an attack like that, and neither, I think, had the Elder. It could have gone much worse. Yet I grieve for Pallas. I had little hope that he or any of his men would survive the initial attack, and I rejoiced that he lived, and hoped that I would have him by my side in the city. Alas, we have lost a great friend."

"What of the black snake, in the smoke, above the heads of the goblins? What happened to it? It just disappeared with the goblins..."

"Smoke and snakes, Thaddeus? I saw neither smoke nor snakes, only the goblins. Was there something else on the plateau, something that only you saw?"

"You didn't see it? The smoke? It had red eyes, like the dragon statue... I don't know what it was. I heard it speak to me, again..."

He was silent for some time, and on we swept, through the dark clouds. Even darker now, for the night was drawing near. The ground was invisible to us, thousands of feet below through the fog and darkness. The chill of the height and the wind cut through my tweed jacket, and my hands were numb as they gripped the cloak of Beow. Before long the darkness was compete, and still we flew. I realized with a start that I had almost fallen asleep, and I had to fight to shake off the fatigue. The adventure of the long day was catching up to me. But to fall asleep would mean a long drop through the darkness and an ignoble end to my strange journey. Beow had felt me slip.

"Hold tight Thaddeus! You have come too far to fail

now."

It seemed that we flew for hours and hours through the darkness and clouds. It was all I could do to keep holding on, for my entire body ached and my hands hurt. Throughout the flight I could hear the beat of the other unicorn's wings, but I never saw them.

"We are nearing our destination Thaddeus," Beow's voice was a whisper carried back on the wind. "From here out we are in as much danger as we were on the cliff. We must be silent and careful."

"But what about the wall?" I whispered back. "Can we just fly over it?"

"That wall was built to keep people in, not to keep them out. But no, we cannot fly over it. We would be shot down in an instant. We must enter the city by one of our secret routes."

All was silent except for the beat of the unicorn's wings. I leaned my head out, looking around Beow to see if I could make out anything through the darkness. At first I could see nothing, but soon I began to make out something far ahead in the gloom. It looked as though there was a line of dark red fire burning in the night.

"What is it?" I whispered.

"They are expecting us. The news of our escape has surely reached them. The beacon lights have been lit, for they expect us to try to fly over the wall if we try to enter the city."

Closer and closer we drew to the wall, and it looked as though the entire rim of the great wall was aflame. I could see the dark red light reflected off the water of the river, and I thought that the river was even wider than I had remembered. It looked like a huge lake. I realized also that we were flying much lower, dropping down quickly till we were no more than one hundred feet above the ground. Before long we were over the water, and the wall towered high above us, the entire rim lit by the beacon fires. I suddenly heard a strange sound, like a high-pitched buzzing of some large insect flying by at high speed. Again

259

and again I heard it, and then actually felt something whip by us from the direction of the wall.

"They have seen us, they are shooting! Hang on!" I heard Beow's tense whisper, and then the unicorn swerved hard to the right. But I was not ready for the sudden movement, and with a cry I slid off the animal, my fingers wrenched from Beow's cloak, and I began to fall. I felt Beow grab for me, but it was too late, and I dropped like a stone through the darkness.

It was just like falling in a dream.

I watched the shadow of the unicorn disappear in the gloom above me, and could just see the firelight reflected off of Beow's panicked face, and then I was just falling. In dreams it is sometimes said that the dreamer will always wake up before he hits the bottom. For a brief moment I wondered if perhaps this was all just a long dream, and now I would wake up safe and sound in my own bed in my parents' house, and my grandfather would be alive, and the only journey that I would attempt would be to walk with my friends to school. Wake up, I told myself, just wake up… and then I struck the water.

The cold darkness knocked the breath out of me as though I had landed on stone, and it closed around me, an inky blanket, and down I sunk, down, down, down. My eyes were open, and above me the red fire reflected off the surface of the water. But deeper I sank, and then all was inky blackness wrapping around me, suffocating me, heavy and cold. And as I sank I despaired.

Farther I sank, and my lungs were screaming. Soon I would have to take a breath, to suck the inky black water into my lungs, and then I would die. I could bear it no more, I must draw that breath, the sterile breath that would be my last. And yet I could not; I had to hold on as long as I could, until my body drew the breath of its own accord. "Not yet, Thaddeus, not yet!" I told myself, "Do not bring death before its time, even a moment before." But I was slipping away, the blackness of the grave even darker than the dark water. All was shadow and haze, and as I began to leave this life I had the strange memory of one of my play-fellows relating something that he had heard, how dying people would see a light, the light of heaven maybe, a light at the end of a tunnel. Would I see that light? Did I see that light? Yes, I think I did, glowing and shimmering through the water. Through the water? But where was the tunnel? And there were other glowing shimmering lights down here, down in the deep. I was far-gone by now, my lungs all but exploding, but I saw something, something in the shimmering, glowing lights. Faces? Were these the faces of angels, perhaps, angels to carry me to my eternal rest? There were more of them now, and all the water was glowing, like the stars of heaven had fallen into the deep. The faces were beautiful, shining, clear as diamonds, and the sea-women angels were all around me. A hand that burned like fire was placed over my mouth, my lungs stopped aching, and my head began to clear.

The sea-women were wrapped in robes of flame, and their hair was silver fire, but liquid flame, and I could not say that they were not somehow the water itself. The burning hands of the fire-women bore me up, up from the deep. As I arose in the light the water was no longer cold, and new strength surged through me. I drew deep breaths, and the very light of the sun seemed to course through my veins. It seemed that we were not rising through dark water but were flying through the very firmament of the heavens, shooting stars in the night sky. And there were cities here, towers and castles of fiery silver and gold, ramparts and flags waving in the light of the stars. Behind us I saw, rank upon rank and file upon file, warriors following us through space, beautiful and terrible to behold, with burning swords in hand. I could hear them singing as they followed, and in their song I thought I heard my name. Faster we arose through the sky, through the water, and the heat in my veins burned till I was a ball of fire.

And then suddenly I was at the surface of the river gasping for air, and splashing around trying to stay afloat. The water around me was dark and cold, but I was hot, burning with a fever. I thought that I could just detect, somewhere far below me, lights, lights blinking in the deep, and then they were gone.

I tried to calm down as I tread water, but I was shaking and, although the water was cold, I was sweating. I kept blinking my eyes, for they felt...white. How shall I describe it? White like melted silver.

In the distance I could see the line of the wall, dark against the night sky, lined with the red beacons. With nothing else to do, I began to swim toward that wall.

Although I was shaking and feverish I seemed to possess strength far beyond my normal meager allotment. I could swim rapidly and I did not tire. I did not allow myself to think what else might be swimming in that dark water, but only to think of the shining light. It was a long way to the shore, and the wall loomed higher and higher.

Finally I dragged myself out of the water and onto the muddy bank. There was a thin, steep strip of land between the water and the wall, enough for two or three men to walk abreast. It was rocky and muddy, and what foliage did grow was coarse and thorny. I thought it wise to try to remain concealed as best I could among the ragged bushes. I was thankful now for the beacon lights, for they cast a dull red glow off the water and I was able to see this little bit of my surroundings.

I sat huddled for some time at the edge of the water, behind the bushes. My head ached with fever, and the cold water that still soaked my clothes did not cool me. My eyes were burning, and I thought that it might be due to the filth in the water, but I could not be sure. Around me on the mud and the plants a faint glow lingered, but I could not place its origin. It was not the sickly red glow from the top of the wall, far overhead. It was a glow like milky moonlight glancing off storm clouds in the night.

What had happened? As I sat in the mud I tried to remember, tried to understand. Had I been dreaming? Had I, in my shock and fear, imagined those underwater beings, and somehow dragged myself ashore without any aid? I

262

could not be sure. But I still had my knife, my key, my empty pistol, and even my little bag of gold, safe and secure beneath my jacket. So I had swum to shore not only fully clothed, but also with the weight of these objects pulling me down... Perhaps there had been no imagining.

As I sat shaking it suddenly occurred to me that I was again in trouble. So disturbed and confused by the water-women was I that I had forgotten that I had lost my guides and protection. But in the moment that my situation came into my consciousness, there was a sudden movement quite close, and a muddy stone nearby spoke in an awed whisper: "Thaddeus? You live! Silently now, over here!"

I had forgotten how well Beow and his men could move silently and unseen. The stone was one of the eight warriors who had escaped with us from the valley. He moved closer as I scrambled towards him, and he threw a dark cloak over me.

"Thaddeus, we thought that you had died. Here, you are shaking. What happened to you, Dragon Slayer? Not now, don't tell me now. We must hurry and join the others. We have been searching for hours after your fall. We must get off the bank before daylight. This was my last sweep of the embankment... I only just saw you from a distance, and turned back. You... you look strange, Thaddeus. Don't speak now, let us hurry."

He spoke thus, quickly and in a hoarse whisper. His voice sounded strange, and I felt like I was burning up under the cloak. We made our way silently, and, as I was moving too slow and stumbling over the muddy ground, he picked me up and carried me the final distance till we met the others. They were congregated at a jumble of stones near a spot where the embankment all but disappeared, and the cold water lapped up against the mass of the wall. The red glow from some immense distance above could still be seen on the water, but it also seemed that there was more light in the sky, the natural light of the dawning sun, just beginning to rise. There were dark clouds in the sky, and a murky fog. In that light I could just see the faces of the warriors, and

263

that of Beow. They stared strangely at me, as though they had never before seen me.

"Here he is, my Lord," whispered the warrior who had found me. "He was sitting by the water, on my fourth pass. I was finally returning when I saw him from a distance…"

"Well done, Caleb. Thaddeus, I am overjoyed to see you. I thought that we had lost you forever. But you survived somehow! Quickly now, we must leave this place. We will be found soon if we tarry. Our brave steeds have flown north, along the wall, to act as a diversion. What time they bought for us may already be over."

Silently and almost invisibly the warriors moved over the boulders and slid into the water by the wall.

"Here Thaddeus," Beow grabbed my arm, and lifted me over the stones. "We must swim now. But we cannot linger in the foul water. There are other creatures that swim in these waters, and they will sense our presence if we are too slow. I thought that your fate had been… Well, I thought that they might have already found you. Can you swim? Well, of course you can! Good, and you must hold your breath for some time. When we go under, hold on to my cloak and do not let go. You will see a light when we come up on the other side. Are you ready to enter the city?"

With those words we dove silently into the dark water, and though I could feel the cold, my body was still warm. We swam some way, and the water was dense with muck and grime. Something like slimy seaweed brushed against my neck, and we had to make our way through a submerged grove of rotten trees that stood out above the water some few feet, looking like the heads of grotesque sea monsters. During that swim I tried to think of the golden sea women, but somehow I could not quite picture them, and wondered again if I had imagined them. Surely they would not live in this awful water. Away in the distance, out toward the deep, we heard a splash.

"Quickly, Thaddeus, we are falling behind!" I heard the urgency in Beow's voice. There was another splash, this

264

time closer, and a small wave washed against my face. Beow was swimming faster now, and was not so concerned with noise. Ahead I could just see the others, and then one by one they reached a spot on the wall and dove under. I glanced out to our right, away from the wall, and away in the gloom I thought I just saw the gnarled tip of another submerged log. And then it disappeared, leaving only a spreading ring of ripples. I opened my mouth to call to Beow, and gagged on the filthy water that sloshed in.

"Here Thaddeus, this is the place. You will have to swim faster than you have ever swum before. Take a breath and follow me!"

He dove under, and as I took a breath to follow I saw out of the corner of my eye a rush of water only a few yards away, and then I dove.

I kicked madly down into the murky darkness, clinging with one hand to Beow's cloak, fear giving me strength. I opened my eyes but saw nothing but murk and gloom, and the filthy water burned my eyes. I could feel the bulk of the wall before us, but then we were moving through a narrow tunnel, with slick, slimy walls, all around us. My lungs were bursting, and I was kicking wildly, trying to get through. Finally we were pushing through a broken grate, and up, up towards the surface. We came up gasping for air, and I could see light ahead. I kept splashing wildly, trying to swim as fast as I could, but Beow grabbed my arm to steady me.

"Calm yourself, Thaddeus! They cannot follow us through that narrow entrance, and we do not want to attract anything that might be on this side. Follow me, we are nearly there." Ahead I could see a bobbing light, and as we moved closer I saw that it was the light of a lantern. The flickering orange glow illumined a large canal, and a cavernous ceiling above us. It was some kind of underground drainage canal, perhaps, and I could see the warriors ahead of us as they climbed out on a flight of stone steps. There were huge, rusty rings in the wall, as though boats had at one time been moored here. All was covered in

265

moss and slime; the air was leaden, and stank of filthy water. We finally reached the steps and crawled out. I was shaking with exhaustion and fear, and even Beow's face seemed ashen and wary in the light of the lantern.

This was held by an old woman who stood on the landing at the top of the stairs. She was hunched and dressed in miserable rags, her face drawn and withered, and in the dancing lantern light she looked like a witch. But her eyes were the same as the others, almond shaped and green.

"Here at last?" Her old voice was cracked and grey. "And so few? You have come to wage war on the queen with only nine and a small boy?" She laughed a squealing, choking laugh. "And this boy? Who is he?"

"Greetings, Stephania," said Beow. "Yes, only we ten. I count Thaddeus among the warriors. We were delayed, and I am glad that you remained here past the appointed time to meet us. Indeed, I almost expected that we would have no welcome down here. How do things fare above? Is all going as planned?"

The old wraith laughed again. "No, mighty Beow, Beow the Brave. No, things do not fare well, nor are any plans being addressed. We live miserably when we live at all, and in the last few days more have died than live. And the dreams grow always worse... We were expecting more than nine, and I do not count children among warriors, and nor will the others. What of the valley? What of mighty Ajax? How is it that you are alone, and why have you tarried? If I am caught down here I will be sent to the dungeon, or to the halls of the Necromancer. And yet here I am. Surely I have not waited in vain?"

The warriors did indeed look exactly as though they had just passed through horrific danger and poisonous water, dripping wet and fatigued. There faces were covered in mud and grime, and they did not look at all like the formidable warriors that I had known only the day before in the valley. Only the day before? It seemed like an eternity. I could only imagine what I looked like. My sopping hood had been hanging over my eyes, and I pulled it back at that

266

moment, uncovering my face. My eyes still felt hot, and I rubbed them to clear away the remains of the river. When I took my hands away, I was startled to see that everyone was staring at me.

"What…" began Stephania. And then she stopped and looked at Beow. The lantern light played over Beow's strong face, and he looked at me as though he had seen a wonder. Then he stepped toward me and pulled my hood back over my head.

"I do," he said, speaking to Stephania in a strong voice, "consider this boy among the warriors. Stephania, this is Thaddeus Micheal, the Dragon Slayer. And if I consider him to be a friend and an ally, then you may be confident that he is. But let us leave from here. We are already late, and we still have a long way to go. Lead us out, Stephania."

The old woman was clearly shaken, and, after one more look at me, turned and led the way over the stone landing to another flight of stairs, and then up again. As we moved to follow, Beow leaned his head down to me and spoke:

"Keep your head covered for now, Thaddeus. I do not know what has happened to you, but you will have time shortly to tell me. Only keep your face from sight, especially when we are above. And speak only to me."

We moved on, through a deep tunnel, and then more stairs, and further through what was a labyrinth of more tunnels and more stairs. Some of the stairs led up, some down, but all the while we were making a steady progress upward.

"We are now below the wall, Thaddeus," Beow told me as we walked. "It is huge, a mass of confusing doors and tunnels, and even our enemy cannot guard every entrance and exit, especially now as she grows weaker. The drain that we swam through is one of many that lead to the river on this side, and, far away, to the west, they lead to the sea. Over the centuries we have discovered many such entrances, and also had many closed up. Sometimes we have lost allies to the guards and watchers, sometimes to the monsters in the river, and some have just disappeared down here, lost forever in this maze. There are many doors down here that should not be opened, and many rooms that should not be entered."

"That is not all, Beow," Stephania had overheard what Beow was telling me. "Do not leave out the most exciting part. There are entrances down here to the Underworld, and an unwary explorer can easily explore too deep." She cackled loudly at this. "Down, down in the Underworld there are the worms. Yes, the worms will find any unwary traveler! Twisting like roots below us now, down, deep down in the Underworld, there are worms."

There were indeed many rooms and passageways that we did not enter, and many doors that we did not open. Some were old metal doors, with strange writing painted on, and some were rotting wooden doors, decrepit and decayed. There were vast chambers that we walked through, some with drainage ditches running through them, and some with huge pieces of strange, intricate machinery, larger than a battleship, filling the expanse of the room, but rusted and silent now. I wondered what the purpose of those machines had been.

We passed one tunnel that looked like an old road, built for wagons or motorcars of some sort, leading down into the darkness, and over the entrance to it was a rusted gate, thick and formidable. But the gate was bent and almost broken, but bent forward, as though some unfortunate soul had tried to escape out from the other side. Our path led up some stairs along side it, and up away. I could feel the air from that road, cold, dead, and earthy.

"Down there, down there, good sirs," cackled the old woman. "There is one entrance to the underworld. I hope the gate holds!" She laughed again.

We had been walking for maybe two hours when the surroundings began to change. The hallways and tunnels began to show signs of use, and were not so old and decrepit. Occasionally, high overhead, light would show

268

through vents or grates. We moved more cautiously now, and Stephania snuffed the lantern out. It was still dark and stuffy, but there was enough natural light to walk by. We finally came to a narrow tunnel leading off to our right, and at the end of this a small metal door. Stephania listened intently at this for some time, and then cautiously opened the door and peered out. Convinced that we were safe, she impatiently waved us through and into a long corridor. One end of the corridor disappeared around a bend some yards away, but the other entered what appeared to be a covered bridge, one that had grated windows spaced along both sides. This we entered, and through the windows I could see that the bridge spanned a large canal, whose sides rose up another forty or fifty feet above the bridge. It was light outside, and it must have been six or seven in the morning. The small bit of the sky that could be seen was grey and dismal, but it was nice to escape the musty confines of the tunnels below the wall.

At the far end of the bridge was another closed door, but we did not open it. We stopped instead at the last window, and Stephania pushed the grate open. It swung up, being hinged at the top. "Hurry now," she whispered. "We do not want to get caught here, do we brave warriors?"

One by one the warriors pushed through the small opening, with Beow and I following last. The window opened over the canal, and it was a fearful drop down. I could see the dark water below, and it was moving fast. But along the wall ran a narrow ledge, just wide enough for a man to stand on, provided he kept his back to the wall. Along this treacherous path we traversed, and it was a very uncomfortable walk. I kept my back pressed against the wall, and did not dare to look down. Beow stayed very close, one hand ready to catch me if I should stumble. I think that my fall from the unicorn was still fresh in his mind.

The canal curved away from the bridge, and it was soon out of site. Soon after we stopped, and the warriors ahead scrambled up what looked like a homemade rope

269

ladder, coarse and frayed, maybe thirty feet high. It hung down from a small hole in the wall where a stone had been dislodged. This was also a treacherous climb, and I was glad to finally scramble through the opening, scraping my knees on the broken stone, and then into what looked like an animal stall in a barn. The floor was covered in rotting straw, and it stank of filthy animals. The tall sides of the stall were wooden, and had tattered bits of tack and rope hanging from hooks. Stephania crawled through the opening last, and then pulled up the rope ladder and covered the opening with some pieces of lumber. The ladder she rolled up and tucked under a brick in the corner. Then she opened the door of the stall, and peered out into the gloom. "Come now, all is safe." Then she swung the door wide and we stepped out into the barn, for barn it was.

Only it was not a country barn. It was rather a working barn in the city, full of animals and all the smells that are associated with such living arrangements, even when properly cleaned and maintained. But this one was not properly maintained, and certainly not clean. Muck and old straw littered the stone floor, and small creatures resembling chickens or pheasants wandered freely. Cattle-like animals with large humped backs were in other stalls, as many as five or six to a stall, cramped and uncomfortable. But the noise of the animals and even the smell was somehow comforting to me. It seemed somehow less strange and foreboding than what I had experienced in the last day or so.

Stephania shuffled up to the wide entrance while we stayed back in the shadows. I could see a small wagon at the entrance, piled with sacks and full of tools. A little old man hobbled out of one of the stalls near the entrance and consulted quietly with Stephania for a minute, and then they waved us forward.

"Quickly now, up on the wagon. You are laborers bound for the construction near the weapons factory. Grillig here will take you as far as the meeting place, and then you can rest, and we will meet at the appointed time tomorrow.

If you make it through the city safely..." She cackled as she spoke. "There are more Dark Men in the burrows now, and there are rumors of the attack on the valley going around. But Grillig will take care of you. He is also a warrior, like you my lords. Or maybe more like the child?" She cackled again, and Grillig motioned us up onto the wagon. He was a small, withered old man, dressed in rags and smelling like the stable. One of his eyes was gone, and around the empty socket were scars, as though his eye had been burned out with a poker. But he smiled warmly, and proved a much more friendly and hospitable guide than Stephania.

The cart was pulled by two shaggy beasts like oxen, only with great tusks that were cut off halfway and wrapped with cloth. I settled comfortably on the cart between Beow and Caleb, grateful for the rest. Beow spoke a word of thanks to Stephania, and then the cart lurched forward, and we left the stable and entered the busy street.

The great city, the City of Dreams... I had waited a long time to finally see it. And what a strange sight it was. And even though I was completely exhausted, I could not help but try to take in all that there was to see.

There were people everywhere, moving to and fro on errands of some kind, and carts like ours clogged the narrow street. The streets were stone, and branched off in all directions like a labyrinth and the clatter of hooves and iron wheels echoed loudly off of them and the sides of the buildings that arose on either side. These buildings looked like a giant child had haphazardly stacked up building blocks, trying to see how high and lopsided he could make them without a collapse. I thought for sure that the whole city would come toppling down at any moment. It was a mass of confusing balconies, windows, stairs and walkways. All the buildings looked as though they never had been quite completed before some new project came up, and the first abandoned. And any and all material was good enough for the job, not only stone and brick, but wood, bits of metal, and broken pieces of old wagons, or unfinished trees. Rickety and ramshackle were the most apt descriptions, I thought. Behind us for the first hour of the trip could be seen the mass of the wall towering in the distance. It cast a great shadow in the morning, in spite of the dense smog.

On the street level were shops of various kinds, with bins of grains, foul looking fish, and carcasses of strange animals hanging from hooks. But everything looked decrepit and poverty stricken, the buildings in shambles and various stages of neglect, the street unclean, and the people dressed in filthy rags. The air was stifling, so polluted and filthy it was. A dense, gritty smoke clung to everything. The sky was brown and orange, the sun barely able to pierce the gloom, and my lungs burned after inhaling my first breath. I remembered seeing, from the plain outside the gate, the smoking clouds and smog that hung over the city. It was every bit as polluted as it looked from the plain.

It was, in spite of the horrible air, an amazing ride that morning. We wound our way through that incredible place, and the shock of the noise, the smells, and the sights lives vividly in my memory. Most of the people who were on the streets were of the same race as Beow and the people of the valley, but there were other peoples here who bore little resemblance. Some looked almost like gophers or moles, with large noses and bulging, glassy eyes, whose sparse hair was black and coarse. They were very short, stocky, and pale skinned, and had large rugged hands whose seven fingers came to bony points at the end. There were strange animals among the crowd as well, some caged, some led by ropes, and some chained. I saw a lizard as large as a crocodile but with six legs and a short head covered in mossy hair of a sickly purple color. This was kept in a cage and carried on a cart. I wondered where it was going.

There were many such strange animals in the city. Rounding one bend we entered a wide plaza full of caged animals, each more marvelous than the next. Indeed, there was even a creature the size of an elephant, but that looked more like a mammoth, held in place with massive chains bolted to the stone pavement. All the animals looked wretched and starving, and some were obviously dead. But

272

the saddest sight of all was that of a captured unicorn, emaciated and filthy, with his wings clipped and his elegant horn hacked off, leaving only a raw stump. His sad eyes were still intelligent, and they caught mine as we passed.

But the strangest thing that I saw on that morning ride was a huddled beggar, one of the many who sat beside the road even more degraded and wretched than the caged animals. This one was lame, his lifeless legs splayed awkwardly in front of him, and each of his fingers on the hand that he held up for alms was cut off at the first knuckle. But it was his eyes that caught my attention. They were pale blue, neither almond shaped nor oversized, but exactly like any Englishman's might be. It was as though I was suddenly transported back to England for an instant, and he was just another beggar outside the train depot. Where had he come from, and how did he end up in this city? I watched him until he was lost in the crowd behind us.

We occasionally passed a group of the Dark Men, three or four, on patrol or simply out to torment the people. The first time this happened I cowered in fear, but Beow whispered into my ear not to be afraid, and to keep my head down. They would take no notice of another cartload of workers headed for some project for the Queen. Indeed, they passed by without even looking in our direction. Once, however, there was an entire line of them, twenty or more, moving quickly and pushing aside the poor people with rough shouts and foul language. The leaders had whips with which to lash those who were too slow to move out of their way. Among this troop were some goblin creatures, similar to the ones who had attacked us on the plateau and killed Pallas, their bodies covered with green and black scales, and their cavernous mouths full of huge fangs. Only these were much smaller than the ones on the plateau, and their heads were far too big for their squat bodies. The people on the street fled to the edges of the road and huddled into the entrance of shops and alleys at the sight of these creatures. Our wagon could not get over quick

273

enough, and the running monsters passed right by us, so close that I could have reached my hand out and touched them. But they took no notice of us, except to curse us in their foul tongue.

The further into the city that we traveled, the more the architecture changed. Although still decrepit and ramshackle, there were more buildings that at least aspired to beauty and to greatness. More were built with stone, and fewer with discarded trash. They too towered up into the dark sky, but looked like they had more of a chance to stay upright, and not go toppling into the crowded streets at any moment. Some looked like they were houses once belonging to wealthy people, with high white walls surrounding courtyards and fountains long since gone dry.

The morning soon turned into a warm, muggy afternoon, and still we jogged on. As we rode, Beow would occasionally tell me about the city, and also about our destination. "We are now going to a safe-house, a home and shop of one of our closest allies. We will be met there tonight by all of the counsel, the group of patriots who lead the rebellion. There you will hear many things, and many questions that you have will be answered. There we will seek advice concerning your own quest."

The city, he told me, was divided into the old and new sections. The older areas stretched away west towards the sea and the Alabaster Castle. Nearest the wall was considered the New City; new, and yet ages old. The newer the area, the more decrepit and poor it was. The older the area, the more advanced architecturally, the more beautiful; and the more empty. Beow described to me the movement of the peoples through the years, after the Queen had risen in power, and after her betrayal of the King. The Great War had devastated much of the city, and the Queen had rebuilt it, using the people here as slave labor. But other things came to live in the city, invited by the Queen, and the old section was abandoned. "The 'Dead City,' it is now called. There are none of our people in the Dead City, Thaddeus," said Beow, "but it is not uninhabited. Indeed, the halls of the

274

Necromancer are in the Dead City, and there are spirits who walk among the silent buildings, they say, the spirits of the dead kings. And there are things worse than spirits..."

The main division was a large canal that split the city along a north-south axis. The main bulk of the New City was along the east side of the canal, including most of the barracks of the Dark Men. "Few venture past that canal. Even the Dark Men do not cross over, unless they have been summoned," said Beow. "The only ones living on that side are the Messengers, and other servants of the Queen who are unfortunate enough to serve in the Alabaster Castle."

In the New City people fared as best they could. All worked in some way at the bidding of the Queen and her ministers who orchestrated the imposed tasks upon the people. There were enormous factories, filled with machinery, smoke, and fire, some for manufacturing weapons, and some for armored wagons and other instruments of war. In these even children were made to work, day in and day out, and more died than grew old. There were mines also, and these were even more wretched and dangerous than the factories. Built right in the city, they belched out toxic fumes and dust, and many laborers died in their depths. But it was dangerous, said Beow, not only because of the terrible conditions, but also because of the depths to which they were forced to tunnel. "Too far they tunneled, and they broke through the crust of the Underworld. Many of the miners do not come back up into the light. The worms find them."

But it was not all these tortures, as terrible as they were, that caused the most suffering. There were the dreams...

The dreams had begun, Beow told me, long ago, drifting down on the city at night, slipping into the minds of the sleepers like serpents. Darkness, he said, the dreams were of darkness. The wretched inhabitants dreaded sleep, and when night finally came, they longed to wake up. They did not want to see what met them in their dreams, night after night. The dreams affected people differently, with

275

some driven nearly insane, and others bearing up resolutely. But across the canal, in the Dead City, they were worse. Indeed, it was the dreams themselves that drove the people ever further east, until the wall was built. The dreams were used by the Queen to control and manipulate her slaves. Those who more readily gave themselves to her were spared, and the intensity of the dreams was diminished, it was said. But for those who resisted, the dreams became more and more vivid, and the nights longer. Most people existed in a state of numb obedience, neither resisting the Queen nor betraying their own. But it was more and more difficult to hold out against the dreams, even for the most determined. It was even worse for the children.

"I do not know how they will affect you, Thaddeus. The dreams do come to me when I am in the city, but they cause me no fear, nor do I dread sleep. But that is not so with others. Even Caleb here tries not to sleep when in the city." His words left me sick, and I thought of my dreams outside the city. I wondered if I could bear dreams even more vivid. What if I finally saw it, the thing in the darkness? I knew that I would be lost.

It was late in the afternoon and still the wagon rattled forward. I suddenly realized with a start and a chill that I was beginning to nod off, despite all that Beow had told me, when old Grillig spoke: "Look there, masters," he croaked. "There, ahead in the sky." We looked, and saw in the distance, rising above the city skyline, a massive pillar of black smoke. It was monstrous in size, and billowed and rolled into the sky like an angry ocean of filth.

"That is the chemical factory, masters. It is where the latest devices and artistry of the Necromancer are built and perfected. Bless me, I am glad that I am just an old stable hand. Poor souls condemned to work in that bit of hell..." Grillig's voice trailed away in a shudder, and I could now see the smokestacks and the mass of buildings that made up the factory, a grim skyline like jagged black teeth, belching flame and ash into the choked air. As the wagon rolled closer the city around us became even more drab and dreary than I had previously seen. There were many people in the crowd, perhaps returning from work in that factory, whose clothes were blackened, and whose faces were covered in grime. Not only dirty, but also hollow and glassy, like people who have seen terrible things about which they dared not speak.

Here it was even more difficult to breathe, and a layer of soot covered all the buildings, and soon covered all our clothes as well. The factory cast a shadow of darkness onto the surrounding city, not only literally but also in the mood and the manner of the people. While the whole city was somber and depressed, here the people seemed stricken also with dread, and all had a look in their eye like they were holding back panic which at any moment might burst out in any number of manifestations. Indeed, the closer we got to that dark place, the more erratic behavior I noticed in the passerby. Occasionally we saw people simply huddled on the ground sobbing, or talking in loud, agitated voices to themselves. One woman, her clothes covered in soot and grime, her hair thin and wretched, just stood by the corner and screamed- short, shrill screams- and my stomach turned at the sight and sound. But the most heart-wrenching sight of all was that of little children, my age and younger, walking chained together in a line toward the factory. They were all crying. The older ones were trying to comfort the younger ones, and though their own faces were streaked with tears, I could see that they were trying to be brave for the younger children. The smallest of these wailed the loudest, his little voice cracking and choking on the foul air. All the people around turned their eyes away, and hurried along to their own business, not wanting to share in the suffering of those children. The children were being led, not by one of the dark men, but by one of Beow's own race. But his green, almond shaped eyes were hard and desperate, and I knew then that not all of these people were our allies.

"The closer we get to the Dead City, and the closer to the work of the Necromancer, the worse the dreams." Beow was whispering to me as we passed them. "These poor souls spend their nights in vivid darkness, and their days in this hell. No one can be well here. It is not surprising that some consider a respite from the suffering more valuable than their souls. Not surprising, but no less despicable."

We abruptly turned a corner, and the line of children vanished from sight. I can't say that I was displeased. There is only so much sadness that a human heart can bear, and I was at a breaking point. How could Beow, Ajax, and the others fight such a hopeless battle? How many had they rescued from this place over the ages? Thousands or even tens of thousands, maybe? And yet here in this wretched city were millions, perhaps, and many willing to sell children into slavery to preserve their own lives. How could anyone hope to win this war? I thought how foolish we would look if our little band was uncovered. Nine men and a little boy, sneaking along, full of intrigues and secret plans. So impotent, so weak and hopeless we seemed now. And I was so tired…

I was jolted out of my thoughts a few minutes later when the wagon turned down a narrow alleyway, and stopped abruptly in front of small café. Beow grabbed my arm, and we hopped down onto the muddy pavement. We stepped through the narrow door and into a room with a few stools and benches, and some tables and chairs. At the back was a bar with a few bottles of some grey liquid, and to the left of this, another door. A giant of a man wielding a short ax stood next to the door, and he waved us through. We went through the door and then up several creaking flights of stairs and onto a crooked landing from which branched several doors and hallways. A woman greeted us here, and led us down one of the hallways, and then into a wide room with high ceilings, several dirty couches and tables, and a huge, open window that led out onto a balcony. She drew the dusty curtains to the window closed, spoke something to Beow, and then she was gone. "Here Thaddeus," said Beow. "Now you can finally get what rest this place will offer, if only for a few hours. Lie on one of these couches and I will call you when it is time to eat. Soon

278

after we will meet with the counsel, and then we may have little time left for rest or food."

I lay down on the nearest couch, wrapped my cloak around me, and thought briefly that my fear of the dreams would keep me awake; then I was asleep.

~

Cassandra, Cassandra, how far you have roamed,
From city, from family, from land and from home.
You've tarried too long, forlorn and alone,
Beneath rock, beneath dirt, beneath clay and cracked stone,
Too long you have dreamed, too long in the night,
Too long you have suffered, too long do you fight.
I heard it, last night, while I walked in the wood,
I heard your name whispered, I stopped and I stood:
"Cassandra, Cassandra," the trees swayed and spun,
"Cassandra, Cassandra, your time was not done."
"Claw your way back, strike back from the dirt,
Cassandra come back, and forgive us the hurt."
But you did not answer, the moon stood above,
Cassandra, Cassandra, I'll find you, my love.
I'll travel to you, to where darkness is woven
I'll find my true love, who darkness has stolen.
Into the dark and into the dreams,
I'll go into the terror, the night, and the screams.
So I said, so I thought, but I never went.
For against the dark dreams, even true love is spent.
Against the Dreamweaver true love cannot hold,
Against the Dreamweaver, not even the bold.
So all of my promises I did not keep,
And nothing was left but to lie down and weep.

~Excerpted from *The Nightmare of Percephilous*, circa
1300AD, translated from the original Latin by Dr. Byron
Fairmont, 1818

Chapter XV

"…We have more ways than one of sacrificing to the rebel angels."
~The Confessions of Saint Augustine

My eyes opened some time later to find that night had fallen.

"Thaddeus," I heard Beow whisper, "it is time to wake up. The hour is late, and we have much work to do."

I sat up, disoriented and still very tired, and could now make out the outline of the large window, and felt the mugginess of the air. It took me a moment to remember where I was.

"In a few minutes we will go join the others in counsel, and I need you to tell me what happened to you after you fell into the river. Even now your eyes are burning. But first, did you dream? I wondered if I should wake you up periodically, so the dreams would not take hold."

The memory came back to me, but it was vague and muddled, and I thought that I had somehow been a stranger and a trespasser in my own sleep. All I could remember was darkness, and that far away. It had left me somehow with a sickly feeling. But I thought that maybe there had been something out there, something in the darkness that was

281

surprised that I was there, that I had stepped into its domain. I had the feeling, however, that, whatever or whoever it was, it couldn't quite see me…

"I did dream, but saw only darkness, as though from a distance."

"Good. That is what I had hoped. The maker of the dreams has not yet found you. Sometimes children in the city can go several years before the dreams really take hold. But tell me: how came you by this transformation? Even now your eyes burn."

Confused as I was, I had no idea what he was talking about. "My eyes?" I asked. "What do you mean they are burning?"

"Look," he answered, and held up to my face a small mirror. I looked into it, and saw reflected back white light, an intense silver glare off the glass. I thought for a moment that a lantern was behind me, distorting the face of the mirror, but I then realized with a shock that it was my own face that I saw, and my own eyes glowing silver, reflected off the glass. I stared for a moment, unsure what exactly I was seeing. How strange I looked, almost fearsome, and I remembered my grandfather's eyes before he had been killed. I handed the mirror back to Beow, shaken and disturbed.

"What is the matter with me, Beow?" I asked. "I don't understand what has happened."

"Tell me the tale, Thaddeus, and perhaps we can decipher this mystery."

And so I relayed to him what had happened to me in the water, as best as I could. It was not easy. I was not sure that it all was not a dream (so many visions I had experienced since arriving at my grandfather's house). But at the end of my story, Beow spoke thus:

"Thaddeus, this is indeed good news. I have not heard such a tale for many ages, and to think that it would be now, in our greatest hour of need, that such a thing has come to pass. What you saw in the river can only mean one thing. It must be as the Elder told us, that the water is

282

awakening, and then perhaps the stars and even the earth. After all these ages, this is unheard of. And you, Thaddeus Dragon Slayer, you have awakened them. How this can be, I do not know. But there is something in you, Thaddeus, some gift of which you are unaware, and perhaps the water recognized it. You awakened the water as the Elder awakened the mountains. Somehow your gift has been revealed, and in the awakening the water your own awakening has begun. The Elder said that he discerned that there was something about you, something hidden. How else can we explain all that has befallen you, and the desire of our enemies to secure you? What else it means I do not know. But we must take heart, and believe that this is a most fortunate sign, a most fortunate turn of events. What shall become of it, or if there is more to be revealed, I cannot tell. But take heart."

I could tell he was smiling, even in the gloom, and he pulled my hood back over my face.

"Keep your face covered, for now at least. We will go and join the counsel, and there you will hear many things, and perhaps we can find a way to further you quest. But take heed. There are very good and brave men among the counsel, courageous souls who have suffered much for our cause. But there are also those who have wavered over the course of our long struggle, and we have rumors of spies among us. Take care to listen closely, and not to speak or uncover your face until I tell you to. Do you understand?"

I told him I did, and followed him through the door and into the crooked hallway. Then down the hallway, and up several more winding flights of stairs, and then to a large double door. In front of this stood the formidable looking man with the axe from the night before. A very small lamp burned next to the door, making him seem even more imposing and menacing than usual. He nodded at Beow, and swung the door open.

Into a large, round room we stepped. It was lit only by a huge window at the far end, by the dim, sad light of the sleeping city. Out this window I could see in the distance the teeth-like outline of the Necromancer's factory, and the fire from the smokestacks burned red. Even against the dark sky, through which no star was ever seen, the belching smoke was blacker. And far, far in the distance, barely discernable was a line of pinpoint red lights, stretching away to the right and the left. That must be the wall, I thought.

Around the edge of the dusty room were seated men and women, old and young, and in the dim light I could not make out their faces. But I did notice some of Beow's men standing along the back of the wall, as well as several other armed guards. Beow's men were recognizable by their cloaks and hoods, and their presence here was a comfort. There were two chairs in front of us, facing the window, pushed out a little from the edge of the circle. In these Beow and I sat. And then the counsel began.

The whole room was silent for a moment, and I could feel all the eyes on us. I pulled my hood lower, and slumped in my chair. At the far end of the room, directly across from us, a figure rose to speak. I could not see his face at all, because of the dim light from behind him, but when he spoke I knew he must have been very old.

"Welcome, friends, to our final counsel. Welcome Beow, and all those who have traveled in stealth from the far mountains. And welcome, stranger, the young boy they call the Dragon Slayer. Whither you have traveled, I do not know, but you travel now under the protection of the mighty Beow, and that is enough for me, even if there are others who would not be so charitable and trusting. Too often have our dearest secrets been betrayed by those we called friends, and our trust has cost us many lives. But," and here his old, shrill voice rose, "Beow is beyond reproach. Therefore we will suffer this boy in our midst."

He spoke with a certain finality, and I realized that my presence here was tolerated, but that I was not truly welcome.

"And," he continued, "it will matter little after tonight whether he is truly a friend or foe. If a friend, he will surely die with the rest of us. And if foe, he will die just the same. We have come to the end of our long war, the war fought by our fathers and their fathers before them. This is the final battle. And little hope remains for victory."

My eyes were becoming adjusted to the dim light, and I could now make out the faces of those surrounding us. There were maybe twenty-five people seated, and ten more standing. All the faces looked worn, tired, and even frightened. They were all thin, emaciated, malnourished, like all the faces that I had seen in this City. So unlike the faces in the valley, and yet, I remembered, those in the valley sometimes wore haunted expressions that revealed their narrow escape. There were a few younger men present, but most were old, and there were several women among the group. The women were old, and looked frightful in the strange light. Not all the faces were severe or unkind, but there were more looks of suspicion and distrust than not. As the counsel progressed, I thought that most of them did not even trust one-another. The speaker continued:

"Beow, since your last visit here we have lost many more allies. Indeed, the number of those who are openly loyal to us has diminished to almost nothing. We have no good news for you, though I see that you hoped there would be some comfort. Most of the inhabitants of this foul city only know of our little group by hearsay and rumor. And most remember us as legends and wives' tales, told them when they were children, in the days when our resistance was more formidable. If any discovers that our group still exists, and still works to overthrow the tyrant in the Alabaster Castle, they hurry to betray and reveal us, hoping for some reward, or some diminution of suffering. And yet we do not let up our constant intrigues and sabotage. But we find there is little hope. And if, as our spies have warned us, it is true that the valley has fallen, and Pallas has been killed, then we shall despair. With our own eyes we saw the hordes of dark men march through the city, seven days ago, and leave through the gate. Dark men and other vile creatures, all armed for war and lusting for blood.

285

Thousands upon thousands there were, and it seemed that all the filth and rot that the Queen keeps in this wretched city had been disgorged. But they never returned, and we heard nothing else. This gave us some hope, for we thought that Pallas and Ajax had eluded them yet again, and perhaps beaten them in open battle. But only this morning has word reached us that some agents of the Queen entered the City, and with them news of Pallas' death, and the destruction of the valley. Speak to us, Beow, and I hope that you have some words of comfort. For how can we continue with our final plan if what we have heard has come about?"

With that, the old man sat down. All eyes turned to us, and Beow rose to speak.

"My fellow conspirators," he began, "it is true what you have heard. The valley has been razed, and Pallas killed."

The faces in the room blanched, and several cried out as if in pain. One old woman spat on the ground and looked away. But Beow continued:

"There is even worse news. The Searcher has been released, after all these years, and he hunts Thaddeus. But we also have reason to hope, and indeed, more reason than we have ever had, in our lifetimes. It is also true that this will be our last stand, and so we must not allow any defeat to dull our resolve. Now is the moment of climax, when all our work either burns like chaff, or flowers like wheat. Listen to me, and I shall tell you what has happened, and why I think even more that now is the best, and last, opportunity for honor that we shall ever have." Beow's strong voice told quickly the story of the last few weeks, from finding me on the plane, to the battle in the cave and in the valley, and finally of our desperate escape off the plateau. But, I noticed, he did not explain my quest to them, and made no mention of the Book.

"And so, my friends," he said, "in the midst of tragedy, we find that still a light of hope burns strong. We killed many of our enemies at the valley, more, I think, of the Queen's army in one day than all the years of our long

286

struggle combined. Her whole strength she expended in one desperate attempt to secure Thaddeus, and, she hoped, to finally destroy our resistance. She failed on both accounts. And in our escape, more of the strange story of Thaddeus Michael has been revealed. Listen, my friends, to what has befallen this child: in our flight over the river Thaddeus lost his balance, and fell into the water. I thought that he must surely have died, either in the fall, or drowned, or pulled under by one of the tentacled creatures that make our entrances into the city so treacherous. But behold, Thaddeus survived all these dangers. We found him, finally, several hours later, on the embankment, alive and well, but with a strange transformation, and an even stranger tale. Deep in the river, Thaddeus said, he opened his eyes to see castles and people, the Women of the Water, awake once again, after all these ages. They saved him, and followed him to the surface, arrayed for battle and singing his name. Thaddeus awakened the water. How can this be, I asked myself? Who is Thaddeus that the Queen fears him, and the water awakens at his most desperate moment of need? But I said that he was transformed by his encounter; behold, the face of a miracle."

With those words Beow turned to me and whispered to me to stand, and throw off my hood. I had heard his words as he spoke, but they seemed to come from far away. At his whisper I looked up, and it seemed as though the room was smaller, and the faces looked at me as though they were looking into a window. I was inside, and they were out. I stood then, and threw off my hood, and the room was lit suddenly by a flash of silver light, and the faces turned away at the sight, as though blinded. They cried out in fear, and then the light faded, and my eyes felt like molten fire. I stood for a moment more looking around the room. The faces stared back at me, confounded and amazed. Then I pulled the hood back over my face, and sat down. No sound was heard in that room.

Finally, Beow spoke again. "So you see, we do have hope, though of what nature I cannot tell."

"You cannot tell, Beow?" The voice was that of an old woman, the one who had spit on the floor. She was hunchbacked and frail, her face pinched and withered, she cackled loudly. "I am much older than you, and I have heard the tales of old. This boy who carries the weapons of kings, who counts among his friends the last of the Bright Ones, and who's eyes glow with the silver flame, I can tell you who he is." Her voice was growing louder as she spoke, and she rose from her seat, her watery eyes wide and wild. "Why are you here, Bellator, and why do you come into this world? Where is your prize? You have not lost it, have you, oh mighty warrior? Your prize is still safe, is it not? But, oh, if it is not safe? What then? Will Beow still speak of hope if you have lost it? You have lost it, you have lost it!" She was almost screaming now, and Beow, moved closer to me. "Look, look, all you poor souls, who have so long labored to free yourselves from the tormenting Queen. Here is the mighty Bellator! Why are you here, Bellator, and only a child? You awaken water, but cannot keep the one thing that is your charge? Where is it? Oh, you have lost it! We are doomed, we are doomed!" She was standing in the middle of the room now, and suddenly she sank to her knees, and began to yank out her thin hair in fistfuls, and to weep loudly, wailing, crying, and screaming, as though her heart had been broken. Two of the men standing guard quickly ran to her, grabbed her by the arms and dragged her wailing from the room.

It was a profoundly disturbing sight. It took some minutes for the room to calm down, and for the old man at the far end of the room (the Regent, he was called) to bring the meeting to order.

"Beow, is this true? Is this the Bellator? But that cannot be... Who is he, Beow, and why is he here?"

A younger man spoke up, interrupting the Regent. "What is a Bellator, Regent? I, for one, have never heard of such a name. And what was Krea saying? What has been lost, and why does it spell our doom?" He was trembling as he spoke, and I was not sure whether out of fear or anger.

288

"What is being kept from us?"

"Peace, Orrin. Krea does not know of what she speaks. She is old, and has seen and suffered terrible things in her time. These torments have frayed her mind, and dulled her wits. She has been a faithful ally, but too much sorrow borne for too long can twist and bend even the most intrepid soul. The Bellator are a myth, a story from long ago, in the time of the Great War. These stories were told not because they were true, but because they were useful, useful for keeping the hopes of children alive. Our Fathers needed to convince their children, and the weak among them, that there was still hope in the fight, that they could still triumph, as long as the Queen still lacked the final key to her ultimate victory. The Bellator were supposed to be the protectors of the Book of Lost Worlds, for which the enemy destroyed our land, and for which she still seeks, roving to and fro among these so called 'other worlds.' These 'Bellator,' the stories said, kept ever ahead of her, always outwitting her, and keeping their treasure safe. Great gifts they had been given, divine gifts, appropriate for their cosmic task. What nonsense, what utter drivel! They are but legends, and this child is not a legend come to life."

He looked at me as he spoke, and it seemed that he hated me at that moment.

"Legends?" asked Beow. "Not all stories told to children are legends and myths. Thaddeus himself told us that he came into our world from another, and that he seeks a Book that his family was sworn to protect. This Book was stolen from him, and by none other than Jacoben the Necromancer. Messengers, Messengers of the Queen who had entered his own world in stealth, he said, killed his own grandfather. Why else would the Queen seek him? And he carries with him a sword wrought of a Krishnag tooth, made for him by Charismata of the Mountain. Thaddeus, show them the knife."

I stood again, and drew the knife from its scabbard. My hand trembled as I brought it forth, and I marveled again at its beauty. It was as light as air, and the silver

289

etchings seemed to glow in the dim room. All were silent as they gazed upon it, and then I replaced it in its leather scabbard, and concealed it under my jacket.

"Do you see, my friends," asked Beow, "that there is truth to what we say? The Elder himself thought that it was possible, and now, after all I have seen, I believe. Thaddeus the Dragon Slayer is the Bellator. He is the guardian of the Book."

"Where then," began the Regent, "is the Book now? If Jacoben has stolen it, why does the Queen still pursue Thaddeus, the 'dragon slayer,' and why does she not now rule all the worlds? Was it not for that reason, if the tales are to be believed, that the War was fought? These myths, these stories, they are not to be trusted. You, among all those present here, should know that, Beow. Now you bring us children with strange eyes and sparkling toys, and you expect us to suddenly become weak-minded fools, like old Krea? Thaddeus, oh mighty 'dragon slayer,' tell us yourself; have you stepped from the tattered pages of myth? Are you the Bellator?"

I had been watching and listening to all of this as though from a distance, as though all was happening outside, and I was seeing it through a window. Weak-minded fools? If so, then I was the greatest fool of all. The Bellator? Was I the Bellator? I heard my grandfather's voice again, as we sat in the garden, and he told me the tales of the lost worlds, the ancient secrets of our family. We were the custodians, he had said, the guardians of the Book. Why else had I followed Jacoben? Why else had I fought the Krishnag? Why had I continued down the mountain, and why was I here now? The Bellator, the Elder had said, had been given certain gifts. Did I have those gifts? But I knew the answer already, and, indeed, I had somehow always known the answer. I had known it from the moment I had seen my grandfather die. I was the Bellator, the last of that line, and the Book was my responsibility.

"I am."

I heard myself speak, but the voice was deep and

strange. It was not the voice of a child only, but that of a warrior. The voice of the Bellator.

All was silent for a moment. And then another of the younger men spoke: "Regent and Beow, you are counted among those who know, and you have heard of this 'Book', and of the Bellator. I, like Orrin, have not. But let us assume, for the moment, that Beow is right, even if it seems so unlikely that this boy, even with his shining eyes, could be he. What then? Krea, in her raving, said that if the Bellator is here, here in the belly of the Queen's domain, than he is searching for what he lost, and thus our doom is sealed. How was the Book lost if it was guarded by so great a warrior, and, most importantly, what do we do now?"

Beow looked at me before he spoke: "The Book was stolen, and through treachery. Thaddeus was only just introduced to his vocation when he was plunged into pitched battle against forces beyond his imagination. The Necromancer infiltrated the ranks of the Bellator, it seems, and deceived Thaddeus's grandfather, Cornelius Ramsey. Jacobin, along with the Messengers, killed Cornelius, and almost killed Thaddeus. How the Necromancer was able to find the last of the Bellator I do not know. How he was then able to deceive, in the end, the one charged with the duty of being ever watchful is a mystery. Indeed, the whole history of the Book, after it disappeared in the Great War, is shrouded and obscure. Even the Elder did not know if the Book still existed. But now, in these last days, it is in the open. But here, my friends, is where the Elder saw a glimmer of light. For the line of the Bellator did not end when Cornelius was killed. The Necromancer himself stood over Thaddeus and thought him dead. Thaddeus evaded the watchful eyes of the Messengers, and found the doorway to the fabled Antechamber, the gateway to all the worlds. In that terrible place he killed the last of the Krishnag serpents, that line of dragons, the stories say, which followed the Bellator into the mountains during the chaos of the Great War, sent by the Queen herself, to kill the warrior and bring back the Book. Thaddeus almost died in the Antechamber. But he was rescued and nursed back to life by none other than Charismata, the Witch of the Mountain. It was she who crafted his weapon, from the tooth that Thaddeus took from the carcass of the dragon. Thaddeus was almost captured on the plain, and we happened to be there at just the right moment. It is because of him that the Queen, in panic, threw her whole strength at the valley and lost. He survived the fall into the river, and he woke the water, asleep since the Great War. And now, here he is before you, as one who has arisen from the pages of a story. And so, my friends, the answer to the last question: whether you believe in him or not, I think it is in our best interest to help him."

"Help him?" The Regents voice cracked as he spoke. "Help him in what way? It is he who should help us, if he is who he claims to be. Let him show his strength against the Queen, and against the Necromancer! What can we do to help him? You fool, Beow! If the legend of the Book is true, and if the Queen has it, then all is lost. There can be no more resistance, not for us, not for all the other worlds. You speak of hope, and of helping this boy, but shining eyes are no match for the power of the Queen, not when the final key to her victory is in her hands. Do you not see the wisdom in our fathers' tales? These alone kept hope alive in the weak. If all you say is true then we are lost. And if what you say is false, then you have stolen the last of our hope. Is the water awake? So is the Searcher! Has the Queen lost many of her minions in the Valley? We have lost Pallas and the Elder! Is this the Bellator? Then the Book is in the hands of our enemy! All is lost, Beow, and you are the greatest of fools!"

There followed a tense silence in the room. Orrin broke it.

"Regent, surely we are beyond such ungracious remarks. Beow, of all of those who fight against the Queen, is not deserving of it. I do not understand what is happening, nor why the 'Bellator' is here, in the visage of a boy. But we must remain calm, and we must decide our

292

course of action with clear minds and steady nerves. Let us not turn on one another."

The Regent did not respond, only looked away. It was Beow who spoke.

"Indeed, Orrin, and I am sorry that our plans have been so far futile. But again, we must hold on to whatever hope we have left. To that end I propose this: Thaddeus needs to find the Book. As far as we know, the Necromancer has it, unless it has already fallen into the Queen's hands. But... Well, there is another element to this strange twist that I have so far left unsaid. Even now I hesitate, only because we have been infiltrated so often with spies and traitors. But all of those here we must consider beyond reproach, or all is lost anyway. There is a possibility, a chance only, that the Book may be so far indecipherable to the Necromancer and the Queen. It is possible that it remains locked in a box that can only be opened by a certain key, one of only a few in existence. I do not know for sure, but it seems that Thaddeus himself has this key, and that the Queen desires him for this reason. But I think it may be more than that. With the Bellator still at large, she will never be safe, and her prize only precariously held. She now needs both the key and Thaddeus. But there are other keys in the worlds, or so the ancient tales say. I know little about them, only that there were at least three made, maybe more. But the Elder saw Thaddeus's key, and thought that it was one of these."

"But Beow," interrupted Orrin, "if she is thwarted by a key, than should we not get the key as far away as we can? Perhaps we can smuggle it over the mountains and across the Endless Desert to the Golden City?"

"It is not ours, for one thing. Thaddeus calls it his 'inheritance.' His father gave it to him. Thaddeus must decide what to do with it. And we do not know for sure if our enemies do not have another key. As I said, it is a possibility only. But we do know this: the Queen will do anything to capture Thaddeus. It might be for the key, or only to kill him and end the line of the Bellator. She may already know that he is in the city, but I do not think so. Right now we must assume that she is so far oblivious to our final preparation, and of the presence of Thaddeus. I propose that we strike quickly, with all the force at our disposal, as we have planned, and simultaneously smuggle Thaddeus across the water to the Dead City."

"To what end, Beow?" The Regent's voice was no longer tinged with anger, but sounded old and tired. "What can he do there? We might be better to simply hand him over to the Queen ourselves and be done with it..."

"Do not speak like that!" Orrin's voice was drawn with almost panic. "Those are traitorous words, and will sow dissention and suspicion amongst us, and could splinter our group."

"Peace, Orrin. I did not mean that we should hand him over, only that both actions will have the same result. But I am willing to try what we can. I do not think that it will matter in the end. Our hope lies in our final attempt to overthrow the Queen by open rebellion. Whatever this boy does or does not do will have little effect, I think. What will he do, Beow, if he can get into the Dead City?"

"I do not know for sure." Answered Beow. "Thaddeus has so far been pursuing the Book. It may be that he will be able to find it and somehow recapture it."

The Regent laughed out loud, a short, desperate laugh.

"Recapture it, Beow? Sneak into the halls of the Necromancer, or into the Allabaster Castle itself, and steal it, maybe when the Necromancer and the Queen turn their backs? It is a fool's errand. But you may do what you wish, Beow. Send the child wherever you think he should go. I will speak no more."

He sat down in his chair and put his head in his hands. Beow spoke again.

"I propose only that we help Thaddeus as much as we are able. It is his decision to go into the Dead City or not. He has already been given the opportunity to end his quest, and he has declined. But let him speak for himself; what will you choose, Dragon Slayer? Will you continue your quest, or will you join us in our final battle? Or will you give up, and go back to your own world, if you are able?"

"I have come this far," I heard myself saying, "I will not give up now. If Jacoben is in the Dead City, then into the Dead city I will pursue. But if you could help me get in, and perhaps tell me how to find the 'halls of the Necromancer,' I would be very grateful."

"You will have no trouble, I think, finding the Halls of the Necromancer, once you are inside the city." One of the old men was speaking, a very old man, wizened and frail, with a long, white beard. His voice was so cracked, halting, and low that I had to strain to hear him. "It is in the center of the city, built on the burial grounds of the kings: a house surrounded by gardens and tombstones, by lawns and crypts. It is a house of mirrors, so they say. It would be easy to lose one's self in there... But the Halls will be easy to find, I think. I was there once, long ago, before all this, before the dreams... as a child I was there- to the burial grounds, before the Necromancer built his house. I remember it clearly. The roads wind to and fro through the city like a labyrinth, through the most majestic city in all the worlds, but they all pass eventually through the grounds, before striking out again for the Alabaster Castle, and the sea. The sea! I saw that too, once, as a child. It is dead now. Only dark men and worse come from across those waters... The water is black."

Here he stopped, his cracked voice trailing off, and his eyes staring out, unseeing, into his memories.

"Yes," Orrin ventured, "thank you, revered father. That is helpful indeed." He spoke as to a young child. "Now Thaddeus can find the Necromancer, with the aid of your memory. That is most helpful."

"Yes, Thaddeus," continued Beow, "we will help you get in, and we will help you find the Necromancer. But, unfortunately, that is all we can do. I cannot accompany you, though I would. Neither can anyone else, even if I would dare to ask. We must carry out our attack here, and

295

try once and for all to break the power of the Queen. If we can, then we will escape from this city, and let the Queen have it to herself. If you fail it might not matter what we do. But if you succeed, then all our intrigues might have been worth the cost."

"Our plan, then," began Orrin, "is to spring our attacks throughout the city simultaneously, in an attempt to destroy the factories and mines, and incite the wretched populace to riot. Because we outnumber our oppressors three to one, the surprise and the swift destruction of their infrastructure, we hope, will be enough to buy us the time to escape, through our preordained routes."

"There, as I have said before, is where I see the greatest flaw in our plan." One of the older men was speaking now. "Even when the valley was intact, it was highly unlikely that we would get that far, even if we could get out of the walls. Where now will we go, with the valley destroyed?"

"Yes, that is indeed a grave concern," answered Beow. "But I think that the odds still break in our favor. We slew so many of the Queen's minions that our initial triumph and escape is far more likely now. There are still routes through the mountains, though they are treacherous and difficult to find, even for me, and I know the mountains better than most. Or we could escape south, following the sweep of the mountains, and seek a refuge in the southern lands among the tribal peoples who still live in those forests. And then, perhaps in time, we could attempt to cross the mountains... But I think we should try for the mountains immediately, and try to cross before the winter snow."

Here the older man who had just spoken interrupted him: "But Beow, what if we succeed in escaping, and with good fortune most of the city escapes with us? How will we all survive? How will we feed so many people with no place of refuge? I fear we will leave through chaos and fire, only to die of exposure on those rocky slopes. It seems to me that the defeat in the valley means that our plans are... if not ruined, then at least subject to profound modification."

"I have long said that we should not abandon the City at all," said Orrin. "This is the home of our fathers, and to cede it forever to the Queen…"

"We do not cede it forever to the Queen," responded Beow. "We take the first step in wrenching it from her evil hand. There is no hope of destroying her power completely, not while the populace suffers under the brutal sway of her dreams. We will do the best we can while our minds are clouded and weary. Light, freedom, and the cleansing breeze of unpolluted air, these will go a long way in the healing of our long-suffering people. In safety and rest we can regroup, and continue our war. Someday, perhaps only in our great-grandchildren's time, we will see the ultimate fall of the Queen."

All was silent for some time. The weary conspirators seemed lost in thought, contemplating, perhaps, the probable end to all their best-laid plans. There were no easy answers, no best options. There was barely a lesser of evil choices. To die, one way or another, was their lot. But, I thought, it was also my own. I too went to certain death, and I too had no better plan. How cruel fate is, I thought, how capricious. Where was hope in times like these? For what could one hope? A miracle, maybe, an intervention by the Divine, and nothing else… Maybe only to do what one should, perhaps, to choose the good, the small, shaken good, in the face of overwhelming evil, and then to die. This alone was left. There was no guarantee of success, no guarantee of even a noble death, locked in a death-struggle with the darkness. A knife in the back would often serve just as well for those who would strike back at the impending shadow. But what else could we do? What other options presented themselves for our consideration? Not to be passively consumed by the shadow, no, that we would not allow. Even futilely we would rage against the night, striking out with pitiful fists, because we would not spit on the gift of life, we could not live as though that very life was ultimately useless and void. Because, I suppose, the good compelled us…

But these thoughts were my own. I did not know what motives drove the others in this room, and relief from suffering might be just as potent. But I thought not. That sort of relief was readily available, I had been told, simply by acquiescing to the Queens' demands. So maybe I was not too far off the mark...

The meeting lasted still several hours longer. The sky outside the huge window began to turn golden-red at the arrival of the dawn, and it looked again, I thought, as though it were on fire. I did not follow much of what else was said. The plans were finalized in specific detail, but because I did not know the names of people mentioned, or location and layout of this or that mine or factory, I lost interest and began to doze. But every time I closed my eyes, I saw the darkness in the distance, and felt that there was something out there, in the darkness, looking for me. And then I would come awake with a start. The darkness was not the darkness merely of closed eyes. I would have welcomed that escape. Rather, it was real darkness, not only (or merely) the absence of light. It was a positive (in that sense) darkness, a rolling, pulsating, inky mist, a wide nothingness; it held terror for me.

Finally the meeting ended. This very evening they would spring their attack, the last battle against the Queen, not leaving her any time to regroup after her partial defeat in the valley. If they failed... well, they would all be dead, or worse, in a few hours. Success would mean escape from the city, with all their women and children, to an uncertain future. Perhaps they would destroy the immediate power of the Queen and escape over the mountains, to the City of Lights in the East. Or, they would escape only temporarily, the power of the Queen being still strong, and be hunted down like animals. But for better or worse, the plans were in place.

I went with Beow and his men to the room with the couches and the balcony, and lay down while they sat around a table and talked in low voices. I could make out only a little of what they were saying, but they had clearly been disturbed by the meeting.

"The Regent I do not trust," I heard Caleb say. "He is on the edge. He might at any moment surrender to the dreams. We should watch him closely till our traps are sprung, and the hour for betrayal past us."

"You are right, Caleb," answered Beow. "Stay with him today, as his 'bodyguard,' until the hour has struck."

They talked for some time, until the morning was late. I could hear the city outside the window coming alive, although it was not a pleasant sound. A normal city coming awake is a wonderfully rich, exciting medley of sounds, while the City of Dark Dreams was like a person waking from a nightmare into a lesser nightmare. It was strange and exotic, while being at the same time sad and depressing. And I wondered what kind of sounds would greet the dawn tomorrow?

"Thaddeus, you can move freely about the house today, but do not venture outside. If you are near a door or window, keep your hood covering your face. Tonight, after our trap is sprung, I will take you to a bridge that I think will be the safest route, and, with luck, you can get into the Dead City unseen. From there, you will follow the road that we told you, and you will come to the old graveyard. It is sprawling, but I think that the Halls of the Necromancer will be easy to find from there. I only hope that the Searcher is still scrambling over the mountains, or looking for you in the submerged Valley. If he is in the city, he will find you… and then there is no one who will be able to protect you.

The morning wore on, and exhaustion was my enemy. I couldn't help but doze, and suffered terribly when I did. Every time I drifted away, the thing in the darkness came nearer and nearer to seeing me, to finding me.

"Sleep is perfect torture, is it not?"

I had just come out of a short doze with a start, and saw the Regent sitting across the room from me. We were downstairs in the "café," (I don't know what else to call it), and the afternoon was well on. Caleb stood near the door, while the huge, axe-wielding man was behind the bar, washing crude, ceramic cups (his great axe was propped against the wall nearby). Beow and the others had left to make the final preparations early that morning, to meet with the leaders of the various cells, and to make sure that all was ready for the night. There were no patrons in the café, and Caleb had said that it would be all right if I sat down here till evening, as long as I sat in the corner, hood down.

"And it gets worse." The Regent never took his eyes off of me. The deep, rolling wrinkles in his forehead seemed to arch in a V over his right eye. "In your dream, it probably has not found you yet, has it? You know of what I speak? It can take time, and for very young children many years, till it finds you. I do not know why. Something seems to protect the very young... But when it finds you, Thaddeus, you will know what we suffer every night. And then we wake to this." He waved his arm around, and his eyes were wild. "This is our life, and has been for ages and ages. You cannot know what we suffer... You have stepped into this world, and proclaim yourself the Bellator, you are friends with Beow, but you cannot know what we suffer..."

"Peace, Regent," Caleb interrupted. "Of course he cannot know. And you do not know what he has suffered, nor the weight of his burden. You have never faced a Krishnag dragon, nor stepped into another world. Do not expect him to know your suffering, just as you cannot know his."

The Regent looked away, and the room grew silent. The giant behind the bar clanked the cups, and a large, fly-like creature buzzed in the humid air. It was a very hot afternoon. The air was stifling, and my lungs burned.

No one had been in to the café for some time. The whole atmosphere was somber and the expectant. Only a few hours away now... Through the dirty windows I could only see the crooked wall of the building across the narrow alleyway, and no sky. Everything looked reddish-orange, as

300

was usual. I wondered if the sky was visible up above, through the space between the two buildings. I got up and walked to the window, threading my way between the randomly strewn tables and chairs. Peering out through the dirty pane I could just make out a patch of filthy sky up through the maze of balconies and overhangs, roofs and stairwells. The buildings were labyrinths, chaotic and misshapen. I looked down the way where the alley met the main road, and could just see the movement of sorrowful people going to and fro. I wondered what the morning would bring for them.

The sky above was beginning to turn red, the same flame that always signaled the end of the day in this wretched city. Very soon night would fall. Behind me I heard a courier come downstairs to speak with the Regent (throughout the day they had been coming and going, traveling by secret ways over the rooftops, bringing word of the all the preparations, and taking messages from the Regent back to the various cells). Caleb joined them, and the three talked quietly in hurried tones, their faces grave. I could only hear pieces of what was being said.

"Maybe he is on his way?" The Regent was speaking. "How long has he been missing?" I did not hear the answer that the courier gave.

"It does not matter, we must act as though the worst has happened. We must light the beacon as soon as night falls." Caleb was speaking now. "Does Beow know?"

"They are trying to reach him," answered the courier. "I don't know if they have succeeded."

"Can Orrin have... No, it is impossible. Not now..." The Regent seemed to be speaking to himself. Then he lowered his voice further, and I could no longer hear any of the hushed, frantic conversation. I turned away to the window.

The sky above looked like a sea of flame, rolling above the spires and rooftops. I glanced back down the alley way toward my left (I could see the road some yards down on both my right and left), and saw a figure clothed in a drab, brown robe, walk slowly by at the very entrance of the alley, disappearing on the far side. And then, suddenly, he reappeared, coming back and rounding the corner into the alley in the same slow, nonchalant pace. The hood of his dusty cloak was over his face, and I could only just make out the chin and nose beneath the hood. A long, hooked nose, and a slight smile lingered on his lips. I could not see the eyes. I thought at first that he might be a beggar. A gnarled stick was in his gloved hand, and he tapped it carelessly on the paving stones and on the sides of the buildings. I wondered if he was a patron, or if he was just passing through, or perhaps come for a handout. His progression was slow, and I began to lose interest, and glanced down the other way. I was startled to see two figures, very much the same, coming down from the other road. Both were dressed in brown, and both seemed to be out for a stroll, so carelessly and aimlessly they walked. Confused, I looked back towards my left, and saw that the first figure was followed by two more, and that behind them, in the street, were others, all slowly making their way towards the alley.

It took only a few seconds for my groggy mind to size up the situation. A strange heat seemed to wrap around my lungs like fingers, and I turned away from the window, stumbled over a chair, and called out to Caleb: "Strangers!"

It was all I could do to get out that word. I was having trouble breathing, and I stumbled towards Caleb and the Regent like a drunken man. Caleb, surprised, reached out to steady me, and at that moment came a quiet knock on the door. At that sound everything grew still, and all four of us in the room silently turned and looked to the door. Caleb then signaled to the giant, who slowly grabbed his axe, and approached the door. Caleb pushed me toward the stairs, whispering fiercely, "Get out of sight!" I moved as quickly as I could, but felt as though lead weights were holding me back. Everything in the café seemed to slow down, as though the hot afternoon had seeped into the fabric of the place, and a great heaviness had fallen on our shoulders.

The knock came again, louder this time. The courier had left some moments before. The giant looked at Caleb, his hand on the knob. The regent had reached under his cloak, and I saw the double handles of long knives. I had reached the stairs and was looking over my shoulder. Caleb's hand was on the hilt of his sword, hidden behind the table. The giant held his axe at his side, hidden from view for when he opened the door. Caleb gave the signal. The giant turned the knob…

The heavy door swung wide, and I could just see the cloaked figure outside, his light smile still on his lips. "What do you seek?" The giant growled. I could see his hand gripping the axe tightly.

"We seek sustenance at the end of a long and tiring day, that is all. Can we find it here? We wish to eat and drink before surrendering again to the dreams. Can we come in?" The voice was low and light, careless almost.

"Not tonight, my friends," answered the giant. "Come back tomorrow, and then we will gladly serve you."

"Ah, but what if tomorrow never comes? What if when the night falls, the darkness is all that is left? Indeed, my dear, dear friend, what if tonight your very soul is required of you?" As he answered I thought his cloak moved suddenly, as though swept by a breeze, and the giant stepped back, jerked oddly, and the stumbled. Then I saw the small crossbow held in the stranger's gloved hand, and the shaft of the arrow buried to the nock in the giant's stomach. The stranger lifted his booted foot and kicked the giant back into the café, sending him crashing through tables and chairs, his axe still gripped in his hand. The stranger then stepped into the room and calmly loosed an arrow at the Regent. But the regent had seen battle before. The twin knives came out, catching the arrow in mid flight, diverting its path with a flash of sparks. The stranger was in the café now, calmly reloading his crossbow with deft and amazing speed, while behind him crowded the other cloaked strangers, pushing into the room. Caleb's sword

303

came up as he leapt over the tables toward the stairs where I stood frozen. I heard the Regent cry out, "Save the Bellator, Caleb!" At that moment also the giant arose suddenly from the floor with a roar, like a Lazarus from the grave, sending tables and chairs in all directions, his great axe high above his head. It fell with such ferocity that it split the stranger nearly in two, the careless smile still fixed, the axe buried for a moment in the wooden floor. He roared again, pulled the axe free, and flung himself upon the strangers, his axe raised over his head. There were at least three strangers in the café now, with more trying to get through the doorway. The giant was met with a volley of arrows from the crossbows, but he didn't pause. He crashed into his enemies like a freight train, the axe ripping through the brown-cloaked bodies, flinging them across the room, over tables and chairs, arms and heads one way, and bodies another. The Regent joined the counter-attack, his knives slipping here and there among the cloaked bodies. But only for a moment did they stem the tide. Even as Caleb was pulling me up the stairs, arrows whipping by us, I saw the giant stumble, an arrow through his neck, his body a huge pincushion, and as he fell the last stroke of his axe swept the legs from under another of his enemies. The brown cloaks swarmed the giant's fallen body like flies, their knives stabbing franticly. The Regent also stumbled, as he turned to escape up the stairs with us. I saw his eyes wide with pain, an arrow through his chest, and then I was up the stairs, sprinting behind Caleb. The battle downstairs was already over, and their defense had bought us only just enough time.

We raced up the steps and onto the landing, and then down the hall past the door to the room with the couches and large window. As we raced by I heard a crash, and saw out of the corner of my eye a brown figure come through the window, rolling and bringing the long curtains and rods with him. I had only an instant to realize that he must have leapt from the far building when we rounded the corner and were on our way up another flight of steps. Behind us we could hear the desperate pursuit. The building was empty now, except for our pursuers and us. All the other inhabitants had errands to run and preparations to make. Caleb turned suddenly, pushed open a small door to a narrow stairwell, and we raced up that. We went through another door, another stairwell, and then burst suddenly onto the roof. It was a stretch of flat roof, like a veranda, and we quickly realized that the danger was not over. The strangers were on the roof.

Across the way we saw three of the strangers huddled over the body of the poor courier, his last message forever undelivered. They looked up as we came out, but were too slow, so concerned were they for their dead prize. Caleb leaped forward, hewing the first one to the ground, and then fell ferociously upon the second. The third narrowly avoided Caleb's rage, and flung himself at me.

I felt no fear, did not even know that I had drawn my knife, and my eyes burned.

The stranger had a short sword in his gloved hand, red with the blood of the courier. I parried the thrust, and stepped under the attack, running the stranger through to the hilt, like through water, then stepped past the moving cloaked stranger as he rolled, my knife raised to strike again. But there was no need.

I was surprised, and looked at the knife in my hand. The silver etching seemed to glow with fury, and it was so light that I almost could not tell where it ended and my arm began. I had killed my first enemy with Charismata's gift.

Caleb looked at me, his two enemies dead at his feet, a strange expression on his face. "Well done, dragon slayer. Or should I now call you Bellator?" And then, turning, we raced to the edge of the roof. Looking down we could just see in the failing light that the street around the building was full of brown cloaks, and among them also were many of the dark men, torches in hand, and even some of the smaller goblins, breaking into every door and window, crawling up the sides, and were even in the buildings opposite ours. The sky above was a blanket of flame, and the light would be completely gone in a few minutes.

305

Arrows skittered past us, bouncing off the edge of the building, and zipping along the roof. One tugged at my sleeve from behind, and more strangers were on the roof.

Caleb grabbed my arm, and we ran along the edge of the wide veranda, to another sloping roof ahead. Up this we scrambled, and heard the cries of the strangers in pursuit.

What followed was a chase that I will never forget. The rooftops, as I have said, were so varied and multileveled, with balconies, spires, bridges and drains, that it was like another world. Over this world we raced through the dying light, followed always by the strangers. Leaping over crevasses between buildings, scrambling over water tanks, trying to escape, it was a perilous flight. More than once I lost my footing and almost plunged over an edge to my death, and more than once Caleb did the same. One of our pursuers did fall, and I heard his cries as he crashed down to his death, six or seven stories below. We had a destination in mind, I soon found out, as Caleb told me between ragged gasps. We had to light the signal flare, to let the rest of the City know that the battle had begun.

"It was not the Regent, I was wrong," said Caleb, over his shoulder. "It was Orrin! The poor fool is even now probably being tortured for whatever information they imagine he might possess. He sold his soul for the hope of comfort, and now will find only a painful death, devoid of glory or a clean conscience."

We could see where we had to go, some distance ahead, though it was no guarantee that we would make it. Above, some distance away, was a high tower, with a narrow opening that held a lantern. This we had to light, or the evening would not go well for the rebels. We would only just make it. Over the balconies and rooftops behind and to the left and right we could see the strangers in brown leaping and scrambling, always getting closer and closer to us. Behind us they seemed to be gaining, and they were trying to cut us off.

At the last moment we burst ahead of our pursuers, only just evading their errant shots. Up a short ladder we scrambled, and we were at the tower. The light was just dying, the fire in the sky going out.

"Thaddeus, light the lamp! I will hold the edge." He turned back toward the ledge, arrows whipping by, and I scrambled up the last small ladder, and then I was in the tower.

It was very high. From here I could see much of the city, now only a sea of lights and shadows, and in the distance I could make out the teeth-like outline of the Necromancer's factory. There was a pile of rags and straw in a large glass lantern, and on the floor next to it a burning wax candle, protected by a ceramic jug. I grabbed the candle, held it for a moment, and then flung it into the great lantern, onto the fuel. The flame sprung up, and I was almost blinded.

It was a flash of orange, and then a brilliant blue light burst forth, shooting rays into the night. It was very hot, and I quickly scrambled out of the tower, and down to Caleb's level. Behind me the blue light shot through the night, and far in the distance over the city, calling the rebels to their finest moment, and to their probable death. In the distance I could see, blinking like blue eyes in the night, answering signals, the message going out into the vast city. For better or worse, the last battle was begun.

~

Weeping, ever weeping, the frightened child lay
In bed next to her mother,
What she'd seen she would not say.
"Looking, ever looking, wild dogs and chains of night,
He'll find us, oh my mother."
Her father barred the doors and shut the windows tight.
"We will to no night noises cow," He said.
But even as he spoke those words, across the wooded hills and
glens
The wolves began to howl.
The tramping of the boots were heard, the rattle of the chains
Claws and fangs and padded paws
Through forests deep and rivers wide, and down the crooked lanes,
Searching, ever searching, until he finds his prey.
Oh sorrow great and tears like rain! That tragic family never saw
The dawning of the day.

~Excerpted From *The Nightmare of Percephilous*, circa
1300AD, translated from the original Latin by Dr. Byron
Fairmont, 1818

Chapter XVI

"I know I am not well, without your telling me, though I don't know what's wrong; I believe I am five times as strong as you are. I didn't ask you whether you believe that ghosts are seen, but whether you believe that they exist."

"No, I won't believe it!" Raskolnikov cried, with positive anger.

"What do people generally say?" muttered Svidrigailov, as though speaking to himself, looking aside and bowing his head. "They say, 'You are ill, so what appears to you is only unreal fantasy.' But that's not strictly logical. I agree that ghosts only appear to the sick, but that only proves that they are unable to appear except to the sick, not that they don't exist."

"Nothing of the sort," Raskolnikov insisted irritably.

"No? You don't think so?" Svidrigailov went on, looking at him deliberately. "But what do you say to this argument (help me with it): ghosts are, as it were, shreds and fragments of other worlds, the beginning of them. A man in health has, of course, no reason to see them, because he is above all a man of this earth and is bound for the sake of completeness and order to live only in this life. But as soon as one is ill, as soon as the normal earthly order of the organism is broken, one begins to realize the possibility of another world; and the more seriously ill one is, the closer becomes one's contact with that other world, so that as soon as the man dies he steps straight into that world. I thought of that long ago. If you believe in a future life, you could believe in that, too."

~Crime and Punishment, **Fyodor Dostoyevsky**

The battle had begun, but it might end very soon for us. Caleb was engaged in a frantic fight with the strangers, who were joined by dark men, all pressing to get up the narrow ladder. Arrows bounced around us, fired from below, but the blue light above cast shadows over us, obscuring us from the shooters. Yet moments after I joined Caleb, the attackers suddenly withdrew, pulling back to the bottom of the ladder, giving us a moment's respite. They too had seen the answering lights in the distance, and we could hear their frantic voices as they planned their next step.

"Well done, Thaddeus," whispered Caleb. "Though we have been betrayed, it may be that we were given just enough time. But we are in a bad place now. We must assume that Beow will not find us. If he is still alive and if he has not been captured, he is certainly now in the thick of battle. So I will get you to the Dead City, or die trying."

"How will we get down from here?" Just as I asked that question the tower seemed to sway beneath us, and a low rumble like an underground train rattled the buildings around us. A spire across the way, just illuminated by the blue light went toppling into the street many stories below. In the distance, across the rooftops, the teeth of the Necromancer's factory were suddenly lit as though from within, like light through a cloth. And then there was a roar that burst upon my ears like cannon fire, and from the teeth exploded a mountain of fire. The pillar of smoke that never ceased to rise from the teeth became in an instant a pillar of fire. It burst high into the sickly night sky, a vast volcanic inferno, lighting the city for miles around. It looked like the monstrous mouth of a demon, vomiting fire. I could feel the heat even here, at this distance. I stared at the mountain of flame for an instant, lost in the wonder of it, when Caleb grabbed my arm.

310

"The first victory, Thaddeus! Come, now is our opportunity." We left the ladder and crawled quickly around to the back of the tower. On this side was nothing but a steep drop into the darkness.

"Just below us, maybe twenty feet down, is a narrow ledge. It is our only chance. I will drop first, and you follow." Without another word he swung himself over the ledge, gripped tight for a moment, then dropped into the darkness below. I heard his whispered voice from the gloom: "Now, Thaddeus! Straight down!"

I have had worse falls, I thought. I swung over the ledge, my fingers griping the edge, and my face against the cold stone; and then I dropped, scraping the side as I fell. It was a short fall. My feet hit the ledge with a jolt, and Caleb grabbed my arm to steady me.

"Quickly now!"

We went along that ledge away from the mountain of fire, still visible above the roofline. It mushroomed now into the thick smog above. Below us we could hear shouts, cries that might have been our pursuers below, and what sounded like the clash of steel, but I could not be sure. The ledge ended, and we were on a long balcony, and then down a flight of stairs, through a passageway, and suddenly we were on the street, several blocks away from the tower. I could see the flashing blue light, but it was dim and obscure against the inferno. The mountain of flame seemed even larger now.

There were people in the streets, but they were clustered in groups, and moving furtively, as though trying to remain unseen. They were all headed away from us, towards the east, where far away lay the great wall. But their presence was a comfort, and we walked quickly along the cobbled streets, keeping to the edge of the buildings.

Strange things were happening. There were shouts and cries from side streets, and the groups of people that we saw became more and more frequent, and more and more bold. Many carried crude weapons, swords and axes, but some had the crossbows favored by the Queen's soldiers, evidently taken from them by force. At one point, several blocks away from where we entered the street, two dark men burst from an alley, running hard, and were immediately followed by a dozen or so of the residents of the City. The dark men were running for their lives, and they did not get far. The rebels caught them a few short steps from where we were, and slew them. We hurried on.

"It is happening, Thaddeus." Whispered Caleb, as we jogged quickly through the dark streets, lit only by the eerie light of the burning factory. "The rebellion has begun. We took the Necromancer's factory within moments of lighting the signal. I had not expected such a speedy victory there. It gives me hope. But these people need to hurry towards the wall. They only have a short window of opportunity, I think. But the word has obviously spread rapidly. We may yet see success."

On we raced through the surreal night. Behind us in the distance other buildings ignited into flame, and more and more people flooded past us, some pushing carts loaded with children and supplies, and others with weapons. Somehow everyone had heard, or could sense, that this was an opportunity, maybe the last, to escape the City of Dark Dreams. We heard sounds of battles in neighboring streets, and we came across the bodies of Dark Men, lying cold in the gutter. And then the people became less frequent, and the sounds more distant, until finally we were alone.

"We are almost at the canal, Thaddeus. I hope that we will find the bridge unguarded."

Soon the blocks and rows of twisted buildings came to an end, and we looked out across a wide road that ran north to south stretching out in front of us. On the far side was a wall, maybe four feet high. Beyond the wall was the canal, as wide as a river. And across the canal, obscured in the gloom, rose the Dead City. The light of the burning buildings behind us seemed incapable of crossing the canal, as though blocked by a shield of darkness. But the road was in good repair, and the wall along the edge of the canal was ornate, with beautiful wrought iron lamps hung periodically. A fog wafted around the road, rising, I thought, from the canal. It looked like a nice stretch of road beside the Thames, a place where fashionable people might walk on a Sunday afternoon. I saw London in my mind's eye, for a moment only, and then saw the same fashionable people walking here, at night, and with a sinister fog about their feet... I felt a chill, and I suddenly wished again that I were staying with Caleb and Beow.

"Down there, Thaddeus," Caleb pointed down to our left. "Down there is the bridge. It is not the main bridge- that is much further up north- and neither is it the best bridge for stealthy crossing. But under these circumstances it will have to do. When you get across, follow the main road that strikes out from the other side. It is wide, and it should lead eventually to the burial ground of the kings, and so to the Necromancer's halls. It will twist and turn through the city, and it may be difficult to follow at times. Take care that you do not lose yourself in the city, Thaddeus. After you find the halls of the Necromancer, I cannot tell you how to proceed. Come, let us try to get across that bridge."

We carefully and quietly made our way down the street, keeping always in the shadow of the buildings, never straying onto the cobbled street itself. I realized now that I did not want to cross that canal, and I did not want to leave Caleb. I had not been alone since I had been rescued on the plain, and I did not want to go back to the fear and the loneliness. I did not want to have to find my own way in the Dead City. In almost a panic I realized that, even if I found Jacoben, and rescued the book, I would never be able to get out of this city alone, and certainly not back to my own world.

We soon came upon the bridge. Looming mysteriously through the fog, it was curved like a rainbow over the span of the canal. Great statues guarded the entrance, one on each side, statues of what looked like kingly and noble men riding horses bred for war. Lanterns of beautifully wrought iron hung from the horses' mouths. The lanterns were molded like twisted vine and flowers, intricate and ornate. The bridge was wide, and all was silent in the fog. The only sound came from behind us in the distance, from the warring city.

"It looks unguarded at the moment," whispered Caleb. "Fortune may yet smile on us. This is your moment, Thaddeus. Your quest is again on your shoulders alone. I do not know what gifts the Bellator have been given, or the meaning of your shining eyes, or how the Witch of the Mountain calls you friend. But I think that you will need every advantage you have to succeed tonight. Farewell my friend. I hope to see you again, in this life or another. The only advice I can give you now is to avoid sleep, once you cross that bridge, and to turn neither to the right nor to the left once you are upon the main road. If you leave the main road, you will surely lose yourself. Hurry now, I will wait here until I see you cross."

I waited a moment longer, looking around for any movement or sign of the enemy. Seeing none, I dashed across the road, and took refuge against the river wall, hiding in the shadow of a jutting piece of stonework. I paused to catch my breath, and then glanced across at Caleb. I could just see him in the shadows. Now or never, I thought. I stepped out of the shadow...

I immediately crouched back in terror. How had I mistaken the statues for the stone shapes of noble men on horseback? I was shaking, trembling at what I now saw. The statues were not of men or horses, but were of huge goats, with open, foaming mouths, and curled horns, their hair wild and flowing. In their cloven hooves they held lanterns of twisting snakes, black dragons like the garden statue. The eyes of the goats and the dragons seemed to glow red, maybe reflecting somehow the burning buildings in the distance. I had seen these statues before somewhere, and in my fear it took a moment to remember. Oh yes, now it came to me: my vision on the plateau. When I had been caught in the fog like a fly in a web...

314

In that moment I heard the sound that I had been dreading. Across the bridge, in the darkness and fog, came the sound of many feet, the clash of steel, and the hammer of hooves on the bridge. I had been seen! Desperately I looked around for a place to run, a place to hide, but there was none. Across the way I could see Caleb's face, and could see the fear in his eyes. His hand was on the hilt of his sword.

The bridge was echoing loudly now, and I knew a great force was crossing. I pressed closely to the wall, trying to lose myself in the shadow. They were almost across now. The echo of the feet and hooves sounded like the roar of waves on the shore, so loud they were. Then the first burst forth from the entrance, a pack of the squat goblins, clothed in chainmail, but instead of turning towards me they drove straight on into the city, never even turning their heads in my direction. Behind them followed, line upon line, dark men, all clad for war, weapons in hand. They flowed into the city like a river, the lust for blood alive in their dead eyes. I pressed into the shadow of the wall, terrified that one would turn and see me, and then rend me limb from limb, hacking me to bits on the dark city street. But they looked only straight on. They were not crossing the bridge to kill me, but to crush the rebellion.

The moving line of dark men seemed to last for hours, and I thought that these would be the end to all the plans of Beow and the rebels. Beow had said that the battle of the valley had destroyed the bulk of the Queen's legions, but the never-ending flood that I saw here tonight shattered that hope. Indeed, I began to think that the sun would rise before this host finished crossing the bridge. I could see that Caleb too was concerned, probably thinking the same thing, and I knew that he wanted to escape and join the rebellion, but he could not move without being seen.

The line of dark men gave way suddenly to a group of huge, hulking monsters, things that looked like the pictures of trolls that I had seen in books. Sharp tusks were protruding from their gaping mouths, their massive heads were covered with barbs and bony spikes, and in their claws were clutched wide swords, curved like scimitars. The noise of their flat, webbed feet echoed down the cobbled street.

Then, group after group, came different creatures, all looking more evil than the last, flowing into the city. Goblins of all different shapes were in the mix, some riding creatures like those killed by Beow and his men on the plain, and some riding creatures that looked something like pictures I had seen of four-legged dinosaurs, with leathery skin and great tusks. They were all running like the devil was behind them, driving them on. I began to ache from crouching for so long in the shadow, and I began to despair of ever getting into the Dead City. And then suddenly the flow began to thin, until only a single line of tall goblins holding battle-axes was running from the bridge to the City.

And then a chill swept over me, and I began to shake uncontrollably. I heard the sound of many hooves on the bridge, and I hoped somehow that whatever was riding now over the bridge would just turn back.

From the bridge came a host of large unicorns, their hair dyed jet black, black as the night, their horns tipped with iron, their eyes wild and shot with blood, foam pouring from their open mouths, and their wings hacked to bloody stumps. Upon their backs road knights clad in black armor, black capes flying behind them, their faces covered by helms of black iron, but painted in chalky white. I knew instantly what they were: Messengers of the Queen. The same terror that I had felt in the library came flooding back to me, and then grief mixed with terror. I saw again in my mind's eye my grandfather's last battle, and saw again his terrible death at the hands of these cruel creatures. This was why the goblins and dark men were running so hard; the devil was indeed after them. I closed my eyes tight, the noise of the hooves pounding through my head like drums, drums beating out a funeral dirge, a wild death march. And then suddenly they were gone, rushing into the City, but the drums still beat in my head.

I opened my eyes and saw Caleb frantically

316

signaling me to cross the bridge. It was now or never. The goat statues seemed to have grown larger and were wilder, as if they had been driven to a frenzy by the monsters that had just crossed their bridge. A memory entered my mind just then of the statues that I had seen with my parents when visiting the cathedral, statues of the saints of old, wild and ecstatic in their love and service for God. Perhaps they were not so different from these statues; perhaps the only difference was the god that they worshiped…

I scrambled up, and crept along the wall until I was a few yards from the entrance. I took one last look at Caleb across the way; he raised his hand in one last gesture of solidarity. And then I gathered my courage and rushed into the opening of the bridge. The eyes of the statues seemed to follow me, and I almost imagined their heads turned as I raced by them, and then I was past, and onto the bridge.

Everything suddenly grew silent. The fog closed around me, shutting off completely the city behind, and I was alone on the bridge. I could only see a few yards ahead, but I crept up the sloping bridge, hoping that there would be no more hordes of the Queen crossing tonight. The silence was unnerving after the cacophony only minutes before. The bridge sloped up, and then down, and in a few minutes I had crossed. I was in the Dead City.

The moment I stepped from the bridge the fog receded somewhat, and by the light of great street lamps I could make out the nearest buildings. I was momentarily stunned. They were huge, ornate and beautiful beyond description. I was standing at the bottom of a canyon; the streets almost literally paved in gold, and as the sides of the canyons stood mountainous buildings. The two that framed the wide street in front of me seemed to swirl and rise up like a palace, and a great golden arch spanned the gap between them. There were words etched into the gold, and though I could not read the language, they seemed at first to be words of welcome, a royal invitation of hospitality. But I looked more closely and saw instead that that they were words of the vilest kind, spiteful and wicked.

The road went to my right and to my left, paralleling the canal, but, taking heed of Caleb's words, I began to follow the wide way that ran straight on in front of me, into the city.

The way was easy to follow, and the only sound that I heard was the echo of my own feet on the paved street. The fog served to dull the noise, and it sounded eerie and foreign to my ears. I walked for some time, my fear much diminished by the beauty of what I saw. The buildings on the right and left were stunning and majestic. Even in the dense fog and dim light the difference between these and the buildings that made up the expanse of the New City could not have been more striking. Where the New City looked like the haphazard work of a child with building blocks, these palaces (that seems the only right word) were the work of an artistic genius of incomparable vision and virtue. They seemed to be carved of pure marble, and that of multiple colors, shades of blue, turquoise, and green highlighted the brilliant white. Balconies and wide windows, relief statues and freestanding statues, fountains and gardens were all incorporated. The statues were of kings and queens, and what looked like winged angels wielding great swords. Beauty and majesty, these were the words that came most quickly to mind. I wondered what this street must have looked like in the light of the sun, filled with people beautifully gowned, and noble in bearing. I was walking in almost a daze, entranced by what I saw. Then, suddenly, I strangely thought that I knew exactly how that would have looked, as though I had, in fact, seen it before. Yes, I remembered now, I had seen it before: the pictures, the pictures in my grandfather's house. The series of pictures of strange but beautiful people, happy and peaceful, the series that ended with a woman among them, the one whose eyes, when viewed from a certain angle, seemed to glow red...

Even as I remembered this I looked again at the buildings that towered above into the fog on the right and left, and wondered how I could have been so blind. How could I have thought that they must have been built by an artistic genius of incomparable virtue? The colors, I saw now, did not perfectly compliment the stunning white, but rather served to mock and distort them. The blues and greens were not like the blue of the sky, or the green of the grass, but were reptilian, ugly and sinister. Even the whites were not really white, but a dull grey, with grime dripping from the edges like black tears. The statues also changed, as I looked, from noble people and winged angels to creatures indescribably hideous, leering and angry. The windows with which I had been so taken now frightened me. They were open graves, and I did not want to know what was beyond them. The buildings seemed now the work of evil, of profane mockery, a perverse mirror image of order. They all looked like massive, distorted skulls- pillars and fountains like the broken teeth, and windows like empty eye-sockets. The fog was smoke, thick and tattered, wafting low to the ground around my feet, but also circling above my head like a storm. It seemed to flow out of the dark windows, like ghosts from the empty sockets of the skull. The street lamps seemed dimmer, and served not to illuminate but to cast shadows. Fear came stalking back to me, and I began to run.

I ran on and on. I did not think of fatigue, but only of finding the end of this city. I did not think of what would happen when I found the Necromancer's house, but only of what might be in the palaces that lined this street. The Dead City they called it? And didn't Beow say that the ghosts of the dead kings still wandered the streets? He had also said that there were other spirits here, and those not of kings, but of something else…

I plunged on through the fog, only able to see about one block in front of me by the dim lamps, and all around me loomed the huge buildings with their terrible openings, and I did not want to know what might be looking out from the darkness. The fog began to feel like a blanket, suffocating me as I ran. I hoped, deep down inside, that all of this was in my imagination, that these were merely old, empty palaces, and the fog merely fog from the sea, which I knew was somewhere ahead of me.

But then I began to see things in the fog.

There were figures and shadows, watching me from balconies or walking quickly across the road in front of me. Some were far up the road, vague shadows in the distance. I saw movement behind the windows and felt dead eyes peering out of those great eye sockets. I did not stop running; panic was growing inside of me. "Oh please," I thought, "do not let these spirits intercept me." But I began to sense that they were speaking to me...

I tried to assure myself that this was not so, that these were all just shadows, that shadows cannot speak, but it was useless. First it was whispers, and then I began to hear them call out to me, saying, "Thaddeus, turn aside, come here, come into the darkness." They wanted me to go with them, into their houses, into the empty sockets, the empty skulls. The voices became louder, and more urgent: "Come away, come away, Thaddeus, come away with us. Come into the darkness." I was becoming frantic. It seemed that I had been in this city for hours and hours, maybe days, and I began to wonder if this road just went in circles. Circles, I thought, like the circles of hell in Dante's Inferno. Which circle was this, and what had I done to merit it? The voices were now a cacophony in my head, and I could see the spirits more clearly now, reaching their hands out the windows towards me, beckoning me from doorways, and from the roads that ran away from the main one. My knife was in my hand, and terror was in my heart. I began to feel like I was losing my mind, like I was no longer in possession of myself: like I was losing myself...

And then as suddenly as the voices had come, the voices were gone.

I drew up, gasping for breath, listening and looking around. Nothing had changed. The fog still hung low, the dead buildings still vaulted high above me, the dim lights still glowed; but the spirits were gone. I stood for a moment, wondering what had happened. It was almost... Almost as

320

though the ghosts themselves were afraid.

They had reason to be. There are other things in the cosmos more frightening than ghosts…

There, ahead of me, sitting on a ledge next to a dry fountain, sat a figure like a man. But a man somehow serpentine in form… I could not quite make him out, for he was strangely obscured. But he seemed nonchalant, carefree almost. He was kicking his feet, and I thought that he was smiling at me. Though I saw him clearly, in a way, I did not really see him at all. It was like a veil was over his face, or maybe over my eyes. I realized suddenly that I *willed* not to see him. And then he spoke:

"We meet again, Thaddeus, and you have been so kind as to walk right into my city. Like a fly into the spider's web…"

It was he, the voice in my nightmares, the darkness in my visions… the voice twisted and broken, a distortion of natures; it looked like the figure of a man, but I knew it was not a man. I could not see it, see it as it really was. I refused to. But somehow, in that strange moment on the street of the Dead City, standing alone with only my knife, I suddenly knew what this was, what had been stalking me since I first arrived at the house of my grandfather. It was a dragon. No, *the* Dragon. Not the Krishnag serpent, no. No the krishnag was but a pet, a plaything to him. This was the real Dragon, the one for whom all the other dragons were but a copy, a feeble derivative, an analogy at best. And it was the Dragon that wanted the Book… I thought that I would react the same way that I had before, that I would go mad with terror, or that I would become immobile, but I did not. I felt only cold, ice cold, and began to tremble.

"Shall I now call you the Bellator, Thaddeus? Did all your friends convince you yet? Do you now think yourself a great warrior? You will not answer? You are afraid, are you not, that if you speak, that if you acknowledge me, that your eyes will be opened, that you will know me as I truly am? That you will see me? As your grandfather would not, as your mother would not… Yes, your mother, Thaddeus. Did you not know? I found her, when she was only a child, younger even than you. I found her, and she almost saw me, Thaddeus. I had been searching for a long time, for over one hundred years for the Bellator, for your family. They had eluded me. It was your great, great grandfather who slipped my grasp. But I found them again, found you mother. But your grandfather thwarted my plans, if only for a while. But your grandmother... you never met your grandmother, did you, Thaddeus? She wavered, in her fear for her daughter, and she opened her eyes, and saw me, saw me as I truly am." I could tell that it was smiling. "She died in despair, Thaddeus. The sickness unto death... She was convinced that I would win this game, that I would find your mother, that I would find the Book for which I have searched all these ages, that it was a hopeless war to fight. And she was right. You do not know your own history, Thaddeus? How your grandfather imagined that he had triumphed, that he had hid the Book and his daughter from me, that he had upheld the great name of the Bellator. And in his greatest moment of triumph, having slain a most valuable servant of mine, having rescued your mother in the very knick of time, he returned to find that I had won the battle... Too late he returned home, returned home triumphant... And now, in the end, he too is dead. So you see, Thaddeus, that all your 'gifts' cannot save you. You will see me also, Thaddeus, as your grandmother did, and as your grandfather did, and you will despair."

Tears were falling unhindered from my eyes. I was shaking, not with cold but with sorrow. This then was why my mother did not want me to meet my grandfather, why my parents did not want me to become the Bellator. Why had they let me, in the end, I wondered? But even in my confusion and sorrow at that moment, as I heard the wicked words of the Dragon, I knew that he was a liar. My grandfather had not died in despair. I had seen him die. He died upholding the name of the Bellator. He died as the Bellator, the protector of the Book, and had passed his vocation to me. My grandfather had, like Elisha, passed his mantle to me, and I hoped, suddenly, that I had received a double portion. I heard the Dragon talk about my grandmother, and I tried to tell myself that these too must all be lies...

"You doubt me, I can see that. Let me show you something, Thaddeus. Your friends here, the ones that you think are so brave and valiant, the ones who you think saved you from my hand and the hands of my servants; they are even now burning. I have shown my servants, the Queen and the Necromancer whom you seek, I have shown them the rebellion, and even now they are crushing it. But there is more, Thaddeus. I will show you something, something that I have been wanting you to see."

And then everything in front of me began to fade away, and in that moment I was suddenly above the New City, watching it burn. All was chaos, and battle raged everywhere. The sky was on fire, like it always appeared to be in the evening and the morning; only now it was actual fire, now the sky was a blanket of burning coal and ash. I looked and saw the great canal that I had crossed, the one that separated the New City from the Dead City. I could see the bridge, and there, further into the city, I saw Caleb. I knew that he was returning to the battle, returning to Beow and the others, returning to help liberate his people. But something was wrong. He had stopped, like he was listening to something. I saw him slowly start again, and then stop again. Something was approaching him, from the raging battles in the New City, toward the Dead City. Something that was running fast... And I heard the rattle of chains, the sound of boots, and the beat of padded paws. Caleb walked slowly to the center of the street, and drew his sword... in the distance I could see a shadow approaching fast, and in the shadow were eyes of fire.

The vision faded suddenly, and I was standing again in the fog, standing alone on the street in the Dead City.

I looked down at my feet, down at the ancient quarried stone, away from the Dragon, and knew somehow that he could not touch me, not now, though I did not know

323

why. But the Searcher could. The Searcher was a slave to the Dragon, I thought. I heard behind me the sound of wolves, far in the distance, and knew that I had to run. Well, we would find out if I could outrun the Searcher. We would find once and for all who could run faster, the Bellator or the Searcher. I looked up again at the Dragon, but he was gone. Yet I could still feel his presence, and could still hear his laugh…

I began to run.

I began to run as I have never run before, not in a panic, but calm and self-possessed, and with a deep sense of urgency that transcended mere self-preservation. I ran because I would not let the Dragon win, not this battle, not tonight. I ran because I had to reach the Book, because I felt the weight of my vocation more clearly than ever before; and I ran because I knew for the first time that the Dragon feared me. I was the Bellator, and the Dragon feared the Bellator. My family had outwitted and out-fought the Dragon through the ages, and even my mother had triumphed. And I did not intend to be the weak link in the chain. The Bellator who had come before me had been in worse danger than this, had had more fear than this, been closer to death that this, but they had not failed. It all came down to me now. And I gave myself, for the first time, to my vocation as the Bellator. We had been given gifts, they had said, gifts to aid us in protecting the Book. I had seen something of that in my grandfather, heard it from Charismata, felt it in waking the water, and now I knew that I would not be left alone without aid. I was the Bellator: everything I needed had already been given. And so I ran.

The fog grew more and more dense, and the lights grew even dimmer. The road turned and curved, with many forks and streets splitting off, but I stayed on the main way. It was wide and smooth, and somehow I remembered the warning that the way to perdition was wide and easy to follow… The houses, mansions and palaces became more and more ornate and huge, and I passed wide parks and huge fountains, with statuary that would have been

324

breathtaking if they were not so revolting. It was as though the Dead City kept swaying between its former glory, when it was alive and vibrant, into the terror of the grave, into the Dead City. One moment it looked too fantastic for words, and the next it would shift, like the setting sun, into a ghost town.

I ran and I did not grow tired. The spirits had returned, and were calling to me again, but I paid them no heed. My only thought was to reach the house of the Necromancer before the Searcher found me. What I thought I would find there, or why I thought somehow that it was a refuge of some kind, a refuge from the Searcher, I did not know. But I did feel it.

It grew colder as I ran; the fog wrapped closer around me, and felt like clammy fingers on my face. I heard again the cry of wolves behind me, only closer now, but still muffled through the fog. I ran faster still, but I knew that the Searcher was gaining on me. Maybe I imagined it, but I began to feel like the fog was holding me back, like it wasn't fog, really, but a sticky web, a web that grew more and more dense. Determination welled inside me, but I began to wonder if it was a false determination, a juvenile bravado, that it was only serving to cover a pure panic. I wanted to run faster, but I felt as though I was starting to slow. "This fog," I thought, "this fog is holding me back."

The cry of the wolves was closer now, and I could tell there were at least three wolves, maybe more. The buildings were nothing but a blur as I raced by, the lamps like smudges of dull orange against the thickening fog. Another sound was coming through the fog, another sound: chains. It was the rattle and crack of chains, and the sound of heavy boots. The Searcher held a pack of wolves, held them with chains.

I began to slash wildly at the fog as I ran, trying to cut through it, as if it were truly a web, but to no avail. My pace was quickening, I knew it had to be, for the buildings were racing by me faster and faster, but it felt as though I was moving like in a dream, like the fog was not around me but in me. The howls seemed to be only a few blocks back now, and I could hear even the foam pouring from their open mouths, hear the gnashing of their teeth. The sound of the chains rang loud, even through the fog, and I could see in my mind's eye the sparks as the chain snapped on the stone street. Only a block or so behind me now…

Suddenly I was running through an open, park-like area, where grass had once grown. There were large stones rising up around me, like giants in the fog. I was in the graveyard.

It had to be close. The road beneath me was now graveled. Somewhere just ahead had to be the house of the Necromancer, if the directions I had been given were true. The howl of the wolves rang in my ears, and the sound of the chains against the paved stone changed suddenly, and I heard the crunch of gravel beneath the boots. "Don't look back," I told myself, "don't look back!"

Ahead of me loomed suddenly a massive shadow, and then I could see the house. So strange it looked, so out of place here. It was a huge colonial house, like those in the American south. A great pillared porch, and a large double door. If I could only make it to that door…

But I wasn't going to make it. I could almost feel the heat of the wolves' breath, and their rabid howls tore through my mind. Almost there…

I heard behind me a snap, and a long rattle of a chain, and I was on the stairs. I reached for the iron hoop on the door, and just looked behind to see the massive shape of a lone wolf, his chain streaming behind, leap through the air, over the steps, its huge mouth open, its jagged teeth stained red, its wide paws up and its claws out. I screamed, slashed wildly, and fell through the opening door. The mass of the creature crashed into me, rolling with me into the house. Warm liquid was everywhere, and the wolf's jaw had fallen away from its face, a face that was laid open to the skull. I kicked at the door, swinging it shut, but even as I did I saw through the fog two more wolves held by chains, racing up the drive. And the chains were held by darkness, a mass of iron studs and gloved hands, great boots, and hooded face. And from deep in the hood glowed two eyes, burning red. The door slammed shut, and I was inside: inside the house of Jacoben the Necromancer.

~

"But why are there beings in the cosmos who are evil? That is, why do some rational beings choose what is considered, at least by traditional moralists, if I may use that term, to be wrong? You understand my question? And please do not bore us with another retelling of the prehistoric 'fall' narrative. That serves merely to obscure the question. We freethinkers have, for millennia, phrased the question thus: if the human person, or any rational being (I include this caveat specifically for the benefit of our guest), has a distinct telos, and a final end, what compels him to seek what is the antithesis of this end? The whole notion of the spiritual realm within the parameters of your anemic mythology, of Angels and Demons, and certainly of an all-powerful 'God,' demands a certain suspension of reason. Surely even a demon would not wish to reject what is manifestly his own good, his own self-preservation? I propose another route, though I do not wish to imply that all my fellow freethinkers would consider this to be an acceptable train of thought. Indeed, I leave the intellectual company of my peers just here: I believe their materialistic conception of reality to be grossly inadequate to the demands of human experience. My interpretation of the facts of the spiritual realm, and of the human encounter with the extra-human domain is the following: if 'God' has indeed granted every rational being, nay, granted every being, a benevolent final end, it is, in fact, not benevolent enough. Ah, I see your reaction! Rather, (follow me here), a better route, a higher end, has been discovered. Indeed, those very beings that you label 'demons,' or 'devils,' always supposedly devising ways to derail the pious, indeed to 'damn' him, are actually the benevolent beings! It is they who have discovered what all the supposed 'Saints' (whom I consider to be the greatest of fools) have missed: that what your 'God' gives is what a father might give a child, some chocolate or a toy, while the true wealth and riches remain untapped, and actually hidden from the child. You, with your talk of other worlds, of a cosmos so vast that we are only indirectly aware of it, you are closer than you think to my point of view. But instead of treating morality, that is, traditional morality, as paramount and necessary to human knowledge and flourishing,

328

you should see it as a veil, an artificial construct, meant by unseen powers to keep you pacified, with your eyes fixed on your supposed 'Divine Being', pacified and submissive. You will never see what lies beyond the veil, you will never truly explore all the cosmos, those other worlds of which you are so convinced, because of these shackles. Indeed, unless you strike the cheek of that 'divine' puppet master, unless you transcend, in thought and deed, the vile urgings of your inbred 'conscience,' true discovery is forever beyond your narrow reach. Rather, take the hands of those beings that reject outright the divine slave master, and learn at their knee. Those beings that, even according to your own mythology, first had the strength of will to ignore the quietly whispered lie, the 'still, small voice.' You see what I mean? Some call it blasphemy; I call it redemption."

~Excerpted from the transcript of the Well-Wisher Society's annual debate, 1893. Christopher Morley is addressing Father Anders Theodus, S.J., Europe's leading exorcist, in response to Fr. Theodus' presentation of his findings on "other worlds", and the implications of these findings for traditional religion. Christopher Morley, the famous atheistic freethinker, was well known at the time for his ferocious anti-religious sentiment, as well as for his dabbling in sorcery, witchcraft, and the occult. Less than six months after this debate, Morley experienced a nervous breakdown, and was admitted to an asylum, where he died shortly thereafter. The readers of this volume will be especially interested to know the nature of the breakdown: Morley claimed to have finally contacted some kind of being, a being, he claimed, of supernatural origin, perhaps like the ones referenced in the above transcript. The encounter apparently served to compromise his sanity. ~*Supernatural Phenomena and the Occult, 1700-1900.* Baker and Sons, 1923.

Chapter XVII

"I don't believe in a future life," said Raskolnikov.

Svidrigailov sat lost in thought.

"And what if there are only spiders there, or something of that sort," he said suddenly.

"He is a madman," thought Raskolnikov.

"We always imagine eternity as something beyond our conception, something vast, vast! But why must it be vast? Instead of all that, what if it's one little room, like a bath house in the country, black and grimy and spiders in every corner, and that's all eternity is? I sometimes fancy it like that."

"But surely, surely you can imagine something more just and comforting than that?" Raskolnikov cried, with a feeling of anguish.

"More just? And how can we tell, perhaps that is just, and do you know it's what I would certainly have made it," answered Svidrigailov, with a vague smile.

This horrible answer sent a cold chill through Raskolnikov. Svidrigailov raised his head, looked at him intently, and suddenly began laughing.

~Crime and Punishment, **Fyodor Dostoyevsky**

I lay gasping for breath, waiting for the door to

crash open, waiting for the Searcher to finish the job; but nothing happened. All was silent. Silent except for what sounded like the loud and steady ticking of a grandfather clock. It took some minutes to register the sound over the noise of my own rapid breathing. But when the door stayed shut, and no other sound was heard, I stood shakily up, and began to examine my surroundings.

The corpse of the beast lay like a massive pile of dirty shag carpet. A pile that stood almost as tall as I did. Its paws were the size of my head, and the claws were daggers. Blood was everywhere. I looked at the Krishnag blade in my hand, expecting it to be covered in grime, but it was not. No filth seemed able to stain this knife. And it had taken but one slash to kill this monster…

The body of the wolf and I were in a wide entryway, one with a wooden floor, and decorated with old pictures, and small mirrors in antique frames. The grandfather clock was near the end of the room, where a long hallway began. The loud tick-tock strained my already frayed nerves. An ornate coat rack stood near the door. It held a well-used raincoat, an umbrella, and two hats, one a tall stovepipe hat, and the other a bowler. I felt as though I had stepped into another world. Or rather, I felt as though I had stepped back into my own world. This could have been an entryway into any upscale home in London (or maybe the American South; I remembered the bizarre architecture outside). Upscale, but also aged, as though the occupant were an elderly statesman, or some wealthy grandparent; or a Necromancer, one who was at least a hundred years old…

Candles in brass holders, spaced regularly along the wall, dimly lit the foyer. I could not see the ceiling, so high above me it was. The candles could not penetrate the gloom at that height. The pictures and mirrors seemed to go up to the ceiling; they disappeared up into the shadow where the light could not reach. Now the sound of the ticking clock was both comforting and eerie…

I felt ill at ease, but, strangely, not because I was in the house of the Necromancer, and just beyond the door was the terrible Searcher, but because of the mess that I had made of the wolf. What would my mother think of this mess, in someone's nice foyer? Indeed, while I did not forget that, only moments before, a monster had chased me through a haunted city, it all seemed somehow distant to me, like something from a dream long ago. I thought only of the blood on the nice plank wood floor. I was a poor houseguest. But then the strangeness of this sensation struck me. I was no houseguest, and the occupant of this house was probably not concerned with formality. But I could not shake the feeling.

As I stood, shaken and confused, I noticed a slight movement near the entrance to the foyer, and a small, old lady shuffled quietly in. She held in her hands a mop and broom, and began to clean up the mess of the wolf. I was surprised, but stood still, watching her as she worked. She was very short, like Jacoben, with grey hair piled on top of her head, and she wore a simple dress, drab in color. She finally glanced at me with glassy eyes, and an expression of vague annoyance. Pointing down the hall, she gestured for me to leave the foyer.

Without considering any other options, I obeyed. I began to make my way through the room. At the end of the foyer two wide staircases swept to the left and the right up into the gloom, but I continued straight down the hall. As I walked, staying on the carpet in the center, I looked more closely at the pictures that were hung on the walls. Some were grainy black and white photographs of different family scenes, of group and single portraits, and all of people who looked something like Jacoben. They were quite diminutive, with similarly shaped heads and ears, the curved, sweeping musical staff ears. Their faces were stern, but not unkind. Some of the men wore great beards. The women wore simple dresses, with their hair done up in complicated styles on top of their heads. Some of the paintings were of outdoor scenes, and these I found most fascinating. The trees and rolling hills looked strangely alien, like very poor imitations of the geography and foliage of England, as if painted by someone who had heard it described, but had never seen it. Sometimes there were buildings, and these looked very much like the house that I was now in.

There were mirrors too that I found vaguely menacing, and I tried not to look into them. They were all different sizes and in different frames. But somehow familiar... Oh yes, I remembered: in my grandfather's library, the dusty mirror with the movement behind the grime that did not quite correspond to my own movement...

The hall ended, and I stepped into a wide room, like a ballroom, with a great chandelier hung from the ceiling. The walls were now covered with murals, murals that should have been lovely, with flowers and dancing, but somehow were not. At the far end was a door, and this just ajar, with a warm light flowing out. I stopped for a moment, unsure how to proceed.

"Come in, Thaddeus. I have been waiting for you."
I had not heard Jacoben's voice for so long that I almost did not recognize it. But it was soft and welcoming in tone, and carried no threat. I approached the door, trembling, and pushed it open.

Golden light spilled out, and I stepped into an impressive library. It was large, but intimate and comfortable, with deep leather chairs, several lamps, and many books. It was not as large as my grandfather's library, but I would have loved to spend some time here, browsing the volumes. There were several closed doors in the room, and straight ahead a low table, stacked high with books and parchments, and against the far wall was a fireplace, several logs aflame, and above it a wide mantle, with a large, framed picture hung above. The picture was of Jacoben, it seemed, but much older, with a grey beard instead of black... No, not Jacoben, I thought, but perhaps a relative.

Jacoben stood in front of the fire, a slight smile on his round face, his little black beard looking even darker against the warm firelight. He wore brown trousers, with a red smoking jacket, and he greeted me as I entered.

"Welcome, Thaddeus, welcome to my home. My adopted home, that is. I wondered if you would make it in one piece."

I didn't know how to answer. I just stood, staring, and suddenly realized that I was a mess, my clothes dirty and stained, and my knife still drawn. His eyes strayed to the knife, and I quickly sheathed it, somewhat embarrassed.

"Do not worry, Thaddeus, I know something of what the Queen has put you through over the last month or so. Without recourse to weapons, you would probably not have made it this far. But you will not need your sword here. That is quite a weapon... I assume Charismata gave that to you? Yes, I know Charismata. Or rather, I know of her. Do you know what she is?"

"I... I heard her called 'the witch of the mountain.'"

"Ha! From what fool did you hear that title applied to Charismata? No, my friend, not a witch. No, Charismata is, possibly, the last of her kind. She is a Winged One, one of those great star-lit beings who were once the protectors of this world. They all died, you know, in the Great War. Or most of them died... The 'Bright Ones' they were called. But our benevolent Queen managed to convince a few of them that they were on the wrong side of things, and through betrayal the Bright Ones were destroyed." He laughed again. "But sit down, Thaddeus, don't stand there staring. Here, on the couch."

I sat down, sinking into the deep couch, while Jacoben sat on the edge of the table, first pushing aside some of the papers and gadgets that cluttered the surface. His legs dangled freely, and he looked at me intently.

"Well Thaddeus? What do you think? I assume, because you are here, that your grandfather convinced you, before he died, that you are the heir, the last remaining Bellator?"

"Yes," I answered, my voice shaking a little, "he convinced me. And not he only, but also Charismata, and the Elder, and Beow..."

334

"Ah, the Elder and Beow! You were there, then, at the battle in the valley? The Queen was apparently convinced of it, though I was not so sure. I originally thought you dead, until I heard someone following me in the depths of the Antechamber. That's when I awakened my pet... I am sorry about that, Thaddeus. I actually thought that it was one of the Queen's Messengers who had followed me."

"Are you also sorry for stabbing me in London?

He looked sharply at me. "Thaddeus, that whole affair was more than distasteful to me. Except for Sylvester, I did not want to see any of you killed, or even the library burned. Sylvester I did not mind stabbing. He has long found me... unsatisfactory. But I did not want to kill you, and certainly not Cornelius. Cornelius had been a faithful friend to me for as long as I had known him. He saved me, you know, in a way. But he would not allow the Book to be accessed, to be used like it was intended. The Book was compiled, Thaddeus, so that the knowledge it held would never be lost. But it is as good as lost if it stays in the Book! It must be read and understood, it must be pondered and pored over. But Cornelius would have none of it..."

He frowned severely, and looked away.

"There was no other way, then, but to kill? And to join forces with someone like the Queen?" My voice was now shaking with anger.

"Join forces? Thaddeus, I have used the Queen as a means to an end, and nothing more. I despise her more than you do. It was ultimately because of her that my own world was dying. But I would never have found the Book without her. You see... well, perhaps you want to hear the story? Yes? I will make it short. I first heard of the Book from my great-grandfather, many, many years ago, when my own world was slipping into darkness. My great-grandfather, a very wise man (that's his portrait there, above the mantle), was my mentor. He had many of the same gifts that I do, only not so powerful, not so developed. He was adamant that I continue to expand my gifts, and to use them for the

335

good of my people, even against the wishes of my father and mother. Indeed, Thaddeus, it is due to my own history that I have so much respect and admiration for you and your own grandfather! You and I have much more in common than you realize. But to continue my story: my great-grandfather was also aware of the other worlds that existed, and had traveled to some. The secrets of these he shared with me. My world was dying, and it would be up to him and to me to save it. But despite his many efforts to extend his own life indefinitely and so be able continue the task, he finally died, leaving the task to me alone. But before he left, he told me of the Book. The Book of Life, the Book of Lost Worlds... Oh how I longed for that Book! My great-grandfather had spent much of his efforts trying to acquire it. He failed, in the end. But he was also aware that there was someone else searching for it, someone who also sought people of... extraordinary ability, to aid her search. He had heard of the Queen of this wretched world. I remember the day, Thaddeus, when one of her despicable minions came to my town. It was offering riches and power to those who would join her, join the Queen, provided they had certain abilities. I was a young man at the time, and I never forgot the message, though I did not join then. Rather, I took the interim years to develop my gifts, and to learn what I could, in hope of helping my own world. But it was of no use. My grandfather died, the shadow finally overtook us, and I watched everything that I loved sink into night. And then I was alone. But my grandfather had taught me well. My gifts were growing stronger, and I exercised them at every opportunity. I wandered for some time through the various worlds, the ones that were still awake, but they were becoming fewer and fewer, and I began to realize that there was only one hope of resurrecting my own world, of actualizing my potency, my destiny. I needed the Book. I needed the key to all the other worlds, to all the wisdom that their discovery would lend me. But how, Thaddeus, how to find the Book?" He was growing excited as he spoke. "Through all the worlds there were rumors of the Queen,

336

rumors of her obsession with the Book. And I still remembered the wretch who had visited my own land. I told myself that I had but to find her and I would be able to find the Book. So I sought her out. But when I finally found her I realized that I would have to allow a certain level of... compromise. I did not like it, but I had to build up a level of trust with her. I had to obey her every command, and help her stomp out the ridiculous rebellion that had plagued her since her original conquest, long ago. I am not proud of this, Thaddeus, but to accomplish what I set out to accomplish it was necessary. And I did earn her confidence. Indeed, I have become the most powerful person in her realm." He was smiling now, his golden tooth flashing in the dancing firelight. "Look at this house, this library. And I am sure you saw my factories? I think they are destroyed now, but that is of no concern. And the dreams, Thaddeus... I was put in charge of the dreams. In fact... Well, perhaps shortly I will show you something, something that I think you will find interesting."

He paused, somewhat distracted, and then continued.

"But think of it! Of all the poor souls who are slaves to the Queen, I had become, in a relatively short period of time, her favorite. I had her complete confidence." He seemed very satisfied with himself, and evidently thought I should be too.

"But," I asked, "what of the Messengers and the Searcher? That is, why did it seem that the Messengers and you were both trying to get the Book, and yet you seemed somehow to be trying to avoid them? And the Searcher... he chased me to your house, but you let me in, and by so doing, I suppose, saved my life? I don't understand..."

"Ah! Yes, of course you do not! You see, Thaddeus (this, you will find, is pure genius), the Queen does not know that I have the Book! The whole plan, from beginning to end, was to get the Book, bring it back here, right in the heart of her wretched kingdom, without her even guessing. This was not easy to make happen, but I did. But you guessed something? Surely you did? Yes, the whole plan was to make the Queen think that Sylvester had escaped with the Book, even as the Messengers killed Cornelius. Your tagging along was not in the plan. I apologize again for Cuthbert's... indiscretion. But, given the circumstances, you can see that we did not know what else to do? And, in the end, I guess Cuthbert paid for his many crimes, no?" He laughed loudly at this, and seemed quite unconcerned with Cuthbert's death.

"So... you tricked the Queen. That does answer some of my questions. But then the Krishnag, and the valley?"

"Yes, I was getting to that. The Krishnag, as I said, was meant to kill the Messenger that I thought had followed me. I did not know it was you. I thought you were lying quite dead in the street where I had left you! Indeed, I still don't know how you survived at all, how you got there that fast, or how you knew where I was going." He looked sharply at me, as if awaiting an answer.

"I... I took the train," was my reply.

Jacoben was obviously not happy with my answer, and his dark eyes flashed. "The train, was it? Very clever of you. I suppose the engineer told you I would be in the Dragon Garden? Never mind, you do not need to answer now. You wanted to know about the valley? Well, I was safe and sound here in my home, ready to unlock the Book, and to learn, once and for all, the secrets of eternal wisdom. The Queen thought that our mission had failed, that the Book was on the move again. Everything had gone exactly according to plan. A classic bait and switch! But the book was locked." Jacobin's eyes grew dark and stormy. "I was thwarted in my moment of triumph. Ah, the agony that I endured at that moment. Your clever grandfather had kept that one little secret from me. I needed the key. And then, in that desperate hour, I received news that a stranger had been spotted on the plain. A young boy... And then I understood! It was you all along, Thaddeus. And if you were pursuing the Book, perhaps you also had the means of opening it. Was I right? Aha, I see in your eyes I was. Do not worry, I am not going to attack you like on that rain-drenched road, or anything so crude. The time for those measures is well past. We will discuss the key later."

He smiled at me, a smile meant to be warm and assuring.

"Where was I? Oh yes, the valley. Your friends rescued you. And, unfortunately, the Queen is not a complete fool. She was quick to see that you might in fact be Thaddeus, the last heir of the Ramseys, the last Bellator. She acted quickly, too quickly, and too passionately. She released the Searcher. How I panicked when I found out! The Searcher is too wild and unruly a weapon even for her. Why do you think he has been locked away all these ages? I had to thwart her plan. I needed to get to you before the Searcher did. But what could I do? I could not let on that I knew it was you, that I suspected your secret. Certainly I could not let on that I knew the real reason that you were here at all. She thinks, I believe, that you were making a rash attempt to avenge your grandfather, or to see for yourself the world where your enemy resides. And she thought that at least you must know where the Book is. When I realized it was you, I thought, 'just like his grandfather!' You know, of course, that your grandfather did the same, once, right after you were born? Yes, he himself crept into this world, and almost discovered my secret identity! He came here because he wanted vengeance, and needed still to protect the Book, even after the disaster that cost the life of your grandmother, and almost cost the lives of you and your mother. He followed the creature that killed your grandmother, back through the dragon statue door (it led straight into this world then, and not into the antechamber), and followed it into this very city, and slew the fiend in the street. Indeed, it was almost too late. The creature, an assassin (one of the many who still roam the worlds, seeking the Book for the Queen), would have revealed the whereabouts of the Bellator, had it made it back to the Alabaster Castle! Your grandfather caught it before it crossed the canal, and threw its body in the water. The Messengers captured him, but did not know who he was. But he was severely wounded, and only escaped because I helped him. Of course, I kept my head, and managed to conceal from him that this wretched city is my... second home, shall we say. I was so shocked that he had entered this world and this city, that I almost gave myself away. It was I who secreted him from the dungeons of the Alabaster Castle, before he was tortured, for then he would have revealed himself, and all would be lost. So I assisted him, and he went into the underworld, and I heard from him no more, until he returned finally to your world. I thought for a time that he had died down in the crust of the earth, but I was sure that the 'gifts,' the 'grace' said to be given to you Bellator would sustain him! Yes Thaddeus, I see you did not know this story. Yet another reason to thank me! I rescued both you and your grandfather from deadly peril. I had to, you see, or I would lose my prize forever.

"But that is ancient history. Whatever the case, to return to my story, the Searcher found the wretched valley within a day. Indeed, he almost caught your party before you made it into the valley! You were probably not even aware of this, were you? (You seem to have the most narrow of escapes, Thaddeus). But, so desperate was she to get to you, that she did not immediately raze the valley. Instead, as you know, she sent the Banshees in disguise to get you out. A foolish plan that failed, and caused the destruction of her army, even if it also destroyed the valley. And you had escaped! Disappeared, it seemed, vanished in the confusion. Oh, the Queen has not been happy since! But, I thought to myself, where could you have gone? Either you were killed in the battle, in the deluge sent by the Elder (yes, I know the Elder. Indeed, I am fascinated by the nature of his power. It almost seems, sometimes, that he is not so different from the earth upon which he treads...), or that you had gone with the others who had, presumably, escaped over the mountains to the endless desert, and then to the Shining City in the east (it is good that you didn't; the Searcher would have found you, eventually, probably on the road before the Shining City, and I don't think your friends could have stopped him). But why, after coming so far, with so many opportunities to turn back, would you have fled to the east, possibly losing the Book and me forever? This question I asked myself, and then it came to me: of course you had not fled! Why, you must even now be on your way to the City of Dark Dreams! You had come to get the Book back, and you would not be dissuaded from your task. You had to: it is your duty!"

Jacoben was up now, pacing the room, his arms gesturing wildly as he spoke, and his eyes flashing brightly.

"But it would not take long for the Searcher to find your trail again. I had to act fast. So, for the last few days, I have been preparing for your arrival. There was only one thing to do. I could not aid you in your quest to find me, not when I did not know where you were, or by what path you would come. But I knew, I just knew, that you would find me. Why, you may ask? How could I be so sure? Because you are the Bellator! You may be the youngest Bellator to have ever held the title, but you are the Bellator nonetheless. You would find a way. So I prepared. That it why, Thaddeus, that is why when you had shut the front door to my house, you were safe. I have used every means at my disposal to protect my home, so that, once you were inside, you would have nothing to fear. Though it was a near thing!"

He was smiling widely at me, sure that I would be grateful to him for his foresight. And I was. I did not want to think what would have happened had he not prepared thus.

"I am grateful to you, for saving me and for saving my grandfather once, if only to betray him later," I responded, "but how long can you hold out? Won't the Queen find out soon enough, and then break through your defenses?"

"Eventually, yes. But your friends have made things more difficult for her. She is momentarily focused on the

341

rebellion. But you are right. She now knows, I think, that you are here, in my home. She now knows of my own rebellion. But do not fear. We have the Book! She has probably guessed this also by now. Why else would you have come here to my home, of all places in her kingdom?" Jacoben laughed loudly at this, completely unconcerned with the possible danger. "She is slow, but not completely hopeless. But it is too late. I have won. She cannot stop us now. Even the Searcher, all brutal, evil strength, but weak of mind, cannot help her now. We are safe, and will be long enough to take advantage of our lead."

"And how do we take advantage of it?" I asked. "How do we use the Book?" I heard myself say it, and I shuddered. The Book should not be used, not by Jacoben, this I knew. Jacoben heard me say it, and was pleased.

"I will show you, Thaddeus. And I think that you will find the process enlightening. How could you not? You understand the power enclosed therein, and you understand why it is so important! I will tell you, Thaddeus, I will tell you what I have found, and how I will use the Book..."

"There is one more question that I have, one that has confused me for some time," I interrupted. Indeed, none of this would make sense unless this question was answered. "What of the Dragon? He said that you were his servant?"

"The Dragon?" Jacoben frowned. "I told you, I had no intention of using the Krishnag to kill you. Indeed, I do not even know exactly how you survived the encounter. But you did, and with a dangerous souvenir. I should not be too surprised, for your grandfather also killed one..."

"No, I mean... I mean the man, or the ghost, or whatever he is. I call him the Dragon, but I don't really know what he is. The one who has been following me in my dreams."

Jacoben was staring at me, and I could see that he did not know what I was talking about.

"Your dreams? Perhaps you mean... Yes, I know who you mean, you are speaking of the Dreamweaver. He

342

has long been up to his mischief, but he is my servant, and I his master. I thought that you would not be affected by the dreams... Because you are the Bellator...? But why would that be so? Of course you were. He, the Dreamweaver, was once like me, you know, that is, he was once a necromancer. Ah, I see you do not like that title. Well, call it what you will. Magician, warlock, whatever... we have certain gifts, gifts that most mortals do not possess, and cannot access. Most do not have the strength of will required. The Queen, long, long ago, as I said, long before my time, employed him, the Dreamweaver, for the task of creating the dreams. The dreams for which this wretched city is named... I told you that I am now tasked with the job? Not of weaving the dreams, no, I am far beyond that, and my powers are far greater! But with maintaining them, and with intensifying them... Did the Dreamweaver come to you in the visage of a dragon? That is unusual..."

I could see that he was confused. He was staring intently at me, unsure of something. Could it be that he did not know the Dragon? But the Dragon... Was that what it really was, a dragon? The Dragon had said that Jacoben was his slave. Somehow I did not think it wise now to explain myself. Jacoben was still staring at me, as dissatisfied as I was.

"So the Dreamweaver has some new tricks up is sleeve, does he? The dreams were waning when I took over. I have worked my magic, don't you know, and have made them more potent, as I said. Do you want to see something Thaddeus? Come with me, I think you will enjoy this. You will appreciate it more than most. Indeed, most would love to see what I will show you, after the terror of the night. That something so... helpless, shall we say, so innocuous, could possibly be the source of so much suffering, this will come as a surprise to you."

He stood up and motioned me to follow. I did, still shaking, and I wondered how much of this to believe. I was confused somewhat, by our whole conversation, for I thought that when I found him it would be a fight to the death, a knife fight or something. I did not expect to be sitting in a warm room talking like old friends. But somehow I thought that he was telling the truth, or at least some of the truth, all evening.

He led me through one of the side doors, and down a series of hallways. The house seemed much larger on the inside than it had looked on the outside. These hallways were carpeted with a deep carpet that muffled our footsteps. Jacoben continued talking over his shoulder as he led the way.

"I have been involved in many interesting projects in my day, and seen many strange things. But this is extraordinary. Here, its just down this way."

We turned a corner, and looked down a narrow corridor with a single closed door at the end. One flickering blue light hung near the door. I felt suddenly cold, and I did not want to know what was behind that door. Jacoben was watching me intently, a strange smile fixed on his face.

"What is wrong, Thaddeus? Surely your curiosity is worth a little fear?" His voice was quiet, and held just a hint of mockery. "Follow me."

The corridor was longer than it seemed, and the walls felt as though they were closing in on us. The blue light kept flickering, casting strange shadows on the wall, but shadows that did not seem to correspond to the flickering. As though something else was in this corridor, something unseen...

"You are familiar with the history of the dreams, are you not? I see that you are, a little. The Queen thought of it long ago, long before me, as a way to control her slaves. It is a brilliant idea, if somewhat crude and unsophisticated. But I have aided her, and now the dreams are even more potent, and grow more effective daily. But where do they come from, you may ask? And who is in them, who or what, is trying to find you when you sleep? Come, I will show you. Behold my masterpiece!" And he threw open the door.

We stepped over the threshold and into the room. It was a very small room, and very dark, though there was

344

what seemed like hundreds of candles burning on the floor, on small tables, and hung from the wall. Even with all the candles, the darkness was overwhelming.

In the center of the room, a figure sat.

Its back was to us, but I could see chains held the figure in the chair, and the chair to the floor. Desperate fear was rising in me, and I was shaking almost uncontrollably. I did not want to know what was in the chair. I wanted to run, to get out of this room, out of this hall, out of this house. Jacoben stepped over the candles to the front of the figure, and he motioned me to join him. I stepped over the candles...

"Behold, Thaddeus, behold the Dreamweaver."

The figure was that of a man, withered and ancient, his mouth hanging open, all teeth rotted out of his black gums, drool falling onto his emaciated chest. His arms were held to the arms of the wooden chair by bolts, bolts that went right through his bony limbs. His neck was held in place by a collar of iron, and chains were wrapped around his body. His feet were likewise bolted to the floor, the bolts pinned right through the rancid flesh of his feet. But it was his eyes... the eyes were not there. Black, gaping eye sockets stared back at me, empty sockets, the eyes seemingly scooped out long ago. I was stuck dumb with horror, a horror not only of the sight in front of me, but with a visceral horror of Jacoben, who stood by my side with a satisfied smile on his face. I wanted in that moment both to stab the creature in the chair, and to stab Jacoben. I had to get out. I stumbled towards the door, knocking over candles, vaguely aware of Jacoben's voice behind me, hoping that the door would not swing shut, locking me in this vile room, locking me forever in hell with the Dreamweaver and with Jacoben. Then I was out, and in the hallway. Jacoben was yelling something behind me, but I just ran until I was out of the hall, and then I vomited.

I crouched in the semi-darkness for some moments, my head spinning, and my hands shaking. I was sweating. I gripped the handle of my knife, but did not draw it. I could

345

hear Jacoben down the hall, cursing to himself as he closed and locked the door to that awful room.

"You have made several messes in my house tonight, Thaddeus. I thought you would have better manners than that." His voice was tinged with annoyance. "My servants have already spent some time cleaning up the mess in the foyer, and now they will have to start again in here. I won't hold it against you, for I know that you have had a very difficult night. But I thought that you Bellator were made of stronger stuff."

I followed him back to the study, like a dog that had been rebuked by its master, feeling ill and weak. Any sense that I had of thankfulness to Jacoben for saving me from the Searcher was gone. I felt as though I had stumbled into hell, and found that hell included a warm study in a mansion. I sank into the couch again, shaking all over. Jacoben resumed his position on the table.

"Well, Thaddeus, I guess that I have misjudged you. That is, not misjudged you, but only your age. I see now that it is not your internal fortitude which has failed you, but only your age. And for this I apologize. It is not just to too quickly show you things that even the very old and wise might balk at. Even your grandfather would probably have hesitated to see what I just showed you."

He was silent for a moment, looking away, his short legs swinging rhythmically.

"Well, Thaddeus, I think now is the time to get to business. We have much to do."

He stood once more, and went to the corner of the room to where a small bell stood on a table. This he rang, and then proceeded to don a hood and cloak that had been hanging near the fireplace. It was brown in color.

"Thaddeus, we will begin, you and I, to unlock the secrets of the universe." His voice shook with excitement. "I have longed for this moment for many years. Let me tell you, Thaddeus, what I tried to tell your grandfather, but he would not hear me: there are other powers in the cosmos, other beings against whose power the Queen's own power is pale and anemic. I have spoken to them, Thaddeus." As I heard his words the light from the fire seemed to dim, and the room seemed to spin. "They are waiting for me. I now have something to give them, and they have something to give me. To them I will give freedom. Yes, freedom. They have been locked in dead worlds for too long, and they want out. I can release them, with the Book. You and I can release them. And they have promised, in return, life and wisdom. These they can grant. They can help me resurrect my own world, and even... perhaps even help me to bring back my great-grandfather. They have the words of eternal life. With the Book I can release them. With the power that they have, they will teach me to be like them. And we will, with the Book, be their masters. And together, you and I, we can restore what has been taken from us. I, my great-grandfather and world, and you, your own grandfather... Yes, Thaddeus, you can bring him back. Indeed, I would not have agreed to strike him down if I did not think I could then bring him back. Would you like that, Thaddeus? And then, with the Book, together we can become masters of the cosmos, we can roam freely throughout the worlds, unhindered by any power. We can smite the Queen, and raze this city to the ground. All will be ours, and ours alone."

His eyes were shining wildly as he spoke, and I saw my grandfather, in my mind's eye, smoking his cigar, smiling at me in his library, telling me that we were the custodians of the Book. If custodians, shouldn't I be able to use the Book, use it for good, to bring him back? Was it possible? But who were these beings of whom Jacoben spoke? Trapped in dead worlds? I didn't understand. How then did they have such power?

The door opened and two little old ladies came in, pulling with them several full-length mirrors in wooden frames. Four mirrors. These they silently moved in front of the fireplace, and then they shuffled out again. The mirrors were like the others, the surface somehow obscured, as though dirty. I did not want to look directly at them.

Jacoben was busy, bringing out a small table and covering it with a red cloth. Upon this he set a single candle in a golden stand. He waved his hand over it, and it sparked to life, a red, wavering flame. Somehow this action, of all the strange things I had seen till now, was profoundly disturbing. I remembered Sylvester's dislike for Jacoben, and I somehow understood, just in this small action.

Jacoben paid me no heed as he continued to prepare. He went to a bookshelf, and moved a couple of volumes over. Behind these was the little metal box that held the Book. I was surprised that he kept it hidden just on the shelf like that. I don't know what I was expecting, but it surprised me. He set the book on the table, and then went to the mirrors. These he positioned side by side, giving me a clear view of all of them from where I sat. Then he turned to me.

"And now, Thaddeus, I will need the key. Do not worry, I will give it back once the Book is opened. It is yours, as is, rightfully, the Book. You will have as much access to it as you like. We are together in this, you and I. I will not withhold anything from you." He held his hand out expectantly.

I paused a moment, and then drew the key from its place around my neck and held it in my hand. It felt heavy, and I remembered the moment in which my father had handed it to me. "This is your inheritance, Thaddeus," he had said. And now I was giving it to my enemy, to the man who had killed grandfather and Sylvester. But what could I do? I handed him the key.

He took it with a smile, and quickly unlocked the little box. He then handed it back. I put it around my neck, but felt as though I had betrayed something, that I was now complicit in evil.

"And now, Thaddeus, the moment of truth."

He opened the box.

I do not know what I expected, a flash of light or something. But nothing happened. The hinge of the box creaked, and he reached in and pulled out the Book. It was small, but dense, a thick leather binding, unmarked, and

348

unremarkable. I almost wondered if this was not the wrong book, that maybe grandfather had tricked all of us. But Jacoben was overjoyed.

"Here it is, Thaddeus, the greatest treasure of all the universe, and it is ours." His hands and voice were shaking. He put the Book on the red cloth next to the candle, and tossed the box unceremoniously onto a nearby couch.

"I hesitate even to open it. Come, behold the talisman of the gods, that which will make us the masters of the cosmos."

I stood and went to his side. He opened the book.

It was printed in a thin golden script, handwritten, and the words were almost too beautiful to look at directly. I could almost hear the words speaking, as though the Book itself was trying to teach me what it said. As I stared it seemed that there must be angels singing somewhere, and my mind felt as though sunlight was shining through it. I almost, in that instant, forgot that I was in the house of the Necromancer, standing next to Jacoben, somewhere in the City of Dark Dreams. I seemed to be pulled down into the script, diving into warmth and light, and I longed to know what was written. Then Jacoben spoke, and the warmth vanished.

"This is it, Thaddeus. You cannot read it? No, and you should not expect to. I cannot read it either. But I think that I will be able to in time. I have given much time and study in the effort of learning the secrets of the ancient language, but have so far been unable to get anything beyond a rudimentary understanding of very basic prose. Soon, with study and practice, I will be able to divine a little of what is written here, but even then it might remain somewhat opaque for a while. In the words of this text will be hidden far more meaning than in any normal speech, of this we can be assured. And I would not dare to read it aloud, not yet, even if I could. These words have not been spoken aloud since it was sealed under the altar, during the Great War. In time, perhaps, when my strength has grown, and I have learned all the Book's secrets. It would be far too dangerous now. But step back now, and I will use the book in the way I know how. There are other ways, secret ways, of divining the messages of this Book, and, more importantly, of harnessing its power. I can recite certain incantations that will, I think, compel the doors to open."

I stepped back and sat down on the couch. I felt sick to my stomach, and my conscience was burning. I knew that I was participating in something that should not be done, something that was in some way wicked. In a certain sense, of course, I had no choice. I was, for all intents, a prisoner here, but I also gave no objection, no condemnation. I did not even try to stop the proceedings.

Jacoben bent his head near the book, and began to slowly turn the pages. I do not know how much he could actually understand. He read, or at least looked, for some time. The light in the room was much dimmer now, as the logs in the fire were dying. Jacoben's face was lit by the red light of the single candle, and I could see it was contorted and strained, as though it was a great effort to read what he did. Finally he looked away.

"And now, Thaddeus, we will try to open the door." He took the book, and laid it on the floor in front of the mirrors. "I first learned the use of these mirrors from your grandfather, in fact. They can be used to harness the doors. The doors exist all over the cosmos, but any door can be opened merely by use of the mirrors. That is, any door not already locked. But with the mirrors and the Book I can open even doors long locked tight. We will attempt it. Thaddeus, you will now witness something that has not ever happened, as far as I know. The door to a dead world will be opened. Opened, after all these years, here in my home! And those beings, Thaddeus, the ones that I spoke of, we will see them finally. I remember when I first heard them speak to me, long ago, when I was very young, in my own world. Their voices frightened me at first, but I spoke back to them, and promised them that I would release them if I could. The first step on my journey, on our journey into complete knowledge and power is about to begin. Can you hear them, Thaddeus, can you hear them now?"

His eyes were wild as he spoke, and his pupils dilated. He then turned away from me and began to whisper violently, his voice growing ever harsher, and the words that he spoke, though hushed, were frightening. He fell to his knees in front of the middle mirror and the book, now open on the floor, and began swaying rhythmically. His hands he clasped together as though praying, and the whispered words came faster and faster. So fast that I do not know how he could even speak them. The only light in the room now came from directly behind the mirror, the light of the dying fireplace. It looked like a red halo around the mirror. Jacoben was shaking now as he swayed, and sweat poured from his brow. The room seemed to contract, and I thought that we were no longer in the library, but in a tiny box of darkness, and only the face of the mirror, and the shadow of Jacoben, were visible. Suddenly, the face of the mirror began to change. Words were pouring so fast from Jacoben's mouth that it seemed that he was no longer in control of what he was saying. The mirror was becoming less opaque, silver lines forming around the edges. Jacoben was raising his hands now, almost screaming in his hysteria, and white light was coming from the face of the mirror.

And then the mirror opened.

I was looking suddenly into a burst of brilliant white light, and an unending sweep of green. A grassy plain rolled away from me, up and up into the sky, like up a vast mountain, and in the distance, far away, was a silver city, shining on the mountaintop, set like a diamond in an endless blue sky. It was a castle in the clouds, like I sometimes imagined that I saw in the sky as a small child, and so breathtaking and beautiful it was that I cried out, almost in pain. How I longed to run up the sweep of that slope, run and run until I came to that city. Happiness was there, light and peace. I think I rose from my seat, ready to leap through the door of the mirror, but then there appeared suddenly in view, knights on white horses, clad in silver, their strangely-lit faces stern and strong. They seemed

351

surprised, and I realized that they could also see us. One rushed forward, his naked sword in hand, riding right towards us, his other hand raised as though to forbid my entrance. I felt suddenly like a trespasser, a thief caught in the act. There appeared two more knights in sight, just in front of us, so close that I could have reached through the frame of the mirror and touched them. I was confused for a moment, not sure what was happening. Darkness was spreading across the face of the mirror, and I realized in that instant that they were closing a door, a door on their side, shutting the door that Jacoben had momentarily opened. There were two screams just then, and the door was closed, and the light went out.

I fell back into the couch, shaking violently, and realized that it was both Jacoben and I who had screamed. I, from the terror of being forever locked out of that place, forever denied running up that grassy slope, forever shut out from the shining city. Tears were in my eyes, and the loss I felt at that moment is indescribable. The other scream was from Jacoben. I looked away from the dark mirror, and saw that he was crumpled on the floor, gnashing his teeth and foaming at the mouth, writhing in apparent agony. I sat shocked for a moment, watching him, unsure what was happening. It took some moments for him to calm down.

He finally sat up, his face red and distorted, his brown cloak soaked with sweat. He sat looking at me for a moment, and there was smoldering hatred in his eyes.

"That... that was not the door that should have been opened," he said at last.

He stood up brushed his cloak off.

"I do not know what vile door that was, but it was the wrong one." He cursed violently. "We will try again. By the gods, I am very shaken up! I am sorry you had to see that, Thaddeus, but there are, apparently, more secrets to be learned before I... before we have complete control of the power of the Book. That must have been... it could only have been another world, a world that shut its doors before the Great War began. I was not expecting that. Someday I will be ready to open that door, and then woe to him who tries to shut it in my face! But I was not ready tonight. But never mind, we will forget about that. Let us proceed again to open the right door."

He took a heavy bookend from the table and threw it suddenly into the mirror. The mirror shattered, throwing shards into the fire behind it. He then moved another mirror into place, directly in front of the fire. Again he opened the Book and laid it on the floor in front of the mirror.

"Let us try again. By the gods, I do not feel as well as I should. That weakened me more than I like to admit. It might take longer than I anticipated, mastering the power of the Book. But once I have the freed those trapped beings, Thaddeus, their power also will be our own."

He turned away from me and kneeled again on the floor in front of the Book and mirror. He breathed deeply, and began again.

This process took even longer than the last. He seemed to be in pain as he whispered his incantations, and he began to writhe on the floor, rolling around before the Book. I could see the beautiful script of the Book glowing, and soon all was dark again, except for the red glow of the fireplace, and the slight, golden light from the Book. But as I watched I began to feel ill, terribly ill, as though Jacoben's words were drawing the health from my body. So vile they were that if I knew what he was actually saying, I think it might have killed me. I remembered the voice in the Dragon Garden, the spigot of death that had been opened, and I was afraid it was open once again.

It was becoming too much to handle. I was beginning to writhe uncomfortably on the couch, my body moving reflexively, completely out of my conscious control. Jacoben was foaming at the mouth, thrashing violently, and I thought that he also might be killed with the effort. The mirror did not change, except to grow darker. And then, as I watched, I realized that the mirror was indeed growing darker, much darker, darker than the night, darker than black ink, as dark as the previous door had been light.

Jacoben saw it too, for he cried out suddenly in joy, and rose to his knees his hands raised in ecstasy. We were having the opposite reactions. I was pushing back into the couch in terror, my hand fumbling for the handle of my knife. If the previous door opened on light and life, this door was opening on something else.

"Can you see it, Thaddeus," screamed Jacoben. "We have done it, we have done it! Oh, welcome to your freedom, blessed friend, welcome to freedom!"

"Jacoben, shut the door!" I yelled, my voice shaking with panic, "shut the door before it gets out!"

I could tell the door was almost completely opened, the deep darkness growing across the surface of the mirror. Jacoben was crying ecstatically, and he began to rise and approach the door.

"I have done it, Thaddeus, I have become the master of the cosmos! I have become god!"

"Jacoben!" My scream was one of sheer horror, shrill and high. Something was approaching the door, approaching from the other side through the darkness, something moving fast, something running. It was a shadow, dark against the shadow of the dead world upon which the door had opened. The shadow was racing towards us, towards Jacoben, whose hands were spread in welcome. It was the shadow of a small child. Not a small child. A shadow of a small child.

"You are free!" Shouted Jacoben.

The shadow child smiled widely as it approached, the dark mouth dark against the darkness, the eyes pinpricks of black ink against a black page, and reached its arms out to Jacoben.

And then the shadow reached through the frame, grabbed Jacoben, pulling him into the darkness, opened wide its mouth, and consumed him.

A short scream of despair, and Jacoben was gone. The shadow child was coming out of the mirror now, a wide smile still fixed on its face. I realized suddenly, through the terror, that it was coming for the Book.

354

I acted without thought, and despite the debilitating fear.

My knife came out and I threw myself at the shadow. I struck the darkness, and it was ice. My breath was gone, sucked out by the cold, and I thought that my life was next. The cold struck so deep that I lost almost all movement. I could see nothing but shadow, and I slashed wildly. The pinprick inky eyes were right in front of me, the wide smile opening to consume me, and the shadow child grabbed at me with ice and pain. As I fell through the door, pulled into the nothing by the shadow child, I frantically grabbed at the frame, and kicked at the base, and then all was falling, and the world itself was upside down and turning. There was a burst of glass and ice, flame and shadow, as the frame and mirror shattered on the wooden floor, sending shards of glass and wood into the dying fire behind it. My head struck the floor, glass pierced my frozen skin, and the knife spun from my hand.

The door was closed, the Book was safe, and Jacoben was gone.

Darkness is a Monster

"The fear that something is out there, an existent, evil being of some kind, something tangible, or at least spiritual, something hidden in the darkness, is a common fear. The fools of our age say that if only we light the lamp, and, behold! There is no evil being present, no monster, no lurking cutthroat, then, well, there was never anything to fear. This is a narrow and perverse misapprehension. That this misapprehension has so thoroughly saturated our common parlance is a testimony to the wretched scientism and materialism of our day. Nay, it is not only the possibility of a being, a creature, or a wicked man who may be hidden in the darkness that we have to fear. There exists, rather, a more primordial reality, something even unspeakably real, a first principle, if you will. This is the truly fearful thing; this is why the darkness is dark. 'The price all men pay for existence,' as the poet says. You may encounter this reality first as a child, or even as an infant in the crib. Oh how you long for the morning light! And you are right to long for it. Perhaps your parents will tell you, just go to sleep, my child, there is nothing there, nothing beneath your bed, nothing hidden in your closet. And they are right. No existent being is there, certainly no corporeal being, not even, perhaps, a ghost or spirit, something stalking in from the netherworld. But you know, the child knows, that his fear is not without foundation. The child has not been poisoned by the spirit of the age, not yet. When the inky blanket surrounds him, when he is alone with only the darkness as a companion, the child meets the dragon; the child meets the monster. Let the man of science scoff, let the fawning parent cast his web of lies, let the so-called teacher distort, it makes no difference to the child. He knows the fear, and well he should. The fear knows him. The darkness knows him. And the darkness is the monster."

~Excerpted from *The Darkness and Her enemies: What lies beyond the Door*, by Daemon Hightower (Unknown Binding, circa 1850).

Chapter XVIII

"Behold the beast with stinging tail unfurled,
That passes mountains and breaks weapon and wall;
Behold him that pollutes the whole wide world."
~The Inferno, Dante

I lay immobile for some time.

My vision was blurry, but I could see my own blood pooling around the broken shards of glass and wood on the floor. The cold was my companion, coldness and sickness. I was so ill at that moment that I was sure that I would die. I could still feel the icy hands of the shadow child, and it seemed that it had wrapped its frozen fingers around my heart. I began to drag myself, slowly, through the debris, towards the dying fire. Warmth, I needed warmth. Very painfully I managed to pull myself up onto the ledge in front of the fireplace. I lay shaking as the fire died, shaking for what seemed like hours. In and out of consciousness I roamed, always drifting away into fear, darkness, and cold, and then coming awake to the same. So sick was I, so sick. I am sure, in fact, that I would have died in that hour, but finally, as I came awake once more, I saw the last glimmer of the dying fire catch the edge of the golden script of the Book, and I remembered who I was. I could not die, not yet.

With great difficulty I managed to pull myself up to a sitting position, and I looked around. Though the light was almost completely gone, I could see that the library was the same. Glass and wood were everywhere, and blood had stained the floor. It looked as though a battle had been fought here.

I stood up shakily, and took a blanket from the couch, wrapping it tightly around me. Then I gingerly picked up the book, closed it, and placed it back into the box. I closed the lid, locked it, and put it in the inside pocket of my cloak. The Bellator was once again the custodian of the Book.

I examined my wounds, and found many deep cuts and lacerations. These I bandaged as best I could, tearing bits of tablecloth to serve the purpose. While these caused me great pain and discomfort, it was the sickness and cold that I found almost unbearable. How do I describe the sickness? Nausea and agony, deep, deep agony... As if those icy fingers had torn my very soul from my body. The cold would not abate, even with the blanket. I began to pile pillows and blankets on the fire, watching it spark up once again and light the room. Then I added the pieces of broken mirror frame, and some warmth began to spread.

Jacoben was gone forever, I was sure. I could not bring myself to rejoice at his death; instead of relief I felt nothing but horror. His sin had exacted from him a heavy price. What a sad, wasted existence. A lifetime spent pursuing forbidden fruit, forbidden power. Vanity, all his life was vanity. And to end just like that, consumed by a being whose very existence lay far beyond my ability to comprehend. Death comes to us all, I suppose, but to some it comes more justly and more ingloriously than to others.

As it was, my sickness was so great that I thought I would surely join Jacoben in that dark place soon, and my death would be no more glorious. My life was even now seeping out of me in sickness and chill... I think I passed out on the couch, for I suddenly opened my eyes, and realized that the fire was almost out again, and that I had been here too long. I needed to leave.

The door to the study opened suddenly, startling me, and two little old ladies shuffled in, paying me no attention. The carried a tray of food and drink, set for two, and placed

358

it on the table. Then they lit some lamps, and began to clean up the mess. I sat and watched for a minute, unsure of what to do. But I was ignored completely. And they seemed quite unconcerned about the whereabouts of Jacoben. They swept up the glass and debris, mopped the floor, relit the fire, and then took the remaining two mirrors out of the room. I was alone again.

I struggled to my feet, and made my way painfully to the table. So great was my illness that I walked only with great effort, and then unstably. I quickly ate and drank, thankful for unexpected meal, which I needed very much. Then I set my mind on the task of escape. I thought that I should leave the way I came in, and face whatever was waiting for me outside. So far I had come, but now was an even greater task: to get home again. I felt the reassuring weight of the Book in my jacket, and was immensely relieved. After all this time and through so much suffering I had retrieved what was mine to protect. And protect it I would, or be killed in the effort.

Something was not right.

I stepped into the circular ballroom, and was struck through with an irrational fear. At first glance all appeared the same. The ballroom was grand, and the lights on the wall still glowed. Several halls led out of the room, presumably towards other wings of the house. But the lights were very dim, and I noticed again the artwork that adorned the walls: it had changed somehow, and at first I could not quite tell how, but it had become even more somber. I closed my eyes and shook my head, for it suddenly seemed that the pictures on the walls were beginning to move as though they were alive. The dim light from the candles on the walls made it impossible to see the paintings clearly, but I grew frightened all the same. The figures on the walls were now moving, dancing a slow somber dance, and at the same time a dance that was vile and unseemly. I could not look at it. I had hoped somehow to be done with the terrors of this house, and face those on the outside, but it appeared that the house was not yet through with me.

I stumbled painfully across the ballroom floor, trying not to look at the walls, and then entered the long hall that led eventually to the front door. Here I stopped, for the sickness and pain made it impossible to go on without a short rest. As I stood, trying to control the nausea, I saw the framed pictures that I remembered, the ones of Jacoben's countrymen. These too had changed. Instead of the kind, if somber, faces, they were now transformed to sneering, proud expressions, or their visages were transmuted into fearful gargoyles, wide-eyed and diabolical. They smiled haughtily with sharp fangs, and their eyes were dark as the night. I gasped and looked away, terrified. But I found no comfort down the hall. It seemed too narrow, and the walls appeared to bend in on me. The light of the lamps that were hung on the walls cast only a thin, dim light, smothering the hallway in shadow and gloom. It was like being in a dream, where the dreamer cannot quite see anything, though he strains to, even with light at hand. The gloom crowded out the rays of the lamps, and the darkness flowed like water from down the hall.

I closed my eyes tightly, fear mixing with nausea. I hoped that this was just a trick that my sick mind was playing. But I knew my mind was playing no tricks. It was Jacoben's last effort, his last sorcery; and maybe in the end his last laugh. I opened my eyes again, and the hall swayed wildly, and the pictures laughed and leered. I stumbled forward into the gloom, trying to keep steady, to just get through to the door that I knew was somewhere down this long hall. The darkness closed around me like a coat, suffocating and thick. The lamps served more to obscure than illumine. I began to panic. I stumbled faster, hoping to see ahead the foyer and the door, but the hall just ran on and on. Yet there, just ahead, now did I see something? A light perhaps, maybe showing the front door?

No. It was not the front door. I was looking down the narrow hall to the wavering blue light that hung, blinking and shaking, before the door of the Dreamweaver's

360

cell.

How did I get here? My knees gave out, and I sank to the floor. But I had followed the right hallway, I was sure, and yet somehow I had arrived here. The blue light seemed to beckon me forward, but I could not move. I would not move. And then I heard something.

There were sounds from beyond the door. A gurgling, rasping sound… It was the sound of some dead thing trying to breathe. A scratching at the door… the handle began to move.

No, no, it could not be. The Dreamweaver was awake, and was loosed from his bonds. The door was opening, and I turned to run.

I stumbled blindly down the hall, the darkness closing in around me. Behind me I could hear the muffled footfalls, the gurgling breath, and I could see in my mind's eye the emaciated figure, whose eyes had been long plucked from his head, and whose wounds from the bolts bled black. The lolling mouth and toothless gums I saw, and the long, broken nails; the nails that would claw out my heart if I stopped running. It was just like the dreams in the City, the ones that made sleep such torture. Something in the darkness, looking for you, following you… And I now knew what was seeking in the darkness.

The halls swayed and spun, and the faces on the pictures sprang to life, snarling at me as I passed. In front of me I could see nothing but shadow, though the lamps still dotted the wall. On and on I ran, and the Dreamweaver ever followed. The house had become a maze, and everywhere I turned I came back again to the wide ballroom. Hall after hall I tried, sure that one must lead eventually to the front door, but again and again I came back to the dancing, the wild revelry that only grew more violent every time I came to that cursed room. I even thought to take refuge in the study, and make a stand in the firelight, but the door to that room was gone. Only the entrance to many hallways led out. And all the halls led again and again into the party of the damned.

I could not go on. I was insane, I thought, driven mad with fear and with this place. It was not as though I were losing my way, but as though I were losing myself. That was it. I was losing myself. The horrid breathing seemed right behind me, and the walls swirled and leered, the darkness enclosed itself about me, and bit-by-bit I was lost.

Nightmare, all was nightmare. Nothing yet existed but the dark, and nothing lived in the darkness but death. In final despair, as I once more found myself back in the hellish ballroom, where the dance of the dead raged on, I fell to the floor, curled in a ball, and closed my eyes to the terror.

I closed my eyes, and remembered.

Standing far away, on a mountainside, from which flowed pure water, where the air was pure and clear... a place where no evil could reach, and whose inhabitant was untouched by the travails of time. "Remember the mountain, Thaddeus, and remember me." My forehead burned anew where she had marked me, and I saw the stars that she loved spin again in their course. "Remember me." The weapon she crafted for me had glowed with silver light, the light of the stars, a weapon that she had said would be redeemed by its use. "Remember me, and remember who you are." Who I was...

My eyes opened suddenly to the ground, and I felt the weight of the darkness. But as they opened, silver light poured out, the light of the stars, and the Bellator arose.

Blackness gave way to the pure silver light, the wild dancers on the wall ran, those who loved the darkness because their deeds were evil, away from the terror of my eyes. I turned and faced my fear, the fear that had entrapped the souls of this city, as he came into the ballroom. The black holes that were his eyes found me, his wasted frame as grey as death, his wounds bleeding black. He came at me with mouth hanging open, hands raised with long broken nails ready to claw out my heart. The Dreamweaver came at the Bellator, thinking to drag with him one last soul to hell, and met his doom.

362

I smote him to the ground, and sundered his ghastly head from his body.

The darkness trembled around me and fled. I stood suddenly in the middle of the ballroom, knife in hand, the body of the Dreamweaver at my feet. I was shaking and my eyes burned. The walls no longer danced, but were now only the sad pictures that I remembered, somewhat faded and worn. Jacoben's sorcery had at last been broken. The dreams would never return to haunt the people of the city.

I stood breathing heavily for a moment, and I realized that if all Jacoben's webs had been unraveled, then the house would no longer be protected against the Searcher and the Queen. Protected or not, I needed to leave this vile house, and face whatever I would find outside. I turned and fled down the main hall.

As I ran I could see that the house had reverted completely to being merely a house. It no longer reeked of sorcery and magic, but of mildew and age. In fact, it smelled something of smoke. Of smoke? How odd, I thought, but I do smell smoke, not the pleasant aroma of tobacco or of logs on a hearth, but bitter smoke, the burning of something unclean. As I raced down the hall I could even see smoke wafting along the ceiling, and seeping through the cracks in the walls. The mighty house of Jacoben the Necromancer was burning.

The hall seemed even longer this time around. In the back of my mind I held a fear that I would once again end up in the ballroom, or at the cell of the Dreamweaver. But there, ahead, lay the foyer. I had made it again to the front door. I rushed forward and laid my hand on the latch, paused for a moment, and then flung the door wide. I stepped onto the porch, and was astonished by what I saw.

The fog was gone, and all the magnificent Dead City lay spread out before me, lit by a wild, unearthly red glow; the sky was burning.

Burning, and instead of blue sky, or grey filth, everything above was fire. For the briefest moment I thought that the sun was rising or setting again, and the light had cast the same tint through the filth and smog that covered the city like a blanket. I remembered being struck by the feeling that the sky seemed a blanket of flame. And now it was. All the soot and filth vomited up by the Queen's mines and factories, that had for centuries befouled the sky above this wretched city, had somehow been lit, and was now an inferno. It was rolling and churning flame and ash, an inverted ocean of fire.

I stood transfixed for a moment, unable to take my eyes from the sight. The heat was ferocious, and many of the taller buildings' roofs were engulfed in the fire. "A consuming fire," I thought. Fog that had made my journey through the Dead City so difficult the night before (or hours before, or days before? I had no idea how long I had been in that house) had cleared in the heat, and the graveyard of the kings stretched before me, five hundred yards or more, till the incredible city reared up. There was no sign of the Searcher.

I thought that the fire in the sky must have been ignited by the eruption of the factory that had been destroyed by the rebels. I remembered the mountain of flame that had shot up into the night sky, and realized that this was the answer. So the whole city would be consumed, regardless of the outcome of the battle. But surely, I thought, this can only fall to the favor of the rebels? The Queen will not be aided by this conflagration. Perhaps this was my chance. Maybe the Queen and her minions have fled, and taken the Searcher with them. I stepped away from the porch, on to the gravel path, and trotted a few yards.

And then looked back.

Jacoben's mansion was indeed on fire, the highest spires and balconies engulfed. But that was not what caught my attention. It was the Alabaster Castle.

Rising above the city like a storm, vast as a mountain, more beautiful than any golden vessel, the Alabaster Castle, the home of Queen Lilith. So radiant and so fair it was that I could only stare in awe. But... Somehow I recognized it, as though I had seen it before. Yes, I had

364

seen it before, only then it was in a dream. I remembered crowds of people, banners hung, trumpets ringing, and a woman... a woman who had seen me too.

The world twisted and turned suddenly, and I knew that another vision was come upon me. I was, in that moment, like a bird in the sky, moving quickly below the blanket of flame, over the city and toward a tower, now onto a great balcony, with windows open to the city, and through that window lay a throne room. Dark against the white walls were the tapestries and rugs, and the throne was black. And on the throne she sat. Her head was bowed; her raiment like the night, her crown was gold. Somehow, I could not quite see her face... But then she looked up, and I beheld my enemy.

She was as beautiful as the night. Face pale as pearls, eyes hollow emeralds, and lips silver lace.

And behind her stood a shadow. A shadow like a man, indistinct, and almost shapeless, and his dark hand was on her shoulder. The Dragon... And the Queen was his servant.

The Queen stared for a moment, and then, like a veil lifted, her green eyes flared ember red, and her lips pulled back from her bare white teeth, and she smiled at me.

The vision passed again from my eyes, and suddenly I could see the great gates of the Tower flung open, and from the mouth issued a hoard of Messengers, their black capes streaming behind, riding like the wind upon unicorns, unicorns with clipped wings and blackened horns. The thunder of their hooves shook the ground.

The vision passed, and I was suddenly on the gravel path in the graveyard, crouched on my knees, shaking. The Book was in the open, and the Queen was in pursuit. Fire still rained from heaven, and the Messengers of the Queen, the same ones who had killed grandfather, knew where I was, and that I had the Book. And somewhere the Searcher was waiting...

I began to run.

Just like I had run to get here. Back down the path

towards the New City, away from the Tower and Jacoben's pathetic mansion, now engulfed in flame. I ran with a fury I had never before known. The buildings all over the Dead City were now burning, and I thought that a fire had also been lit in me. My eyes blazed silver, I could feel them, and the word *veritas* on my knife glowed. Pieces of ash and cinder fell all around me but I paid it no heed. I had to win, I had somehow to win; I was so close...

I was running through the very narrows of hell. The heat was a branding iron, searing me to my soul. I gasped for breath of stale air through the smoke, and in my head I thought I heard the hammer of the hooves. On I ran, faster and faster, the burning buildings a blur as I passed. I thought nothing of what ghosts might be here, or whether the Dragon would meet me again. I would not stop for anything. Not even for him.

I began to hear a rumbling behind me.

Still far away, but I could hear it. Would this wretched city never end? The rattle of black armor mixed with the thunder of hooves, and the screams of the Messengers with the clang of steel weapons. They were gaining on me.

"Don't look back," I told myself through ragged gasps, "don't look back!"

Rumble and clang, rumble and clang, and the screams echoed off the vaulted library ceiling. No, not the library, but off the burning houses and buildings. But like grandfather in the library, I would be killed by those demons. They were nearer now.

Panic was seizing me, and I thought to duck down an alley or side road and try to hide, try to lose them in this vast city. But to what end? I would be burned alive, if I could have hidden, and where could I hide where they would not find me? No, I had to get out of this city.

Only two blocks behind now...

There, up ahead, the street widened, and I could see the sweep of the low wall along the canal. The bridge was just ahead.

The screams were drowning out even my thoughts, and the street beneath me was shaking.

I burst out into the open way along the canal, and saw the bridge.

And I lost all hope.

There upon the far side of the bridge he stood, towering darkness, clad in hood, leather and iron, and with two leaping, slavering wolves held in check with great chains. The Searcher was waiting for me. A great black beard he wore, like burned thistle, and his wild eyes were red, billowing, roiling red, like two cinders had fallen from the inferno above and into the sockets on his terrible face. Fangs stained crimson curled up around his foaming lips, and his mouth was black. He towered high, massive and savage, and yet was somehow crouched, his elbows and knees strangely bent, as though he would drop at any moment to all fours and run like the wolves he held at bay. His thick neck twisted strangely, and his fanged mouth cracked into a smile when he saw me. His black hair was knotted like ropes, and spun and swung wildly around his shoulders. He was a monstrous cloud of darkness and void, a tear in the fabric of creation. A dark and terrible storm he seemed, standing on the far side of the bridge. A storm from which no one caught in its deluge could ever escape.

I came to a halt, between the Dead City and the bridge. The buildings were all towers of fire, the sky ripped with furious flame. Ahead of me stood the Searcher, an embankment of black cloud, and behind me the Messenger's of the Queen.

I looked back at the Messengers, who had pulled up at the edge of the city. A wall of darkness they were, and naked swords were in their hands. They stopped at the edge of the road, as though they themselves were frightened, and did not want to face the storm. I looked back at the Searcher, the dark cloud, and he released his wolves. With savage roar they leaped slavering across the bridge, and bore down on me with gaping jaws.

And so it was that I, Thaddeus Michael, the last

Bellator, on the streets of the Dead City, made my hopeless stand.

My eyes burned, and I met the beasts head-on. They clawed me viciously, and I hewed them with all my strength. I was flung to the stone street, and rose again to strike. Again and again I hacked, stabbed and cut, and again and again they mauled me. With the last of my ebbing strength I ran my knife through the great mouth of one, killing it even as it tried to tear my arm from my body. The other was moving towards me, but one of its legs was gone, and it teetered and stumbled. I stepped forward and stabbed it in the heart, running the blade through it as through a sponge.

I looked up from the carnage, and saw the wall of my enemies before me, and behind me the Searcher began to move. I was bleeding, and fell to my knees.

"How strange," I thought, "to die this way. Like my grandfather had died. After such a journey, to end this way, on this street, in this world... The last of the Bellator."

The world seemed to be going dark, but I struggled to rise. I would face my death like a man, like my grandfather had, like my father would want me to. The Searcher was advancing across the bridge, running now with ferocious speed and with a roar like a depraved lion; he had reached the summit. His red eyes seamed to spout fire, his terrible beard and Medusa hair was an eruption of chaos and disorder, and he lashed the chains like a whip.

And as I rose I heard a noise.

It was a noise like a rushing wind, cold and ancient, fluid and cool, and in the noise I thought I heard singing. And in the singing I heard my name... The bridge and road were shaking, and the singing grew louder. I thought for a brief, distracted moment that two trains had left the track and were barreling from both sides towards the bridge in the canal. But they were not trains.

With a noise like thunder, clear blue water exploded up into the air around the bridge with terrible strength, and the Searcher stumbled as the bridge swayed beneath him.

368

He cast confusedly around as the waves leaped up from the deep canal, on both sides of the bridge, and I saw in the waves warriors with flowing hair and eyes of cold blue. In their hands were long swords, and the Women of the Water reached up to the Searcher and struck at him. It was a mountain of water, yet an army of Women warriors, and the Searcher stumbled, cut through by the lashing waves, the waves that were swords. He swung his chain one time, and then with savage roar, his black mouth open in a snarl, and his red eyes bulging with rage, his knotted hair and beard writhing like Medusa's snakes, was pulled from the bridge with a surge of many waters, and the Women of the Water bore him down into the depths, cutting him to pieces as he fell, and the Searcher was no more. It was as though a terrible storm cloud had been engulfed by the dawn, as though the night itself had disappeared into the water.

I was overwhelmed by the sight for only an instant, and then stumbled up and ran towards the bridge, a spark of hope now lit, and heard behind me the rush of hooves and rattle of armor. The water was exploding up and around the bridge, and washing across it as I ran, and I had the strange thought as I ran that I remembered this very story, as though I were reading it now and not living it, as though I were outside looking in, of Moses, in the Egyptian desert, escaping the Pharaoh through the waters of baptism. The waves rose around me like walls. I was only a few yards in when I felt the hooves of my pursuers strike the bridge. And as they did the bridge trembled, cracked, and began to crumble. As if it was made of clay it broke beneath the hooves of the Messengers, and with screams at once choked by the cold water, a mass of them plunged headlong into the rushing torrent. The stone seemed also to simply disappear under my feet, to vanish into the deep, and the crush of the waves overwhelmed me, and for an instant I was sure that I too would die, drowned and crushed beneath falling stone, deep down where the Searcher and the Messengers now lay. I could not see or hear anything but the roar of water, and the pressure was terrible. But in an instant I was suddenly tossed and rolling onto the stone street, coughing and gasping for air.

I was on the far side of the canal, safe from my enemies.

The bridge was gone, vanished into the arms of the crashing waves, and the messengers were screaming and clashing their arms, and frantically racing to and fro on the far side. Several leaped their steeds across the canal, an impossible distance, and were pulled down into the deluge by the waves. The noise was deafening, the sight overwhelming. Tears were racing down my face, and my clothes were soaked with blood and water. I turned away from the violent sight across the canal, and stumbled toward the New City, now almost completely engulfed in flame. But as I turned to run, I saw, walking calmly among the frantic Messengers, a shadow, cold and dark.

I could not believe I had come this far. I could not believe what I had just beheld. I had escaped in the most fantastic manner, and the Searcher, the bane of so many, the horror of the worlds, had, just like that, in an instant, been destroyed. But I was bleeding badly, and the smoke was suffocating. I still had to make it to the gate. Miles yet.

On I ran, hoping somehow to make it through the City before I was consumed. The ceiling of fire was lower now, and all the buildings of the city were engulfed. The dead from the battle last night were strewn and piled everywhere, and most were the dark men or the squat goblins. There were no living creatures, either men or goblin, in the city now. I hoped that the rebels had made it out.

I was not going to make it out. Everything was cinder and ash, and the smoke engulfed the burning city like a shroud. The fire in the buildings had almost reached the ground floors, and soon after I would be consumed. My wounds still bled freely, and I began to stumble and sway as the world turned from red to black.

I collapsed to the street. It was cooler down here, and the smoke was less dense. I crawled forward some yards,

370

but it was no use. I was passing out, and then reviving, every few minutes. Soon I would pass out and never wake up.

The Book felt comforting and secure in my jacket. The last Bellator had succeeded at least in rescuing the Book from Jacoben. But what a sorry victory it was. Now the Book would be destroyed in the inferno, along with its keeper. A fitting end, I supposed. But maybe the Book wouldn't be consumed. Maybe the Book is protected in its case even from the heat of the flames? Then it would be found one day, and maybe by the Queen. So I will have lost in the end. So much effort, and I would remain the weak link. Victory snatched from my hand at the very last moment.

I had stopped even crawling now. My eyes were open and looked at the ancient stone of the street. Ash and cinder fell in my view, and I wondered if I should take the Book out of the case, and let it burn with me. But I couldn't do it. It would not be right, for I could not imagine every possibility, every outcome, nor yet had I the right to intentionally destroy that which was in my care. I was the custodian, and not the owner. I had once already given in to weakness, and handed the key to Jacoben. I would not fail again. No, even if I, the last Bellator, died here in hell, I would not destroy the Book. I was merely a player in the arch of its existence. I would exit its stage. There are powers greater than I that control the drama; the Book would endure.

As I lay, I thought of my parents, and wept. Would they ever know what had befallen me? Or what had befallen grandfather? I wished suddenly that I had just stayed home, that I had never thought to pursue Jacoben. But it was a vain wish. I had done my duty; I had done what I should. And I could not regret it; I did not regret it. No, I had given myself to my vocation. I had been entrusted with it, and I had given my all. Nothing had been held back.

Down the street I heard a sound, the sound of someone walking, slowly and steadily, through the fire and rubble towards me, but I was too far gone to run, fight, or even turn to look at who had found me. But I knew who it was, I knew what it was, that was coming towards me with slow, steady step. I had felt this shadow too many times before: the Dragon had found me. Despair descended like a curse. Even in my last moment my enemy would be at hand, whispering his vile lies in my ear.

I was slipping into darkness. The sound of the steps was near, just by my head. Even with my eyes tightly closed I could sense the shadow, feel the presence. The Dragon stood staring at me for some time. I think that I would have been screaming in terror if I were not already about to die, with or without the Dragon.

"Do you feel death calling your name, Thaddeus? Even now he rides closer, I can see him on the horizon. His scythe is sharpened, and he seeks you. How does it feel, Thaddeus, to have lost after all this? How does it feel, to join your grandfather in the dust, to know defeat? Even to join your beloved mother and father in the grave? Yes, Thaddeus, as you die, despair! The dark rider has not been idle, and his scythe has not been blunted. You, the last Bellator, shall join your wretched family in the dirt, the food of maggots and worms. There will be no peace in death for you, not for such a failure. And I will have your prize. You have lost. My servants shall find the Book, and all your pitiful friends shall know the power of my hand. You have only made my servant the Queen stronger, more powerful and wonderful. I can see him now, Thaddeus, I can see the dark horseman. He is coming for you, mighty Bellator. And when he is through with you, you will see me as I truly am. You will behold what you fear. Despair and die."

He spoke softly, and his words choked my mind. Such agony and sadness I had never before known. I was dying, as my parents had died...

But suddenly the Dragon snarled.

So terrible was the sound that my eyes opened at once, and the shadow was gone. The Dragon was gone. Only debris, fire, and the crooked flagstones of the street were in my view. But the Dragon was gone.

372

I rolled my head slightly, confused and in a stupor, and looked down the winding street, strewn with burning wreckage, dead bodies that I would soon join, and smoke. I watched this scene for a moment, and began to feel myself drifting off into unconsciousness, from which I knew I would never return. At least I could die in peace, without the poisoned words of that monster in my mind. That at least was a mercy. As I closed my eyes, I saw my mother far down the street, clad in silver and blue raiment that shone like the moon, walking lightly among the flame and smoke, her bare feet never touching the ground.

With great effort I opened again my eyes. It must have been another vision, an apparition brought on by my impending death. I blinked several times, smoke swirling around my face and burning my eyes. But there, in silver light, sparkling and shimmering, I saw her again, walking towards me with a smile on her face. Only, no, it was not my mother that I saw, but an angel. Yes, it had to be an angel. The fire bent and moved around her, and the light of the fire was made dim by the light of her face. In her hand she held a naked sword, and wings were at her back. "An angel sent to take me away, take me to heaven," I thought, as darkness closed around me again. "How wonderful..."

But as I drifted away, somehow happy and content, I heard her voice call my name: "Thaddeus, Thaddeus, why do you sleep? The day is not yet over, nor yet has the battle ended. Thaddeus, awake, and face the day! You must finish the fight you have begun!"

I heard this voice as in a dream, but I felt a touch like golden fire on my hand, and I opened my eyes. I looked up, and behold, Charismata, the 'witch of the mountain,' the last of the Bright Ones, my friend, robed with the stars and cloaked with the moon, had taken hold of my hand, and with a laugh lifted me to my feet. I stood trembling and afraid in the light of her face, afraid of her terrible light, afraid that this was but another vision, from which I would wake up in darkness again, but pain and sorrow fled from my body like shadows in morning light.

"Do not be afraid, Thaddeus, for I have been sent to you, to bring you out of the City of Dark Dreams. My time has at last come, and I have much work to do. And your work has not been finished, Thaddeus, or do you not remember who you are? Behold, the earth, sky, and water are awake at last: and the one for whom the Book was made now walks the pathways of the worlds! Rejoice, and take my hand! I will lead you out of the city, and then you must finish your task. Follow me.

With a smile that burned me to my heart, the angel turned, and taking my hand led me through the fire, walking as the fire gave way before her.

Never shall I forget that walk.

I had been raised from the dead, like Lazarus, called forth. I was Dante led by Beatrice into Paradise. As we walked new strength came over me, and the fire receded before us, seemingly bowing before Charismata as she walked, her feet never touching the ground. The stone of the ancient streets became smooth before her, the shimmer and light cast by Charismata seemingly transforming the hardened stone into a path of deep crystal. Her hand was fire, but pure, purgatorial fire. I moved as though in a dream.

The ugly, furious fire above had now consumed the entire city; all the ancient buildings and structures were engulfed, consumed in the raging flame. Burning buildings on our left and right, the sky above was rolling fire, and before us the way was wide and clear. Ahead I could now see the great wall that had contained this city for so long, now a wall of fire, and the wreckage of the gates lay splintered and broken on the ground. Out of the burning city we walked, and into open sky and plain. Across the bridge we strode, hand in hand, and the light of the sun beat down on my upturned face. The same bridge before which I had crouched in fear (so long ago it seemed) I now walked across triumphant. And the Book weighed heavily and comfortingly in the pocket of my tweed jacket.

At the end of the bridge we stopped. Charismata

turned to me and spoke: "Here I will leave you, Thaddeus. You will be safe now. Do not fear, and be comforted. You have done well. The name of Bellator has not been sullied while in your care. But know that you still have much work to do. The vineyard of the worlds still needs laborers. The Bellator still plays a role. Be at peace, and know that you have not failed your vocation. Goodbye for now, Thaddeus Michael. Thaddeus, the Bellator."

With those words she lifted from the ground, her white wings spreading with a flash of silver and gold, and she was gone. Only shimmering air she left behind.

I sat down on the dusty road, and looked back towards the city. What a sight it was. A wall of fire as far as the eye could see along the other side of the river, to the north and to the south, and the light glimmered and shone on the surface of the dark water. As high as the eye could see were mountains of flame and black smoke. What an end to such a great and ancient city. But on this side of the river, no smoke blew and no ash fell. The air was pure and fresh, and the sun was high in the sky. It must have been around two o'clock.

I lay back onto the street, the pain and sickness returning. Nausea and pain, but gone was the fear and trembling that had been my companion in the city. I think my wounds were bleeding again, but I was too tired to consider binding them. I vaguely hoped that I would not bleed to death, as I drifted to sleep, watching the inferno in the sky.

I was awakened suddenly, a short time later, by the sound of my name.

"Thaddeus, Thaddeus, are you still living?"

I opened my eyes and looked into the worn and worried face of Beow. So he had survived the battle. I tried to sit up, but the pain was too great.

"He lives! Quickly now, he is badly wounded."

I was lifted up, and carried to a waiting unicorn. I tried to speak, but my mouth was too dry to get any words out. I clasped my hand over my chest, and felt the shape of

375

the Book under my torn jacket. Beow swung up behind me on the steed, and away we rushed, up into the air at great speed, followed by several more of Boew's men. Away from the city we flew, and towards the mountains.

We alighted a short while later, just in the tree line of the first fingers of the mountains, and I saw there a great encampment of people, hundreds, perhaps thousands, of people, men, women, and children, surrounding fires and makeshift tents. It was both a comforting sight and a sad one. It was a refugee camp, full of the wounded and suffering. The people had escaped, but at great cost.

I was moved quickly to a large tent, and I collapsed onto a pile of rags on the ground. An old woman, apparently skilled in medicine, came to my aid, and began to attend to my many wounds. My jacket was removed, and I found my voice and strength enough to grab it before it was taken from my side.

"No, leave that beside me," I gasped.

My wounds were many, and they were deep. Glass and fang had torn my body in many places. But from the sickness that returned like a storm I suffered the most. For several days I was in and out of consciousness, and the time was lost to me.

Some days later I awakened, and though still sick and in pain, I was now coherent. I sat up and took some food, thin soup, and Beow came to me.

We sat for some time, and he told me of the terrible battle that was fought, and the heavy losses that were sustained.

"We would not have triumphed, I think, but for the fire. We fought like madmen to make the gate, but that they held against us, and we could not break through. Black arrows they rained on us, and we despaired. But the fire, which we did not expect, consumed them. The gates we were able to throw down, and the remnant that you see here escaped. All others perished."

He was quiet for a moment, his face downturned.

"All others?" I asked. "Even Caleb?"

He looked up, his face clouded and sad.

"My men found Caleb on the street some several miles from the gate. He had been killed in a most brutal way. His body was torn and savaged almost beyond recognition. We thought that you too had been killed along with him, or captured. But he had not sold his life cheaply. His sword was notched and bloody. We buried him in the plain, along with those few others that we could carry with us from the wreckage. The rest were burned on the pyre of the city."

He paused for a moment.

"But you survived, Thaddeus. My men had been watching the gate after our escape, to see if any others might emerge unscathed. No one did. They had almost given up hope, and were about to return, when they saw you walk out. The sheet of flame parted like curtains, they said, before you as you walked. They said, 'it is a little boy, but he walks in light, as though the moon and stars were his guide.' I could not believe it at first, but here you are. How is it that you escaped, and did you accomplish your quest?"

I did not answer, but only looked away. How could I speak of what that I had endured? How could I tell of the icy hands that tried to pull me into the darkness, or of the Dreamweaver, or of the Searcher? Of the Dragon…

"Yes, I did accomplish my task. The Dreamweaver is dead, and so is Jacoben, the necromancer, who was the Dreamweaver's puppet master. And the Searcher is also dead. I accomplished my task, but suffered dearly for it. I grieve also for Caleb. He saved me, and brought me to the bridge unscathed. I hoped that he would have survived…"

"And the Queen? Has she finally been killed, after all these ages?"

"No, I do not think so. I saw her, but only in a vision. Unless she was killed in the fire, she still lives. But somehow I don't think that she was killed. I don't think this fire was hot enough for the task."

"But you know that the others are dead? How is that? Did you kill them?"

I looked up, for Beow's voice sounded strange.

"Only the Dreamweaver. Him I killed. Jacoben was killed by...something. I don't really know by what. Something he called up, called up through sorcery, using the Book. Something from a dead world... It almost killed me. It... it made me ill by its touch. I cannot speak of that further... But the Women of the Water killed the Searcher. The same ones who rescued me from drowning, if you remember. When I fell from the unicorn. They found me, somehow, and because of them I was able to evade the Messengers. They leapt out of the river, the canal, and pulled the Searcher in. I... it was a marvel. I don't know how to describe it. I wish you had seen it."

We were silent for some time. Beow sat as if in deep thought. It was evening now, and the firelight danced through the wide tent, and shadows played across the tired face of Beow.

"This is quite a tale, and even though I know that you are withholding much, it is still marvelous. When you are well I hope that you will tell me more. But your wounds are still fresh, and you have been stricken with a strange illness, one that is unknown even to those among us most skilled in the art of medicine. Rest now. Tomorrow we must begin our journey, and you must choose what you will do. Indeed, you have once before been faced with this same choice: will you go with us, to the Shining City across the mountains and the endless desert, or will you go alone to your home by another path?"

He rose, and looked at me kindly.

"Rest now, Thaddeus Michael, dragon slayer. Your journey has been strange and wondrous, and perhaps is not yet finished. You have done well. Rest now."

And he left me there as the fire died. I stayed awake for some time, listening to the sounds of the encampment settling down for the last night before leaving forever the sight of the city. I heard the soft sounds of laughter, and the clatter of dishes. Closing my eyes, I thought that I could remember those sounds from long ago and far away. Maybe

378

it was the sound of my parents, laughing and talking quietly in the kitchen, while cleaning up after the evening meal. It was a pleasant, reassuring sound, reminding me that there were places of light and hope sill left in the many worlds. The faces of my mother and father danced in my mind as I fell finally to sleep.

~

"We have so far examined several of the more enduring suppositions concerning the contents of the Book, and so far have not arrived at an explanation with which to confidently assert the nature of the text. Indeed, it has been most strenuously argued that attempting to solve a mystery so insoluble, which most certainly will never deign to disclose its secrets completely, is an effort in futility and vanity. We do not think this is the case. We who love wisdom, who beg ceaselessly at her door, we do not think the pursuit to be wasted, even with no guarantee of securing, in our own persons and in this life, the full rewards of that wisdom. Rather, as we grow in wisdom and knowledge, and we discover that we are enlightened not only by that which we may grasp with our intellect, and secure by our effort, or by the merely useful knowledge, but also, and most importantly, by that which is given. Given, that is, from the immutable hand of the Divine. The splinters of light that refract from His person, these we cling to and guard jealously. This light is given gratuitously to those who seek, and doors are opened to those who knock. It is in this light that we can understand more fully the reasons that our forefathers of old, who were given more, who were privileged to have had more of nature disclosed to them, and, more than this, were even given the extraordinary grace to tread the many paths between the diverse and varied worlds, believed the contents of the Book worth saving, even against all odds. And, more importantly, they were certain that there would emerge someday from the masses of persons among all the varied worlds, one capable of looking and understanding, of searching the contents of the Book and of being therein enlightened. Enlightened, but to what end, the critic asks? This is the question thrown carelessly in the face of all who seek to know, to discern, all those who love wisdom for her own sake, and has been thrown since man first applied himself to understanding. We need not attempt a defense here; such an effort would be futile. If the critics would not listen to Socrates, nor yet to the exhortations given in the text of the Sacred Scriptures, then neither will they listen to us. Content to remain fools, content *with rooting in the insubstantial musings of their own minds, they cannot see the treasures that wisdom holds forth in her hand, with which she beckons us. But we are convinced of the value of wisdom, and so also of the value of the Book; and if the Book gives a practical exposition of all the many paths between the worlds and of the means whereby we may enter through the many doors, or if it is the key to unlocking all the many mysteries of the cosmos, and so giving man a map by which he may craft a kingdom more blessed, so much the better. But if what it gives can only be understood and valued by lovers of wisdom, as we ourselves suspect, then even in finding the Book all other seekers will not in any way be enlightened. More likely they will therein be destroyed. The man who cannot bear to look upon the Divine light is the man with the grasping hand of power. In its light such a hand is exposed for what it truly is: the miserable hand of impotent pride. A consuming fire the Book will become for such a man. But come, let us apply ourselves to the greater question, the question most pertinent to whether any of our searching has merit: if the Book has survived all these long ages, and is finally unearthed, who is it that may arise and take hold of the text? Who can understand what lies therein? Does such a man yet exist, or will he ever? And if so, from which world will he come? This is, we think, a most important question, and hope that someday soon the answer will be given..."*

~Excerpted from *The Book and its Contents: A Likely Scenario*, by Jacques Leon (Paladium Publishing, 1703), translated from the original French by Mr. A. Abrams.

Epilogue

Dust in the air suspended
Marks the place where the story ended.
~T.S. Eliot, Four Quartets

Now, Father, you know my story, and now your question is answered. You were curious about my original inspiration, and asked an innocent question about the catalyst for my academic career. For an answer I have given you an overlong tale, and one not quite believable. You are, even now, free to disbelieve all that I have written above, and I would not blame you. But an honest answer to your question, and due justice to our long friendship, required nothing less than what I did write. I am sure that you now understand why I had to tell you all, and how my present career as an academic follows naturally from my strange and unusual role. My responsibility as the Bellator means, among other things, that the history of the Book must not be lost completely while it is in my care. The tale must not vanish into the dust and shadow of time. Because of the young age at which I assumed the mantle of the Bellator, and the too early death of my grandfather, I did not have the opportunity afforded many of my predecessors, and certainly my grandfather, to learn and remember the history of the Book. Indeed, because of my grandfather's death, the ruin of his extensive library (which, I am sure, housed the largest collection of anything relating to the Book), and also the death of all his collaborators at the hands of the Messengers and Jacoben, I was compelled to begin anew. That has been my life's work. To learn, to understand, to document, to sift through obscure and strange texts, and to discern between falsity and truth, this has been the focus of my academic life. And also, perhaps, my life as an academic has served as a handy cover to hide my vocation as the Bellator.

You see now that it was no academic or esoteric inquisitiveness, but rather a desire to more clearly understand the full story surrounding my own tale that led me to pursue the question of other worlds, doors, and a strange Book behind them all. I did not seek then, nor do I now, as the skeptical, agnostic theologian seeks God, nor as a cosmopolitan professor of comparative religion seeks truth. Rather, I believe, and so plunge into my studies not as one above, in thought and in faith, the mysteries of the cosmos, but rather as a humble beggar at wisdom's door, who truly and desperately wants what lies beyond the door. I truly believe that the door upon which I knock will one day be opened.

But, in a certain respect, my work has been in vain. To be sure, I have uncovered some of the Book's long history, and have documented much of the stories, myths and legends relating to the other worlds. Nevertheless, whether and in what way the history of the Book and of the doors to other worlds intersects with and plays a role in our own understanding of the vast universe is, in our age of stultifying materialism and science without context, an outmoded question. What mysteries could possibly matter when modern luxuries and entertainment can fill any existential vacuum that might make itself felt, and an appeal to the authority of some popular scientist will serve to smother any dissatisfied murmur in our own souls? No, no one will look at my research, I think, and if someone does, he will not take seriously the questions posed, or the possible answers. I suppose, however, that I am no different than any man who seeks wisdom. Wisdom must be loved for her own sake, and truth as such must compel the lover of wisdom. I have, in life and in my research, attempted to see into the mysteries of the universe, but more than this, to see behind them, to see the ultimate first principle, if you will, who has Himself veiled the universe in secrecy. To 'see' in the metaphysical sense, which truly is, I think, nothing other than to love. But you are not unfamiliar with the problems of which I speak. And I will not ask whether my story has affected you beyond making you less free with your questions...

So I leave my story here, though my strange journey did not end immediately on the slopes of those mountains, among the remnant of the poor citizens of the City of Dark Dreams. Rather, with Beow and the others I journeyed over the mountains and into the desert. Across that wasteland, through great peril and sorrow, we came finally to the City of Lights. But the enemy was not yet finished with us. War was waged, and treachery was a constant menace. My escape was managed only by the narrowest of margins. I have not written that part of my tale, for I suppose it is less relevant, at least to your question. I have related to you the most important aspect of my story, how I recaptured the Book and discovered my vocation. What happened after that, while compelling, is not directly related to your question. If you find what I have written worthwhile, and you are able to believe that it is true, then you might be able to persuade me to write the rest down, for friendship's sake.

I will say that I eventually found a way home, just in time, and stumbled back into my own world through an obscure door. You will laugh, for I found myself suddenly in an American museum. It was a local history museum in rural Connecticut. I created quite a stir. Apparently the door is an ancient carved stone, quite large, and one covered with Native American hieroglyphics. A fisherman had long ago pulled it out of a lake in Maine, and had donated it to the museum. And so I appeared, far from home, wandering confused in a museum. But I was back in my own world,

384

and the Book with me.

But I had grown older, and the world had not waited. I was unknown to all, save my most excellent aunt and uncle, who embraced me even after my long absence, as one come back from the grave. Indeed, my reappearance created quite a stir in some circles, and I still have a couple of aged newspaper clippings, 'young boy, heir to the Ramsey fortune, who disappeared, found alive in America,' something like that. It was assumed that in the chaos of the war I had been lost or kidnapped, and I said nothing to discourage this misapprehension. I think also that many people believed my sanity to be somehow compromised.

My parents, dear to my heart, had died. My father was killed in the war, and my mother died soon after of a broken heart, or so I was told. I stood many hours next to their graves, and wept. The sadness that I suffered then, and still suffer to this day, is unspeakable. I had hoped that the Dragon's whispered words were lies. And always I wondered if I had made the right choice. What if, instead of following Jacoben on that rain-soaked night, I had just gone home?

Of my friends who had lived at my grandfather's castle, Mrs. Phelps and the Sedgwicks, only Mrs. Phelps I found again, some years after my return. She lived in the nearby town, and was very happy and surprised to see me. I think that by then her views on many matters had changed, not the least being her antipathy to all things strange and unusual. She fainted when I revealed my name, thinking me long dead as a child. The Sedgwicks' had disappeared after the destruction of the Castle. No one had heard of them or seen them since, according to Mrs. Phelps. I have often wondered where they went. I think, perhaps, that they found a way to return to their true home, wherever that might be. Or at least I hope that was their fate.

My grandfather's ruined home and healthy fortune I inherited, and so I went to school, and have poured my strength into the study and search of all things related to the many worlds and their doors. I feared that my enemies would immediately follow me into this world again, and that I was endangering my family. But they did not, at least not right away. In fact, it was not until many years later that I began to hear rumors of assassins on the move between the worlds again. Assassins and other creatures... But I quickly realized that they did not know who they were looking for, or even what world the Bellator was in. Such was the chaos and destruction that was unleashed by the burning of the City of Dark Dreams, and the war with the City of Lights. My enemies were thrown into confusion, at least for a time. Yet there have still been some remarkably close shaves, and I am never able to relax my diligence.

I have asked that you keep the above manuscript secret; I now repeat that plea. Even if you doubt my tale, I ask it as an old friend. My enemies do not sleep, and though they have not yet found me, it is not for want of trying. For this reason only I have hesitated in disclosing to you my secret: I fear for your life if somehow my enemies find me, after all these long years. If somehow they learn that you too know of the whereabouts of Book or of the Bellator, they will seek your life. And they will find you. I have leaned heavily on your discretion in the past. I do so again. And this for both our sakes... I have devoted much effort to hiding the Book, and to eluding my enemies. I hope, in the end, that this manuscript does not become the undoing of all my labor.

Now I must mention something else, something that I am sure has crossed your mind. The Book is safe, it is hidden, but my enemy still seeks it. But I am old, and have no progeny (as you know, I have never married). Who, then, will carry on the work of the Bellator when I am gone? To this question I have given much thought. For the Bellator has always been, as far as I know, of a single family, and the title has passed from father to son, or grandfather to grandson. And yet I wonder... Surely, in the long history of the Bellator, there have been those who were unable to marry? Or whose children died young, or any other conceivable scenario? There must have been those who were in a situation not unlike my own. And, if so, there is precedent for passing on the mantle of the Bellator to someone unrelated by blood. Dimly analogous, I suppose, to the apostle Paul, chosen from the mass of humanity to supplement those twelve who made up the inner circle, so to speak. Such was the conclusion I came to. I think, therefore, that this Bellator will soon relinquish his title to someone worthy of the task, and worthy of the gifts that accompany it. Who that will be, I do not yet know for sure, but I have an idea…

And when, I wonder, will the age of the Bellator be ended? When will the 'one for whom the Book was written' be revealed? I do not know, but I look for that day with eager gaze. Charismata seemed to say that he was alive even now, and even now was roaming somewhere among the worlds. But prophecies and visions often lead the literalist astray, and there is so much about the Book that remains for me a mystery. Whether and in what way the 'one' may be revealed is unknown to me. Though I look for his coming, I do not really know what I am looking for, or if I will recognize him when I see him. Maybe he will be revealed in my lifetime, and maybe not. As I grow older, I think it more likely that I will not live to see that day, to see the one of whom Charismata spoke. And yet I still remain, alive and well, and God has not seen fit to end my sojourn. Who knows what events may yet unfold, ere I leave?

And so, Father, that is my story. The story of my youth, though I still feel the physical effects of that journey to this day. I have yet to heal completely from my wounds (you yourself have noted the shock of white on my grey head), and from the sickness that infected me when I was gripped by the demon I have never recovered. It comes back still, usually at night, and I awake in nightmare and pain. But these troubles I bear as my cross, and I have no regret. There is, however, something else from which I suffer, something that lies on my heart like a stone, or rather like a burning coal, alive and searing, a great and mysterious desire. It was awakened when I beheld the world beyond the door, the door that Jacoben opened by mistake, the one that opened on the sweep of green grass rising to a great mountain, and above that mountain the city in the clouds, white against the blue sky. I have been smote to the heart, and now can never be free of the torment. It is an unimaginable torment, but a torment that is, strangely, like the vice-grip of joy. Oh how I long to go there, to go to that castle in the clouds! I think about it night and day while awake, and it returns often in my dreams when I sleep, and then I weep at the returning dawn. And I am getting much older, Father, as you know well. I think that it will not be much longer now until I finally surrender to our mortal condition. I hope that if it has not been granted to me to enter that realm in this life, then by the grace of God it may be granted in the next. Meanwhile, here in this life, I have no rest. I suppose that no one, having glimpsed a greater kingdom, a wilder, more beautiful land can ever truly be at rest, can ever lose his inquietude. You, I am sure, know precisely what I feel. Let us both hope and pray that the day will swiftly draw near, and we can continue the strange journey of existence and life in that faraway land where all roads meet, and all stories have their ultimate fulfillment. I look forward with you in hope to that day.

Affectionately yours,
Thaddeus Michael

The End